# THE PROSPECTOR

# THE PROSPECTOR

## A TALE OF THE CROW'S NEST PASS

BY

RALPH CONNOR

AUTHOR OF "THE SKY PILOT," "BLACK ROCK,"
"THE MAN FROM GLENGARRY,"
"GLENGARRY SCHOOL DAYS,"
ETC.

FLEMING H. REVELL COMPANY
NEW YORK, CHICAGO, TORONTO
LONDON AND EDINBURGH

PR
6013
O5
P7

New York: 158 Fifth Avenue
Chicago: 63 Washington Street
Toronto: 27 Richmond Street, W.
London: 21 Paternoster Square
Edinburgh: 30 St. Mary's Street

# CONTENTS

CHAPTER                                                          PAGE

I.      A Social Impossibility . . . . . . . . . .    11

II.     'Varsity versus McGill . . . . . . . . .      24

III.    The Voice in the Wilderness . . . . . . .     55

IV.     Only One Claim . . . . . . . . . . . .        62

V.      "Yea, and His Own Life Also" . . . . . .      83

VI.     On the Trail . . . . . . . . . . . . .       103

VII.    The Outpost . . . . . . . . . . . . .        121

VIII.   The Old Prospector . . . . . . . . . .       133

IX.     Tim Carroll . . . . . . . . . . . . .        146

X.      The Turf Meet . . . . . . . . . . . .        164

XI.     "I Was a Stranger, and Ye Took Me In" . .    180

XII.    His Keeper . . . . . . . . . . . . . .       197

XIII.   The President of Guy's, London . . . . . .   215

XIV.    Old Prospector's Awaking . . . . . . . .     234

XV.     Ejected and Rejected . . . . . . . . . .     263

# CONTENTS

XVI.    "Stay at Your Post, Lad" . . . . . . . 290

XVII.   Betty's Last Words . . . . . . . . . 312

XVIII.  The Don's Recovery . . . . . . . . . 331

XIX.    The Region Beyond . . . . . . . . . . 353

XX.     The New Policy . . . . . . . . . . . 377

XXI.    The Waiting Game . . . . . . . . . . 391

# THE PROSPECTOR

## I

## A SOCIAL IMPOSSIBILITY

IT was one of November's rare days. The kindly
air, vital with the breath of the north wind and
mellow with the genial sun, was full of purple
haze; the grass, still vividly green, gave no hint
of the coming winter; the trees, bony and bare but
for a few rags of summer dress, russet-brown and
gold, stood softened of all their harshness in the
purple haze and slanting, yellow light of the autumn
afternoon. Nature wore a face of content. She had
fulfilled her course for another year, and, satisfied
with her achievement, was obviously thinking of
settling herself into her winter's sleep.

It was a good day to be alive. The tingle in
the air somehow got into the blood.

So it felt to a young girl who danced out from
under the trees on the west boundary of the University campus.

"Oh!" she cried to her statelier, taller sister, who
with a young man followed more sedately into the
open. "Oh, what a day! What a picture!"

She was a bonny maid just out of her teens, and,
with her brown gown, brown hair and eyes, red

cheeks, and wholesome, happy face, she fitted well into the picture she herself looked upon.

"Dear old 'Varsity," said her sister in a voice quiet, but thrilling with intense feeling. "There is nothing so lovely in all this city of Toronto."

"Toronto!" exclaimed the young man at her side. "Well, I should say! Don't you know that a distinguished American art critic declares this building the most symmetrical, the most harmonious, the most perfectly proportioned bit of architecture on the American continent. And that is something, from a citizen of the 'biggest nation on dry land.'"

They walked slowly and silently along the border of the matchless velvety lawn, noting the many features of beauty in the old grey face of the University building—the harmonious variety of lines and curves in curious gargoyles, dragons, and gryphons that adorned the cornices and the lintels, pausing long to admire the wonderful carved entrance with its massive tower above.

"Great, isn't it?" said Lloyd. "The whole thing, I mean—park, lawn, and the dear old, grey stones."

At this moment some men in football garb came running out of the pillared portico.

"Oh, here's the team!" cried Betty, the younger sister, ecstatically. "Are they going to play?"

"No, I think not," said Lloyd. "Campbell would not risk any scrimmaging or tackling this evening, with McGill men even now in town thirsting for their blood. He's got them out for a run to limber up their wind and things for to-morrow."

The sisters were football enthusiasts. For the past four years the beautiful Rosedale home of the Fairbanks had been the rendezvous for students, and, as many of these had been football men, the young ladies had become as devoted to the game and almost as expert in its fine points as any of its champions.

"Don't they look well and fit," exclaimed Betty as the string of runners went past.

"Yes, and fit they are every man," replied Lloyd. "There's Campbell! He's a truly great captain, knows his men, and gets out of them all that is possible."

"Yes, and there's Brown; and McNab, isn't it? Aren't they the quarters?" asked Betty excitedly.

Lloyd nodded. "And yonder goes 'Shock,' the great Shock."

"Oh, where?" cried Betty. "Yes, yes. Now, do you know I think he is just as mean as he can be. Here I have been bowing and smiling my best and sweetest for four years, and though he knows a lot of the men we know he is just as much a stranger as ever," and Betty pouted in a manner that would have brought deep satisfaction to Shock had he seen her.

"Here are the three halves, aren't they?" inquired Helen, the elder sister.

"Yes," replied Lloyd. "There's Martin and Bate. Fine fellow, Bate—and——"

"Oh!" broke in Betty, "there's the 'The Don.' I do wish they would look. They needn't pretend they don't see us, the horrid things."

"Of course they see you," answered Lloyd, "but

they are engaged in serious business. You surely don't expect to divert their attention from the pursuit of their noble art. Why, who, or what do you conceive yourself to be?"

But Betty only smiled serenely, and shook her curls back saucily.

"Oh, I know," replied Lloyd, "I know what you are saying. 'Some day, some day they will grovel.' Alas, only too soon! And, indeed, here comes The Don on his second round. I'll ask him what he means."

"If you dare!" cried Betty.

"Mr. Lloyd!" said Helen haughtily, and Mr. Lloyd thought better of it.

But "The Don" did not even glance toward the group.

"Look at that, now," said Lloyd disgustedly. "Did anyone ever see such besotted devotion to a barbarous vocation."

"He did not see us at all," insisted Betty. "But why is Mr. Balfour called 'The Don'?"

"Obviously, I should say, from his Don-like appearance, bearing, carriage, etc. But I am not an authority. Ask little Brown, your special slave. He knows all about both Shock and The Don."

"What absurd names you have," exclaimed Betty. "Now, what is the reason for Shock's name? Is it the shock of his charge in the scrimmage?"

"Not bad, that. I rather fear, however, it has to do with his most striking feature, if feature it be, for when you pull him feet first out of a scrimmage, a

young days young people never thought of amusement. We had no time for such follies."

"Oh, nonsense!" exclaimed Betty impatiently. "Has she no other interest in life than Shock?"

"None. Her church,—she would regard your prelacy with horror,—and Shock, and Shock's doings and goings—and football, of course, as I have said. Shock plays, you see."

"Then I have an idea," cried Helen. "We'll——"

"Do go on," appealed Brown.

"Better give it to him," said Lloyd. "An idea, you know, is to some people a rare and valuable asset."

"Not now. Perhaps later I may impart it," said Helen.

"It would be a great kindness," said Brown humbly, "if you could let me have it soon."

"Nature abhors a vacuum, you know," put in Lloyd.

At this point the bell rang and The Don came in. He was a young man of striking appearance, handsome, dark, well set up, with the eyes of his Spanish mother, but with the head and jaw of his Scotch sea-captain father. With all his ease of manner there was a shy, proud reserve about him, and a kind of grand air that set him apart from any company in which he might appear.

After saluting the young ladies with a somewhat formal bow, he announced, "I want you, Brown."

"Oh, sit down," cried Betty. "Sit down, Mr. Balfour. We are not going to allow you to carry off our visitor in this abrupt manner."

" Yes, take yourself off," cried Brown. " You see I can't be spared."

" Please sit down," urged Helen. " We want to ask you about the match."

" I really cannot," replied The Don. " I am on duty, you see."

" On duty? "

" Yes. Looking after men who would stay out to all hours, and regale themselves upon cake and all sorts of indigestible stuff. And more than that, Shock is outside waiting."

" Oh," cried Betty, " do bring him in. For years Helen and I have known him, and yet we don't know him. Bring him in."

" Can you not persuade him to come in? " urged Helen.

" I am sure I cannot. But if you were to try——" The Don paused, looking doubtfully at her. Helen hesitated.

" Oh, he's awful, I know. He will hardly speak to me," interrupted Betty. " But if you'll come with me I'll humble myself before him."

In a moment or two, sure enough, they returned, with Shock following.

He was a big man, gaunt and bony, with a mighty pair of shoulders topped by a square, massive head on which bristled a veritable shock of coarse, yellow hair. But he had a strong, honest face, and good, deep blue eyes. He seemed too big for the room, and after shaking hands awkwardly with Helen, who had gone forward to meet him, he subsided into a deep arm-chair, struggling with his hands and feet.

The contrast between Shock on the one hand, and the elegant Lloyd and the handsome Don on the other, could hardly be more striking. All in the room were conscious of this contrast and sought in every way to minimise it. Betty plunged into football talk, to which Shock listened for the most part smilingly silent.

She was determined to draw her unhappy visitor from his shell. But her most brilliant efforts were in vain. Poor Shock remained hopelessly engaged with his hands and feet, and replied at unexpected places in explosive monosyllables at once ludicrous and disconcerting. Not even The Don, who came to her assistance, could relieve the awkwardness of the situation. Shock was too large to be ignored, and too unwieldy to be adjusted.

After a few minutes of hopeless endeavour The Don gave up the attempt and rose to go, saying: " You will need to excuse us. We are due at a meeting to-night. Come along, Brown."

The alacrity which Shock displayed in getting upon his feet gave abundant testimony to the agony he had been suffering during the last half hour.

" Yes, we must be off," said Brown, far more eager to go than was his wont.

" Will you not come again? " said Betty to Shock, as she shook hands with him. " My mother would be glad to see you."

But Shock could only look at her blankly, evidently

wondering what her mother might wish to see him for, and when Betty tried to extract a promise from him he muttered something about being " far behind in his work and very busy."

But Betty was not to be baulked.

" I should like to call on your mother," she said. But again Shock looked blank, while Brown began to make faces at her from behind his back.

" When will your mother be in? " she persisted.

" Oh, she's in every day, except when she goes out for a walk, or——"

Brown kept up his signalling, and The Don began to look puzzled and annoyed.

" Well," said Betty desperately, " I would like to go and see her some day."

Shock hesitated, blushed, and then answered: " We have no friends in the city, and we do not visit much, and——"

" Oh, I'll tell you, Miss Betty," burst in Brown. " Get a sharp attack of typhoid and Mrs. Macgregor will then come and see you. She's a great nurse."

" That she is," said Shock enthusiastically. " She would be glad to come."

" Come along, Brown," broke in The Don. " We are late now. Come along, Shock," and the three men went off together, leaving Lloyd behind.

" Isn't he awful? " said Betty. " And didn't I humiliate myself? "

" You certainly deserved humiliation," said her sister indignantly. " You might have seen he was dreadfully shy, and you ought to have left him alone. And now for my great idea. I will take you both into my confidence. I am going to drive Mrs. Macgregor to the match to-morrow."

"Splendid!" exclaimed Betty. "And I'll go with you. But how can you persuade her?"

"I have thought about that," said Helen. "We'll ask Mr. Brown to drive around with us a little before, and I'm sure she will go."

"Will you allow me to join the party?" humbly asked Lloyd, "or is there someone else?"

"Oh," said Betty, "we are sure to need somebody, and you will do as well as any other."

In obedience to an invitation conveyed by Lloyd, Brown appeared at the Fairbanks house in the early morning. Eagerly the young ladies propounded their plan. At once Brown entered heartily into it, and calling with them in the afternoon persuaded the old lady that she ought to attend the great match, emphasising especially the fact that Shock would be delighted to see her there, and would be stimulated to do his very best by her presence.

"It will likely be his last game, too," urged Brown.

This finally decided the matter, and so it turned out that perhaps the most enthusiastic, and certainly the most picturesque, of all the groups that surrounded the campus next day was that which filled the Fairbanks carriage, consisting of two young ladies, an elegantly attired young man, and a quaint, plainly dressed, but undeniably dignified, old lady.

# II

# 'VARSITY VERSUS McGILL

IT is a glorious autumn day. The smoky air with just a nip of the coming frost in it hangs still over the trees, through whose bare tops and interlacing boughs the genial sunlight falls in a golden glory upon the grass below. The nip in the air, the golden light, the thrilling uncertainty of the coming match, the magnitude of the issue at stake, combine to raise the ardour of football enthusiasts to the highest pitch.

The record of each team is unique. Each has gone through the championship series without a single reverse. Perhaps never in their history have both universities been more worthily represented than by the teams that are to contest to-day the championship of the Dominion.

The McGill men are the first to appear on the campus, and are welcomed with loud and generous cheers, which are, however, redoubled upon the appearance of the 'Varsity champions.

Many eyes are turned upon the Fairbanks carriage. The young ladies are well known in University circles; but the quaint old lady, looking so handsome in spite of her plain black bonnet, awakens the curiosity of the crowd, which only increases when it becomes known that she is Shock's mother.

" Do you see Hamish, my dear? " inquires the old

lady. " They are so much alike I cannot distinguish him."

" Go and bring him," cries Betty, and Lloyd returns in a moment with Shock and little Brown.

" Mother! mother! This is awful. You won't like it a bit. You'll think I'm getting killed many a time."

But the old lady only smiles placidly. " Indeed, and I'm not afraid for you. Run away, Hamish, and be careful of the laddies."

" Don't tell him that, Mrs. Macgregor," pleads Brown. " He's far too gentle as it is."

Some few minutes are spent in arranging for the kick-off.

" Oh, I do wish they would start," exclaims Betty, standing up in the carriage. " If they would only start!" she repeats. "I want to have a chance to shriek."

" There they go!" exclaims Lloyd.

It is McGill's kick. Huntingdon, the big captain and centre forward, takes it magnificently, following up hard with his whole team. Pepper, the 'Varsity full back, however, is at the spot and returns into touch. In the throw-in McGill secures the ball, and by a swift rush makes fifteen or twenty feet, when, amid the cheers of the spectators, both teams settle down into their first scrimmage.

These are the days of close scrimmage play, when nine men on each side put their heads down with the ball between them, and shove for dear life. Picking out, heeling out, or kicking out is strictly forbidden and promptly penalised.

The first scrimmage results in a dead ball. Once more a scrimmage is formed, but again the result is a dead ball. Over and over again this play is repeated with very little gain on either side. It gradually becomes apparent, however, that McGill in a scrimmage is slightly heavier. Foot by foot they work their way toward the 'Varsity goal.

The cries of " Hold them, 'Varsity! Hold them, 'Varsity!" and, " You've got 'em, McGill! You've got 'em!" indicate the judgment of the spectators.

"Ay," says the old lady, " they are a bit heavy for them, I doubt."

" Who!" inquires Betty, much amused.

" The Montreal lads. But we will be waiting a meenute."

It is a very slow game for the crowds that line every side of the field. Neither team will let the ball out. Again and again the quarters nip up the ball and pass, but the tackling is so hard and swift that the halves cannot get away, and by passing ground is almost always lost.

" Keep it in!" is the word. Inch by inch towards the 'Varsity goal the McGill forwards fight their way.

Suddenly the McGill scrimmage weakens and breaks up. Their quarter seizes the ball, passes it low and swift to Bunch, who is off like the wind across the field, dodges through the quarters, knocks off Martin and Bate, and with The Don coming hard upon his flank, sets off for the 'Varsity line with only Pepper between him and a touch-down.

But Pepper is waiting for him, cool and steady. As Bunch nears him he crouches like a cat, creeping slowly to meet his coming foe. Ten feet from the line straight at the full back goes Bunch. At two paces distance he changes his mind and swerves to the left with the hope of dodging past.

But he has ventured too far. Pepper takes two short steps, and like a tiger springs at his foe, winds his arms round his hips and drags him down, while The Don from the side leaps fiercely on him and holds the ball safe, five feet from the line.

'Varsity goes wild with relief.

"Pepper! Pepper! Red hot Pepper!" they chant rapturously in enthusiastic groups here and there, as Pepper's red head emerges from the crowd piled upon him and the prostrate Bunch. Again and again rises the chant, as the full back returns at a slow trot to his place behind the line.

"Indeed, it is Pepper is the grand laddie," says the old lady approvingly. "Many's the game he has saved, Hamish will be telling me."

"Now, McGill!" calls out a Montreal man, leading his fellows. "Stone wall! Stone wall! Shove 'em in! Shove 'em in!"

But the 'Varsity captain is alive to his danger, and getting his men low down he determines to hold the enemy fast till the fury of their attack be somewhat spent, or till fortune shall bring him aid.

"Get up! Get up there, 'Varsity!" yells the McGill contingent.

"Look at 'em saying their prayers!" shouts a boy.

" They need to," answers another.

" Get up, 'Varsity! Get up! Don't be afraid!" they yell derisively.

" Make 'em stand up, referee," a Montreal man insists.

Again and again the McGill captain appeals to the referee, who remonstrates, urges, and finally orders the 'Varsity to get up or be penalised.

Campbell perceives that something must be done. He moves Shock from the centre to the left wing of the scrimmage and calls in Martin and Bate from half.

By this time every 'Varsity man is on his feet, for he knows that Shock is about to lead the " screw " and before the scrimmage is well formed the McGill stone wall is broken, and Campbell is boring through it with the ba l, gaining a good ten feet and by a quick re-form ten more.

" Man, man, take heed.   Yon's a dangerous game, I'm thinking," murmurs Shock's mother anxiously, to the amazed amusement of Lloyd, who replies, " Why, Mrs. Macgregor, you seem to know the game as well as the rest of us."

" Ay, Hamish has often showed me the working of the screw, and it is not to be depended upon in a place like yon."

The 'Varsity team breathe freely again and go in with new vim, while McGill settles down on the ball to recover steadiness.

But the 'Varsity captain has seen the screw work and resolves to try it again.   Once more he moves

Shock to the wing, signals to the quarters, and again the Montreal stone wall is demoralised. But instead of Campbell boring over the prostrate form of his big centre with the ball the McGill captain, securing it, passes to Carroll, his quarter, who dashing off as a feint to the right, passes far across the field to Bunch on the left.

Bunch as usual is in his place, catches beautifully and is off down the field like a whirlwind, dodging one, knocking off another, running round a third, till between him and the goal line he has only the half back, Martin, and the full.

The McGill people go wild again. "Bunch! Bunch!" they yell frantically, crowding down the line after him. "He's in! He's in!"

But not yet. Red Pepper is swiftly bearing down upon him, and as he comes within reach springs at him. But the wily Bunch has learned to measure that long reach, and dodging back sharply, he slips round Pepper and makes for the line ten yards away.

A long groan goes up from the 'Varsity support, while from a hundred McGill throats rises the cry again—"He's in! He's in! A touch! A touch!"

But close upon him, and gaining at every foot, is The Don, the fleetest man in the 'Varsity team. For half a second it looks as if Bunch must make the line, but within three yards of the goal, and just as he is about to throw himself toward it, Balfour shoots out his arm, grasps his enemy by the back of the neck, and turning round, hurls him back with terrific

force to the ground and clambers on top of him.  It
is a fierce tackle, giving great satisfaction to all the
'Varsity supporters, but to none more than to Mrs.
Macgregor, who, as she sees the unfortunate Bunch
hurled to earth, exclaims with quiet satisfaction,
" That will be doing for ye, I'm thinking."

" Isn't she a great old warrior? " says Lloyd aside,
to the young ladies.

" The Don! The Don!" cry the 'Varsity contingent.  " We—like—Don!  We—like—Don!" they
chant, surging across the corner of the field in the
wildest enthusiasm.

" Keep back! Keep back! Give him air."  The
referee, and the captains with their teams, push the
crowd back, for Bunch is lying motionless upon
the ground.

" It's simply a case of wind," says little Carroll,
the McGill quarter, lightly.

" The want of it, you mean," says big Mooney,
hauling Carroll back by the neck.

In a few minutes, however, the plucky McGill half
back is up again, and once more the scrimmage is
formed.

Gradually it grows more evident that McGill is
heavier in the scrimmage, but this advantage is offset
by the remarkable boring quality of the 'Varsity captain, who, upon the break up of a scrimmage, generally succeeds in making a few feet, frequently over
Shock's huge body.  As for Shock, he apparently
enjoys being walked upon by his captain, and
emerges from each successive scrimmage with his yel-

low hair fiercely erect, his face covered with blood, and always wreathed in smiles. No amount of hacking and scragging in a scrimmage can damp his ardour or ruffle the serenity of his temper.

"Isn't he ghastly?" exclaims Lloyd to the young ladies at his side.

"Perfectly lovely!" cries Betty in return.

"Ah, the old story of the bloodthirsty sex," replies Lloyd. "Hello, there goes half time," he adds, "and no score yet. This is truly a great game." Eagerly the men are taken charge of by their respective attendants, stripped, rubbed, slapped, and sponged.

Up come Shock and Brown. The blood on Shock's face gives him a terrifying appearance.

"Oh!" cries Helen anxiously, "you are hurt."

"Not a bit," he replies cheerily, glancing in surprise at her.

"How do you like it, Mrs Macgregor?" inquires Brown.

"Man, laddie, they are a grand team, and it will be no easy matter to wheep them."

"Don't you think now that Shock is a little too gentle with them?" asks Brown wickedly.

"Well, it will not do to allow them to have their own way altogether," she replies cautiously. "But run away, Hamish, and get yourself put right. There is much before you yet."

"Say, old man," says Brown as they trot off, "it's no credit to you to be a great centre. You'd disgrace your blood if you were anything else."

Into the 'Varsity dressing room strolls old Black,

the greatest captain of the greatest team 'Varsity has ever seen.

"Well, old chap," he calls out cheerfully to Campbell, "how goes it?"

"All right," says Campbell. "They are a great team, but I think we are holding them."

"They are the greatest team McGill ever sent here," replies Black.

"Oh, thanks, awfully," says Campbell, "but they are hardly up to the team of four years ago."

"Quite, I assure you, and you are holding them down."

"Do you think so?" There was no anxiety in the captain's tone, but there was a serious earnestness that somehow caught the ear of all the men in the room.

Black noticed it.

"Yes, you are holding them so far, without a doubt. Their weight tells in the scrimmage, and of course we do not know their back play yet, and that fellow Bunch Cameron is a wonder."

"That's what!" sings out little Brown. "But what's the matter with The Don?"

Immediately the roar comes back, "He's—all—right!"

"Yes," replies Black quietly, "Balfour is swifter, and harder in tackle."

"Have you anything to suggest?" asks Campbell, with a reverence which a man in the struggle feels for one who has achieved. The men are all quiet, listening. But Black knows his place.

" Not in the least. You have a great team, and you are handling them perfectly."

" Hear that now, will you?" cries little Brown. " We're It!"

" Do you think we had better open up a little?" But Black is a gentleman and knows better than to offer advice.

" I really cannot offer an opinion. You know your men better than I. Besides, it is better to find out your enemy's tactics than to be too stuck on your own. Remember, those fellows are doing some thinking at this blessed minute. Of course," he went on hesitatingly, " if they keep playing the same close game—well—you might try—that is—you have got a great defence, you know, and The Don can run away from any of them."

" All right," said the captain. " We'll feel 'em first, boys. Keep at the old game. Close and steady till we get inside their heads. Watch their quarters. They're lightning in a pass."

It turns out that old Black is right. The McGills have been doing some thinking. From the kick-off they abandon the close scrimmage for a time, playing an open, dribbling, punting game, and they are playing it superbly. While they are sure in their catching and fierce in their tackle, their specialty is punting and following up. In this they are exceedingly dangerous. For the first ten minutes the 'Varsity men are forced within their own twenty-five yard line and are put upon their defence. The quarters and forwards begin to "back," a sure sign of coming doom.

"What in thunder are you doing back here!" roars Martin to little Brown. "Do you see anything wrong with this line?"

Nothing so maddens a half back as to see the forward line fall back into defence. Little Brown, accepting his rebuke with extraordinary meekness, abandons the defence and with the other quarters and forwards, who had been falling back, goes up where Campbell and Shock are doing their best to break the punting game and are waiting their chance for a run.

Every moment is dangerous; for the McGills have the spirit of victory strong upon them, and from their supporters on the side lines the triumphant and exasperating refrain is rising:

"Got 'em going, going, going,
Got 'em going home."

And indeed for a few minutes it looks like it. Again and again the McGill forward line, fed carefully and judiciously by their defence, rush to the attack, and it is all Campbell can do to hold his men in place. Seizing the opportunity of a throw-in for 'Varsity, he passes the word to his halves and quarters, "Don't give away the ball. Hold and run. Don't pass," and soon he has the team steady again and ready for aggressive work. Before long, by resolutely refusing to kick or pass and by close, hard tackling, 'Varsity forces McGill to abandon open play, and once more the game settles down into the old, terrible, grinding scrimmage.

" Oh, why don't they let The Don have it?" exclaims Betty. " I am sure he could get through."

The crowd seem to hold the same opinion, for they begin to call out, " Let it out, Alec. Let The Don have it."

But Campbell still plays cautiously a close game. His men are staying well, and he is conscious of a reserve in his back line that he can call upon at the fitting moment. For that moment, however, he waits anxiously, for while his scrim is playing with bulldog grit it is losing snap. True, Shock comes out of every tussle bloody, serene, and smiling as usual, but the other men are showing the punishment of the last hour's terrible scrimmage. The extra weight of the McGill line is beginning surely to tell.

It is an anxious moment for the 'Varsity captain, for any serious weakening of the scrimmage line is disastrous to the morals of a team.

" You are holding them all right, old chap," says old Black, taking advantage of a pause in the play while little Brown's leg is being rubbed into suppleness.

" I'd like to open out, but I'm afraid to do it," replies Campbell.

" Well, I think your back line is safe enough. Their scrimmage is gaining on you. I almost think you might venture to try a pass game."

It is upon the passing of his back line that Campbell has in previous matches depended for winning, and with ordinary opponents he would have adopted long ago this style of play, but these McGill men are so hard upon the ball, so deadly in tackling, and so sure in their catch that he hesitates to give them the opportunities that open play affords. But he has every confidence in The Don, his great half back; he has never played him in any match where he has not proved himself superior to everything in the field, and he resolves to give him a chance.

At this moment something happens, no one knows how. A high punt from behind sends the ball far up into the 'Varsity territory, and far before all others Bunch, who seems to have a kind of uncanny instinct for what is going to happen, catches the ball on the bound and makes for the 'Varsity line with a comparatively open field before him. Fifteen yards from the line he is tackled by Martin, but ere he falls passes to Huntingdon, his captain, who, catching neatly and dodging between Campbell and another 'Varsity man, hurls his huge weight upon Pepper, who is waiting for him, crouched low after his usual style.

The full back catches him fairly and throws him over his shoulder. As both come heavily to the ground there is a sickening crack heard over the field. The McGill captain, with Pepper hanging desperately to his hips, drags himself over the line and secures a touchdown for McGill.

At once there rises a wild tumult of triumph from the McGill contingent, but after a minute or two the noise is followed by an anxious hush, and when the crowd about the prostrate players is dispersed Pepper is seen lying on his face tearing up the grass. Two or three doctors rush in from the crowd, and before long Pepper is carried off the field. His leg is broken.

A number of people begin to leave the field.

"Oh, isn't it horrible," groans Betty, turning very pale. "Shall we go home, Mrs. Macgregor?"

Helen looks at the old lady anxiously.

"Here is Hamish," she replies quickly. "We will wait."

Shock runs up, much disturbed.

"Awful, is it not?" he says to Helen, who is the first to meet him. "I am sorry, mother, you are here."

"Will they be stopping, think you, Hamish?" asks his mother. There is a shade of anxiety in her voice.

"No, mother, we must play it out."

"Then I will just be waiting for the end," says the old lady calmly. "Poor laddie—but he was bravely defending his post. And you must just be going, Hamish man."

As Shock moved off the young ladies and Lloyd looked at her in amazement. It was in some such spirit that she had sent her husband to his last fight twenty years ago.

A cloud of grief and foreboding settles down upon the 'Varsity team, for Pepper is not only a great favourite with them, but as a full back they have learned to depend upon him. Huntingdon is full of regrets, and at once offers Campbell and the referee to forego the touchdown, and to scrimmage at the point of tackle.

"He would have held me, I know, bar the accident," he says.

The referee is willing, but Campbell will not hear of it.

"Put off a man," he says shortly, "and go on with the game."

Bate is moved from half to full, a man is taken from the scrimmage to supply his place, McGill makes a similar shift, and the game proceeds.

Huntingdon fails to convert the touchdown into a goal. Bate kicks back into touch, and with desperate determination 'Varsity goes in to even the score.

Campbell resolves now to abandon the close game. He has everything to win, and to lose by four points is as much a loss as by a dozen.

"Play to your halves every time," he orders the quarters, and no sooner is play begun than the wisdom of the plan is seen. With a brilliant series of passes the 'Varsity quarters and halves work the ball through the McGill twenty-five line, and by following hard a high punt, force the enemy to a safety touch. No sooner has the McGill captain kicked off than the ball is returned and again McGill is forced to *rouge*.

The score now stands four to two in favour of McGill, but the 'Varsity men have come to their strongest and are playing with an aggressiveness that cannot be denied. Again and again they press their opponents behind their twenty-five line.

"Oh," exclaims Betty, "if there is only time they can win yet. Do find out," she says to Lloyd, "what time there is left." And Lloyd comes back to announce that there are only six minutes to play.

"Hamish will be telling me that a game is often won in the last minute," remarks the old lady encouragingly.

As Campbell perceives his desperate case, he begins to swear low, fierce oaths at his quarters. In all their experience of their captain the 'Varsity men have never heard him swear, and they awake to the fact that they are face to face with a situation entirely unparalleled in their history as a team. They are being defeated, and about to lose their one chance of the proud distinction of holding the championship of Canada.

From man to man Campbell goes as he finds opportunity, his face white, his eyes ablaze, adjuring, urging, entreating, commanding, in a way quite unusual with him.

A new spirit seizes the men. Savagely they press the enemy. They are never off the ball, but follow it as hounds a hare, and they fling themselves so fiercely at their foe that in every tackle a McGill man goes down to earth.

But try as they may it seems impossible to get the ball to The Don. The McGill men have realised their danger and have men specially detailed to block the great 'Varsity half. Again and again The Don receives the ball, but before he can get away these men are upon him.

At length, however, the opportunity comes. By a low, swift pass from Brown, Martin receives the ball and immediately transfers it to The Don. Straight into the midst of a crowd of McGill men he plunges, knocking off the hands reaching for him, slipping through impossible apertures, till he emerges at the McGill line with little Carroll hanging on to his shoulders, and staggering across falls fairly into the arms of big Mooney.

Down they go all three together, with hands on the ball.

"What is it? Oh, what is it?" shrieks Betty, springing upon the box.

"I am thinking it is what they will be calling a *maul in goal*, and it is a peety we cannot be seeing it," replies the dauntless old lady.

"Oh, it's The Don," exclaims Betty anxiously. "What are they doing to him? Run, oh, run and see!" and Lloyd runs off.

"It's a *maul* sure enough. Two of them have The Don down," he announces, "but he'll hold all right," he adds quickly, glancing keenly at Betty.

"Let me go," cried Betty. "I must go."

"Betty," says Helen, in a low voice, "be quiet."

"Oh, I don't care," cries Betty passionately. "I want to go."

"He'll hold all right," says Lloyd confidently, and Betty grows suddenly quiet.

"Ay, that he will, yon chap," agrees Mrs. Macgregor, standing up and trying to see what is going on.

"If The Don can hold for three minutes it will count two for his side; if Mooney and Carroll can get the ball away it will only count one," explained Lloyd.

About the three players struggling on the ground the crowd pours itself, yelling, urging, imploring, shrieking directions. Campbell stoops down over The Don and shouts into his ear. "Hold on, Don. It means the game," and The Don, lying on his back, winds his arms round the ball and sets himself to resist the efforts of Mooney and Carroll to get it away.

In vain the police and field censors try to keep back the crowd. They are swept helpless into the centre. Madder and wilder grows the tumult, while the referee stands, watch in hand, over the struggling three.

"Stop that choking, Carroll," says Shock to the little quarter, who is gripping The Don hard about the throat.

"Get off, Mooney," cries Campbell. "Get off his chest with your knees. Get off, I say, or I'll knock your head off."

But Mooney persists in boring into The Don's stomach with his knees, tugging viciously at the ball. With a curse Campbell springs at him. But as he springs a dozen hands reach for him. There is a wild rush of twenty men for each other's throats. Too close to strike they can only choke and scrag and hack each other fiercely. The policemen push in, threatening with their batons, and there is a prospect of a general fight when the referee's whistle goes. Time is up. The *maul* is over. 'Varsity has its two points. The score now stand even, four to four, with two minutes to play.

They lift The Don from the ground. His breath is coming in gasps and he is trembling with the tremendous exertions of the last three minutes.

"Time there!" calls out Shock, who has Balfour in his arms.

The smile is all gone from Shock's face. As he watches The Don struggling in deep gasps to recover his breath, for the first time in his football life he loses himself. He hands his friend to a couple of men standing near, strides over to Mooney, and catching him by the throat begins to shove him back through the crowd.

"You brute, you!" he roars. "What kind of a game do you call that! Jumping on a man when he is down, with your knees! For very little," he continues, struggling to get his arm free from the men who are hanging on it, "I would knock your face off."

Men from both sides throw themselves upon Shock and his foe and tear them apart.

"That's all right, Shock," cries The Don, laughing between his gasps, and Shock, suddenly coming to himself, slinks shamefacedly into the crowd.

"It is not often Hamish forgets himself in yon fashion," says his mother, shaking her head. "He must be sorely tried indeed," she adds confidently.

"I am quite sure of it," replies Helen. "He always comes out smiling." And the old lady looks at her approvingly a moment, and says, "Indeed, and you are right, lassie."

In a few minutes The Don is as fit as ever, and slapping Shock on the back says pleasantly, "Come, along, old fire-eater. We've got to win this game yet," and Shock goes off with him, still looking much ashamed.

McGill kicks from the twenty-five line, but before the scrimmage that follows is over time is called, with an even score.

The crowd streams on the field tumultuously enthusiastic over a game such as has never been seen on that campus. Both sides are eager to go on, and it is arranged that the time be extended half an hour.

Old Black gets Campbell aside and urges, "Take ten minutes off and get your men into quarters." Campbell takes his advice and the rubbers get vigorously to work at legs and loins, rubbing, sponging, slapping, until the men declare themselves fresh as ever.

"Not hurt, Don?" inquires Campbell anxiously.

"Not a bit," says The Don. "It didn't bother me at all. I was winded, you see, before I fell."

"Well," says Campbell, "we're going to give you a chance now. There's only one thing to do, men. Rush 'em. They play best in attack, and our defence is safe enough. What do you say, Black?"

"I entirely agree. But begin steady. I should use your whole half back line, however, for a while. They will lay for Balfour there."

"That's right," says the captain. "Begin steady and pass to Martin and McLaren for the first while, and then everyone give The Don a chance.

"And Shock," calls out little Brown, "don't be a fool, and stop fighting," at which everybody roars except Shock himself, who, ashamed of his recent display of temper, hurries off to the field.

Once more the campus is cleared. Battered and bloody as to features, torn and dishevelled as to attire, but all eager and resolved, the teams again line up, knowing well that they have before them a half hour such as they have never yet faced in all their football career.

It is 'Varsity's kick. Campbell takes it carefully, and places it in touch well within the McGill twenty-five. After the throw in, the teams settle down to scrimmage as steady as at the first, with this difference, however, that 'Varsity shows perceptibly weaker. Back step by step their scrimmage is forced toward the centre, the retreat counterbalanced somewhat by the splendid individual boring of Campbell and Shock. But both teams are alert and swift at the quarters, fierce in tackle and playing with amazing steadiness.

Suddenly Carroll nips up the ball and passes hard and swift to the half back immediately behind him, who in turn passes far out to Bunch on the left wing. With a beautiful catch Bunch, never slacking speed, runs round the crowd, dodges the quarters, knocks off Martin, and with a crowd of men of both teams close upon his heels, makes for the line.

Before him stands Bate alone. From his tall, lank make one might easily think him none too secure on his legs. Bunch determines to charge, and like a little bull rushes full at him.

But Bate's whole football life has been one long

series of deceptions, and so he is quite prepared for this kind of attack. As Bunch comes at him he steps lightly aside, catches the half back about the neck, swings him round and lands him prone with such terrific impact that the ball flies out of his grasp.

Immediately little Brown has it, passes to Martin, who on being tackled passes to The Don. The field before him is full of the enemy, but The Don never hesitates. Doubling, twisting, knocking off, he eludes man after man, while the crowds on the line grow more and more frantic, and at length, clearing the main body, he sets off across the field to more open country on the 'Varsity left. Behind him come Campbell, Shock, Martin and others, following hard; before him stand three of the McGill defence. Dorion, McDonnell, and Mooney. He has already made a great run, and it looks as if he cannot possibly make through.

First Dorion springs at him, but The Don's open hand at the end of a rigid arm catches him full in the neck, and Dorion goes down like a stick.

Big McDonnell bears swiftly down upon him and leaps high at him, but The Don lowers his shoulder, catches McDonnell below the wind and slides him over his back; but before he can get up speed again little Carroll is clutching at his hips, and Mooney, the McGill full back, comes rushing at him. Swinging round, The Don shakes Carroll partly off, and with that fierce downward cut of his arm which is his special trick, sends the little quarter flying, and just as Mooney tackles, passes the ball over his shoulder to Shock, who is immediately pounced upon by half a dozen McGill men, but who, ere he is held, passes to Campbell, who in turn works forward a few yards, and again on being tackled, passes to The Don. It is a magnificent bit of play.

The spectators have long since passed all bounds of control, and are pouring on the field, yelling like mad people. Even the imperturbable old lady loses her calm for a moment, and griping Helen's arm exclaims, "Look at that, now! Man, man, yon is a grand laddie."

There is no chance for The Don to run, for a swarm of the McGill men stand between him and the line only a few yards off. Then he does the only possible thing. Putting his head down he plunges into the crowd in front of him.

"Come on, Shock," yells Campbell. Instantly a dozen 'Varsity men respond to the cry and fall in behind Campbell and Shock, who, locking arms about The Don, are shoving him through for dear life.

There are two minutes of fierce struggle. Twenty men in a mass, kicking, scragging, fighting, but slowly moving toward the McGill line, while behind them and around them the excited spectators wildly, madly yelling, leaping, imploring, adjuring by all kinds of weird oaths to "shove" or to "hold." In vain the McGill men throw themselves in the way of the advancing mass. Steadily, irresistibly the movement goes on. They are being beaten and they know it.

"Down! down!" yells big Huntingdon, dropping on his knees on the line in front of the tramping, kicking 'Varsity phalanx.

A moment's pause, and there is a mass of mingling arms, legs, heads and bodies, piled on the goal line.

"Held! held!" yell the McGill men and their supporters.

But before the referee can respond Shock seizes The Don below the waist, lifts him clear of the mob, and trampling on friend and foe alike, projects him over the struggling mass beyond the enemy's line, where he is immediately buried beneath a swarm of McGill men, who savagely jump upon him and jam his head and body into the turf.

"He's in! he's in!" shrieks Betty, wildly waving her hand.

"Will it be a win, think ye?" anxiously inquires Shock's mother. "It will hardly be that, I doubt. But, eh—h, yon's the lad."

"Down! down!" cries the 'Varsity captain. "Get off the man! Get off the man! Let him up, there!"

But the McGill men are slow to move.

"Get up!" roars Shock, picking them off and hurling them aside.

"Get up, men! Get up! That ball is down," yells the referee through the din, into the ears of those who are holding The Don in a death grip.

With difficulty they are persuaded to allow him to rise. When he stands up, breathless, bleeding at the mouth, but otherwise sound, the crowd of 'Varsity admirers go into a riot of rapture, throwing up caps, hugging each other in ecstatic war dances, while the team walk quietly about recovering their wind, and resisting the efforts of their friends to elevate them.

"Quit it!" growls Campbell.   "Get off the field! Get back, you hoodlums!"

Meantime Huntingdon is protesting to the referee.

"I claim that ball was fairly held, back there. Balfour was brought to a dead stand."

"How do you know, Huntingdon?" returns Campbell.   "Your head was down in the scrim."

"I could see his legs.   I know his boots."

It is true that The Don has a peculiar toe on his boots.

"Oh," jeers Campbell scornfully, "that's all rot, you know, Huntingdon."

"Look here, Campbell, listen to what I say.   I want you to remember I am speaking the truth."

Huntingdon's quiet tone has its effect.

"I would never think of challenging your word," replies Campbell, "but I think it is quite impossible that you could absolutely know that The Don came to a dead stand."

"I repeat, I can pick out Balfour's boots from a whole crowd, and I know he was brought to a stand. I am prepared to swear that.   Can any man swear to the contrary?"

"Why, certainly," cries Campbell, "half a dozen men can.   There's Shock, who was right behind him."

But Shock thus appealed to, hesitates.   He has an unfortunate conscience.

" I can't say for sure," he says, looking piteously at his captain.

" Weren't you moving all the time, Shock?"

" Well, I was shoving all the time."

" But hold on," says Huntingdon. " Will you say that Balfour was never brought to a stand? Will you swear that?"

" Well, I cannot say for sure," replies Shock in great distress. " It was not very long, anyway."

Yells of triumphant laughter break from the McGill crowd.

The referee is in great difficulty. He has a reputation for courage and fairness. He hesitates a moment or two, and then, while the crowd wait breathless for his decision, says, " You can all see that it is almost impossible to be certain, but on the whole I shall give it a ' hold.' "

It was a bitter moment to the 'Varsity men, but Campbell is a true sport.

" Shut up, men," he says in answer to the loud protests of his team. " Get behind the ball."

Every second is precious now, and the line is only three feet away.

Again the field is cleared. The teams, springing to their places in the scrimmage, began to shove furiously before the ball is in play.

" Get up, men!" says the referee. " You must get up. Let me get this ball in. Get up, McGill! Get off your knees!" for the McGill men are on their goal line in an attitude of devotion.

Again and again the scrimmage is formed, only to

be broken by the eagerness of the combatants. 'At length the referee succeeds in placing the ball. Instantly Shock is upon it, and begins to crawl toward the line with half a dozen men on his back, gripping him by nose, ears, face, throat, wherever a hand can find a vulnerable spot.

"Hold there!" calls the referee.  "'Varsity ball."

"Get off the man!  Get off!" cry the 'Varsity men, pulling the McGill fellows by legs and heads, till at length Shock rises from the bottom of the heap, grimy, bloody, but smiling, grimly holding to the ball. He has made six inches.  The line is two feet and a half away.

It is again 'Varsity's ball, however, and that means a great deal, for with Campbell lies the choice of the moment for attack.

Placing Shock on the wing, and summoning his halves and quarters, Campbell prepares for a supreme effort.  It is obviously the place for the screw.

The McGill men are down, crouching on hands and feet, some on their knees.

Campbell refuses to play and appeals to the referee in a tone of righteous indignation, "What sort of game is this?  Look at those fellows!"

"Get up McGill!  Get up, or I'll penalise you," says the referee.  Everyone knows he will keep his word.  There is a movement on the part of McGill to rise.  Campbell seizes the opportunity, lowers his head, and with a yell drops the ball in front of Shock. In the whirl of the screw the ball slips out to Brown, who tips it to The Don, but before he can take a single step half a dozen men are upon him and he is shoved back a couple of feet.

"Man, man," ejaculates the old lady, "will you not be careful!"

"I say!" exclaims old Black to a McGill enthusiast whom he had fought in the famous championship battle four years ago. "This is something like."

"Great ball," replies his friend. "We'll hold them yet. I've often seen a ball forced back from two feet off the line."

It is still the 'Varsity ball. The crowds are howling like maniacs, while the policeman and field censors are vainly trying to keep the field decently clear.

The Don resigns the ball to the captain and falls in behind. Every man is wet, panting, disfigured, but eager for the fight. Again the scrim forms, only to fall upon the ball.

"Dead ball," announces the referee, and both teams begin to manœuvre for advantage of position. A few inches is a serious thing.

Again the ball is placed and the men throw themselves upon it, Shock as usual at the bottom of the heap with the ball under him.

Old Black runs up through the crowd and whispers in Campbell's ear, "Put Balfour and Martin in the scrim. They are fresher." He has noticed that the scrim line on both sides is growing stale, and can do no more than grimly hold on. At once Campbell sees the wisdom of this suggestion. The Don, though not so heavy as Shock, is quite as strong, and is quicker than the big centre, who is beginning to show the effect of the tremendous series of scrimmages he has just passed through. Martin, though neither so strong nor so heavy, is like an eel.

Quietly Campbell thrusts the halves into the first line on the right, whispering to Shock, " Let Balfour have it, and back him up."

As The Don gets the ball Campbell throws himself behind him with the yell, " 'Varsity! now!" At the same instant The Don drops the ball, and with the weight of the whole team behind him begins to bore through the enemy.

For a few moments both teams hang in the balance, neither giving an inch, when old Black, yelling and waving wildly, attracts the attention of Bate.

" Go in!" he cries. " Go in!" and Bate, coming up with a rush, throws himself behind the scrim.

His weight turns the scale. Slowly at first, but gaining momentum with every inch, the mass yields, sways, and begins to move. The McGill men, shoving, hacking, scragging, fighting fiercely, finally dropping on their knees, strive to check that relentless advance. It is in vain. Their hour has come.

With hoarse cries, regardless of kicks and blows, trampling on prostrate foes, and followed by a mob of spectators tumultuously cheering, the 'Varsity wedge cleaves its way, till on the other side The Don appears with the ball hugged to his breast and Huntingdon hanging to his throat. A final rush and the ball is down.

" The ball is down!" cries the referee, and almost immediately time is called.

The great match is over. By four points 'Varsity holds the championship of the Dominion.

"The greatest match ever played on this ground," cries old Black, pushing through the crowd to Campbell, with both hands outstretched.

After him comes the Montreal captain.

"I congratulate you most heartily," he says, in a voice that breaks in spite of all he can do.

"Thanks, old man," says Campbell quietly. "It was a case of sheer luck."

"Not a bit of it," replies Huntingdon, recovering himself. "You have a great team. I never saw a better."

"Well," replies Campbell heartily, "I have just seen as good, and there's none we would rather win from than McGill."

"And none," replies Huntingdon, "McGill would rather lick than 'Varsity."

Meantime Shock, breaking from a crowd of admirers who are bound to carry him in on their shoulders, makes for the Fairbanks carriage, and greets his mother quietly.

"Well, mother, it's over at last."

"Ay, it is. Poor fellows, they will be feeling bad. But come along, laddie. You will be needing your supper, I doubt."

Shock laughs loud. He knows his mother, and needs no words to tell him her heart is bursting with pride and triumph.

"Come in. Let us have the glory of driving you home," cries Betty.

" In this garb? " laughs Shock.

" That's the garb of your glory," says Helen, her fine eyes lustrous with excitement.

" Come, Hamish man, you will get your things and we will be waiting for you."

" Very well," he replies, turning away. " I will be only a minute."

He is not allowed to escape, but with a roar the crowd seize him, lift him shoulder high, and chanting, " Shock! Shock! we—like—Shock!" bear him away in triumph.

" Eh, what are the daft laddies saying now?" inquires the old lady, struggling hard to keep out of her voice the pride that shone in her eyes.

" Listen," cries Helen, her eyes shining with the same light. " Listen to them," and beating time with her hand she joins in the chant, " Shock! Shock! we —like—Shock. "

# III

## THE VOICE IN THE WILDERNESS

THE Superintendent had come from the West on his spring round-up. New settlements in anticipation of and following the new Railway, old settlements in British Columbia valleys formed twenty years ago and forgotten, ranches of the foot-hill country, the mining camps to the north and south of the new line—these were beginning to fire the imagination of older Canada. Fresh from the new and wonderful land lying west of the Great Lakes, with its spell upon him, its miseries, its infamies, its loneliness aching in his heart, but with the starlight of its promise burning in his eyes, he came to tell the men of the Colleges of their duty, their privilege, their opportunity waiting in the West. For the most part his was a voice crying in the wilderness. Not yet had Canadians come to their faith in their Western Empire. Among the great leaders were still found those who poured contempt upon the project of the trans-continental railway, and even those who favoured the scheme based their support upon political rather than upon economic grounds. It was all so far away and all so unreal that men who prided themselves upon being governed by shrewd business sense held aloof from western enterprises, waiting in calm assurance for their certain collapse. Still, here and there men like Bompas, McLean, McDougall, and Robertson were holding high the light that fell upon prairie and foot-hill, mountain peak and canyon, where speculators, adventurers, broken men, men with shamed names seeking hiding, and human wolves seeking their prey were pouring in.

Discouraged with the results of his work in the Eastern Colleges, the Superintendent arrived at Knox, and to-night he stood facing the crowd of students and their friends that filled the long Dining Hall to overflowing. With heart hot from disappointment and voice strident with intensity of emotion, he told of the things he had seen and heard in that great new land. Descriptions of scenery, statistics, tales hu-morous and pathetic, patriotic appeal, and prophetic vision came pouring forth in an overwhelming flood from the great man, who e tall, sinewy form swayed and rocked in his passion, and whose Scotch voice burred through his sonorous periods. " For your Church, for your fellowmen, for Canada," rang out his last appeal, and the men passed out into the cor-ridor toward the Entrance Hall, silent or conversing in low, earnest tones. There was none of the usual chaffing or larking. They had been thinking great thoughts and seeing great visions.

" I want to thank you for asking me in to-night, Lloyd," said The Don. His voice was quiet and his fine eyes were lustrous with light. " That man ought to be in Parliament. I shall see that country soon, I

hope. What a master he is! What a grasp! What
handling of facts! There's a great Canadian, I say,
and he ought to be in Parliament."

The men gathered round, for the great 'Varsity
half back was well known and well liked in that company; but they all knew him as one of the gay 'Varsity set, and some of the older men knew, too, that in
his early college career were passages that neither he
nor his friends cared to remember. Hence all of
them, but especially Shock, whom he loved, and Lloyd,
whom he greatly admired, listened with surprise to
The Don's enthusiastic words, for they both had stood
beside him in those dark days, and had played toward
him the brother's part. The men waited in silence for
Lloyd's reply. They knew him to be by far the
strongest man in the college, the readiest in debate,
as well as the most popular in the pulpit; but, with
the sure instinct of college men, they had come to
recognise his ambitious spirit, and, indeed, to be more
influenced by it tha.1 they would have cared to
acknowledge.

"Yes," said Lloyd, "it was certainly a statesman-
like address. It contained all the elements of a great
speech. But he—of course—well—he sees only one
thing—The West."

"That's right," said little Brown, who had come in
at Shock's earnest invitation, and because he was
anxious to hear about the new country from one who
was coming to be recognised as an authority, "he
sees one thing sure enough. I say, what a drummer
he'd make! Talk like that is worth $100 a minute

to any firm. I'll put my Governor on to him. When that chap opened his sample case he wouldn't talk weather and politics, and then sidle up to business. Not much! He'd give them Brown's Axle Oil, Brown's Baking Powder, or anything else of Brown's he was showing, till his customer would see nothing but Brown's Axle Oil and Brown's Baking Powder all over his shop, and he'd be reaching for the whole output. One thing! You bet!"

A general laugh of approval followed Brown's speech.

"That's true enough," said Lloyd in a tone of calm superiority, "but there is other work to do and other places to do it in."

"The Park Church, for instance, eh, Lloyd?" suggested the voice slyly.

"Why not?" answered Lloyd. "The centres must be manned—that's a safe principle in strategy."

"Certainly," cried another voice ironically. "Our neglected masses!"

"Yes, and neglected classes, too." Lloyd's tone was earnest and sincere.

"I agree with you, Lloyd," said The Don emphatically, "if any fellows need to be, ah—well—shaken up, you know, it's us poor devils who attend the city churches. For my part, I would like to see you in the Park Church, and I promise you I would go regularly."

On all sides there was frank approval of The Don's position, while Lloyd, flushed and laughing, lightly replied: " Oh, there won't be any trouble, I fancy, in getting a man for the Park Church."

" Not in the least, I assure you," said Brown. " Brown Bros., Commission Merchants, etc., etc., will undertake to supply men in half-dozen lots willing for a consideration to offer themselves upon the altar of Park Church."

" There's more than willingness necessary, unfortunately, and besides, lots of men would be willing to go West," answered Lloyd.

" Yes, and lots of men deucedly unwilling, too, from what your old man there says, not to speak of the young lady, who apparently must also be willing. Oh! I say, wasn't that a great yarn; and if ever that chap gets a look at himself from that particular point of view, that 'll be the time to buy him."

" Brown, my boy," said The Don solemnly, " your limitations are obvious. The commercial in you has run to seed."

" That may be, but I can spot a man that knows how to show his goods, and when that old gentleman set forth the West in those high lights of his, I tell you what, I almost wished I was a Theologue."

" What a pity you are not," replied The Don thoughtfully, " for apparently they want strong men." At which the crowd again laughed.

" What's the matter with Shock? " suggested someone; " he's a good strong man." There was a general laugh.

" You're the man, Shock. You would clear out those saloons."

" Can you ride a broncho, Shock? "

At the good-natured chaff Shock blushed a deeper red than usual.  No one expected much of poor Shock. Indeed, most of his classmates wondered if he would ever " get a place," and none more than Shock himself.

But Brown, resenting the laugh and its all too evident implication, replied indignantly: " You bet Shock's the man for the West, or any place else where solid men are wanted, and where Shock goes there will be something doing!  And," striking an attitude, " the country will be the better for it!  Oh, I am a Canadian! " he continued, smiting his breast dramatically.  " Come along, Shock, we've got an appointment," and Brown, linking his arm affectionately through that of his big friend, stuck his cap on the back of his head and marched off whistling " The Maple Leaf."

" Say! " he cried, as he passed out into the street, " won't a lot of those fellows volunteer, or will they hunt round for a nice little bunk in Ontario? "

" Many would like to go if they could," said Shock thoughtfully, " but you know there are many things that must be considered."

" Young ladies, eh? " asked Brown with a laugh. " Oh! didn't he tell that yarn well?  It was great. But I'd hate to be the fellow."

" But you are not fair," replied Shock.  " A man can't answer every appeal.  He must think what he is fit for, and, in short, where he is called to work. There's Lloyd, now——"

"Oh, Lloyd!" broke in Brown impatiently. "He's a quitter."

"Not he. He's anything but that."

"No," owned Brown, "he's not a quitter, but he puts in overtime thinking of what's good for Lloyd. Of course, I do that sort of thing myself, but from a fellow like Lloyd one expects something better."

Soon they were at Shock's door.

"Come in," said Shock cordially, "mother will be glad to see you."

And Brown went in.

# IV

## ONLY ONE CLAIM

IT always gave Brown a sense of content to enter the Macgregor cottage. Even among the thrifty North country folk the widow Macgregor's home, while not as pretentious as those of the well-to-do farmers, had been famous as a model of tidy housekeeping. Her present home was a little cottage of three rooms with the kitchen at the back. The front room where Mrs. Macgregor received her few visitors, and where Shock did most of his reading, except when driven to his bedroom by the said visitors, was lighted by two candles in high, polished, old-fashioned brass candlesticks, and by the fire from the hearth, which radiated a peace and comfort which even the shiny hair-cloth chairs and sofa and the remaining somewhat severe furniture of the room could not chill. It was the hearth and mantel that had decided Mrs. Macgregor and Shock in their purchase of the little cottage, which in many eyes was none too desirable. On the walls hung old-fashioned prints of Robbie Burns and his Highland Mary, the Queen and the Prince Consort, one or two quaint family groups, and over the mantel a large portrait of a tall soldier in full Highland dress. Upon a bracket in a corner stood a glass case enclosing a wreath of flowers wrought in worsted, and under it in a frame hung a sampler with the Lord's Prayer similarly wrought. On one side of the room stood a clock upon a shelf, flanked by the Family Bible and such books as "The Saint's Rest," "Holy Living," "The Fourfold State," "Scots Worthies," all ancient and well worn. On the other side stood a bookcase which was Shock's, and beside it a table where he did his work. Altogether it was a very plain room, but the fireplace and the shining candlesticks and the rag carpet on the floor redeemed it from any feeling of discomfort, while the flowers that filled the windows lent an air of purity and sweetness.

"Come away, my lad, come away," said Mrs. Macgregor, who sat knitting by the fire. "The night is chill enough. Come away up to the fire."

"Thanks, Mrs. Macgregor," said Brown, "it does me good to look at you by the fire there with your knitting. When I'm an old man I only hope I'll have a cozy hearthstone like this to draw up to, and on the other side a cozy old lady like you with pink cheeks like these which I must now kiss."

"Tut, tut, it's a daft laddie you are whatever," said the old lady, blushing a little, but not ill-pleased. "Sit ye down yonder."

Brown, ever since his illness, when Mrs. Macgregor and Shock had nursed him back from death's door two years ago, was one of the family, and, indeed, he used endearments with the old lady that the undemonstrative Shock would never have dared to use.

"Ye're late, Hamish. Surely yon man had much

to say," said his mother, looking lovingly upon her great, sturdy son.

"That he had, mother, and great it was, I can tell you."

Then Shock proceeded, after his habit, to give his mother a full share of what he had been enjoying. Mrs. Macgregor listened intently, pausing now and then in her knitting to ejaculate, "Well-a-well!" "Look at that, now!" "Hear to him!" When Shock had finished, Brown broke in: "It was truly magnificent, I assure you, Mrs. Macgregor, and the enthusiasm of the man! And his yarns! Oh, he is truly great!"

"And what would he be doing at the college?" enquired the old lady. "There would not be much money there, I doubt."

"Men, mother, men," cried Shock with some excitement. "Volunteers for the Great West, and a hard time he is having, too, what with the foreign field, and needy vacancies in this country, and city pulpits, and the like."

Mrs. Macgregor sat silent, her needles flying fast and her lips pressed together.

"I wish you could have heard him, Mrs. Macgregor," said Brown, enthusiastically. "He has a tongue like a rasp, and at times it takes off the skin. That was fine, Shock, about the fellows who could not give him answer till they had asked the Lord about it. 'I find a good many men,' the old chap said, 'who, after anxiously enquiring as to the work expected of them, remuneration, prospects of advance, etc., always want to lay the matter before the Lord before giving their answer. And I am beginning to think that the Lord has some grudge against the West, for almost invariably He appears to advise these men to leave it severely alone.' Oh, it was great!" Little Brown hugged his knee in delight at the memory of that rasping tongue.

" But surely there are plenty of men," said Mrs. Macgregor a little impatiently, " for there's no want of them whateffer when a congregation falls vacant."

" That's so," replied Brown ; " but you see he wants only first-class men—men ready for anything in the way of hardship, and not to be daunted by man or devil."

" Ou ay!" said the old lady, nodding her head grimly ; " he will not be finding so many of yon kind."

" But it must be a great country," went on Brown. " You ought to hear him tell of the rivers with sands of gold, running through beds of coal sixty feet thick."

The old lady shook her cap at him, peering over her glasses. " Ye're a gay callant, and you will be tak-ing your fun off me."

" But it's true. Ask Shock there."

" What? " said Shock, waking up from a deep study. Brown explained.

" Yes," said Shock. " The sands of the Saskatch-ewan are full of gold, and you know, mother, about the rivers in Cariboo."

" Ay, I remember fine the Cariboo, and Cariboo

Cameron and his gold.  But not much good did it do him, poor fellow."

"But," said Shock, gazing into the fire, "it was terrible to hear his tales of these men in the mines with their saloons and awful gambling places, and the men and women in their lonely shacks in the foot-hills. My! I could see them all."

Mrs. Macgregor looked sharply into her son's face, then laying her kitting down in her lap she turned to him and said severely, " And what took them out yonder?  And did they not know what-na country it was before they went out? "

"Yes," said Shock, still looking into the fire, "but there they are, Mother, there they are, and no living soul to speak a good word to them."

"Well then," said the old lady, even more impatiently, "let them put up with it, as better before them have done to their credit, ay, and to their good as well."

"Meantime the saloons and worse are getting them," replied Shock, "and fine fellows they are, too, he says."

"And is yon man wanting the lads from the college to go out yonder to those terrible-like mines and things so far from their homes?  Why does he not send the men who are wanting places? "  Mrs. Macgregor's tone was unusually sharp.  Both Shock and Brown looked at her in surprise.

"Yes, you may look," she went on, "but I say let them that's not needed here go out yonder, and there will be plenty of them, I warrant."

"'And they'd none of them be missed,'" sang Brown.

"I doubt they wouldn't do," said Shock, shaking his head sadly.

"Well, mother," cried Brown, "you'll have a chance of hearing him yourself to-morrow morning, for he is going to preach in your church, I see."

The old lady shrugged her shoulders. "Indeed, and I wish our meenister wouldn't be so ready with his pulpit for every Bill and Bob that comes the way. He will not be needing a rest again, will he?"

Shock gazed at his mother in sheer amazement. He had never seen her like this before. This bitter impatience was so unlike her usual calm, dignified self-control.

"But mother," he ventured, "the cause will be needing money and the people will need to hear about it, surely."

"Oh, as to that," she answered in a relieved tone, "it is not much that we can give, but what we can we will, and, indeed, there are many of them in that Kirk that would be the better of giving a little of their money. But, lad," she added as if dismissing a painful subject, "you must be at your books."

"Which means I must go. I know you, Mother Macgregor," said Brown, using his pet name for the woman who had for two years been more of a mother to him than his own.

"Ay, and within a few weeks you will be wishing, as well, that someone had set you to your books, for the examinators will be upon you."

"And, doubtless, shear me as bare as Delilah did Samson of old. But I am not promising you I am going to work. My physician warns me against work on Saturday nights, so I am going to hunt up The Don."

"Indeed then, you will know well where to look for him," said the old lady shrewdly.

"Ah, mother, you're too sharp for any of us. Not much escapes your eyes."

"Indeed, one does not require eyes to see some things, and yon laddie is daft enough."

"Daft's the word," said Brown, "and has been for the last three years. Is not it astonishing and profoundly humiliating," he added solemnly, "to see a chit of a girl, just because she has brown curls and brown eyes with a most bewildering skill in using them, so twiddle a man? It passes my comprehension."

The old lady shook her head at him. "Wait you, my lad. Your day will come."

"I hear The Don has got the offer of a great appointment in connection with the new railway in that country and I fear that means trouble for him. There are those who would be delighted to see him out of the way for a couple of years or so."

But the old lady would not gossip, so Brown was forced to drop the subject with the remark, "But I'll do what I can to assist the Fates, and I'll begin by bringing both those young ladies to hear your big gun to-morrow if I can, Shock. They ought to know more about their own country."

Shock glanced up quickly as if to speak, but seemed to think better of it and poked the fire instead.

"I doubt they would be more profited in their own church," said Mrs. Macgregor. "'Traivellin' sheep are sair tae keep,' as they say in the South country. No, it's little enough the poor things will be getting in yon church of theirs with their read prayers and their bit sairmon—a sairmonette, they will be calling it. Ay, a sairmonette!" The old lady indulged herself in a quiet chuckle of indescribable contempt.

"Why, mother," said Shock in a reproving tone, "don't you know that their minister is just a splendid preacher. There is no better in the city."

"And that's not saying much," said the old lady. "But I'm glad to hear it."

"My! mother, but you are censorious to-night. You can't expect to find men like Candlish, Chalmers, and Macdonald of Ferintosh in every age."

"Ay," said the old lady with an emphatic shake of her head, "and that's a true word. Men like yon are not to be found, and like McCheyne and Burns and Guthrie and the rest of them. Oh! it iss manys the Sabbath morning when I wass a lass, that I walked with my shoes and stockings in my hand down the glen to hear these men preach. And yon was the preaching. Yon was the preaching. None of your puny, peeping, fifteen-meenute sairmonettes, but preaching, terrible heart-smiting preaching." The old lady had ceased her knitting and was sitting erect in her chair gazing straight before her. The young men sat silent, fearing to break the spell that was upon her, and waiting eagerly for what they knew was coming.

" Man ! man ! " she continued, " those were the days ! and those were the men !   I have heard such preaching as would cause your heart to quake within you and make you to listen with the fear of death upon you lest it should stop."

" It must have been terrible preaching, indeed," said Brown softly.

" Terrible ! ay, terrible's the word.   Lad, lad," said the old lady, turning upon Brown her piercing blue-grey eyes, " in the old Mullin Church I have seen the very rafters throbbing, and strong men and women swaying like the tree-tops in the glen while Burns was raging forth upon them like the Tummel in spate, while visions of the eternal things—the throne of God and the Judgment Day—filled our eyes."   She paused a few moments and then sinking back into her chair she went on, " Ay, terrible preaching, yon, like the storm-blast sweeping the hillsides and rending the firs in the Pass.   Yes ! yes !   But gentle at times and winning, like the rain falling soft at night, wooing at the bluebells and the daisies in the glen, or like a mother croonin. over the babe at her breast, till men wept for love and longing after Himself.   Ay, lad, lad, yon was the preaching."

There was a long silence while they waited for her to continue.

" What was that sermon, mother, at Mullin that time upon the words ' Will ye also go away ? ' you remember ? " at length asked Shock cunningly.

His mother sighed. " Ay, and that was a sairmon to draw the heart out o' you. That was the melting day, while the big men gripped their sticks hard and the women wiped at their eyes that would never be done running, and that man's voice soughing over them like the wind in the pines in the evening, Yes! yes! But," suddenly recalling herself, " come, lads, you must be off to your books."

The young men sat a few moments silently gazing into the fire, and then Brown rose and said, " Good-night, mother. You're the greatest preacher I know, and I would not mind a whole hour from you." His voice was earnest and his eyes soft and tender as he stooped and kissed her cheek.

" Good-night, laddie," answered Mrs. Macgregor, patting his hand gently. " I doubt, after all, the fault nowadays is not with the preaching so much as with the hearing."

" Well, I'm off. You will see me to-morrow with my flock of straying sheep. But I warn you that after you hear that man from the West you will all be volunteering as missionaries."

The old lady took up her knitting again and after the door had closed upon Brown sat back in her chair with a weary sigh.

" You're tired to-night, mother," said Shock gently.

" Tired? And what for would I be tired? No, no, but the day is long."

" Yes, some days, mother. But the longest pass."

She glanced quickly at her son, but save for a quivering of the lips usually so firm, there was no sign of the pain which both knew lay at the heart of each. Her mood of impatience had passed. She was once more herself, calm and strong, looking with steadfast eyes into the future, knowing well that whatever the days might bring, He who for fifty years had been her refuge and her strength would not fail her.

The appeal for the West was the theme of conversation at the Fairbanks home, where the usual company had assembled. The Don was describing the Superintendent's address at the College and thrilling his listeners with his own enthusiasm, when Brown entered.

"Hello! At it again?" cried Brown. "If he doesn't avoid that fiery cross fellow, The Don will be off for the West first thing you know."

"Tell us," cried Betty, "was he as great as all that? Mr. Balfour here would have us believe that this Western man is really something wonderful."

"Well, I don't know," said Brown. "You never think of whether he is wonderful or not, but one thing I know, he makes you see things—the mountains and that foot-hill country, the mining camps and all that saloon and gambling-hell business, till you can smell the brimstone and you want to be in it."

"What? Into the brimstone?" laughed Lloyd.

"I am rather incoherent, I confess. But that old chap suits me. If I were a Theologue, and unattached, I'd be there."

"There's no doubt it is a great country, with vast opportunities," said The Don, glancing at Betty.

"Yes," said Mrs. Fairbanks, frowning as she noted

the glance, " and doubtless any young man who has the necessary enterprise and courage will make his fortune with the growth of that country."

" But why unattached?  What do you mean by that? " enquired Betty.

" Unattached?  Why, you know, just like me—a man with no family ties to speak of.  Did you tell them that yarn, Lloyd?  Well, I'll tell you.  You know the Superintendent was telling the fellows of the difficulty he had in securing men.  Well, he managed to get a man from an Eastern College whom he appointed to the Cariboo—right sort of chap, too, apparently—accepted the appointment—everything was arranged—happened, however, he was engaged to a young lady brought up in the lap of luxury, and that sort of thing.  When she heard of her young man being appointed to this outlandish place, she promptly collapsed into a faint, sister went into hysterics, mother into a blind rage, result—young man resigned.  ' So you see, gentlemen,' said the old chap dryly, ' when you have to consider the tastes and temperament, not only of the young man, but of his young lady and of all her near family relatives, the difficulty of securing men for the West is sensibly increased.' "

" I think that is just horrid of him," exclaimed Betty indignantly.  " The young lady ought to be consulted.  Don't you think so? " turning to Lloyd.

" Why certainly, and yet——"

" Most assuredly," said Mrs. Fairbanks.  " Would you ask a young lady to go out and bury herself alive in such a country as that, or ask her to wait an indefinite number of years till the young man should return? Why it is simply monstrous." And Mrs. Fairbanks fixed her glasses firmly on her nose and gazed at Brown as if she would annihilate him.

"Why certainly I would," replied Brown, quite unabashed; "and if she loved me," placing his hand over his heart, "she would be glad to do either. I would simply remark, 'My love, I'm off for Greenland.' 'Wait, my dear,' she would promptly reply, 'till I get my furs.'"

"All the same," said Lloyd seriously, "it would be a terrible life for any woman, and a man should hesitate before asking her to share it."

"No society, nothing congenial in environment! Quite impossible!" exclaimed Mrs. Fairbanks with great emphasis. "And quite absurd to dream of it."

"Then," replied Brown warmly to Lloyd, "the only available men for your Chief, apparently, are hopeless old bachelors or young men, however worthy like myself, who are still unappropriated."

"Exactly," said Mrs. Fairbanks with an air of finality.

"But, Mrs. Fairbanks," exclaimed The Don, "what of our soldiers and officers who go to India and other outlandish places? They take their wives along with them, I understand?"

"That's quite a different thing, Mr. Balfour," said Mrs. Fairbanks. "These men go out to serve their Queen and country, and it is recognised as the proper thing, and—well, you see, it is quite different."

"I must say," exclaimed Helen, hastening to forestall the hot answer she knew to be at The Don's lips, "I agree with Mr. Brown. If a man's work calls him to Greenland, his wife ought to go with him or she ought to be willing to wait his return."

"Helen, you speak like a sentimental school-girl," replied Mrs. Fairbanks with a touch of haughty scorn. "Of course if a man is married and duty calls him to a foreign land, he must go. But why should a girl throw away her prospects and condemn herself to a life of obscurity and isolation by attaching herself to a man who chooses to take up some fantastic mission in some outlandish place or other?"

"Why? Because she loves a man whose duty calls him there," exclaimed Helen, her grey eyes glowing.

"Bravo!" replied Brown. "If I see a Western missionary wanting a helpmeet—that's the proper word, I believe—I shall know where to send him."

"Nonsense," cried Mrs. Fairbanks quite crossly, "but surely we need not discuss the question any further."

"Well, if I may offer an opinion," said The Don in a deliberate, strained voice, "that country is the place for men with enterprise who believe in themselves, and I think no man is throwing his prospects away who identifies himself with it—nor woman either, for that matter. And what is true of other professions ought to be true of the ministry."

"I agree," cried Brown, adding wickedly, "just the spot for you, Lloyd."

"Why, I should like nothing better," said Lloyd, " if circumstances indicated that my work lay there."

" Well, well, what's come to you all? " cried Mrs. Fairbanks, holding up her jewelled hands in despair.

" The Occidental microbe," suggested Brown.

" And the monumental nonsense it is," said Mrs. Fairbanks, " for men of high culture and special training to lose themselves in such a country as that."

" But," persisted Brown, " they say that that's the very place for such men.   Why, that country is full of high-class chaps—University grads, Lords, Dukes, and such, as well as the professional gambler, and other highly technical experts.   The Superintendent declared to-night he wouldn't have any but high-class men—hence, Lloyd!" and Brown waved his hand toward that gentleman.

" I have no doubt," said Mrs. Fairbanks with severe deliberation, " that Mr. Lloyd has the good sense to perceive that his special training fits him for something quite different, and I think he will not be mad enough to throw away his brilliant prospects in any such silly manner.   But come, let us have some music. Mr. Lloyd, you and Betty sing something for us."

As they moved to the piano, Brown looked up at The Don.   His handsome, haughty face was set hard and in his eyes burned a light that Brown had often seen there on the football field.

" He's going to tackle and tackle hard, too, poor old chap.   Not much chance, though, against that combination of Church and State."

" Oh, that we two were Maying," sang Lloyd in

his fine tenor voice, with Betty responding in like sentiment.

"Well, I rather hope not," muttered Brown to himself as he crossed the room to where Helen was seated. Pausing a moment beside her he said in a low tone, "The Don has had an offer on the new railway construction in the West—two years' appointment. Go and talk to him about it. Looks fierce, doesn't he?" And Helen, nodding intelligently, lingered a moment and then moved to where The Don sat, while Brown went toward the piano. "Must get these youngsters inoculated with the Occidental microbe," he muttered as he took his place beside Mrs. Fairbanks, who was listening with pleased approval to the "Maying" duet, the pauses of which Brown industriously employed in soothing her ruffled feelings. So well did he succeed that when he proffered the humble request that the young ladies should be allowed to accompany him to Shock's church in the morning, Mrs. Fairbanks gave a reluctant assent.

"Undoubtedly, I am a great strategist," said Brown to himself next morning as he sat watching with surreptitious glances the faces of the young ladies beside him. The preacher was at his best. The great land where his life mission lay, with its prairies, foot-hills, mountains, and valleys, and all their marvellous resources, was spread out before the eyes of the congregation with all the passionate pride of the patriot. The life of the lonely rancher and of his more lonely wife, the desperate struggle for manhood by the men of the mine and the railroad and the lumber camp, the magnitude of the issues at stake; the pathos of defeat, the glory of triumph, were all portrayed with a power that compelled the sympathy of his hearers, while the shrewd common-sense vein that ran through all convinced their intellects and won their confidence. Perplexity, wonder, horror, compassion, filled their hearts and were reflected with rapid succession on their faces, as he told his stories of the wreck of human lives and consequent agony of human hearts.

"By Jove! they've got it," exclaimed Brown to himself. "The dear Mrs. Fairbanks has no anti-toxine for this microbe." His eyes turned to Shock and there were held fast. "He's got it, too, confound him," he grumbled. "Surely, he wouldn't be beast enough to leave his old mother alone." The mother's face was a strange sight. On it the anguish of her heart was plainly to be seen, but with the anguish the rapt glory of those who triumph by sacrifice.

As the congregation broke up the young ladies hurried to greet Mrs. Macgregor. From the day of the football match they had carefully and persistently nursed the acquaintance then begun till they had come to feel at home in the Macgregor cottage. Hence, when Betty fell into severe illness and they were at their wits' end for a nurse, they gladly accepted Mrs. Macgregor's proffered help, and during the long anxious weeks that followed, the whole family came to regard with respect, confidence, and finally warm affection, the dignified old lady who, with such kindly, shrewd, and tender care, nursed the sick girl back to strength. Helen especially, who had shared the long watch with her, had made for herself a large place in her heart. To-day, after an exchange of greetings, Helen drew Mrs. Macgregor back and allowed the others to go on. For some time they walked in silence, Helen holding the old lady tight by the arm.

"Well, what do you think of that?" she said finally. "Wasn't it wonderful? It makes one proud to be a Canadian. What a country that must be! If I were only a man! It's too bad that men have all the good things. Wouldn't you like to go yourself?"

"That I would," said the old lady eagerly, "that I would. But I doubt it's not for me. But yon's a man."

"Yes," cried Helen enthusiastically, "he is a man to follow. Of course, it was a strange sermon for a church—those stories of his, I mean, and all those figures about coal beds and gold and cattle. I'm not used to that sort of thing and I don't like to see the people laugh."

"Ay, he's wise," replied the old lady shrewdly. "When a man laughs he's nearer to letting his money go. Ay, he's wise, yon man."

"Of course, I think he's extreme," said Helen. "You would think to hear him there was no place but the West and that every young minister must go out there and give up everything."

"There's few to go, I doubt," said the old lady in a musing tone, "and yon are terrible-like places for those lads to live."

"Yes, but everyone can't go."

"No, no. That's it. That's just it. Not many

can go and not many are fit to go.   But those that can—— " the old lady paused, drawing her breath in sharply.

" But surely a man may do his work without giving up everything he holds dear," persisted Helen.

" ' Forsaketh not all that he hath,' " quoted the old lady softly.

" Yes, but that's not for everybody," insisted Helen.

" ' Whosoever,' " quoted Mrs. Macgregor again, with a stern relentlessness in her tone.   " Ay, there will be no slipping out from under yon."

" But surely," argued Helen, " it is not reasonable to think that every young minister is bound to forsake home and friends, and all that, and go out to these wild places."

" Not every one will be called.   The application will not be easy for any of us, I doubt.   Oh, no! it will not be easy."

" But surely, Mrs. Macgregor, there are other claims upon men."

" There iss only one claim, lassie, only one claim. His claim is the first.   All other claims will just be working out that first one.   Ay, that's it," she said, as if arriving at decision, " only one claim.   God peety us!   One claim," she added with a sudden break in her voice.

At that break Helen glanced at the old lady.   The strong face was working strangely.   The tears were slowly making their way down the wrinkled face.

" Oh, Mrs. Macgregor! " exclaimed Helen, " that seems an awfully hard doctrine.   Do you think God ever wants a man to leave father, mother, wife, help-less behind? "

" No, no, lassie, not helpless. But——," she could go no further. " But," she continued after a moment or two, clutching Helen by the arm, " he—will—be—going—away, lassie, he will be going away. He will be leaving me and—it iss the will of the Lord. Oh! lassie, lassie, heed me not. He must never see the tears on my face."

" Don't! don't! " cried Helen in a sudden anguish. She had no need of further words to tell her what the old lady meant. " He would never do such a thing! He could not do it! "

" Could not? " answered Mrs. Macgregor. " Ay, he could," she said proudly. " Thank God he could. He will not be shaming his blood. But oh! it iss himself will carry a sore heart away with him and leave a sore heart behind."

" Oh, Mrs. Macgregor! " cried Helen, while her breath came fast and her hand went to her own heart, " perhaps he will not think it to be his duty. Per-haps he will not——"

" Indeed, indeed, and I saw it in hiss face last night, and clearer than ever to-day. He hass heard the voice and it iss for him to obey—and for us."

They were near Mrs. Macgregor's home, where the others stood waiting for them at the gate.

" May I come to see you? " said Helen hurriedly.

" Ay, come," said Mrs. Macgregor with a keen look at her, " you will be needing—I will be needing help."

The others they found eagerly discussing the ser-

mon, but there was little criticism.   The Superintendent had won his volunteers.   On Shock's face sat the
serenity of a great decision, in his deep blue eyes the
light of a great enterprise.   As he said good-bye to
Helen, she became aware that his usual hesitating,
nervous awkwardness had given place to quiet,
thoughtful dignity.   A great resolve and a great
sacrifice had lifted him far above things small and
common.

## V

## "YEA, AND HIS OWN LIFE ALSO"

WHEN Helen entered her own room she had leisure to analyse the tumult of emotion filling her heart. Amazement, shame, anger, dismay, grief, were surging across her soul.

"How can he think of leaving his mother? It is a shame!" she cried indignantly to herself. But why this hot sense of shame? "Nonsense!" she protested vehemently to herself, "it is that poor, dear old lady I am thinking of." She remembered that sudden stab at her heart at the old lady's broken words, "He will be going away, lassie," and her cheek flamed hot again. "It is all nonsense," she repeated angrily, and there being no one to contradict her, she said it again with even greater emphasis. But suddenly she sat down, and before long she found herself smiling at the memory of the old lady's proud cry, "Could not? Ay, he could." And now she knew why her heart was so full of happy pride. It was for Shock. He was a man strong enough to see his duty and brave enough to face what to him was the bitterness of death, for well she knew what his mother was to him.

"He will go," she whispered to her looking-glass,

" and I'd go with him to-morrow. But"—and her
face flamed hot—" he must never know."

But he did come to know, to his own great amazement and overwhelming, humbling gladness.

Shock's determination to offer himself to the far
West awakened in his friends various emotions.

" It is just another instance of how religious fanaticism will lead men to the most fantastic and selfish
acts," was Mrs. Fairbanks' verdict, which effected in
Brown a swift conversion. Hitherto he had striven
with might and main to turn Shock from his purpose, using any and every argument, fair or unfair,
to persuade him that his work lay where it had been
begun, in the city wards. He was the more urged to
this course that he had shrewdly guessed Helen's
secret, so sacredly guarded. But on hearing Mrs.
Fairbanks' exclamation, he at once plunged into a
warm defence of his friend's course.

" The finest thing I ever heard of," he declared.
" No one knows what these two are to each other, and
yet there they are, both of them, arriving at the
opinion that Shock's work lies in the West."

" But to leave his mother alone ! " exclaimed Mrs.
Fairbanks indignantly.

" She is not to be alone," said Brown, making there
and then a sudden resolve. " By the greatest of luck
for me I am turned out of my quarters, and she is to
take me in, and while I can't fill Shock's place, still
I am somebody," added Brown, fervently hoping the
old lady would not refuse him shelter.

" I am not sure that a man is ever called to leave

his mother to the care of strangers," said Lloyd, who, after long indecision and much consultation with various friends, had determined that his particular gifts and training fitted him for Park Church.

"Oh! blank it all!" said Brown to Helen, "I can't stand that rot!"

"I beg your pardon," said Mrs. Fairbanks, looking haughtily at Brown through her glasses.

"I was about to say," replied Brown, in the sweetest of tones, "that if these two who are most interested, and who are extremely sane and reasonable persons, have come to an agreement upon a question, I'd bank on that decision as being about the thing." At which Helen gave his arm a quick squeeze.

"Well, mother," said Betty, "I think he's fine, and I never admired him so much as now. You know he may never see her again, and she has the whole of his heart."

"Not quite, I guess," said Brown in a low tone to Helen, who, blushing vividly, replied in like tone, "You seem to be remarkably well informed."

"I know," said Brown confidently. "But he is a mine of blind stupidity! If some one would dig him up, explore him—blast him, in short! Confound him!"

But when the Superintendent learned of all that Shock's decision involved, he made a point to insert among his multitudinous engagements a visit to the Macgregor cottage.

"It was a great scene, I assure you," said Brown, who was describing it afterwards to the young ladies.

" Those two old Spartans, all ice and granite outside, all molten lava within, stood up looking at each other a minute or two without the quiver of an eyelid and then the old chief burred out:

" ' You are to be congratulated upon your son, Mrs. Macgregor.' "

" 'Ay,' said she in a matter of fact tone, ' he will be doing his duty, I warrant.' "

" 'And, believe me, your mutual sacrifice has not been unnoticed.' "

" ' It is not great beside His own, but it iss all we could. It iss our life.' "

" The old chap bowed like a prince and then his voice burred like a buzz saw as he answered, ' Remember I did not ask you for him!' "

" ' No, it wass not you.' "

" 'But I want to tell you,' said the chief, ' I am proud to get a son who for the Cause can forsake such a mother, and I thank God for the mother that can give up such a son.' "

" And then he gripped her hand with that downward pull of his,—he gave it to me once when he heard I was Shock's friend, and nearly jerked me off my feet,—and without more words he was gone, while I stood behind them like a blubbering idiot."

" Oh, isn't she a dear!" exclaimed Betty, " poor thing."

" Poor thing!" echoed Helen warmly, " indeed she doesn't think so. She's as proud of him as she can be, and feels herself rich in his love; and so she is."

Her tone and manner struck Brown with sudden pity.

"Hang his stupidity!" he said to himself, "can't the old bloke see. But he has not such a blamed low opinion of himself that he can't imagine any girl, much less a girl like that, looking at him, and even if he did come to see it he would not think of asking her to share the life he's going to out there; and, by Jove! it would be hard enough for her. I guess I won't take the responsibility of interfering in this business."

But Brown had no need to interfere. Mrs. Fairbanks, of all people, did what was necessary. On the morning of Shock's departure it was she who declared that someone should take pity on "that dear old lady," and should stand by her in her hour of "desertion."

"So I think I shall drive over this afternoon; and, Helen, perhaps you had better come with me. You seem to have great influence with her."

But Helen was of quite another mind. She shrank from intruding upon what she knew would be a sacred hour to mother and son. But when Mrs. Fairbanks expressed her determination to go Helen finally agreed to accompany her.

"Oh, let's all go, mother," said Betty.

"I do not think they will want you, Betty, but you may go along," and so the three ladies proceeded in the afternoon to the Macgregor home.

But at the parting of Shock and his mother there were no tears or lamentations, or at least none that any could witness. Through the long night before, they each knew the other to be keeping the watch of love and agony; yet, each alone, they drank the cup of sacrifice. It was only when the morning was nearing that Shock could bear it no longer, and hastily dressing he came into his mother's room and kneeling by her bedside put his arms about her.

"Mother, mother, why have you not been sleeping?" he whispered.

His mother turned to him and took his head to her bosom in a close embrace, but no words came from her.

"But, mother, don't be grieving like this," sobbed Shock, "or how can I leave you at all."

"Laddie, laddie, why did you come in to me? I had minded to give you up without tears, and this iss my hour of weakness. There now, let your head lie there. Whist! lad, och-hone. It iss twenty-four years since first you lay there, lad, and though grief hass come to me many's the day, yet never through you, never once through you, and you will be remembering that, lad. It will comfort you after—after—after I'm gone."

"Gone, mother!" cried Shock in surprise.

"Yess, for this iss the word given to me this night, that you will see my face no more."

"Oh, mother! mother! don't say that word, for I cannot bear it," and poor Shock buried his face in the pillow, while his great frame shook with sobs.

"Whist now, laddie! There now. It iss the Lord."

Her voice grew steady and grave. "It iss the Lord, and He gave you to me for these few happy years, and, Shock, man, you will be heeding me."

Shock turned his face toward her again and laid his face close to her cheek.

"Remember, I gave you to Himself in convenant that day, and that covenant you will keep now and—afterwards, and I must be keeping it too."

"Yes, mother," said Shock brokenly, while he held her tight. "But it is only for two years, and then I will be coming home, or you to me, and before that, perhaps."

"Yes, yes, laddie, it may be—it may be," said his mother soothingly, "but whether or no, we will not be taking back with the one hand what we give with the other. I had minded to give you without tears, but—but—oh, lad, you are all—all—all—I have. There is no one left to me."

There was a long silence between them. Under cover of darkness they let their tears freely mingle. In all his life Shock had never seen his mother sob, and now he was heart-stricken with grief and terror.

"Whist now, mother, you must not cry like that. Surely God will be good to us, and before long I will get a little place for you yonder. Why should you not come to me? There are missionaries' wives out there," he said.

"No, lad," his mother replied quietly, "I will not be deceiving myself, nor you. And yet it may be the Lord's will. But go away now and lie you down.

You will need to sleep a bit, to-morrow will be a hard day to you."

For twenty years and more she had thought first of her boy, and now, even in the midst of her own great sorrow, she thought mostly of him and his grief.

" Let me stay here, mother," whispered Shock. And so in each other's arms they lay, and from sheer exhaustion both soon fell asleep.

The morning's sun was shining through the chink by the curtain when Mrs. Macgregor awoke. Gently she slipped out of the bed and before dressing lighted the kitchen fire, put on the kettle for the tea and the pot for the porridge. Then she dressed herself and stepping about on tiptoe prepared breakfast, peering in now and then at her sleeping son.

It was with a face calm and strong, and even bright, that she went in at last to waken him.

" Now, mother," exclaimed Shock, springing off the bed, " this is really too bad, and I meant to give you your breakfast in bed to-day."

" Ay, it's myself knew that much," she cried with a little laugh of delight.

" Oh, but you're hard to manage," said Shock severely, " but wait until I get you out yonder in my own house."

" Ay, lad," answered his mother brightly, " it will be your turn then."

They were determined, these two, to look only at the bright side to-day. No sun should shine upon their tears. The parting would be sore enough with

all the help that hope could bring. And so the morning passed in last preparations for Shock's going, and
the last counsels and promises, and in planning for
the new home that was to be made in the shadow of the
Rockies in the far West.

"And the time will soon pass, mother," said Shock
cheerfully, "and it will be good for you to have
Brown with you. He will need your care, you know,"
he hastened to add, knowing well that not for her own
sake could she have been persuaded to receive even
Brown into her little home.

"Ay, I will do for him what I can," she replied,
"and indeed," she added warmly, "he's a kind lad,
poor fellow."

"And the young ladies will be looking in on you
now and then, so they said," and Shock bent low over
his trunk working with the roping of it.

"Yes, indeed," replied his mother heartily, "never
you fear."

And so with united and determined purpose they
kept at arm's length the heart's sorrow they knew
would fall upon each when alone.

To go to the ends of the earth in these globe-trot-
ting days is attended with little anxiety, much less
heart-break, but in those days when Canada was cut
off at the Lakes, the land beyond was a wilderness,
untravelled for the most part but by the Indian or
trapper, and considered a fit dwelling place only for
the Hudson Bay officer kept there by his loyalty to
"the Company," or the half-breed runner to whom
it was native land, or the more adventurous land-

hungry settler, or the reckless gold-fevered miner. Only under some great passion did men leave home and those dearer than life, and casting aside dreams of social, commercial, or other greatness, devote themselves to life on that rude frontier. But such a passion had seized upon Shock, and in it his mother shared. Together these two simple souls, who were all in all to each other, made their offering for the great cause, bringing each their all without stint, without measure, without grudging, though not without heart-break, and gaining that full exquisite joy, to so many unknown, of love's complete sacrifice.

To none but themselves, however, was the greatness of the sacrifice apparent. For when the carriage arrived with Mrs. Fairbanks and her daughters there was no sign of tears or heart-break in the quiet faces that welcomed them. And Mrs. Fairbanks, who had come prepared to offer overflowing sympathy to the old lady " deserted " by her " fanatical " son, was somewhat taken aback by the quiet dignity and perfect control that distinguished the lady's voice and manner. After the first effusive kiss, which Mrs. Fairbanks hurried to bestow and which Mrs. Macgregor suffered with calm surprise, it became difficult to go on with the programme of tearful consolation which had been prepared. There seemed hardly a place for sympathy, much less for tearful consolation, in this well-ordered home, and with these self-sufficient folk.

" We thought we would like to come over and—and —help, perhaps drive you to the station to see your son off," said Mrs. Fairbanks, who was readjusting her scenery and changing her rôle with all speed.

"That was kind, indeed," said Mrs. Macgregor, "but Hamish will be walking, I doubt, and I will just be waiting at home."

She had the instinct of the wounded to hide in some sheltered and familiar haunt.

"I shall be glad to remain with you, Mrs. Macgregor, if I can be of any service," repeated Mrs. Fairbanks.

"It will not be necessary; everything is done, and there is nothing needed."

The voice was more than quiet, as if it came from a heart whose passion had been spent.

"It is very kind, indeed, and we are grateful," said Shock, feeling that his mother's manner might be misunderstood.

"Yess, yess," said the old lady hastily, "it iss very good of you and of the young ladies," turning to look at Helen with kindly eyes. "You will not be thinking me ungrateful," she added with a suspicion of tears in her voice. "I have been spoiled by Hamish yonder," turning her face toward her son.

"Whist now, mother," said Hamish to her in a low tone, in which depreciation and warning were mingled. He knew how hard the next hour would be for himself and for his mother, and he knew, too, that they could not indulge themselves in the luxury of uttered grief and love. At this moment, to the relief of all, Brown entered with an exaggerated air of carelessness.

"Here's a man for your 'settler's effects,'" he

cried cheerily.   " Lucky dog, aint he," he cried, turning to Helen, " and don't I wish I was in his place.
Think of the times he will have riding over the claims
with those jolly cowboys, not to speak of the
claims he will be staking, and the gold he will be wash-
ing out of those parish streams of his.   Don't I wish I
were going!   I am, too, when I can persuade those old
iron-livered professors to let me through.   However,
next year I'm to pass.   Mrs. Macgregor is to see
to that."

" Indeed, I hope so," cried Betty, " an hour's study,
at least, before breakfast and no gallivanting at night.
I will help you, Mrs. Macgregor.   We will get him
through this time."

" Ay, I doubt I will not be much the better of your
help," replied Mrs. Macgregor, with a shrewd kindly
smile.

" There now, take that," said Brown to Betty, adding ruefully to Shock, " You see what I'm in for."

" You'll survive," said Shock.

Then he rose and lifted his coat from the peg behind the door.   At the same instant Helen rose hurriedly and with paling face said to her mother:  " Let
us go now."

" Well, Mrs. Macgregor, if we cannot serve you we
will be going," said Mrs. Fairbanks;  " but we would
be glad to drive Mr. Macgregor to the station."

She was anxious to justify her visit to herself and
her friends.

" That's a first-rate idea," cried Brown, " that is, if
you can give me a lift, too."

" Of course," cried Betty.

" Thank you, I shall be very glad," said Shock, seeing it would please Mrs. Fairbanks.

" Come along, then," said Betty. " I suppose we have not too much time."

" Good-bye, for the present," said Mrs. Fairbanks, offering her hand to the old lady, who was standing erect, white but calm, facing the hour whose bitterness she had already tasted.

" Good-bye," said Betty softly, kissing the white cheek, and trying to hurry her mother towards the door.

At this, Helen, who had been standing with face growing whiter and whiter, went to Mrs. Macgregor and put her arms around her and kissed her good-bye. When she was nearing the door she came hurriedly back. " Oh, let me stay with you. I cannot bear to go," she whispered.

The old lady turned and scrutinised steadily the young face turned so pleadingly toward her. Slowly under that steady gaze the red crept up into the white cheek, like the first dawning of day, till the whole face and neck were in a hot flame of colour. Yet the grey, lustrous eyes never wavered, but, unshrinking, answered the old lady's searching look. At that revealing wave of colour Shock's mother made as if to push the girl away from her, but, with a quick change of mood, she took her in her arms instead.

" Ay, poor lassie, you too! Yes, yes, you may stay with me now."

The motherly touch and tone and the knowledge

that her secret had been read were more than Helen could bear. She clung to Mrs. Macgregor, sobbing passionate sobs.

At this extraordinary outburst Mrs. Fairbanks came back into the room and stood with Shock and the others gazing in utter amazement upon this scene.

"Whist now, lassie, whist now," Mrs. Macgregor was saying, "never you fear, he'll come back again."

"What on earth is this nonsense, Helen?" Mrs. Fairbanks' voice was haughty and suspicious. "What does this mean?"

"It means," said Mrs. Macgregor with quiet dignity, "what neither you nor I can help or harm."

"Helen, speak to me."

At the stern command Helen lifted her face, still hot with blushes, and stood looking straight into her mother's eyes. Her mother turned from her impatiently.

"Do you know what this means?" she said to Shock.

"What? I don't understand," replied Shock, gazing helplessly at the haughty, angry face turned toward him.

"Have you dared to speak to my daughter?"

"Oh, mamma," cried Helen, in an agony of mortification, "how can you?"

"You may well be ashamed," said Mrs. Fairbanks, who had quite lost control of herself, "throwing yourself at the head of a man so far beneath you, with no prospects, and who does not even want you."

"So far beneath, did you say?" cried Mrs. Macgregor quickly. "Woman, say no more. You shame yourself, let alone your child. Whist,"—checking the other's speech—" the blood in the veins of Hector Macgregor yonder" (pointing to the portrait of the Highland soldier on the wall) "was as proud as that in any Lowland trader of you."

"What sort of conduct, then, is this?" answered Mrs. Fairbanks angrily. "Have you encouraged your son?"

"Hush, mother," said Shock, suddenly awakening to an understanding of what was happening, "let me speak."

The stern voice compelled silence. Shock was a new man to them all. He was thinking quickly now for his mother, for himself, but most of all for the girl he loved, who stood with face turned away and eyes cast down in intolerable humiliation.

"Mrs. Fairbanks," said Shock, speaking slowly and with quiet dignity, "if I have not spoken of love to your daughter, it is not because I have not loved her well and for long, but because I could not feel myself worthy of her. Hush, mother; I am not worthy of her, nor shall I ever be, not by reason of any difference in blood,—for there is no difference,—but because of what she is herself, so far above me. I have never spoken with my lips of love, and yet for many and many a day I have feared that my eyes, and all else that could speak, must have told her I loved her. And if it should be—for I will not pretend to misunderstand you—if it should be that it is possible she should ever love me, then there has come to me a joy greater than I could have hoped, and whatever may come of it, this day is the happiest of my life."

As Shock began to speak, Helen lifted her face, and as she listened her look of grief and shame fled, and in her eyes a light of joy began to dawn, then grew till it seemed to overflow in waves across her beautiful face. And as Shock continued his calm, manly words pride mingled in her joy, and her head lifted itself with a grace and dignity that matched that of the old lady standing by her side.

Mrs. Fairbanks stood fairly speechless at Shock's words and at the look of joy and pride she saw upon her daughter's face.

"This is absurd!" she cried at length. "It's preposterous, and it must end now and forever. I forbid absolutely anything in the way of—of engagement or understanding. I will not have my daughter tie herself to a man with such prospects."

"Wait, mother," said Shock, putting his hand out toward the old lady, who was about to speak. "Mrs. Fairbanks," he continued quietly, "far be it from me to take advantage of your daughter in any way, and I say to you here that she is as free now as when she came into this room. I shall not ask her to bind herself to me, but I will be false to myself, and false to her, if I do not say that I love her as dearly as man ever loved woman, and come what may, I shall love her till I die."

The ring in Shock's voice as he spoke the last words thrilled everyone in the room.

"Ay, lad, that you will," said his mother proudly.

"Oh, aint he great," whispered Brown to Betty, who in her excitement had drawn close to him.

Betty responded with a look, but could not trust herself to speak.

The moment was pregnant with possibilities.

As Shock finished speaking, Helen, with an indescribable mingling of shy grace and calm strength, came and stood by his side. For the first time Shock lost control of himself. He flushed hotly, then grew pale, then with a slightly defiant look in his face, he put his arm lightly about her.

"Time for that train," said Brown, who had slipped to the outer door. "That is," he continued in his briskest manner, "if you're going."

With a quick gasp Helen turned towards Shock. He tightened his arm about the girl, and putting his hand upon her shoulder, turned her face toward him and looked down into her face.

"Good-bye," he said gently. "Remember you are free, free as ever you were. I have no claim upon you, but don't forget that I will always love you. I will never forget you."

"Good-bye, Shock," she replied in a low, sweet tone, lifting her face to him. "I will not forget. You know I will not forget."

She slipped her arm around his neck, and while his great frame trembled with emotion she held him fast. "I'll not forget," she said again, the light in her great grey eyes quenched in a quick rush of tears. "You know, Shock, I will not forget." Her lips quivered piteously.

Then Shock cast restraint to the winds. "No," he cried aloud, " you will not forget, thank God, you will not forget, and you are mine!"

He drew her close to him, held her a moment or two, looking into her eyes, and as she lay limp and clinging in his arms he kissed her on the brow, and then on the lips, and gave her to his mother.

"Here, mother," he said, "take her, be good to her, love her for my sake."

He put his arms around his mother, kissed her twice, and was gone.

"He'll never get that train," cried Betty.

"Take the carriage," said Mrs. Fairbanks shortly, " and follow him."

"Come along! hurry!" said Betty, catching Brown's arm.

"The station, John!"

"Oh, I say," gasped Brown, seizing Betty's hand and crushing it ecstatically, "may I embrace you? It's either you or John there."

"Do be quiet. It seems to me we have had as much of that sort of thing as I can stand. Wasn't it awful?"

"Awful? Awfully jolly!" gasped Brown, hugging himself. "Haven't had a thrill approaching that since the McGill match, and even that was only a pale adumbration of what I've just been through."

"I'm sure I don't know what to think. It's so dreadfully startling."

"Startling!" cried Brown. "Come now, Miss

Betty, you don't mean to say you haven't seen this growing for the past six months!"

"No, truly I haven't."

"Well, that's only because you have been so occupied with your own affairs."

"Nonsense," cried Betty indignantly, with a sudden flame of colour in her cheeks. "You're quite rude."

"I don't care for anything now," cried Brown recklessly. "My prayers, tears, and alms-giving haven't been without avail. The terrors and agonies I've endured this last few days lest that old blockhead should take himself off without saying or doing anything, no man will ever know. And he would have gone off, too, had it not been for that lucky fluke of your mother's. Do you mind if I yell?"

"Hush! Here, let my hand go, it's quite useless," said Betty, looking at that member which Brown had just relinquished.

"John," gravely enquired Brown, "are you using both your hands?"

"I beg pardon, sir," enquired the astonished coachman, half turning round.

"Here, do stop your nonsense," cried Betty in a shocked voice.

"Oh, all right, John, this will do," said Brown, seizing Betty's hand again, as John gave his attention to the horses.

"I say, pull up beside Mr. Macgregor there, will you? Here, Shock, get in. You'll miss your train. Here, you old bloke, come along, don't gape like a sick duck. Get in here. You have got to get that train *now*."

"Mr. Brown," said Betty in a severe whisper, "mind, don't say a word to him about this business. I can't stand it."

"Certainly not," said Brown, in a matter of fact tone. "There's nothing to be said."

But there was one last word to be said, and that was Betty's.

"Good-bye, Shock," she whispered to him, as he stepped upon his train. "I think—I know—I'm very glad."

Poor Shock could only grasp her hand in mute farewell. It was just dawning upon him that he had some further offering to bring to make his sacrifice complete.

# VI

## ON THE TRAIL

"T HAT'S the trail. Loon Lake lies yonder."

Shock's Convener, who had charge for his Church of this district, stood by the buck-board wheel pointing southwest. He was a man about middle life, rather short but well set up, with a strong, honest face, tanned and bearded, redeemed abundantly from commonness by the eye, deep blue and fearless, that spoke of the genius in the soul. It was a kindly face withal, and with humour lurking about the eyes and mouth. During the day and night spent with him Shock had come to feel that in this man there was anchorage for any who might feel themselves adrift, and somehow the great West, with its long leagues of empty prairie through which he had passed, travelling by the slow progress of construction trains, would now seem a little less empty because of this man. Between the new field toward which this trail led and the home and folk in the far East there would always be this man who would know him, and would sometimes be thinking of him. The thought heartened Shock more than a little.

"That's the trail," repeated the Convener; "follow that; it will lead you to your home."

"Home!" thought Shock with a tug at his heart and a queer little smile on his face.

"Yes, a man's home is where his heart is, and his heart is where his work lies."

Shock glanced quickly at the man's tanned face. Did he suspect, Shock wondered, the homesickness and the longing in his heart?

Last night, as they had sat together in late talk, he had drawn from Shock with cunning skill (those who knew him would recognise the trick) the picture of his new missionary's home, and had interpreted aright the thrill in the voice that told of the old lady left behind. But now, as Shock glanced at his Convener's face, there was nothing to indicate any hidden meaning in his words. The speaker's eyes were far down the trail that wound like a wavering white ribbon over the yellow-green billows of prairie that reached to the horizon before and up to the great mountains on the right.

"Twenty miles will bring you to Spruce Creek stopping-place; twenty miles more and you are at Big River—not so very big either. You will see there a little school and beside it, on the left, a little house— you might call it a shack, but we make the most of things out here. That's Mr. McIntyre's manse, and proud of it they all are, I can tell you. You will stay with him over night—a fine fellow you will find him, a Nova Scotian, very silent; and better than himself is the little brave woman he has for a wife; a really superior woman. I sometimes wonder—but never mind, for people doubtless wonder at our wives: one can never get at the bottom of the mystery of why some women do it. They will see you on your way.

Up to this time he was the last man we had in that direction. Now you are our outpost—a distinction I envy you."

The Convener's blue eye was alight with enthusiasm. The call of the new land was ever ringing in his heart, and the sound of the strife at the front in his ear.

Unconsciously Shock drew in a long breath, the homesickness and heart-longing gave back before the spirit of high courage and enterprise which breathed through the words of the little man beside him, whose fame was in all the Western Church.

"Up these valleys somewhere," continued the Convener, waving his hands towards the southern sky-line, "are the men—the ranchers and cowboys I told you of last night. Some good men, and some of them devils—men good by nature, devils by circumstance, poor fellows. They won't want you, perhaps, but they need you badly. And the Church wants them, and"—after a little pause—"God wants them."

The Convener paused, still looking at the distant flowing hills. Then he turned to Shock and said solemnly, "We look to you to get them."

Shock gasped. "To me! to get them!"

"Yes, that's what we expect. Why! do you remember the old chap I told you about—that old prospector who lives at Loon Lake?—you will come across him, unless he has gone to the mountains. For thirteen years that man has hunted the gulches for mines. There are your mines," waving his hand again, "and you are our prospector. Dig them up.

Good-bye. God bless you. Report to me in six months."

The Convener looked at his fingers after Shock had left, spreading them apart. "Well, what that chap grips he'll hold until he wants to let it go," he said to himself, wrinkling his face into a curious smile.

Now and then as he walked along the trail he turned and looked after the buckboard heading toward the southern horizon, but never once did his missionary look back.

"I think he will do. He made a mess of my service last night, but I suppose he was rattled, and then no one could be more disgusted than he, which is not a bad sign. His heart's all right, and he will work, but he's slow. He's undoubtedly slow. Those fellows will give him a time, I fear," and again the Convener smiled to himself. As he came to the brow of the hill, where the trail dipped into the river bottom in which the little town lay that constituted the nucleus of his parish, he paused and, once more turning, looked after the diminishing buckboard. "He won't look back, eh! All right, my man. I like you better for it. It must have been a hard pull to leave that dear old lady behind. He might bring her out. There are just the two of them. Well, we will see. It's pretty close shaving."

He was thinking of the threatened cut in the already meagre salaries of his missionaries, rendered necessary by the disproportion between the growth of the funds and the expansion of the work.

"It's a shame, too," he said, turning and looking once more after Shock in case there should be a final signal of farewell, which he would be sorry to miss.

"They're evidently everything to each other." But it was an old problem with the Convener, whose solution lay not with him, but with the church that sent him out to do this work.

Meantime Shock's eyes were upon the trail, and his heart was ringing with that last word of his Convener. "We expect you to get them. You are our prospector, dig them up." As he thought of the work that lay before him, and of all he was expected to achieve, his heart sank. These wild, independent men of the West were not at all like the degraded men of the ward, fawning or sullen, who had been his former and only parishioners. A horrible fear had been growing upon him ever since his failure, as he considered it, with the Convener's congregation the night before. It helped him not at all to remember the kindly words of encouragement spoken by the Convener, nor the sympathy that showed in his wife's voice and manner. "They felt sorry for me," he groaned aloud. He set his jaws hard, as men had seen him when going into a scrim on the football field. "I'll do my best whatever," he said aloud, looking before him at the waving horizon; "a man can only fail. But surely I can help some poor chap out yonder." His eyes followed the waving foot-hill line till they rested on the mighty masses of the Rockies. "Ay," he said with a start, dropping into his mother's speech, "there they are, 'the hills from whence cometh my help.' Surely, I do not think He would send me out here to fail."

There they lay, that mighty wrinkling of Mother Earth's old face, huge, jagged masses of bare grey rock, patched here and there, and finally capped with white where they pierced the blue. Up to their base ran the lumbering foot-hills, and still further up the grey sides, like attacking columns, the dark daring pines swarmed in massed battlions; then, where ravines gave them footing, in regiments, then in outpost pickets, and last of all in lonely rigid sentinels. But far above the loneliest sentinel pine, cold, white, serene, shone the peaks. The Highland blood in Shock's veins stirred to the call of the hills. Glancing around to make sure he was quite alone—he had almost never been where he could be quite sure that he would not be heard—Shock raised his voice in a shout, again, and, expanding his lungs to the full, once again. How small his voice seemed, how puny his strength, how brief his life, in the presence of those silent, mighty, ancient ranges with their hoary faces and snowy heads. Awed by their solemn silence, and by the thought of their ancient, eternal, unchanging endurance, he repeated to himself in a low tone the words of the ancient Psalm:

> " Lord, Thou hast been our dwelling-place,
>     In generations all,
>   Before Thou ever hadst brought forth
>     The mountains, great or small ! "

How exalting are the mountains and how humbling! How lonely and how comforting! How awesome and how kindly! How relentless and how sympathetic! Reflecting every mood of man, they add somewhat to his nobler stature and diminish somewhat his ignobler self. To all true appeal they give back answer, but to the heart regarding iniquity, like God, they make no response. They never obtrude themselves, but they smile upon his joys, and in his sorrow offer silent sympathy, and ever as God's messengers they bid him remember that with all their mass man is mightier than they, that when the slow march of the pines shall have trod down their might's dust, still with the dew of eternal youth fresh upon his brow will he be with God.

Then and there in Shock's heart there sprang up a kindly feeling for the mountains that through all his varying experiences never left him. They were always there, steadfastly watchful by day like the eye of God, and at night while he slept keeping unslumbering guard like Jehovah himself. All day as he drove up the interminable slopes and down again, the mountains kept company with him, as friends might. So much so that he caught himself, more than once after moments of absorption, glancing up at them with hasty penitence. He had forgotten them, but unoffended they had been watching and waiting for him.

A little after noon Shock found the trail turn in toward a long, log, low-roofed building, which seemed to have been erected in sections, with an irregular group of sod-roofed out-houses clustering about.

An old man lounged against the jamb of the open door.

"Good day," said Shock politely.

The old man looked him over for a moment or two and then answered as if making a concession of some importance, "Good day, *good* day! From town? Want to eat?"

A glance through the door, showing the remains of dinner on a table, determined Shock. "No, I guess I'll push on."

"All right," said the old man, his tone suggesting that while it was a matter of supreme indifference to him, to Shock it might be a somewhat serious concern to neglect to eat in his house.

"This is Spruce Creek?" enquired Shock.

"Yes, I believe that's what they call it," said the old man with slow deliberation, adding after a few moments silence "because there ain't no spruces here."

Shock gave the expected laugh with such heartiness that the old man deigned to take some little interest in him.

"Cattle?" he enquired.

"No."

"Sport?"

"Well, a little, perhaps."

"Oh! Pospectin', eh? Well, land's pretty well taken up in this vicinity, I guess."

To this old man there were no other interests in life beyond cattle, sport, and prospcting that could account for the stranger's presence in this region.

"Yes," laughed Shock, "prospecting in a way, too."

The old man was obviously puzzled.

" Well," he ventured, " come inside, anyway. Pretty chilly wind that for April. Come right in !"

Shock stepped in. The old man drew nearer to him.

" Pain-killer or lime-juice? " he enquired in an insinuating voice.

" What? " said Shock.

" Pain-killer or lime-juice," winking and lowering his voice to a confidential tone.

" Well, as I haven't got any pain I guess I'll take a little lime-juice," replied Shock.

The old man gave him another wink, long and slow, went to the corner of the room, pushed back a table, pulled up a board from the floor, and extracted a bottle.

" You's got to be mighty careful," he said. " Them blank police fellers, instead of attending to their business, nose round till a feller can't take no rest at night."

He went to a shelf that stood behind the plank that did for a counter, took down two glasses, and filled them up.

" There," he said with great satisfaction, " you'll find that's no back-yard brew."

Shock slowly lifted the glass and smelt it. " Why, it's whisky ! " he said in a surprised tone.

" Ha ! ha ! " burst out the old man. " You're a dandy ; that's what it is at home."

He was delighted with his guest's fine touch of humour. Shock hesitated a moment or two, looking down at the whisky in the glass before him.

" How much? " he said at length.

" Oh, we'll make that fifty cents to you," said the old man carelessly.

Shock put down the money, lifted his glass slowly, carried it to the door and threw the contents outside.

" Hold on there! What the blank, blank do you mean? " The old man was over the counter with a bound.

" It was mine," said Shock quietly.

" Yours," shouted the old man, beside himself with rage; " I aint goin' to stand no such insult as that."

" Insult! "

" What's the matter with that whisky? "

" All right as far as I know, but I wanted lime-juice."

" Lime-juice! " The old man's amazement somewhat subdued his anger. " Lime-juice! Well, I'll be blanked! "

" That's what I asked for," replied Shock good-naturedly.

" Lime-juice! " repeated the old man. " But what in blank, blank did you throw it out for? "

" Why, what else could I do with it? "

" What else? See here, stranger, the hull population of this entire vicinity isn't more than twenty-five persons, but every last one of 'em twenty-five 'ud told you what to do with it. Why didn't you give it to me? "

" Why," said Shock in a surprised tone, " I don't know the ways of your country, but where I come from we don't take any man's leavings."

This was new light upon the subject for the old man.

"Well, now, see here, young man, if ever you're in doubt again about a glass of whisky like that one there, you just remark to yourself that while there may be a few things you might do with it, there's just one you can't. There's only one spot for whisky, and that's inside some fellow that knows something. Heavens and earth! Didn't know what to do with it, eh?"

He peered curiously into Shock's face as if he found him an interesting study.

"No," said Shock seriously, "you see, I couldn't drink it—never did in my life."

The old man drew nearer to him. "Say," touching him with his forefinger on the chest, "if I could only be sure you'd keep fresh I'd put you in a case. They'd come a mighty long way in this country to see you, you bet."

Bill Lee's anger and disgust were giving place to curiosity.

"What are you, anyway?" he enquired.

"Well, my boss told me to-day I was a prospector." Shock's mind reverted, as he spoke, to that last conversation with his Convener.

"Prospector," echoed the old man. "What for, land, coal?"

"No, men."

"What?" The old man looked as if he could not have heard aright.

"Men," said Shock again simply and earnestly.

Bill was hopelessly puzzled.   He tried to get at it another way.

"What's your Company?" he enquired.   "I mean who are you working for?"

Before answering Shock paused, looking far past Bill down the trail and then said solemnly, "God."

Bill started back from his companion with a gasp of surprise.   Was the man mad?   Putting the incident of the whisky and this answer of his together, he might well be.

"Yes," said Shock, withdrawing his eyes from the trail and facing Bill squarely.   "That's my business. I am after men."   He drew from his pocket a small Bible and read, "Follow me and I will make you fishers of men."

When Bill saw the Bible he looked relieved, but rather disgusted.

"Oh, I git you now!   You're a preacher, eh?"

"Well," said Shock in a tone almost confidential, "I'll tell you I'm not much of a preacher.   I don't think I'm cut out for that, somehow."   Here Bill brightened slightly.   "I tried last night in town," continued Shock, "and it was pretty bad.   I don't know who had the worst of it, the congregation or myself.   But it was bad."

"Thinkin' of quittin'?"   Bill asked almost eagerly, "Because if you are, I know a good job for a fellow of your build and make."

"No, I can't quit.   I have got to go on."   Bill's face fell.   "And perhaps I can make up in some other ways.   I may be able to help some fellows a bit." The sincerity and humble earnestness of Shock's tone quite softened Bill's heart.

"Well, there's lots of 'em need it," he said in his gruff voice. "There's the blankest lot of fools on these ranches you ever seen."

Shock became alert. He was on the track of business.

"What's wrong with them?" he enquired.

"Wrong? Why, they aint got no sense. They stock up with cattle, horses, and outfit to beat creation, and then let the whole thing go to blazes."

"What's the matter with them?" persisted Shock, "Are they lazy?"

"Lazy! not a hair. But when they get together over a barrel of beer or a keg of whisky they are like a lot of hogs in a swill trough, and they won't quit while they kin stand. That's no way for a man to drink!" continued Bill in deep disgust.

"Why, is not this a Prohibition country?"

"Oh! Prohibition be blanked! When any man kin get a permit for all he wants to use, besides all that the whisky men bring in, what's the good of Prohibition?"

"I see," said Shock. "Poor chaps. It must be pretty slow for them here."

"Slow!" exclaimed Bill. "That aint no reason for a man's bein' a fool. I aint no saint, but I know when to quit."

"Well, you're lucky," said Shock. "Because I have seen lots of men that don't, and they're the fellows that need a little help, don't you think so?"

Bill squirmed a little uneasily.

"You can't keep an eye on all the fools unless you round 'em up in corral," he grunted.

"No. But a man can keep from thinking more of a little tickling in his stomach than he does of the life of his fellowman."

"Well, what I say is," replied Bill, "every fellow's got to look after himself."

"Yes," agreed Shock, "and a little after the other fellows, too. If a man is sick——"

"Oh! now you're speakin'," interrupted Bill eagerly. "Why, certainly."

"Or if he is not very strong."

"Why, of course."

"Now, don't you think," said Shock very earnestly, "that kicking a man along that is already sliding toward a precipice is pretty mean business, but snatching him back and bracing him up is worth a man's while?"

"Well, I guess," said Bill quietly.

"That's the business I'm trying to do," said Shock. "I'd hate to help a man down who is already on the incline. I think I'd feel mean, and if I can help one man back to where it's safe, I think it's worth while, don't you?"

Bill appeared uncomfortable. He could not get angry, Shock's manner was so earnest, frank, respectful, and sincere, and at the same time he was sharp enough to see the bearing of Shock's remarks upon what was at least a part of his business in life.

"Yes," repeated Shock with enthusiasm, "that's

worth while. Now, look here, if you saw a man sliding down one of those rocks there," pointing to the great mountains in the distance, " to sure death, would you let him slide, or would you put your hand out to help him? "

" Well, I believe I'd try," said Bill slowly.

" But if there was good money in it for you," continued Shock, " you would send him along, eh? "

" Say, stranger," cried Bill indignantly, " what do you think I am? "

" Well," said Shock, " there's a lot of men sliding down fast about here, you say. What are you doing about it? " Shock's voice was quiet, solemn, almost stern.

" I say," said Bill, " you'd best put up your horse and feed. Yes, you've got to feed, both of you, and this is the best place you'll find for twenty miles round, so come right on. You're line ain't mine, but you're white. I say, though," continued Bill, unhitching the cayuse, " it's a pity you've taken up that preachin' business. I've not much use for that. Now, with that there build of yours "—Bill was evidently impressed with Shock's form—" you'd be fit for almost anything."

Shock smiled and then grew serious.

" No," he said, " I've got to live only once, and nothing else seemed good enough for a fellow's life."

" What, preachin'? "

" No. Stopping men from sliding over the precipice and helping them back. The fact is," and Shock looked over the cayuse's back into Bill's eyes, " every man should take a hand at that.   There's a lot of satisfaction in it."

"Well, stranger," replied Bill, leading the way to the stable, "I guess you're pretty near right, though it's queer to hear me say it.   There aint much in anything, anyway.   When your horse is away at the front leadin' the bunch and everybody yellin' for you, you're happy, but when some other fellow's horse makes the runnin' and the crowd gets a-yellin' for him, then you're sick.   Pretty soon you git so you don't care."

"'Vanity of vanities, all is vanity,'" quoted Shock.  "Solomon says you're right."

"Solomon, eh?   Well, by all accounts he hit quite a gait, too.   Had them all lookin' dizzy, I reckon. Come on in.   I'll have dinner in a shake."

Fried pork and flapjacks, done brown in the gravy, with black molasses poured over all, and black tea strong enough to float a man-of-war, all this with a condiment of twenty miles of foot-hill breezes, makes a dinner such as no king ever enjoyed.   Shock's delight in his eating was so obvious that Bill's heart warmed towards him.   No finer compliment can be paid a cook than to eat freely and with relish of his cooking.   Before the meal was over  the men had so far broken through the barriers of reserve as to venture mutual confidences about the past.   After Shock had told the uneventful story of his life, in which his mother, of course, was the central figure, Bill sat a few moments in silence, and then began:  "Well, I never knew my mother.   My father was a devil, so I guess I came naturally by all the devilment in me, and that's a few. But "—and here Bill paused for some little time—" but I had a sweetheart once, over forty years ago now, down in Kansas, and she was all right, you bet. Why, sir, she was—oh! well, 'taint no use talkin', but I went to church for the year I knowed her more'n all the rest of my life put together, and was shapin' out for a different line of conduct until——" Shock waited in silence. " After she died I didn't seem to care. I went out to California, knocked about, and then to the devil generally." Shock's eyes began to shine.

" I know," he said, " you had no one else to look after—to think of."

" None that I cared a blank for. Beg pardon. So I drifted round, dug for gold a little, ranched a little, just like now, gambled a little, sold whisky a little, nothing very much. Didn't seem to care much, and don't yet."

Shock sat waiting for him to continue, but hardly knew what to say. His heart was overflowing with pity for this lonely old man whose life lay in the past, grey and colourless, except for that single bright spot where love had made its mark. Suddenly he stretched out his hand toward the old man, and said: " What you want is a friend, a real good friend."

The old man took his hand in a quick, fierce grip, his hard, withered face lit up with a soft, warm light.

" Stranger," he said, trying hard to keep his voice steady, " I'd give all I have for one."

" Let me tell you about mine," said Shock quickly.

Half an hour later, as Bill stood looking after Shock and rubbing his fingers, he said in soliloquy: "Well, I guess I'm gittin' old. What in thunder has got into me, anyway? How'd he git me on to that line? Say, what a bunco steerer he'd make! And with that face and them eyes of his! No, 'taint that. It's his blank honest talk. Hang if I know what it is, but he's got it! He's white, I swear! But blank him! he makes a fellow feel like a thief."

Bill went back to his lonely ranch with his lonely, miserable life, unconsciously trying to analyse his new emotions, some of which he would be glad to escape, and some he would be loath to lose. He stood at his door a moment, looking in upon the cheerless jumble of boxes and furniture, and then turning, he gazed across the sunny slopes to where he could see his bunch of cattle feeding, and with a sigh that came from the deepest spot in his heart, he said: "Yes, I guess he's right. It's a friend I need. That's what."

# VII

## THE OUTPOST

UPON a slight swell of prairie stood the Outpost manse of Big River, the sole and only building in the country representative of the great Church which lay behind it, and which, under able statesmanship, was seeking to hold the new West for things high and good. The Big River people were proud of their manse. The minister was proud of it, and with reason. It stood for courage, faith, and self-denial. To the Convener and Superintendent, in their hours of discouragement, this little building brought cheer and hope. For, while it stood there it kept touch between that new country and what was best and most charteristic in Canadian civilisation, and it was for this that they wrought and prayed. But, though to people and minister, Convener and Superintendent, the little manse meant so much, the bareness, the unloveliness, and, more than all, the utter loneliness of it smote Shock with a sense of depression. At first he could not explain to himself this feeling. It was only after he had consciously recognised the picture which had risen in contrast before his mind as the home of the Fairbanks, that he understood.

" I could never bring her to such a house as this," was his thought. " A woman would die here."

And, indeed, there was much to depress in the first look at the little board building that made a home for the McIntyres, set down on the treeless prairie with only a little wooden paling to defend it from the waste that gaped at it from every side. The contrast between this bare speck of human habitation and the cosy homes of his native Province, set each within its sheltering nest of orchard and garden, could hardly have been more complete. But as his eyes ran down the slope of the prairie and up over the hills to the jagged line of peaks at the horizon, he was conscious of a swift change of feeling. The mighty hills spoke to his heart.

" Yes, even here one might live contented," he said aloud, and he found himself picturing how the light from those great peaks would illumine the face that had grown so dear within the last few months.

" And my mother would like it too," he said, speaking once more aloud. So with better heart he turned from the trail to the little manse door. The moment he passed within the door all sense of depression was gone. Out of their bare little wooden house the McIntyres had made a home, a place of comfort and of rest. True, the walls were without plaster, brown paper with factory cotton tacked over it taking its place, but they were wind-proof, and besides were most convenient for hanging things on. The furniture, though chiefly interesting as an illustration of the evolution of the packing box, was none the less service-

able and comfortable. The floors were as yet un-
carpeted, but now that April was come the carpets
were hardly missed. Then, too, the few choice pictures upon the walls, the ingenious bookcase and the
more ingenious plate- and cup-rack displaying honest
delf and some bits of choice china, the draping curtains of muslin and cretonne, all spoke of cultivated
minds and refined tastes. Staring wants there were,
and many discrepancies and incongruities, but no vul-
garities nor coarseness nor tawdriness. What they had
was fitting. What was fitting but beyond their means
these brave home-makers did without, and all things
unfitting, however cheap, they scorned. And Shock,
though he knew nothing of the genesis and evolution
of this home and its furnishings, was sensible of its
atmosphere of quiet comfort and refinement. The
welcome of the McIntyres was radiant with good
cheer and hearty hospitality.

It was partly the sea-rover in his blood, making
impossible the familiar paths trodden bare of any experience that could stir the heart or thrill the imagination, but more that high ambition that dwells in noble
youth, making it responsive to the call of duty where
duty is difficult and dangerous, that sent David Mc-
Intyre out from his quiet country home in Nova
Scotia to the far West. A brilliant course in Pictou
Academy, that nursing mother of genius for that
Province by the sea, a still more brilliant course in
Dalhousie, and afterwards in Pine Hill, promised
young McIntyre anything he might desire in the way
of scholastic distinction. The remonstrance of one

of his professors, when he learned of the intention of his brilliant and most promising student to give his life to Western mission work, was characteristic of the attitude of almost the whole Canadian Church of that day.

"Oh, Mr. McIntyre!" said the Professor, "there is no need for such a man as you to go to the West."

Equally characteristic of the man was McIntyre's reply.

"But, Professor, someone must go; and besides that seems to me great work, and I'd like to have a hand in it."

It was the necessity, the difficulty, and the promise of the work that summoned young McIntyre from all the openings, vacancies, positions, and appointments his friends were so eagerly waving before his eyes and set him among the foot-hills in the far front as the first settled minister of Big River, the pride of his Convener's heart, the friend and shepherd of the scattered farmers and ranchers of the district. Once only did he come near to regretting his choice, and then not for his own sake, but for the sake of the young girl whom he had learned to love and whose love he had gained during his student days. Would she leave home and friends and the social circle of which she was the brightest ornament for all that he could offer? He had often written to her, picturing in the radiant colours of his own Western sky the glory of prairie, foot-hill, and mountain, the greatness and promise of the new land, and the worth of the work he was trying to do. But his two years of missionary experience had made him feel the hardship, the isolation, the meagreness, of the life which she would have to share with him.  The sunset colours were still there, but they were laid upon ragged rock, lonely hill, and wind-swept, empty prairie.  It took him days of hard riding and harder thinking to give final form to the last paragraph of his letter:

"I have tried faithfully to picture my life and work.  Can you brave all this?  Should I ask you to do it?  My work, I feel, lies here, and it's worth a man's life.  But whether you will share it, it is for you to decide.  If you feel you cannot, believe me, I shall not blame you, but shall love and honour you as before.  But though it break my heart I cannot go back from what I see to be my work.  I belong to you, but first I belong to Him who is both your Master and mine."

In due time her answer came.  He carried her letter out to a favourite haunt of his in a sunny coolie where an old creek-bed was marked by straggling willows, and there, throwing himself down upon the sloping grass, he read her message.

"I know, dear, how much that last sentence of yours cost you, and my answer is that were your duty less to you, you would be less to me.  How could I honour and love a man who, for the sake of a girl or for any sake, would turn back from his work?  Besides, you have taught me too well to love your glorious West, and you cannot daunt me now by any such sombre picture as you drew for me in your last letter. No sir. The West for me! And you should be ashamed —and this I shall make you properly repent— ashamed to force me to the unmaidenly course of in- sisting upon going out to you, ' rounding you up into a corral '—that is the correct phrase, is it not?—and noosing, no, roping you there."

When he looked up from the letter the landscape was blurred for a time. But soon he wondered at the new splendour of the day, the sweetness of the air, the mellow music of the meadow-lark. A new glory was upon sky and earth and a new rapture in his heart.

" Wonderful! " he exclaimed. " Dear little soul! She doesn't know, and yet, even if she did, I believe it would make no difference."

Experience proved that he had rightly estimated her. For a year and a half she had stood by her husband's side, making sunshine for him that no clouds could dim nor blizzards blow out. It was this that threw into her husband's tone as he said, " My wife, Mr. Macgregor," the tenderness and pride. It made Shock's heart quiver, for there came to him the picture of a tall girl with wonderful dark grey eyes that looked straight into his while she said, " You know I will not forget." It was this that made him hold the little woman's hand till she wondered at him, but with a woman's divining she read his story in the deep blue eyes, alight now with the memory of love.

" That light is not for me," she said to herself, and

welcomed him with a welcome of one who had been so recently and, indeed, was still a lover.

The interval between supper and bed-time was spent in eager talk over Shock's field. A rough map, showing trails, streams, sloughs, coolies, and some of the larger ranches lay before them on the table.

"This is The Fort," said McIntyre, putting his finger upon a dot on the left side of the map. "Twenty-five miles west and south is Loon Lake, the centre of your field, where it is best that you should live, if you can; and then further away up toward the Pass they tell me there is a queer kind of ungodly settlement—ranchers, freighters, whisky-runners, cattle thieves, miners, almost anything you can name. You'll have to do some exploration work there."

"Prospecting, eh?" said Shock.

"Exactly. Prospecting is the word," said McIntyre. "The Fort end of your field won't be bad in one way. You'll find the people quite civilised. Indeed, The Fort is quite the social centre for the whole district. Afternoon teas, hunts, tennis, card-parties, and dancing parties make life one gay whirl for them. Mind you, I'm not saying a word against them. In this country anything clean in the way of sport ought to be encouraged, but unfortunately there is a broad, bad streak running through that crowd, and what with poker, gambling, bad whisky, and that sort of thing, the place is at times a perfect hell."

"Whisky? What about the Police? I have heard them well spoken of," said Shock.

"And rightly so. They are a **fine** body of men,

with exceptions.    But this infernal permit system
makes it almost impossible to enforce the law, and
where the Inspector is a soak, you can easily understand that the whole business of law enforcement
is a farce.    Almost all the Police, however, in this
country are straight fellows.  There's Sergeant Crisp,
now—there is not money enough in the Territories
to buy him.    Why, he was offered six hundred dollars
not long ago to be busy at the other end of the town
when the freighters came in one night.    But not he.
He was on duty, with the result that some half dozen
kegs of whisky failed to reach their intended des-
tination.    But there's a bad streak in the crowd, and
the mischief of it is that the Inspector and his wife
set the pace for all the young fellows of the ranches
about.    And when whisky gets a-flowing there are
things done that it is a shame to speak of.    But they
won't bother you much.    They belong mostly to
Father Mike."

"Father Mike, a Roman Catholic?"

"No, Anglican.    A very decent fellow.  Have not
seen much of him.    His people doubtless regard me
as a blooming dissenter, dontcherknow.    But he
is no such snob.    He goes in for all their fun—
hunts, teas, dances, card-parties, and all the rest
of it."

"What, gambling?" asked Shock, aghast.

"No, no.    I understand he rakes them fore and
aft for their gambling and that sort of thing.    But
they don't mind it much.    They swear by him, for
he is really a fine fellow.  In sickness or in trouble

Father Mike is on the spot. But as to influencing their lives, I fear Father Mike is no great force."

"Why do you have a mission there at all?" enquired Shock.

"Simply because the Superintendent considers The Fort a strong strategic point, and there are a lot of young fellows and a few families there who are not of Father Mike's flock and who could never be persuaded to attend his church. It doesn't take much, you know, to keep a man from going to church in this country, so the Superintendent's policy is to remove all possible excuses and barriers and to make it easy for men to give themselves a chance. Our principal man at The Fort is Macfarren, a kind of lawyer, land-agent, registrar, or something of that sort. Has cattle too, on a ranch. A very clever fellow, but the old story—whisky. Too bad. He's a brother of Rev. Dr. Macfarren."

"What? Dr. Macfarren of Toronto?"

"Yes. And he might be almost anything in this country. I'll give you a letter to him. He will show you about and give you all information."

"And is he in the Church?" Shock's face was a study. McIntyre laughed long and loud.

"Why, my dear fellow, we're glad to get hold of any kind of half-decent chap that is willing to help in any way. We use him as usher, manager, choirmaster, sexton. In short, we put him any place where he will stick."

Shock drew a long breath. The situation was becoming complicated to him.

"About Loon Lake," continued McIntyre, "I can't tell you much. By all odds the most interesting figure there is the old Prospector, as he is called. You have heard about him?"

Shock bowed.

"No one knows him, though he has been there for many years. His daughter, I understand, has just come out from England to him. Then, there's Andy Hepburn, who runs a store, a shrewd, canny little Scot. I have no doubt he will help you. But you'll know more about the place in a week than I could tell you if I talked all night, and that I must not do, for you must be tired."

When he finished Shock sat silent with his eyes upon the map. He was once more conscious of a kind of terror of these unknown places and people. How could he get at them? What place was there for him and his mission in that wild, reckless life of theirs? What had he to bring them. Only a Tale? In the face of that vigorous, strenuous life it seemed at that moment to Shock almost ridiculous in its inadequacy. Against him and his Story were arraigned the great human passions—greed of gold, lust of pleasure in its most sensuous forms, and that wild spirit of independence of all restraint by law of God or man. He was still looking at the map when Mr. McIntyre said:

"We will take the books, as they say in my country."

"Ay, and in mine," said Shock, coming out of his dream with a start.

Mrs. McIntyre laid the Bible on the table. Her husband opened the Book and read that great Psalm of the wilderness, " Lord, thou hast been our dwelling place," and so on to the last cry of frail and fading humanity after the enduring and imperishable, " Let the beauty of the Lord our God be upon us; and establish thou the work of our hands upon us: yea, the work of our hands establish thou it."

As he listened to the vivid words that carried with them the very scent and silence of the hungry wilderness, there fell upon Shock's ears the long howl and staccato bark of the prairie wolf. That lonely voice of the wild West round them struck Shock's heart with a chill of fear, but following hard upon the fear came the memory of the abiding dwelling place for all desert pilgrims, and in place of his terror a great quietness fell upon his spirit. The gaunt spectre of the hungry wilderness vanished before the kindly presence of a great Companionship that made even the unknown West seem safe and familiar as one's own home. The quick change of feeling filled Shock's heart to overflowing, so that when Mr. McIntyre, closing the Book, said, " You will lead us in prayer, Mr. Macgregor," Shock could only shake his head in voiceless refusal.

" You go on, David," said his wife, who had been watching Shock's face.

As Shock lay that night upon his bed of buffalo skins in the corner, listening to the weird sounds of the night without, he knew that for the present at least that haunting terror of the unknown and that disturbing sense of his own insufficiency would not trouble him. That dwelling place, quiet and secure, of the McIntyre's home in the midst of the wide waste about was to him for many a day a symbol of that other safe dwelling place for all pilgrims through earth's wilderness.

" Poor chap," said McIntyre to his wife when they had retired for the night, " I'm afraid he'll find it hard work, especially at The Fort. He is rather in the rough, you know."

" He has beautiful honest eyes," said his wife, " and I like him."

" Do you? "

" Yes, I do," she replied emphatically.

" Then," said her husband, " in spite of all appearances he's all right."

# VIII

## THE OLD PROSPECTOR

LOON LAKE lay in the afternoon sunlight, shimmering in its glory of prismatic colours, on one side reflecting the rocks and the pines that lined the shore and the great peaks that stood further back, and the other lapping the grasses and reeds that edged its waters and joined it to the prairie. A gentle breeze now and then breathed across the lake, breaking into myriad fragments the glassy surface that lay like sheets of polished multi-coloured metal of gold and bronze and silver, purple and green and blue.

A young girl of about sixteen years, riding a cayuse along the lake shore, suddenly reined in her pony and sat gazing upon the scene.

"After all," she said aloud, "it is a lovely spot, and if only father could have stayed, I wouldn't mind."

Her tone was one of discontent. Her face was not beautiful, and its plainness was increased by a kind of sullen gloom that had become its habit. After gazing across the lake for some minutes she turned her horse and cantered toward a little cluster of buildings of all sizes and shapes that huddled about the end of the lake and constituted Loon Lake village. As she drew near the largest of the houses, which was dignified by the name of Loon Lake Stopping Place, she came upon a group of children gathered about a little cripple of about seven or eight years of age, but so puny and poorly developed that he appeared much younger. The little lad was sobbing bitterly, shriek-ing oaths and striking savagely with his crutch at the children that hemmed him in. The girl sprang off her pony.

"Oh, shame on you!" she exclaimed, rushing at them. "You bad children, to tease poor Patsy so. Be off with you. Come, Patsy, never mind them. I am going to tell you a story."

"He was throwin' stones at us, so he was," said his brother, a sturdy little red-headed lad of six. "And he hit Batcheese right on the leg, too."

"He pu—pu—pulled down my mountain right to the ground," sobbed Patsy, lifting a pale, tear-stained face distorted with passion.

"Never mind, Patsy," she said soothingly, "I'll help you to build it up again."

"And they all laughed at me," continued Patsy, still sobbing stormily. "And I'll knock their blank, blank heads off, so I will!" And Patsy lifted his crutch and shook it at them in impotent wrath.

"Hush, hush, Patsy! you must not say those awful words," said the girl, laying her hand over his mouth and lifting him onto her knee.

"Yes, I will. And I just wish God would send them to hell-fire!"

" Oh, Patsy, hush! " said the girl.  " That's awful. Never, never say such a thing again."

" I will! " cried Patsy, " and I'll ask God to-night, and mother said He would if they didn't leave me alone."

" But, Patsy, you must not say nor think those awful things.  Come now and I'll tell you a story."

" I don't want a story," he sobbed.  " Sing."

" Oh, I'll tell you a story, Patsy.  I'll come into the house to-night and sing for you."

" No, sing," said the little lad imperiously, and so the girl began to sing the thrilling love story of The Frog and The Mouse, till not only was Patsy's pale face wreathed in smiles, but the other children were drawn in an enchanted circle about the singer.  So entranced were the children and so interested the singer that they failed to notice the door of the Stopping Place open.  A slovenly woman showed a hard face and dishevelled hair for a moment at the door, and then stole quietly away.  In a few moments she returned, bringing her husband, a huge man with a shaggy, black head and repulsive face.

" Jist be afther lookin' at that now, will ye, Carroll! " she said.

As the man looked his face changed as the sun breaks through a storm-cloud.

" Did ye iver see the loikes av that? " she said in a low voice.  " She'd draw the badgers out av their holes with thim songs av hers.  And thim little divils have been all the mornin' a-fightin' and a-scrappin' loike Kilkenny cats."

"An' look at Patsy," said her husband, with wonder and pity in his eyes.

"Yis, ye may say that, for it's the cantankerous little curmudgeon he is, poor little manny."

"Cantankerous!" echoed her husband. "It's that blank pain av his."

"Whist now, Tim. There's Thim that'll be hearin' ye, an' it'll be the worse f'r him an' f'r you, beloike."

"Divil a fear have Oi av Thim," said her sceptical husband scornfully.

"Aw, now, do be quiet, now," said his wife, crossing herself. "Sure, prayin' is jist as aisy as cursin', and no harrum done, at all." She shut the door.

"Aw, it's the beautiful singer she is," as the girl struck up a new song. "Listen to that now."

Full, clear, soft, like the warbling of the thrush at evening, came the voice through the closed door. The man and his wife stood listening with a rapt look on their faces.

"Phat in Hivin's name is she singin', at all?" said Mrs. Carroll.

"Whisht!" said her husband, holding up his hand. "It's like a wild burrd," he added, after listening a few moments.

"The pore thing. An' it's loike a wild burrd she is," said Mrs. Carroll pityingly. "Left alone so soon afther comin' to this sthrange counthry. It's a useless man altogether, is that ould Prospector."

Carroll's face darkened.

"Useless!" he exclaimed wrathfully, "he's a blank

ould fool, crazy as a jack rabbit! An' Oi'm another blank fool to put any money into 'im."

"Did ye put much in, Tim?" ventured Mrs. Carroll.

"Too much to be thrown away, anyhow."

"Thin, why does ye do it, Tim?"

"Blanked if Oi know. It's the smooth, slippin' tongue av 'im. He'd talk the tale aff a monkey, so he would."

At this moment a loud cry, followed by a stream of oaths in a shrill childish voice, pierced through the singing.

"Phat's that in all the worrld?" exclaimed Mrs. Carroll. "Hivin preserve us, it's little Patsy. Tim, ye'll 'av to be spakin' to that child for the swearin'. Listen to the oaths av 'im. The Lord forgive 'im!"

Tim strode to the door, followed by his wife.

"Phat the blank, blank is this yellin' about? Phat d'ye mane swearin' loike that, Patsy? Oi'll knock yer blank little head aff if Oi catch ye swearin' agin."

"I don't care," stormed little Patsy, quite unafraid of his father when the other children fled. "It's that blank, blank Batcheese an' Tim there. They keep teasin' me an' Mayan all the time."

"Let me catch yez, ye little divils!" shouted Carroll after the children, who had got off to a safe distance. "Go on, Marion, an' sing phat ye loike. It's loike a burrd ye are, an' Oi loikes t' hear ye. An' Patsy, too, eh?"

He took the little cripple up in his arms very gently and held him for some minutes.

"You're a big man, dad, aint ye?" said Patsy, putting his puny arm round his father's hairy neck. "An' ye can lick the hull town, can't ye?"

"Who wuz tellin' ye that, Patsy?" asked his father, with a smile.

"I heard ye meself last week when the big row was on."

"Ye did, be dad! Thin Oi'm thinkin' ye do be hearin' too much."

"But ye can, dad, can't ye?" persisted the boy.

"Well, Oi'll stick to phat Oi said, anyway, Patsy boy," replied his father.

"An' I'll be a big man like you, dad, some day, an' lick the hull town, won't I?" asked Patsy eagerly.

His father shuddered and held him close to his breast.

"I will, dad, won't I?" persisted the lad, the little face turned anxiously toward his father.

"Whisht now, laddie. Sure an' ye'll be the clivir man some day," said the big man huskily, while his wife turned her face toward the door.

"But they said I'd niver lick anybody," persisted Patsy. "An' that's a blank lie, isn't it, dad?"

The man's face grew black with wrath. He poured out fierce oaths.

"Let me catch thim. Oi'll break their backs, the blank, blank little cowards! Niver ye heed thim. Ye'll be a betther man thin any av thim, Patsy avick, an' that ye will. An' they'll all be standin' bare-headed afore ye some day. But Patsy, darlin', Oi want ye to give up the swearin' and listen to Marion yonder, who'll be afther tellin' ye good things an' cliver things."

"But, dad," persisted the little boy, "won't I be——"

"Hush now, Patsy," said his father hurriedly. "Don't ye want to go on the pony with Marion? Come on now, an' Oi'll put ye up."

"Oh, goody, goody!" shouted little Patsy, his pale, beautiful face aglow with delight.

"Poor little manny!" groaned Carroll to his wife, looking after the pair as they rode off up the trail. "It's not many ye'll be after lickin', except with yer tongue."

"But, begorra," said his wife, "that's the lickin' that hurts, afther all. An' it's harrd tellin' what'll be comin' till the lad."

Her husband turned without more words and went into the house. Meantime Marion and Patsy were enjoying their canter.

"Take me up to the Jumping Rock," said the boy, and they took the trail that wound up the west side of the lake.

"There now, Patsy," said Marion, when they had arrived at a smooth shelf of rock that rose sheer out of the blue water of the lake, "I'll put you by the big spruce there, and you can see all over the lake and everywhere."

She slipped off the pony, carefully lifted the boy down and set him leaning against a big spruce pine that grew seemingly up out of the bare rock and leaned far out over the water. This was the swimming place for the boys and men of the village; and an ideal place it was, for off the rock or out of the overhanging limbs the swimmers could dive without fear into the clear, deep water below.

"There now, Patsy," said the girl after she had picketed her pony, "shall I tell you a story?"

"No. Sing, Mayan, I like you to sing."

But just as the girl was about to begin he cried, "Who's that comin', Mayan?" pointing down the trail.

The keen eyes of the lad had descried a horseman far away where the long slope rose to the horizen.

"I don't know," answered the girl. "Who is it, Patsy? A cowboy?"

"No," said Patsy, after waiting for a few minutes, "I think it's Perault."

"No, Patsy, that can't be. You know Perault went out with father last week."

"Yes, it is," insisted Patsy. "That's father's pony. That's Rat-tail, I know."

The girl stood up and gazed anxiously at the approaching rider.

"Surely it can't be Perault," she said to herself. "What can have happened?"

She unhitched her horse, rolled up her picket rope, and stood waiting with disturbed face. As the rider drew near she called, "Perault! Ho, Perault!"

"Hola!" exclaimed Perault, a wizened, tough-looking little Frenchman, pulling up his pony with a jerk. "Bo jou, Mam'selle," he added, taking off his hat.

Perault's manner is reassuring, indeed quite gay.

" What is it, Perault? Why are you come back? Where is father? " The girl's lips were white.

" Coming," said Perault nonchalantly, pointing up the trail. " We strak de bad luck, Mam'selle, so we start heem again."

" Tell me, Perault," said the girl, turning her piercing black eyes on his face, " tell me truly, is father hurt? "

" Oui, for sure," said Perault with an exaggeration of carelessness which did not escape the keen eyes fastened on his face, " dat ole boss, you know, he blam-fool. Hees 'fraid noting. Hees try for sweem de Black Dog on de crossing below. De Black Dog hees full over hees bank, an' boil, boil, lak one kettle. De ole boss he say 'Perault, we mak de passage, eh?' 'No,' I say, 'we try noder crossing.' ' How far? ' he say. 'Two—tree mile.' 'Guess try heem here,' he say, an' no matter how I say heem be blam-fool for try, dat ole boss hees laf small, leele laf an' mak de start. Well, dat pony hees going nice an' slow troo de water over de bank, but wen he struk dat fas water, poof! wheez! dat pony hees upset hessef, by gar! Hees trow hees feet out on de water. Bymbe hees come all right for a meenit. Den dat fool pony hees miss de crossing. Hees go dreef down de stream where de high bank hees imposseeb. Mon Dieu! Das mak me scare. I do'no what I do. I stan' an' yell lak one beeg fool me. Up come beeg feller on buckboard on noder side. Beeg blam-fool jus' lak boss. Not 'fraid noting. Hees trow rope cross saddle. De ole boss hees win' heem roun' de horn. Poof! das upset dat pony once more. Hees trow hees feet up on water, catch ole boss on head an' arm, knock heem right off to blazes. 'Good bye,' I say, 'I not see heem more.' Beeg feller hees loose dat rope, ron down on de bank hitching rope on willow tree an' roun' hees own shoulder an' jump on reever way down on bend an' wait for ole boss. For me? I mak dis pony cross ver' queek. Not know how, an' pass on de noder side. I see beeg feller, hees hol' de ole boss on hees coat collar wit hees teef, by gar! an' sweem lak ottar. Sap-r-r-e! Not long before I pull on dat rope an' get bot on shore. Beeg feller hees all right. De ole boss hees lie white, white and still. I cry on my eye bad. 'Go get someting for dreenk,' say beeg feller, 'queek.' Sac-r-re! beeg fool messef! Bah! Good for noting! I fin' brandy, an' leele tam, tree-four minute, de ole boss hees sit up all right. Le Bon Dieu hees do good turn dat time, for sure. Send beeg feller along all right."

The girl stood listening to Perault's dramatic tale, her face growing white.

" Is father not hurt at all, then? " she asked.

" Non. Hees tough ole man, dat boss," said Perault. Then he added lightly, " Oh! hees broke some small bone—what you call?—on de collar, dere. Dat noting 'tall."

" Oh, Perault! " exclaimed the girl. " You're not telling me the truth. You're keeping back something. My father is hurt."

" Non, for sure," said Perault, putting his hand over his heart. " Hees broke dat bone on de collar.

Dat noting 'tall. He not ride ver' well, so hees come on beeg feller's buckboard. Dat's fine beeg feller! Mon Dieu! hees not 'fraid noting! Beeg blam-fool jus' lak boss." No higher commendation was possible from Perault.

"But why is father coming back then?" asked the girl anxiously.

"Mais oui! Bah! Dat leele fool pony got hisself dron on de Black Dog, an' all hees stuff, so de ole boss he mus' come back for more pony an' more stuff."

"When will they be here, Perault?" asked the girl quietly.

"Ver' soon. One—two hour. But," said Perault with some hesitation, "de ole boss better go on bed leele spell, mebbe."

Then the girl knew that Perault had not told her the worst, turning impatiently from him, she lifted little Patsy on to the saddle and, disdaining Perault's offered help, sprang on herself and set off toward the village about a mile away at full gallop.

"Das mighty smart girl," said Perault, scratching his head as he set off after her as fast as his jaded pony could follow. "Can't mak fool on her."

Half way to the village stood the old Prospector's house, almost hidden in a bluff of poplar and spruce. A little further on was Perault's shack. At her father's door the girl waited.

"Perault," she said quietly, "I left the key at your house. Will you get it for me while I take Patsy home?"

"Bon," said Perault eagerly. "I get heem an' mak fire."

"Thank you, Perault," she replied kindly. "I'll be right back."

But it took some time to get Patsy persuaded to allow her to depart, and by the time she had returned she found Perault had the fire lit and Josie, his bright-eyed, pretty, little wife, busy airing the bed-clothes and flitting about seeking opportunities to show her sympathy.

"Ma pauvre enfant!" she exclaimed, running to Marion as she entered and putting her arms about her.

"Josie," warned Perault gruffly, "shut up you. You go for mak fool of yousef."

But Josie paid no attention to her husband and continued petting the girl.

"Josie," cried Marion, fixing her eyes upon the Frenchwoman's kindly face, "tell me, is my father badly hurt? Perault would not tell me the truth."

"Non, ma petite, dat hur's not so ver' bad, but de cole water—das bad ting for fader, sure."

The cloud of gloom on the girl's face deepened. She turned away toward the door and saying, "I'll go and get some crocuses," she mounted her pony and rode off toward the Jumping Rock.

Within half an hour the girl came galloping back.

"Josie," she cried excitedly, springing off her pony, "they're coming. I saw them up the trail."

She tossed her flowers on the table and hurried to arrange them in basins, cups, old tin cans, and all available vessels, till the whole house seemed to be running over with those first and most exquisite prairie spring-flowers. And for many following days the spring-flowers filled the house with their own hope and cheer, when hope and cheer were both sorely needed.

## IX

## TIM CARROLL

THERE stood at the door Perault, Josie, and Marion, waiting for Shock and the Old Prospector to drive up. The contrast between the two men in the buckboard was striking. The one, a young man with muscular frame, a strong, fresh face innocent of worldly wisdom and marked by the frankness of an unspoiled faith in men and things; the other, an old man, tall, slight, with a face worn and weary, delicately featured and kindly enough, but with a mask of inscrutable reserve tinged with that distrust of men and things that comes of a bitter experience of the world's falsities. For fifty years Walter Mowbray had looked out of the piercing black eyes that gleamed like coals of fire through his pallid face upon a world that had continuously allured and mocked him. The piercing eyes were those of an enthusiast, not to say fanatic. The fire in them still burned deep and bright. The indomitable spirit, refusing to accept defeat, still lived and hoped with a persistence at once extraordinary and pathetic.

A gleam of light shot across his pale impassive face as his eyes fell upon his daughter who, in the presence of a stranger, shrank back behind Josie. He beckoned her to him.

"Come, my daughter," he said in a clear, musical voice.

Then she forgot her shyness and threw herself at him.

"Oh, father!" she cried in a low, smothered voice, her whole frame shaking as she clung to him.

For a single instant the old man held her to him, his pale face once more illumined by that momentary gleam, then loosening her arms from his neck, he said in calm tones, in which mingled surprise, raillery, almost rebuke, "Why, my child, this is indeed an extraordinary welcome home."

At the tone the girl shrank back, and with marvellous self-control regained her ordinary quiet manner.

"You are hurt, father," she said so quietly that her father glanced with quick surprise at her. He hardly knew as yet this daughter of his, who had come to him only two months ago, and whom for fifteen years he had not seen.

"A mere touch," he answered carelessly. "A broken collar-bone, inconvenient, but neither painful nor dangerous, and an additional touch of rheumatism, which, though extremely annoying, will prove only temporary. After a few days of your nursing we shall be able to resume our march, eh, Perault?'

"Oui! bon! dat so," said Perault, grinning his eager acquiescence. "De ole boss he stop for noting."

"But now we shall get with all speed between the blankets, my girl. Hot blankets, Josie, eh?"

"Oui, certainment, tout suite!" cried Josie, darting into the house.

The old man began carefully to raise himself off the seat of the buckboard.

"Ha!" catching his breath. "Rather sharp, that, Mr. Macgregor. Oh! I forgot. Pardon me," he continued, with fine, old-time courtesy. "Permit me to introduce you to my daughter. Marion, this is Mr. Macgregor, but for whose timely and heroic assistance I might even now be tumbling about at the fitful fancy of the Black Dog. We both have cause to be grateful to him."

With a surprised cry the girl who, during her father's words, had been looking at him with a white face and staring eyes, sprang towards Shock, who was standing at the pony's head, seized his hand between hers, kissed it passionately, flung it away, and returned hurriedly to her father's side.

"It was nothing at all," said Shock, when he had recovered from his confusion. "Any one would have done it, and besides——"

"Not many men would have had the strength to do it," interrupted the Old Prospector, "and few men the nerve to try. We will not forget it, sir, I trust."

"Besides," continued Shock, addressing the girl, "I owe something to your father, for I was helplessly lost when he found me."

With a wave of his hand the old man brushed aside Shock's statement as of no importance.

"We shall hope for opportunity to show our gratitude, Mr. Macgregor," he said, his clear voice taking a deeper tone than usual. "Now," he continued briskly, "let us proceed with this somewhat serious business of getting into blankets. Just lift my feet round, my daughter. Ah! The long ride has stiffened the joints. Oh! One moment, my dear." The old man's face was wet and ghastly pale, and his breath came in quick gasps. "A difficult operation, Mr. Macgregor," he said apologetically, "but we shall accomplish it in time. Wait, my dear, I fancy I shall do better without your assistance. At least, I shall be relieved of uncertainty as to responsibility for my pains. An important consideration, Mr. Macgregor. Uncertainty adds much to the sum of human suffering. Now, if I can swing my legs about. Ah-h-h! Most humiliating experience, Mr. Macgregor, the arriving at the limit of one's strength. But one not uncommon in life, and finally inevitable," continued the old philosopher, only the ghastly hue of his mask-like face giving token of the agony he was enduring.

Then Shock came to him.

"Let me carry you," he said. "It will give you less pain, I am sure."

"Well, it can hardly give more."

"Put your arms about my neck. There. Now don't try to help yourself."

"Most sound advice. I surrender," said the old man, his philosophic tone in striking contrast to his ghastly face. "But one most difficult to accept."

Gently, easily, as if he had been a child, Shock lifted him from the buckboard, carried him into the house and laid him upon his bed. The old man was faint with his pain.

"Thank you, sir—that was distinctly easier. You are—a mighty man. Perault! I think—I——"

His voice faded away into silence and his head fell back. The girl sprang forward with a cry of fear, but Shock was before her.

"The brandy, Perault! Quick!" he said. "Don't fear, Miss Mowbray, he will soon be all right."

The girl glanced into Shock's face and at once grew calm again. Soon, under the stimulus of the brandy, the old man revived.

"Ah!" he said, drawing a long breath and looking with a faint apologetic smile at the anxious faces about, "pardon my alarming you. I am getting old. The long drive and the somewhat severe pain weakened me, I fear."

"Indeed, you have no need to apologise. It is more than I could have stood," said Shock in genuine admiration.

"Thank you," said the old man. "Now we shall get into blankets. I have the greatest faith in blankets, sir; the greatest faith. I have rolled myself in wet blankets in mid-winter when suffering from a severe cold, and have come forth perfectly recovered. You remember the Elk Valley, Perault?"

"Oui, for sure. I say dat tam ole boss blam-fool. Hees cough! cough! ver' bad. Nex' mornin', by gar! he's all right."

"And will be again soon, Perault, my boy, by the help of these same blankets," said the old man confidently. "But how to negotiate the business is the question now."

"Let me try, sir. I have had some little experience in helping men with broken bones and the like," said Shock.

"You're at least entitled to confidence, Mr. Macgregor," replied the Old Prospector. "Faith is the reflection of experience. I resign myself into your hands."

In half an hour, with Perault's assistance, Shock had the old man between heated blankets, exhausted with pain, but resting comfortably.

"Mr. Macgregor," said the old man, taking Shock by the hand, "I have found that life sooner or later brings opportunity to discharge every obligation. Such an opportunity I shall eagerly await."

"I have done no more than any man should," replied Shock simply. "And I am only glad to have had the chance."

"Chance!" echoed the Old Prospector. "I have found that we make our chances, sir. But now you will require lodging. I regret I cannot offer you hospitality. Perault, go down to the Stopping Place, present my compliments to Carroll and ask him to give Mr. Macgregor the best accommodation he has. The best is none too good. And, Perault, we shall need another pony and a new outfit. In a few days we must be on the move again. See Carroll about these things and report. Meantime, Mr. Macgregor, you will remain with us to tea."

"Carroll!" exclaimed Perault in a tone of disgust. "Dat man no good 'tall. I get you one pony cheap. Dat Carroll he's one beeg tief."

The little Frenchman's eyes glittered with hate.

"Perault," replied the Old Prospector quietly, "I quite understand you have your own quarrel with Carroll, but these are my affairs. Carroll will not cheat me."

"Ah! Bah!" spat Perault in a vicious undertone of disgust. "De ole boss he blam-fool. He not see noting." And Perault departed, grumbling and swearing, to make his deal with Carroll.

Timothy Carroll was a man altogether remarkable, even in that country of remarkable men. Of his past history little was known. At one time a Hudson Bay trader, then a freighter. At present he "ran" the Loon Lake Stopping Place and a livery stable, took contracts in freight, and conducted a general trading business in horses, cattle—anything, in short, that could be bought and sold in that country. A man of powerful physique and great shrewdness, he easily dominated the community of Loon Lake. He was a curious mixture of incongruous characteristics. At the same time many a poor fellow had found in him a friend in sickness or "in hard luck," and by his wife and family he was adored. His tenderness for little lame Patsy was the marvel of all who knew the terrible Tim Carroll. He had a furious temper, and in wrath was truly terrifying, while in matters of trade he was cool, cunning, and unscrupulous. Few men had ever dared to face his rage, and few had ever worsted him in a "deal." No wonder Perault,

who had experienced both the fury of his rage and
the unscrupulousness of his trading methods, approached him with reluctance. But, though Perault
had suffered at the hands of the big Irishman, the
chief cause of his hatred was not personal. He
knew, what many others in the community suspected,
that for years Carroll had systematically robbed and
had contributed largely to the ruin of his " old boss."
Walter Mowbray was haunted by one enslaving vice.
He was by temperament and by habit a gambler. It
was this vice that had been his ruin. In the madness
of his passion he had risked and lost, one fatal night
in the old land, the funds of the financial institution
of which he was the trusted and honoured head. In
the agony of his shame he had fled from his home,
leaving in her grave his broken-hearted wife, and
abandoning to the care of his maiden sister his little
girl of a year old, and had sought, in the feverish
search for gold, relief from haunting memory, redemption for himself, and provision for his child.
In his prospecting experiments success had attended
him. He developed in a marvellous degree the prospector's instinct, for instinct it appeared to be; and
many of the important prospects, and some of the
most valuable mines in Southern British Columbia,
had been discovered by him.

It was at this point that Carroll took a hand. Act-
ing in collusion with the expert agent for the British
American Gold and Silver Mining Company, he had
bought for hundreds of dollars and sold for thousands
the Old Prospector's claims. Not that the old man

had lost that financial ability or that knowledge of human nature that had given him his high place in former days, but he was possessed of a dream of wealth so vast that ordinary fortunes shrank into insignificance in comparison. He had fallen under the spell of an Indian tale of a lost river of fabulous wealth in gold that disturbed all his sense of value. In one of his prospecting tours he had come upon an old Indian hunter, torn by a grizzly and dying. For weeks he nursed the old Indian in his camp with tender but unavailing care. In gratitude, the dying man had told of the lost river that flowed over rocks and sands sown with gold. In his young days the Indian had seen the river and had gathered its "yellow sand and stones"; in later years, however, when he had come to know something of the value of this "yellow sand and stones" he had sought the river, but in vain. A mountain peak in one vast slide had filled up the valley, diverted the course of the river, and changed the whole face of the country. For many summers the Indian had sought with the unfaltering patience of his race the bed of the lost river, and at length, that very summer, he had discovered it. Deep down in a side canyon in the bed of a trickling brook he had found "yellow sand and stones" similar to those of the lost river of his youth. As the dying Indian poured out from his buckskin bag the glittering sand and rusty bits of rock, there entered into the Old Prospector the terrible gold-lust that for thirteen years burned as a fever in his bones and lured him on through perils and privations, over mountains and along canyons, making him insensible to storms and frosts and burning suns, and that even now, old man as he was, worn and broken, still burned with unquenchable flame.

Under the spell of that dream of wealth he found it easy to pay his " debts of honour " to Carroll with mining claims, which, however valuable in themselves, were to him paltry in comparison with the wealth of the Lost River, to which every year brought him nearer, and which one day he was sure he would possess. That Carroll and his confederate robbed him he knew well enough, but finding Carroll useful to him, both in the way of outfitting his annual expeditions and in providing means for the gratifying of his life-long gambling passion, by which the deadly monotony of the long winter days and nights was relieved, he tolerated while he scorned him and his villainy.

Not so Perault, whose devotion to his " ole boss " was equalled only by his hate of those who robbed while they derided him, and he set himself to the task of thwarting their nefarious schemes. For this Perault had incurred the savage wrath of Carroll, and more than once had suffered bodily injury at his hands.

The Stopping Place was filled with men from the ranges, freighters from the trail, and the nondescript driftwood that the waves of civilisation cast up upon those far-away shores of human society. With all of them Perault was a favourite. Carroll was out when he entered. On all sides he was greeted with exclamations of surprise, pleasure, and curiosity, for all knew that he had set out upon another "annual fool hunt," as the Prospector's yearly expedition was called. "Hello, Rainy, what's happened?" "Got yer gold dust?" "Goin' to retire, Rainy?" "The Old Prospector struck his river yit?" greeted him on every side.

"Oui, by gar! He struck heem, for sure," grinned Perault.

"What? The Lost River?" "What? His mine?" chorused the crowd, awakened to more than ordinary interest.

"Non, not Los' River, but los' man, blank near." And Perault went on to describe, with dramatic fervour and appropriate gesticulation, the scene at the Black Dog, bringing out into strong relief his own helplessness and stupidity and the cool daring of the stranger who had snatched his "ole boss" out of the jaws of the Black Dog.

"By Jove!" exclaimed a rancher when the narrative was finished, "not bad, that. Who was the chap, Rainy?"

"Do' no me. Tink he's one what you call pries'. Your Protestan' pries'."

"What, a preacher?" cried the rancher. "Not he. They're not made that way."

"I don't know about that, Sinclair," said another rancher. "There's Father Mike, you know."

"That's so," said Sinclair. "But there are hardly two of that kind on the same range."

"Fadder Mike!" sniffed Perault contemptuously. "Dat beeg feller hees roll Fadder Mike up in one beeg bunch an' stick heem in hees pocket. Dat feller he's not 'fraid noting. Beeg blam-fool, jus' lak ole boss, for sure."

"I guess he must be good stuff, Rainy, if you put him in that class."

"Dat's hees place," averred Rainy with emphasis. "Jus' lak ole boss."

At this point Carroll came in.

"Hello, Perault!" he said. "What the blank, blank are ye doin' here?"

Perault spat deliberately into the ash-pan, tipped back his chair without looking at the big Irishman, and answered coolly:

"Me? After one pack pony an' some outfit for de ole boss."

"Pony an' outfit, is it?" shouted Carroll. "What the blank, blank d'ye mane? What 'av ye done wid that pack pony av moine, an' where's yer blank ould fool av a boss?"

Carroll was working himself up into a fine rage.

"De boss, he's in bed," replied Perault coolly. "De pony, he's in de Black Dog Reever, guess."

"The Black Dog? What the blank, blank d'ye mane, anyway? Why don't ye answer? Blank ye f'r a cursed crapeau of a Frenchman? Is that pony of moine drowned?"

"Mebbe," said Perault, shrugging his shoulders, "unless he leev under de water lak one mush-rat."

"Blank yer impudence," roared Carroll, "to be

sittin' there laughin' in me face at the loss av me property.  It's no better than a pack of thieves ye are."

"Tieves!" answered Perault, in quick anger. "Dere's one beeg, black, hairy tief not far 'way dat's got hees money for dat pony two—three tam overe."

Choking with rage, Carroll took one step toward him, kicked his chair clean from under him, and deposited the Frenchman on the floor amid a shout of laughter from the crowd.  In blazing wrath Perault was on his feet with a bound, and, swinging his chair around his head, hurled it full in the face of his enemy.  Carroll caught it on his arm and came rushing at the Frenchman.

"You one beeg black tief," shrieked Perault, drawing a knife and striking savagely at the big Irishman.

As he delivered his blow Carroll caught him by the wrist, wrenched the knife from his grasp, seizing him by the throat  proceeded to choke him.  The crowd stood looking on, hesitating to interfere.  A fight was understood in that country to be the business of no man save those immediately concerned.  Besides this, Carroll was dreaded for his great strength and his furious temper, and no man cared to imperil his life by attacking him.

"Blank yer cursed soul!" cried Carroll through his clenched teeth.  "It's this Oi've been waitin' f'r many a day, an' now by the powers Oi'll be takin' the life of yez, so Oi will."

His threat would undoubtedly have been carried out, for Perault was bent far back, his face was black, and his tongue protruded from his wide open mouth. But at this moment the door opened and Shock quietly stepped in. For a single instant he stood gazing in amazement upon the strange scene, then stepping quickly behind Carroll, whose back was toward the door, he caught his wrist.

"You are killing the man," he said quietly.

"Oi am that same!" hissed Carroll, his eyes blood-shot with the light of murder in them. "An' by all the powers of hell Oi'll be havin' yer heart's blood if ye don't kape aff."

"Indeed, then, he's too small a man for you, and as to myself, we can see about that later," said Shock quietly.

He closed his fingers on the wrist he held. The hand gripping Perault's throat opened quickly, allow-ing the Frenchman to fall to the floor. Swinging round with a hoarse cry, the big Irishman aimed a terrific blow at Shock's head. But Shock, catching the blow on his arm, drew Carroll sharply toward him, at the same time giving a quick downward twist to the wrist he held, a trick of the Japanese wrestlers the 'Varsity men had been wont to practise. There was a slight crack, a howl of pain, and Carroll sank writhing on the floor, with Shock's grip still on his wrist.

"Let me up," he roared.

"Will you let the little man alone?" asked Shock quietly.

"Let me up, blank ye! It's yer heart's blood will pay for this."

" Will you leave the little man alone? " asked Shock in a relentlessly even tone.

"Yis, yis," groaned Carroll. "Me wrist's bruk, so it is. But Oi'll be afther doin' f'r yez, ye blank, blank——"

Carroll's profanity flowed in a copious stream.

"As to that," said Shock, quietly stepping back from him, "we can discuss that later; but it is a shame for a man like you to be choking a little chap like that."

The old football scrimmage smile was on Shock's face as he stood waiting for Carroll to rise. The whole incident had occurred so unexpectedly and so suddenly that the crowd about stood amazed, quite unable to realise just what had happened.

After a time the big Irishman slowly rose, holding his wounded wrist and grinding out curses. Then suddenly seizing with his uninjured hand the chair which Perault had thrown at him, he raised it aloft and with a wild yell brought it down upon Shock's head. With his yell mingled a shrill cry. It was little Patsy. He had stolen in behind his father, and with eyes growing wider and wider had stood listening to his father's groans and curses.

Gradually the meaning of the scene dawned upon little Patsy's mind. His father had been hurt, and there stood the man who had hurt him. In a fury the little lad hurtled across the room, and just as his father delivered his terrific blow he threw himself, with crutch uplifted, at the astonished Shock and right in the way of the descending chair.

Instead of starting back to avoid the blow, as he might easily have done, Shock without a moment's hesitation sprang towards the child, taking the full weight of the blow upon his arm and head, but without entirely saving Patsy. Together they fell, Shock bleeding profusely from a deep cut on the head.

Two men sprang to his aid, while Carroll stood stupidly gazing down upon the white face of the little boy.

"Never mind me," said Shock, recovering consciousness quickly, "look to the child. Is he hurt?"

"He's dead, I guess," said Sinclair.

"It's a lie!" cried Carroll, in a hoarse voice. "It's a blank lie, I tell you!"

His face was white and his terrible eyes, so lately suffused with the light of murder, were filled with startled terror. He dropped beside his child and lifted him in his arms, crying softly, "Patsy, boy! Aw, now Patsy, darlin'. Spake to me, Patsy."

But the long lashes lay quietly upon the white cheeks, and the little form remained limp and still. Carroll lifted an amazed and terror-stricken face to the company.

"What have I done? Sure he's not dead!" he said in an awed whisper.

"No, no," said Shock, wiping the blood out of his eyes and leaning over the little white face. "Water, Perault, and brandy," he cried. "Quick!"

The men who had stood aghast at the tragic ending of what had been simply a row of more than ordinary interest now hastened to give help. Water and brandy were immediately at hand. Ignoring his own wound, Shock bathed the face and hands of the unconscious child, but there was no sign of life.

"Guess he's gone out, right enough," said a cowboy.

"Liar! Liar! Blank your cursed soul for a liar!" cried Carroll, in a tone of agony.

"Man, man!" said Shock, in a stern, solemn voice, "would you provoke the Almighty to anger with your oaths? You ought rather to beseech His mercy for your own soul. Why should He give your child to the care of such a man as you? Give me the lad."

Without a word of remonstrance Carroll allowed Shock to lift the lifeless child and carry him into the open air, where, laying him on the ground, he began to vigorously chafe his hands and feet. After some minutes of bathing and rubbing the eyelids began to flutter and the breath to come in gentle sighs.

"Brandy now, Perault," said Shock. "There now, laddie. Thank God, he is coming to!"

"Dad, dad, where's dad?" said little Patsy faintly, opening his eyes. "I want dad."

"Here! Here! Patsy mannie," cried his father quickly, coming from behind the crowd where he had been standing dazed and stupid. "Stand back there! Let me have my boy," he added savagely.

He swept both Perault and Shock angrily aside, gathered the little lad tenderly in his arms and strode off into the house, the white face of the child resting on his father's shoulder and his golden curls mingling with the black, coarse masses of his father's hair and beard.

"Well, I'll be blanked!" said one of the men. "Wouldn't that pall you!"

"Blank cantankerous cuss!" said the cowboy. "Never a 'thank you' for gittin' half killed in place of his kid."

Perault walked up to Shock, and offering his hand, said in a voice husky and broken, "Dat's two for you dis evenin'—me an' dat leele feller. For me—I can't spik my heart," smiting himself on the breast, "but my heart—dat's your own now, by gar!" He wrung Shock's hand in both of his and turned quickly away. But before he had taken many steps he returned, saying, "Come on wit me! I feex up your head." And without further words Shock and Perault passed into the Stopping Place.

The men looked at each other in silence for a time, then the cowboy said with unusual emphasis, "Boys, he's white! He's blanked white!"

# X

## THE TURF MEET

THE great brown shadows of the rolling hills had quite filled the hollows between and were slowly climbing up the western slope of every undulation when Shock reached the lip of the broad river bed in which lay the little fort town.

The white clump of buildings standing by themselves he knew to be the barracks of the North-West Mounted Police. The flag floating above showed that, as well as the air of military neatness about them.

The town straggled along two intersecting streets, and then frayed out over the flats in isolated and dejected-looking shacks. The more imposing buildings on the main street Shock guessed were the hotels and stores. One of the latter he recognised from its flag as that of the ancient and honourable Hudson's Bay Company. On a back street here and there stood a house surrounded by a garden and scrubby trees, a pathetic attempt to reproduce in this treeless country what in other lands had been fondly called home.

Away on every side stretched the vast sweep of rolling prairie to where the amber of the sky-line mingled with the grey blue of the earth.

How insignificant, how miserable and wretched in the midst of this expanse of sky and earth, seemed the huddling bunch of dejected buildings, and yet the whole interest of heaven above and earth around centred in those straggling shacks, for they were the abodes of men.

From feasting his heart upon the marvellous beauty of the expanse of rounded hills, with their variegation of sunlight and shadow, and the expanse of cloudless sky, deep blue overhead and shading by indefinable transitions through blues and purples into pearl greys and rose tints, and at last into glorious yellow gold at the horizon, Shock, with almost a shudder, turned his eyes to the little ragged town beneath him. How marvellous the works of God! How ugly the things man makes!

It was partly the infinitude of this contrast that wrought in Shock a feeling of depression as he followed the trail winding down the long slope toward the town. As he became aware of this depression, he took himself severely to task.

"What's the matter with me, anyway?" he asked himself impatiently. "I'm not afraid of them." And yet he had a suspicion that it was just this that troubled him. He was afraid. The feeling was not one with which he was unfamiliar. Often before a big match he had been shamefully conscious of this same nervous fear. He remembered how his heart had seemed too big for his body, till he felt it in his throat. But he remembered now, with no small comfort, that once the ball was kicked his heart had always gone back to its place and its work and gave him no further concern, and to-day he hoped this might be his experience again.

It was a great day at the Fort, nothing less than the Spring Meeting of the South Alberta Turf Association; and in that horse country, where men were known by their horses rather than by personal characteristics, the meeting of the Turf Association easily took precedence over all other events, social or political.

This spring, to the interest naturally centring in the races, there was added a special interest, in that, behind the horses entered for the Association Cup, there gathered intense local feeling. The three favourites were representative horses. The money of the police and all the Fort contingent in the community had been placed on the long, rangey thoroughbred, Foxhall, an imported racer who had been fast enough to lose money in the great racing circuits of the East, but who was believed to be fast enough to win money here in the West.

The district about the fort town was divided into two sections, the east and the west. In the eastern section the farming industry was carried on to an almost equal extent with ranching; in the west, up among the hills, there was ranching pure and simple. Between the two sections a strong rivalry existed. In this contest the east had "banked" on Captain Hal Harricomb, rancher and gentleman farmer, and his black Demon. The western men, all ranchers, who despised and hated farmers and everything pertaining to them, were all ranged behind the Swallow, a dainty little bay mare, bred, owned, and ridden by a young Englishman, Victor Stanton, known throughout the Albertas, south and north, as "The Kid," or, affectionately, "The Kiddie," admired for his superb riding, his reckless generosity, his cool courage, and loved for his gentle, generous heart.

Already two heats had been run, one going to the Demon and one to the Swallow, Foxhall sustaining his Eastern reputation as a money-loser.

The excitement of the day had gradually grown in intensity, and now was concentrated in the final heat of the Association Cup race.

All unconscious of this excitement and of the tremendous issues at stake, Shock sent his little cayuse peacefully trotting along the trail to where it met the main street. The street was lined on either side with men and horses. Something was evidently going on, but what Shock could not see.

But no sooner had he turned up the street than there was a fierce outburst of yells, oaths, and execrations, and at the same moment he heard behind him the pounding of hoofs.

Hastily glancing over his shoulder, he saw thundering down upon him half a dozen or more mounted men. In vain he tugged at his cayuse. The little brute allowed his stubborn head to be hauled round close to the shaft, but declined to remove his body; and, indeed, had he been ever so eager, there would hardly have been time. A big black horse was plunging wildly not more than ten feet behind him. A fierce oath, a shower of dust and gravel in his face, a flash of legs and hoofs, and the big black was lifted clear over Shock and his cayuse, and was off again down the street between the lines of yelling men.

"Here, blank your blank head! Git off the course! Don't you know nothin'?"

When Shock came to himself, he was aware that a tall, lanky cowboy in chaps, woollen shirt, and stiff, broad-brimmed hat was pounding his cayuse over the head with his heavy whip.

Shock never knew how it happened. All he remembered was a quick rush of blood to his brain, a mad desire to punish the man who was brutally beating his pony, and then standing by the shaft of his buckboard waiting for the man to get up.

"Gad, sir!" exclaimed a voice over his shoulder, "that was a clever throw!" There was genuine admiration in the voice.

Shock looked up and saw an old gentleman, with white, close-cropped hair and moustache and erect military form, regarding him with admiration. He was riding a stout hunter, docked in English style.

"And served you perfectly right, Ike," continued the old gentleman. "What business have you to strike any man's horse?"

"What the blank blank is he doing on the course?" said Ike wrathfully, as he slowly rose from the ground and came toward Shock.

"I say, stranger," he said, coming over near to Shock and looking him carefully in the eye, "I'll give you twenty-five dollars if you do that agin. You took me unbeknownst. Now, git to work."

Shock's heart had got back to its right place and was beating its steady beat. The old scrimmage smile was on his face.

"But I do not want to do it again, and I did take you unawares."

"Look-a-here," said Ike, touching Shock with his forefinger on the breast, "do you think you kin do it agin?"

"Don't know that I could," said Shock quietly. "But I do know that I do not intend to try. And, in fact, I do not know how it was done."

"Ikey does," drawled a voice.

There was a delighted roar from the crowd that had gathered round. Ike looked round the circle of grinning men for a second or two.

"Say," he said slowly, "if any blank, blank son of a she-ape thinks he knows how to do that trick when I'm a-watchin', here's his opportunity right naouw—fer fun, or fer money, or," lowering his voice and thrusting forward his face a little, "fer blood."

The laugh died out from the crowd. There was a silence for a moment or two, and then the same voice drawled, "Nobody's hungry, I guess, Ikey," and Ike turned from them with a grunt of contempt.

"Now," he said, coming back to Shock, "I'd like to hear you talk."

Ike threw himself into an attitude of defence, but Shock's position never changed, nor did the smile fade from his face.

"I have nothing to say except that I do not know how it happened. I saw my horse being abused, and —well, I acted a little hastily, I fear."

"Hastily!" exclaimed the old gentleman, who had remained in the crowd. "Nonsense! Perfectly right, I say, and Ike knows it. What would you do, Ike, if you saw a fellow pounding Slipper over the ears?"

"Poundin' Slipper?" said Ike slowly, pausing to turn his quid of tobacco in his cheek. "Poundin' Slipper," he repeated with even greater deliberation. "Knock his blank face into the back of his head."

"Then it seems to me, Ike, you were let off easy." The old gentleman smiled grimly down upon the cowboy, who was still wrathful, but more puzzled than wrathful. The smiling man at the pony's head looked so thoroughly good-natured that it was hard to push a quarrel, but still Ike's dignity had been injured.

"What I beg to remark is," he continued, returning to the attack, "kin he do it agin? Does he have any lingerin' suspicion that he is capable of that act?" Ike reserved his best English for serious occasions. "If he does, I'm willin' he should extemporise at it."

"Good man, Ikey!" drawled the voice again from the crowd. "I'll back Ikey to his last pant's button."

Shock stood silent and smiling, while Ike stood facing him, more and more puzzled. Shock was an entirely new experience. He would not fight, he would not run away, he would not even get angry.

At this point the old gentleman interfered.

" Now, Ikey," he said, " it is time you were learning some manners. This gentleman is no pugilist. He has neither the desire nor the intention of fighting you, which is perhaps all the better for you. That is a poor way to treat a stranger the first day he arrives in our town. Perhaps you will allow me to be of some service to you," he said, turning to Shock.

" Thank you," said Shock simply. " I am in need of a doctor first of all. Two of my friends at Loon Lake are very ill. Is there a doctor in this town? "

" There is," replied the old gentleman. " Dr. Burton. But I very much fear that he will hardly be fit for service to-day. Unfortunately, our doctor, though a remarkably clever practitioner, is not always—well, to be quite frank, he is very frequently drunk. Get him sober and he will do you good service."

" How shall I accomplish that? " asked Shock, with a feeling of despair in his heart, thinking of the Old Prospector in his pain and of little Patsy lying in semi-unconsciousness in the back room of the Loon Creek Stopping Place. " I must have a doctor. I cannot go back without one."

" Then," said the old gentleman, " you will need to kidnap him and wait till he sobers off."

" I shall try," said Shock quietly.

The old gentleman stared at him.

" By Jove! " he said, " I believe you mean to. And if you do, you'll succeed."

" Can you direct me to the house of Mr. Macfarren? " inquired Shock.

"Certainly. That is his house among the trees," pointing to a cottage with a verandah about it, which stood back some distance from the main street. "But if you wish to see Mr. Macfarren, you will find him down at the other end of the street at the finishing post. He will be very busily engaged at the present, however, being one of the judges in this race, and if it is not of immediate importance I would advise your waiting till the race is over. But stay, here he comes. The man in the centre is Mr. Macfarren."

As he spoke he pointed to a tall man, with a long, grizzled beard, riding a pony, followed by two younger men splendidly mounted. The elder of these was a man strongly built, face open and honest, but showing signs of hard living. He rode a powerful black horse, whose temper showed in his fierce snatching at the bit. Just now the horse was covered with foam, reddened at the flanks and mouth with blood.

His companion was much younger, a mere boy, indeed. His fair hair, blue eyes, and smooth face accentuated his youthful appearance. It was his youthful face and boyish manner that gave him his name among the cattle men, and his place in their hearts. But though they called him "The Kid," and often "The Kiddie," and thought of him with admiring and caressing tenderness, no man of them failed to give him full respect; for boy as he was, he had a man's nerve, a man's grip, his muscles were all steel, and with all his smiling gentleness none of them would think of taking a liberty with him. Earlier in the day he had won from a dozen competitors that

most coveted of all honours in the ranching country,
The Bucking Belt, for he had ridden for the full
hundred yards without " touching leather," the *out-
law* specially imported from the other side.

As the three men rode up the rider of the black
horse was heard to say, " That's the fellow that nearly
spilled me. And if Demon hadn't been mighty quick
in recovering, it would have been a blank nasty mess."

" I say," said Macfarren, in a loud, blustering tone,
" don't you know enough to keep off a race-course
when a race is being run? "

Shock was much taken aback at this greeting.

" I beg your pardon, but I didn't know this was a
race-course, nor did I know that a race was on."

" The deuce you didn't! Hadn't you eyes to see? "

To this Shock made no reply, but taking a letter
from his pocket said quietly, " You are Mr. Macfarren, I believe. I have a letter for you from Mr.
McIntyre."

At this the other two rode away. Mr. Macfarren
opened the letter with a scowl. As he read the flush
on his face deepened.

" What the deuce does this mean? " he burst out,
in an angry tone. " I wrote both the Superintendent
and McIntyre last week that it was a piece of folly to
plant a man here, that we didn't require and didn't
want a man. The community is well supplied already
with church services, and as far as the Presbyterians
are concerned, they would find the support of a minister an intolerable burden."

For a moment or two Shock stood in speechless

amazement. It was disconcerting in the extreme to be told by the man upon whom he had chiefly depended for support and counsel that he was not wanted.

"Your letters would not have reached them in time, I suppose," he said at last.

"Well, that's the fact, at any rate," replied Macfarren roughly. "We won't want a minister. We are thoroughly well supplied. We don't need one, and we cannot support one."

He was turning away without further words when he was arrested by the sharp and peremptory voice of the old gentleman, who had remained behind Shock during the conversation.

"Macfarren, this gentleman is a stranger, I presume. Will you kindly present me?"

"Oh—ah—certainly," said Macfarren, wheeling his pony and looking rather ashamed. "Mr. ——" looking at the letter.

"Macgregor," said Shock quietly.

"Mr. Macgregor, this is General Brady, one of our leading ranchers."

"I am delighted to make your acquaintance, sir," said General Brady, shaking Shock warmly by the hand. "You will find us rough and wild, but, sir, I am glad to say we are not all a blank lot of boors."

"Thank you, sir," said Shock, with a sudden flush on his face.

"Oh—ah—certainly we are glad to have you visit our town," said Macfarren, as if trying to atone for his former rudeness. "And, of course, it is no fault of yours, Mr.—ah——"

"Macgregor," said the General shortly.

"Yes, Mr. Macgregor. There's a deuce of a mistake been made, but I take it you will not suffer. There are plenty of—ah—positions—places, I believe, where you will find—ah—opportunity. But if you will excuse me, I am busy for the moment. I shall doubtless see you again before you leave."

Shock bowed in silence.

"Blank cad!" muttered the General. Then turning to Shock he said, with hearty interest showing in his tone, "Where do you put up, Mr. Macgregor?"

"I do not know the town at all. I shall have to look about for a boarding place of some kind, I suppose." Shock's smile was rather uncertain.

The General was evidently interested in this stranger, and touched by his forlorn condition.

"The Royal there," pointing down the street, "is the best hotel. They do you there not so badly. They may give you accommodation for a night, but I fancy it will be rather difficult to find a boarding house. But," he added heartily, "why not come to me in the meantime? Mrs. Brady and myself will be most happy to have you visit us for a few weeks, till you find quarters. I have, unfortunately, an engagement that will keep me late in town to-night, else I should insist on your accompanying me at once—an engagement which I cannot well break. In short, this is our annual spring meeting of the Turf Association, and there is in connection with it some sort of social function to wind the thing up to-night, and Mrs. Brady, being one of the patronesses, and I myself being more or less interested—the president of the Association, indeed—we cannot avoid putting in an appearance. And indeed, we enjoy it, sir. We thoroughly enjoy it. It brings to our present crude and somewhat limited life a little bit of the past. But to-morrow I shall be glad to ride down for you, sir, and bring you up to my little place."

The cordial kindness of this stranger, upon whom he had no claim, touched Shock greatly.

"Thank you again," he said. "I cannot tell you how much I feel your kindness. But if you will allow me, I would rather accept your invitation later. I feel I must get settled to my work at once. I have been long on the way, and my work is waiting me." Then, after a pause, he added simply, "But your kindness makes me think of a word I have read, ' I was a stranger, and ye took me in.' "

The General bowed in silence, and seeing that Shock was not to be persuaded, shook hands with him once more. "Come when you will, sir, and stay as long as you can. The sooner you come and the longer you stay, the better we shall be pleased." And with another courteous bow the General rode off to attend to his duties as President of the Turf Association.

As Shock turned back to his buckboard he found Ike waiting him. Ike had been an interested witness of all that had taken place, and while his sympathy had gone completely with Shock and against Macfarren, he had not been quite able to shake off the feeling of humiliation under which he suffered.

"Say, stranger," he said, touching Shock on the shoulder, and speaking in a low and almost respectful tone, "there aint a man in the Territories has ever put the dust onto Ike Iveson's pants. Here's twenty-five dollars," diving deep into his hip pocket and pulling out a plug of tobacco, a knife, and a roll of bills, "which is a standin' offer to any man who can circumvent that there trick. And I want to say," he continued, with a subdued eagerness in his tone, "I'll make it fifty if you do it agin."

Ike's tone was persuasive. There was nothing of resentment in it. It was the tone of a man who had come upon an interesting and puzzling experience, and was anxious to investigate.

"No," said Shock, backing away from Ike, "I cannot take that. Besides, it was not a fair throw."

"Well," said Ike, much mollified, "that's so, that's so. And I consider it something handsome in you sayin' so. But that offer stands."

"All right," said Shock, smiling a little more broadly. "I'll remember. And when I want fifty dollars very badly I may come to you. But," he added, looking Ike up and down, "I'll have to be pretty hard pushed before I try."

"It's a bargain, stranger," said Ikey, offering a languid hand. Shock grasped it warmly. A slight tremour ran over Ike's lanky frame as Shock's hand closed on his.

"Je-roo-sa-*lem!*" he ejaculated, drawing in his breath, as Shock turned away. "I'll be ready fer you next time. I prefer a grizzly myself." He looked down at his finger nails. "Didn't expect to see 'em on," he observed. "And say, boys," turning to the crowd, "I surmise he's a preacher, a blank fire-escape."

At once Ike became the object of various comments.

"A preacher, Ike? Say, you'll have to change your ways and go to meetin'."

"What's Ikey's church, anyway?"

"Don't know as I ever heard."

"Oh, Ikey aint mean, he treats 'em all the same."

"Well, I guess Ikey'll have to dust toward the sky-line."

Ike listened for a time unmoved, and then drawled out quietly, "What I want to remark to you jay birds is, that if ever you have any misunderstandin' with that there ascension ladder, he'll make you say more prayers in a minute than you've said for the last ten years of your mortal life. And if ever he gits after you the only thing that'll save you will be your dust."

So saying Ike slouched off down the street, keeping his eye on Shock's buckboard. He watched him go into the Royal and in a few minutes come out again, followed him to the International, and soon after to the Ranchers' Roost.

"Guess he's purty nigh tangled up now," said Ikey, with considerable satisfaction. He had a scheme of his own in mind. "There aint a six-foot hole in this hull town, and he'd take purty nigh seven. Now, what's his next move?"

Shock appeared undecided. There was evidently

no place for him in the town. He had a deepening sense of being not wanted. The town was humming with life, but in that life there was no place for him. Awakening a strange sense of fellowship the words came to him, " He was rejected of men."

# XI

## " I WAS A STRANGER, AND YE TOOK ME IN "

A S Shock stood, uncertain as to his next move, he noticed that out of the confused mingling of men and horses order began to appear. The course was once more being cleared. The final heat, which the Swallow had won, and which had been protested by the owner of the Demon, on the ground that his course had been blocked by Shock and his cayuse, was to be run again. Shock was too much occupied with his own disappointment and uncertainty to take much interest in the contest that was the occasion of such intense excitement to the throngs on the street. With languid indifference he watched the course being cleared and the competitors canter back to the starting point. Behind them followed a cavalcade of horsemen on all sorts of mounts, from the shaggy little cayuse, with diminishing rump, to the magnificent thoroughbred stallion, stall-fed and shining. In the final heat it was the custom for all the horsemen in the crowd to join at a safe distance behind the contestants, in a wild and tumultuous scramble.

Shock's attention was arrested and his interest quickened by the appearance of Ike in the crowd, riding a hard-looking, bony, buckskin broncho, which he guessed to be Slipper.

In a short time the Demon and the Swallow were in their places. Far behind them bunched the motley crowd of horsemen.

The start was to be by the pistol shot, and from the scratch. So intense was the stillness of the excited crowd that, although the starting point was more than half a mile out on the prairie, the crack of the pistol was clearly heard.

In immediate echo the cry arose, " They're off! They're off! " and necks were strained to catch a glimpse of the first that should appear where the course took a slight turn.

In a few seconds the two leading horses are seen, the riders low over their necks, and behind them, almost hidden by the dust, the crowd of yelling, waving, shooting horsemen.

The Demon is leading, the Swallow close on his flank. As they come within clear view the experienced eyes of the crowd see that while the Demon, though as yet untouched by whip or spur, is doing all that is in him, the Swallow is holding him easily. On all sides the men of the west raise a pæan of victory, " The Swallow! The Swallow! Good boy, Kiddie! Let her go! Let her go! " " You've got him standing! " " Bully boy! "

Fifty yards from the winning post The Kid leans over his mare's neck and shakes out his fluttering reins. Like the bird whose name she bears the Swallow darts to the front, a length ahead. In vain the Captain calls to the Demon, plying fiercely whip and spur. With nostrils distended and blood-red, with eyes starting from their sockets, and mouth foaming bloody froth, the noble animal responds and essays his final attempt.

It is a magnificent effort. Slowly he creeps up to the Swallow's flank, but beyond that he cannot make an inch, and so they remain to the winning post.

Down the street behind the leaders, yelling wild oaths, shooting off their guns, flinging hats in the air, and all enveloped in a cloud of dust, thunders the pursuing cavalcade.

Just as the Swallow shoots to the front, out from the cloud of dust behind, with his cowboy hat high in one hand and his reins fluttering loosely in the other, Ike emerges on his beloved Slipper. At every bound the buckskin gains upon the runners in front, but when level with the Demon, Ike steadies him down, for he would not be guilty of the bad taste of "shoving his nose into another man's fight," nor would he deprive the little mare, who carried the fortunes of the men of the west, of the glory of her victory.

The riot that follows the race passes description. The men from the west go mad. About The Kid and his little mare they surge in a wave of frantic enthusiasm. Into the Ranchers' Roost they carry the rider to wash down the dust, while as many as can find room for a hand get vigorously to work upon the Swallow.

After the riot had somewhat subsided and the street had become partially clear, side by side, threading their way through the crowd, appeared the two competitors for the Cup. On all sides they were greeted with renewed cheers, and under the excitement of the hour they abandoned the customary reserve of the cowboy, and began performing what seemed to Shock impossible feats of horsemanship.

"I bet you I'll ride her into the Roost, Captain," cried The Kiddie.

"Done, for the drinks!" replied the Captain.

The boy cantered his mare across the street.

"Out of the way there!" he cried. "Out of the way, you fellows! I'm coming!"

As he spoke he put the little mare straight at the flight of steps leading up to the door of the Roost. The crowd parted hastily, but the Swallow balked and swerved, and but for the fine horsemanship of the rider he would have been thrown.

With an oath, the Kid took hold of his horse again, and riding carelessly, faced her once more at the steps. But again she plunged, reared, swung round, and set off at a run down the street.

The lad rode her easily back, brought her up to the steps at a walk, quieted her with voice and hand, and then, cantering across the street, came back again at an easy lope to the steps. The mare made as if to balk again.

"Up, girl!" cried the boy, lifting her with the rein; and then, as she rose, touching her with the spur, Like a cat the little mare clambered up the steps, and before she could change her mind she found herself through the door, standing in the bar-room with her rider on her back.

Through the outer entrance thronged the crowd of men, giving vent to their admiration in yells and oaths, and lining up at the bar waited for the payment of the bet.

Shock, who had been singularly attracted by the handsome, boyish face of the rider, walked up to the door and stood looking in, his great form towering above the crowd of men that swayed and jostled, chaffing and swearing, inside. As he stood looking at the boy, sitting his horse with such careless grace, and listening with pleased and smiling face to the varied and picturesque profanity in which the crowd were expressing their admiration, the words of his Convener came to his mind, " They may not want you, but they need you."

" Yes," he muttered to himself, " they need me, or someone better."

A great pity for the lad filled his heart and overflowed from his eyes.

The boy caught the look. With a gay laugh he cried, " I would drink to your very good health, sir! " his high, clear voice penetrating the din and bringing the crowd to silence. " But why carry so grave a face at such a joyous moment? " He lifted his glass over his head and bowed low to Shock.

Arrested by his words, the crowd turned their eyes toward the man that stood in the door, waiting in silence for his reply.

A quick flush rose to Shock's face, but without moving his eyes from the gay, laughing face of the boy, he said in a clear, steady voice, " I thank you,

sir, for your courtesy, and I ask your pardon if my
face was grave. I was thinking of your mother."

As if someone had stricken him the boy swayed
over his horse's neck, but in a moment recovering
himself he sat up straight, and lifting high his glass,
he said reverently, as if he had been toasting the
Queen: " Gentlemen, my mother! God bless her!"

" God bless her!" echoed the men.

Drinking off the glass he dismounted and, followed
by the cheers of the crowd, led his horse out of the
room and down the steps, and rode away.

Meantime Shock went in search of the doctor. In
a corner of the International bar he found him in a
drunken sleep. After vain efforts to wake him, without more ado Shock lifted him in his arms, carried
him out to the buckboard and drove away, followed
by the jibes and compliments of the astonished crowd.

But what to do with him was the question. There
was no room for himself, much less for his charge,
in any of the hotels or stopping places.

" May as well begin now," Shock said to himself,
and drove out to a little bluff of poplars at the river
bank near the town, and prepared to camp.

He disposed of the doctor by laying him in the
back of his buckboard, covered with the buffalo. He
unhitched and tethered the pony, and, according to
his crude notions of what a camp should be, began to
make his preparations. With very considerable difficulty, he first of all started a fire.

" Hello! Rather chilly for campin' out yit?"

He looked up and saw Ike.

" I guess you aint lived much out of doors," continued his visitor, glancing at the apology for a fire, and noticing the absence of everything in camp-making that distinguishes the experienced camper.

" No, this is my first camp," said Shock. " But I suppose every man must make a beginning."

" Yes," agreed Ike, " when he's got to. But I have a lingerin' suspicion that you'd be better inside to-night. It aint goin' to be pleasant."

" Oh, I'll be all right," replied Shock cheerfully. " I have a small tent, a couple of coats, a pair of blankets, and my pony has got his oats."

" Yes," drawled Ike, regarding the cayuse with contemptuous eyes, " he's all right. You can't kill them fellers. But, as I remarked, you'd be better inside."

He walked around the buckboard and his eyes fell upon the doctor.

" What the——" Ike checked himself, either out of deference to Shock's profession or more likely from sheer amazement.

He turned down the buffalo, gazed at the sleeping figure with long and grave interest, then lifting his head he remarked with impressive solemnity, " Well, I be chawed and swallered! You *have* got him, eh? Now, how did you do it? "

" Well," said Shock, " it was not difficult. I found him asleep in the International. I carried him out, and there he is."

" Say," said Ike, looking at Shock with dawning admiration in his eyes, " you're a bird! Is there anythin' else you want in that town? Guess not, else it would be here. The General said you'd kidnap him, and he was right. Now, what you goin' to do when he comes to? There aint much shelter in this bluff, and when he wakes he'll need someone to set up with him, sure. He's a terror, a dog-goned terror!"

"Oh, we'll manage," said Shock lightly. "I mean to start early in the morning."

"Before he gets up, eh? As I remarked before, you're a bird!"

For some moments Ike hung about the camp, poking the fire, evidently somewhat disturbed in his mind. Finally he said in a hesitating tone, "It aint much to offer any man, but my shack kin hold two men as well as one, and I guess three could squeeze in, specially if the third is in the condition he's in," nodding toward the doctor. "We kin lay him on the floor. Of course, it aint done up with no picters and hangin's, but it keeps out the breeze, and there aint no bugs, you bet."

Shock's experience of Western shacks had not been sufficiently varied and extensive to enable him to appreciate to the full this last commendation of Ike's. Ike's hesitation in making the offer determined Shock.

"Thank you very much," he said cordially. "I shall be delighted to go with you."

"All right, let's git," said Ike, proceeding to hitch up the pony, while Shock gathered his stuff together. In a few minutes they were ready to start.

"Guess he'll ride comfortable where he is," said

Ike. " You can't kill a drunk man. Strange, aint it? "

It was growing dusk as they drove through the town, but the streets, the hotel stoops, and bars were filled with men in various stages of intoxication. As they caught sight of Ike and recognised his companion, they indulged themselves in various facetious remarks.

" Hello, Ike. Goin' to meetin'? "

" No," retorted Ike shortly. " Goin' to school fer manners. Want to come? "

" Ikey's got religion. Caught on to the fire-escape you bet."

" No, he's goin' to learn that rasslin' trick."

" Ikey's showin' the stranger the town. He's on for a bust, you bet."

" Blank lot of jay birds," said Ike grimly, in a low tone. " I'll see 'em later. You'd think they'd never seen a stranger before."

" That is all for me, I suppose, Ike," said Shock apologetically.

" Don't you worry. It won't give me any grey hair." Ike emphasised his indifference by tilting his hat till it struck on the extreme back of his head, and lounging back in his seat with his feet on the dashboard.

" They all seen you givin' me that h'ist this afternoon," he continued, " and they can't get over that we aint fightin'. And," he added, hitting the hub of the wheel with a stream of tobacco juice, " it is a rather remarkable reminiscence."

Ike had a fondness for words not usually current among the cowboys, and in consequence his English was more or less reminiscent, and often phonetic rather than etymoligical.

Ike's shack stood at the further side of the town. Upon entering Shock discovered that it needed no apology for its appearance. The board walls were adorned with illustrations from magazines and papers, miscellaneous and without taint of prejudice, the *Sunday Magazine* and the *Police Gazette* having places of equal honour. On the wall, too, were nailed heads of mountain sheep and goats, of wapiti and other deer, proclaiming Ike a hunter.

Everything in the shack was conspicuously clean, from the pots, pans, and cooking utensils, which hung on a row of nails behind the stove, to the dish-cloth, which was spread carefully to dry over the dish-pan. Had Shock's experience of bachelors' shacks and bachelors' dishes been larger, he would have been more profoundly impressed with that cooking outfit, and especially with the dish-cloth. As it was, the dish-cloth gave Shock a sense of security and comfort.

Depositing the doctor upon a buffalo skin on the floor in the corner, with a pillow under his head, they proceeded to their duties, Ike to prepare the evening meal, and Shock to unpack his stuff, wondering all the while how this cowboy had come to hunt him up and treat him with such generous hospitality.

This mystery was explained as they sat about the fire after the tea-dishes had been most carefully washed and set away, Ike smoking and Shock musing.

" That old skunk rather turned you down, I guess,"
remarked Ike, after a long silence; " that old Macfarren, I mean," in answer to Shock's look of enquiry.

" I was surprised, I confess," replied Shock. " You
see, I was led to believe that he was waiting for me,
and I was depending upon him. Now, I really do not
know what to think."

" Movin' out, perhaps? " said Ike, casting a sharp
look at him from out of his half-closed eyes.

" What? Leave this post, do you mean? " said
Shock, his indignant surprise showing in his tone.
" No, sir. At least, not till my chief says so."

A gleam shot out from under Ike's lowered eyelids.

" The old fellow 'll make it hot for you, if you don't
move. Guess he expects you to move," said Ike
quietly.

" Move! " cried Shock again, stirred at the remembrance of Macfarren's treatment that afternoon.
" Would *you?* "

" See him blanked first," said Ike quietly.

" So will I," said Shock emphatically. " I mean,"
correcting himself hastily, " see him saved first."

" Eh? Oh—well, guess he needs some. He needs
manners, anyhow. He'll worry you, I guess. You
see, he surmises he's the entire bunch, but a man's
opinion of himself don't really affect the size of his
hat band."

Shock felt the opportunity to be golden for the
gathering of information about men and things in

the country where his work was to be done. He felt that to see life through the eyes of a man like Ike, who represented a large and potent element in the community, would be valuable indeed.

It was difficult to make Ike talk, but by careful suggestions, rather than by questioning, Ike was finally led to talk, and Shock began to catch glimpses of a world quite new to him, and altogether wonderful. He made the astounding discovery that things that had all his life formed the basis of his thinking were to Ike and his fellows not so much unimportant as irrelevant; and as for the great spiritual verities which lay at the root of all Shock's mental and, indeed, physical activities, furnishing motive and determining direction, these to Ike were quite remote from all practical living. What had God to do with rounding up cattle, or broncho-busting, or horse-trading? True, the elemental virtues of justice, truth, charity, and loyalty, were as potent over Ike as over Shock, but their moral standards were so widely different that these very virtues could hardly be classified in the same categories. Truth was sacred, but lying was one thing and horse-swapping another, and if a man was " white to the back " what more would you ask, even though at poker he could clean you out of your whole outfit?

Hitherto, a man who paid no respect to the decencies of religion Shock had regarded as " a heathen man and a publican," but with Ike religion, with all its great credos, with all its customs, had simply no bearing. Shock had not talked long with Ike until he began to feel that he must readjust not only his whole system of theology, but even his moral standards, and he began to wonder how the few sermons and addresses he had garnered from his ministry in the city wards would do for Ike and his people. He was making the discovery that climate changes the complexion, not only of men, but of habits of thought and action.

As Shock was finding his way to new adjustments and new standards he was incidentally finding his way into a new feeling of brotherhood as well. The lines of cleavage which had hitherto determined his interests and affinities were being obliterated. The fictitious and accidental were fading out under this new atmosphere, and the great lines of sheer humanity were coming to stand out with startling clearness. Up to this time creed and class had largely determined both his interest and his responsibility, but now, apart from class and creed, men became interesting, and for men he began to feel responsibility. He realised as never before that a man was the great asset of the universe—not his clothes, material, social or religious.

It was this new feeling of interest and responsibility that made him ask, " Who was that lad that rode the winning horse to-day? "

" That chap? " replied Ike. " He's my boss. The Kid, they call him."

Men of laconic speech say much by tone and gesture, and often by silence. In Ike's tone Shock read contempt, admiration, pity.

"A rancher?" he enquired.

"Well, he's got a ranch, and horses and cattle on it, like the rest of 'em. But ranchin'——" Ike's silence was more than sufficient.

"Well," said Shock, with admiring emphasis, "he seems to be able to ride, anyway."

"Ride! I should surmise! Ride! That kid could ride anythin' from a he-goat to a rampagin', highpottopotamus. Why, look here!" Ike waxed enthusiastic. "He's been two years in this country, and he's got us all licked good and quiet. Why, he could give points to any cattle-man in Alberta."

"Well, what's the matter with him?"

"Money!" said Ike wrathfully. "Some blamed fool uncle at home—he's got no parents, I understand—keeps a-sendin' him money. Consequently, every remittance he cuts things loose, with everyone in sight a-helpin' him."

"What a shame!" cried Shock. "He has a nice face. I just like to look at him."

"That's right!" answered Ike, with no waning of his enthusiasm. "He's white—but he's soft. Makes me so blank mad! He don't know they're playin' him, and makin' him pay for the game. The only question is, will he hold out longer'n his money."

"Why! hasn't he any friends here who would remonstrate with him?"

"Remonstrate! Remonstrate!" Ike rolled the word under his tongue as if it felt good. "You try to remonstrate, and see him look at you, and then smile, till you feel like a cluckin' hen that has lost her nest. Not any for me, thank you. But it's a blank pity! He's a white kiddie, he is."

"And that friend of his who was riding with him—who is he?"

"Harricomb—Captain Hal Harricomb, they call him. Good sort of fellow, too, but lazy—and considerable money. Goin' at a pretty good lick. Wife pulls him up, I guess. Good thing for him, too. Lives up by the General's—old gent, you know, sat by when you set me down out yonder. Mighty slick, too. Wasn't on to you, though."

"No," Shock hastened to say, "it was a fluke, of course. General Brady, you mean. Yes, he was very kind, indeed."

"Oh, the General's a gentleman, you bet! Horse ranch. Not very big, but makes it go."

"Could not a man like the General, now, help that young fellow—what is his name?"

"His name? Well, he goes by 'The Kid.' His name's Stanton, I think. Yes, Stanton—Vic Stanton. Though he never gets it."

"Well, could not the General help him?" repeated Shock.

"Help The Kid? Not he, nor anyone else. When a horse with blood in him gets a-goin', why, he's got to go till his wind gives out, unless you throw him right down, and that's resky. You've got to wait his time. Then's your chance. And that reminds me," said Ike, rising and knocking the ashes out of his pipe, "that I've got a job on hand. There'll be doin's to-night there after the happy time is over."

Shock looked mystified.

" They'll get the ladies off, you know, and then the fun'll begin."

" Fun? "

Ike winked a long, significant wink. " Yes. Lit'-rary Society, you know. A little game in the back room."

" And are you going to play, Ike? "

" Not to-night, thank you. I aint no saint, but I aint a blank fool altogether, and to-night I got to keep level. To-day's the boss's remittance day. He's got his cheque, I've heard, and they're goin' to roll him."

" Roll him? "

" Yes, clean him out. So I surmise it'd be wise for me to be on hand."

" Why, what have you got to do with it, Ike? "

Ike paused for a few moments, while he filled his pipe, preparatory to going out.

" Well, that's what I don't right know. It aint any of my own business. Course he's my boss, but it aint that. Somehow, that Kiddie has got a hitch onto my innards, and I can't let him get away. He's got such a blank slick way with him that he makes you feel like doin' the things you hate to do. Why, when he smiles at you the sun begins to shine. That's so. Why, you saw that race this after-noon? "

" Yes, the last heat."

" Well, did you observe Slipper come in? "

" Well, yes, I did. And I could not understand

why Slipper was not running.  Why didn't you run him, Ike?"

"Why?" said Ike, "that's what I don't know. There aint nothin' on four legs with horsehide on in these here Territories that can make Slipper take dust, but then—well, I knowed he had money on the Swallow.  But I guess I must be goin'."

"But what are you going to do?"

"Oh, I'll fall down somewheres and go to sleep. You see lots of things when you're asleep, providin' you know how to accomplish it."

"Shall I go with you?" asked Shock.

Ike regarded him curiously.

"Guess you wouldn't care to be mixed up in this kind of thing.  But blame it, if I don't think you'd stay with it if it was in your line, which it aint."

"But suppose you get into difficulty."

"Well," said Ike, smiling a slow smile, "when I want you I'll send for you," and with that he passed out into the night.

# XII

## HIS KEEPER

TILL long after midnight Shock sat over the fire pondering the events of the day, and trying to make real to himself the strange series of happenings that had marked his introduction to his work in this country. His life for the last month had been so unlike anything in his past as to seem quite unnatural.

As he sat thus musing over the past and planning for the future, a knock came to the door, and almost immediately there came in a little man, short and squat, with humped shoulders, bushy, grizzled hair and beard, through which peered sharp little black eyes. His head and face and eyes made one think of a little Scotch terrier.

"Ye're the meenister?" he said briefly.

"Yes," replied Shock, greatly surprised at his visitor, but warming to the Scotch voice.

"Aye. Ye're wanted."

"Wanted? By whom?"

"The man that lives in this hoose. He's deein', I'm thinkin'."

"Dying!" said Shock, starting up and seizing his hat. "What! Ike?"

"Aye, Ike. He's verra ill."

"Go on, then," said Shock. "Quick!"

"Aye, quick it is." And the little man, without further words, plunged into the darkness.

A few minutes' swift walk through the black night brought them to the Ranchers' Roost. There, in a corner of the room at the back of the bar, he found Ike lying almost unconscious, and apparently very ill.

"Why, what's the matter?" cried Shock, dropping on his knees beside Ike. But Ike seemed stupefied, and mumbled a few incoherent words. Shock caught the words, "the gang," and "dope."

He looked in an agony of helplessness at the little Scotchman, who stood by looking down upon the sick man with face quite unmoved.

"Do you know what he says?" enquired Shock.

"He's no sayin' much," said the the little Scotchman calmly.

Again Ike tried to speak, and this time Shock caught the words, "The boss—gang's got him—Smiley Simmons—back room—fetch him."

"What does he mean?" cried Shock.

"It's ha-r-r-d to tell that," said the little Scotchman. "He's talkin' about some boss or other."

"Oh, yes, I know what that means. He is referring to his boss, young Stanton."

"Oh, ay!" said the little Scotchman, with a light breaking on his face. "I saw the bodies. They've gaen o'er to the creature Simmons'."

"Show me the way," said Shock. "Quick!"

"Come, then," said the little Scotchman, leading once more into the darkness.

Some distance down the street stood Smiley—or as some preferred to call him Slimy—Simmons' general store. At the back of the store there was a side door.

"They're in yonder," said the little Scotchman, and disappeared.

Shock knocked at the door, but there was no response. He turned the handle, opened the door, and walking in found himself in the back of the store, in a room dimly lighted by a hanging lantern. Seated on a stool at a high desk, evidently busy with his ledger, sat a man, tall, slender, and wiry. He had a sharp, thin face, with high forehead, protruding nose, and receding chin. The moment he spoke Shock discovered at once how it was he came by his nickname. His smile was the most striking characteristic of his manner. Indeed, so permanent and pervasive did his smile appear, that it seemed almost to be a fixed feature of his face.

He came forward to Shock, rubbing his hands.

"Ah, good evening," he said, in a most insinuating voice. "Is there anything I can do for you?"

"Yes," said Shock, instinctively shrinking from him. "I want to see Mr. Stanton."

"Mr. Stanton—Mr. Stanton? Let me see. I saw Mr. Stanton some hours ago. Let me think. Was it at the International? Yes, I think it was the International. No, in the Royal. I have no doubt you will find him there. I shall be pleased to show you, for I see you are a stranger. We are always delighted to see strangers and we try to make them welcome to our town."

He moved toward the door as he spoke. Shock knew at once he was lying.

"Mr. Stanton is not at the Royal. I have been informed he is in this building somewhere."

"In this building?" murmured Smiley, in a puzzled tone. "In this building?" He glanced up at the ceiling as if expecting to see the missing man there. "Strange," he continued. "Now, I have been here for some time, for hours, indeed. I am a busy man, Mr. ——"

"Macgregor," replied Shock.

"Mr. Macgregor. I find it necessary to pursue my avocation into the hours we generally devote to slumber. And to-day business has been unusually interrupted. But I have failed to notice Mr. Stanton enter."

At the further end of the room Shock's eyes fell upon a door, through the cracks of which a light was shining.

"It is possible," said Shock, "he is in that room," pointing to the door.

"Hardly, my dear sir, hardly."

But even as he spoke a voice, loud and clear, rang out. "Now, my dear fellow, go to the deuce. That comes to me."

The reply Shock could not catch.

"I think," he said, turning to Smiley, "we shall find Mr. Stanton in there."

As he spoke he walked toward the door. But Smiley slipped before him.

"Pardon me, my dear sir, that is a private room—

some friends of mine who would greatly dislike being disturbed. I am exceedingly sorry I cannot oblige you."

"I must see Mr. Stanton," said Shock, putting his hand upon the door knob.

"My dear sir," said Simmons, his thin lips drawn back over his yellow teeth, "I regret to say it is impossible. If Mr. Stanton is in there—mark me, I say *if* he is in there, which is extremely unlikely—but if he is in there, he would be very unwilling to be disturbed at this hour. However, since you are so anxious, I shall take him a message."

As Smiley said this he bowed with an air of gracious condescension, as if he expected Shock to be profoundly impressed with this concession to his persistence. But Shock was not at all impressed.

"I cannot wait longer," he said. "It is a matter of life and death. I must enter that room."

"My dear sir," said Simmons, rubbing his hands, his smile becoming more and more expansive, "this is my house, that door is my door. If you break it I should be grieved to have to exact the full penalty of the law."

Shock hesitated. He had never willingly broken a law in his life. It would be a most unfortunate beginning for his mission in this town, and, after all, what business had he to interfere? If this young fool was determined to waste his money, let him do so. But he thought of Ike, and the entreaty in his voice as he whispered out his broken words, and he thought of the look of reverence and love on the lad's face that afternoon when he gave his toast, "My mother! God bless her!" Shock's face set hard.

"I must see him," he said simply, but with such an air of determination that Simmons weakened.

"Well, if you wait a few minutes," replied Smiley, "I will see if he will speak to you."

Shock waited till Smiley opened the door, whereupon, stepping quickly forward, he set his foot against the lower panel, and pushed the door wide open.

In a small room, bare of furniture except for tables and chairs and a hanging lamp, sat four men, of whom Shock recognised two. The Kid was one, and Macfarren the other. Across the table from these sat two men, one by his uniform the Inspector of the Mounted Police. The face of the other had to Shock a familiar look, but where he had seen him he could not remember.

As Shock opened the door the man in uniform started up with an oath, and Macfarren blew out the light.

"What's that for, Macfarren?" said The Kid.

"Shut up, you fool," growled Macfarren.

"What did you say, sir?" enquired The Kid, in a voice somewhat thick and unsteady.

"Get him out of here," said Macfarren, in a low tone.

"I want to have a few words with Mr. Stanton," said Shock, standing in the doorway.

"Here you are. Fire away," replied the boy. "The light is not good, but I can hear in the dark."

"You are wanted, Mr. Stanton, very earnestly by a friend of yours."

"Let him walk right in if he wants me," replied The Kid.

"That he cannot do. He is very ill."

"Ah! who is he, may I ask?" enquired Stanton, striking a match.

It was promptly blown out.

"I wouldn't do that again," he said gently. "Who is it?" he repeated, striking another match and lighting the lamp.

"It is Ike," said Shock. "He is very ill—dying, for all I know, and he wants you."

For answer there was a contemptuous laugh from the Mounted Policeman, in which Macfarren joined.

"Rather good that," said Macfarren.

"Excuse me, gentlemen," said the boy, making a strenuous effort to pull himself together. "I hate to leave this good company, but I must go. I happen to pay Ike wages, but he is my friend. He has asked for me, and I am going to him."

"Oh, blank it all! Don't be a fool," said the policeman. "Ike's all right. He has been taking an extra drink, but you can't kill Ike. Wait for half an hour, and we'll go down and see how he is."

The young lad hesitated. The stranger made a signal to Smiley, and suddenly Shock found himself pushed backward from the entrance, and the door slammed in his face.

"Open that door!" he heard The Kid cry.

There was a murmur in response.

"Open it, I say, Simmons."

Again a murmur.

"No, I am going. I will go myself. Ike wants me." The boy's voice was loud and hard.

"That's mine," the voice cried again. "Let that go at once!"

There was a sound of scuffling and of falling chairs. With a kick Shock sent the door flying open, and saw three men struggling with Stanton. Smiley had wound his long arms about him from behind, the Inspector held his arm in a firm grip with one hand and with the other had hold of the stranger, who had The Kid by the throat. Macfarren was still at the table, evidently gathering up what lay upon it.

In an instant Shock sprang into the fray. With a single jerk he tore Smiley from his victim and flung him on the floor. Reaching for the stranger, who was choking The Kid, he caught his wrist and gave it a slight turn. With a yell of pain the stranger turned upon him and aimed a blow at Shock's face. Catching the blow on his arm, Shock seized his assailant by the shoulder, jerked him clear of his feet, and flung him far into the corner of the room. At this the policeman immediately gave back.

For a few seconds The Kid stood swaying unsteadily. Then, after he recovered his breath he turned to Shock and said, "I hardly expected to ever feel grateful to you, but I assure you I appreciate your timely help."

Then turning to the others, and regaining his wonted smile and easy manner, he continued,

"Gentlemen, you are somewhat insistent in your hospitality. It is always instructive, and sometimes pleasant, to extend our knowledge of our friends, and now let me say that a more blackguardly lot of thieves I have never met, and if this gentleman who has dropped in so opportunely will kindly stand at my back for a few minutes, I shall be delighted to make good my words by slapping your faces." The Kid's tone was low and gentle, even sweet.

"Mr. Macfarren, your venerable beard prevents me. Simmons, your general sliminess protects you, but as for you, Inspector Haynes, it gives me great pleasure to express my opinion of you—thus!" His open hand flashed out as he spoke and caught Haynes on the cheek a stinging blow.

With an oath the Inspector jerked out his pistol and sprang at him. "I arrest you, sir, in the name of the Queen. Move your hand and you are a dead man."

"So be you, Mr. Inspector," drawled a quiet voice in the door.

Shock turned, and to his unspeakable amazement saw his sick friend standing with his gun covering the Inspector.

"One step back, please, Mr. Inspector. Quick! This trigger goes mighty easy. Now, right wheel!" The Inspector hesitated a second. "Quick!" cried Ike sharply. "Don't you fool too long obeyin' orders. I aint used to it. I'm here exercisin' a public function, preventin' murder, in short, and I'll drop you in your tracks if you don't move at the next word. You here me? And if you don't intend to move at the next word, say your prayers in this interval. Now then, back up to that table and put down that gun. Correct. Very nice, indeed."

Ike's voice took on more and more of its customary drawl.

"Now, two steps forward. Right. Now, you can —go—to—the—devil!'"

Ike stepped to the table, took up the pistol, and returned to his place at the door, saying:

"Say, boss, this prayer meetin's over. Let's go home."

"Not until the Inspector says so," said The Kid, who had recovered himself, and who was now quite sober. "He has the word now, Ikey, so don't interfere."

"All right, Kiddie, play your game. You're equivalent to it, I surmise."

"I think so," said the Kid sweetly. Then, turning to the Inspector, he continued in a voice of gentle consideration, "There is something on your cheek, Inspector Haynes. You have not observed it. Allow me to point it out to you."

He moved forward as he spoke, but Shock interposed.

"I think that is enough, Mr. Stanton," he said. "Let the matter drop now."

The boy turned quickly, and looking steadily into Shock's face, began in a quiet, even voice, "Mr.— ah——"

"Macgregor," supplied Shock.

" Mr. Macgregor, you are a stranger. In this country in a matter of this kind we never allow interference."

" And yet," said Shock in a voice equally quiet, " interference is not unwelcome at times."

" What you say is quite true," replied the boy, " and, as I have said, I am not ungrateful for your timely assistance."

" Oh, I was thinking of Ike," said Shock hurriedly. " But surely you will let this matter drop now."

" Drop!" roared the Inspector. " Blank your impudence! He has called me a thief, and he has slapped my face while doing my duty. I will have the lot of you arrested for interference with justice. And as for you, Stanton, we shall settle this again."

So saying, the Inspector made for the door.

At the door Ike still stood on guard.

" When you want me, Mr. Inspector," he said, " don't have any delinquency in sendin' for me. I surmise I can contribute some valuable evidence on the point of guns, games, and such."

The Inspector glared at him.

" I'll take my gun," he said.

" Your gun? Why, cert! Did you drop it somewheres? Perhaps if you look round when the light's good you'll find it. Slimey, here, will help you. I'm pretty nigh certain you'll extradite that weapon in the morning. Good-night."

With a curse the Inspector passed out.

" Now, Ikey," said The Kid coolly, " stand aside,

for there is a cur here that had the audacity to throttle me."

With these words he sprang past Shock, seized the stranger by the throat, cuffed him with his open hand, and dragging him to the door sent him forth with a parting kick and an imprecation.

" Now, Macfarren," he said, turning to that gentleman, who still sat by the table, " you have some money not belonging to you. Put it on the table."

Without a moment's hesitation Macfarren hastily poured forth from his pocket poker-chips, gold pieces, and bills.

" I assure you, Mr. Stanton," he hurried to say, " I was simply holding them till the—ah—trouble should be over."

" That was most kind," replied Stanton. " I have no very clear remembrance, but I was under the impression that it was your suggestion to lock the door." As he spoke he swept the money into his pocket.

" Certainly, but my only intention was to keep out—ah—strangers and—intruders. You know, Mr. Stanton, I would be no party to robbery, and, indeed, I do not believe for a moment that any robbery was intended. It was an unfortunate eagerness on the part of Crawley to secure his winnings that precipitated the trouble. I really hope you do not think me capable of anything of the sort."

Macfarren's manner was abject, but his tone was evidently sincere.

" You were unfortunate in your company, then, Mr. Macfarren. Come on, Ike. We are done with this gang. Lucky I was not quite slewed, or my creditors would have been in mourning to-morrow. Mr. Macgregor, where do you put up?"

"He's with me to-night," said Ike, "and a mighty fortunate circumstance it was for us all. This here business had got beyond my capabilities. Some of us need a keeper."

"That's me, Ikey. Yes, I know. Rub it in. It's a keeper I need. Well, I give you my word I am done with this **gang**. Fool! Fool!" he continued bitterly, "a cursed fool, Ikey. Three years of it now."

"That's what," said Ikey, leading the way down the street. "For the past two years, boss, you know you've beat me. Though I don't hold myself out as no sort of paradox——"

"Paragon, Ikey," said The Kid, with a gentle laugh. He always found his cowboy's English amusing.

"Paragon, eh? Well, all the same, I aint no sort of paragon, but I know where to stop."

"Where are we now, Ike? At the end of the rope, eh?"

"No, by the livin' Gimmini! but gettin' there on the jump," said Ike, with grave emphasis.

Without further conversation they made their way through the dark streets till they reached Ike's shack. The doctor lay still asleep in the corner.

"He kidnapped him," was Ike's explanation to The Kid, nodding his head toward Shock. "So I'd advise that you hitch on to the preacher here for a period. Give him the job of windin' you up."

" Could you undertake that, do you think? " There was a curious smile on the boy's face, but an undertone of seriousness in his voice.

" No," said Shock gravely, " I could not undertake that."

" You see, Ike, I am too uncertain. Too far gone, I guess."

Ike was too puzzled to reply. He had a kind of dim idea that in Shock there was some help for his boss, and he was disappointed at Shock's answer.

For some time Shock sat in silence, looking at the fire. His heart was sore. He felt his helplessness. This clever, gay-hearted young fellow, with all his gentleness of manner, was unapproachable. He belonged to another world, and yet Shock yearned over him with a tenderness inexplicable to himself. The Kid gave him no opening. There was a kind of gay defiance in his bearing, as if he had read Shock's heart and were determined to keep him at arm's length. Instinctively Shock knew that he must wait his opportunity.

" Well, guess we'd better turn in," suggested Ike. " Can you two bunk together? That bed'll hold you both, I guess."

" No, thanks," said Shock decidedly. " That is your bed. I'll spread my blankets on the floor."

" In this country," said Stanton, " we give the stranger the bed, so you need not scruple to turn Ike out of his. Ike and I will take the floor."

" Not this time," said Shock firmly. " I am thankful enough for shelter, without taking a man's bed.

Besides," he added, suddenly remembering, "Ike needs his bed to-night, after his sick turn."

"Yes, by Jove! By the way," exclaimed Stanton, "what happened, Ike?"

"A sudden and unexpected predisposition which takes me now and then," turning his back upon Shock and solemnly winking at The Kid; "but I recover just as quickly, and when I do I'm as slick as ever, and slicker. These here turns work off a lot of bad blood, I guess."

During his speech he continued winking at The Kid. That young gentleman gazed at him in amazed silence. Gradually, a light broke in upon him.

"Look here, Ike, what in thunder do you mean?"

"I say, boss," said Ike persuasively, "just go easy. You oughn't to excite yourself. 'Taint good for you, and 'taint good for me, either. My doctor says so. I wouldn't persecute your enquiries at this late hour of the night."

Ike's gravity was imperturbable.

"Well, I be blanked! I beg your pardon, Mr. Macgregor. Ike, you're a cool one. You've got the nerve of——" Here The Kid began to laugh, and Shock, all unsuspecting of Ike's scheme for getting his boss out of the clutches of his spoilers, gazed from the one to the other with an air of such absolute perplexity that The Kid went off into immoderate fits of laughter. Ike's gravity remained unbroken.

"All the same, boss," he said, "you want to keep an eye on that outfit. They'll get even. That man Crawley and the Inspector aint goin' to rest easy where they are. Marks like what you put on 'em burn to the bone."

"They cannot hurt me, Ike," said the Kid lightly, "and I think they will be afraid to try. But Mr. Macgregor here has got into trouble. Is not Macfarren a church warden, or something, in your Church?"

"He is a manager, I think," said Shock. "Pretty much the same thing."

"Well, he is a man to look out for. I can get along without him, but you cannot, can you? I mean, he can hurt you."

"No," said Shock quietly, "he cannot hurt me. The only man that can hurt me is myself. No other man can. And besides," he added, pulling a little Bible out of his pocket, "I have a Keeper, as Ike said."

As Shock opened the little Bible he became conscious of a sense of mastery. His opportunity had come.

"Listen to this," he said, and he read in a voice of assured conviction:

> "The Lord is thy keeper.
> The Lord shall keep thee from all evil.
> He shall keep thy soul.
> The Lord shall keep thy going out and thy coming in.
> From this time forth and forevermore."

He closed the book and put it in his pocket.

"No," he said, "no man can hurt me." Then turning to Ike he said quietly, "I always say my

tations, prayers, blessings, and entreaties. Within the room, seated beside the bed, was Carroll, gloomy and taciturn.

The doctor drew back the blind and let in the morning light. It showed poor little Patsy, pale and wasted, his angelic face surrounded with a golden aureole of yellow curls that floated across the white pillow. The doctor was startled and moved.

"What is this?" he cried. "What is the matter?"

"Just an accident, doctor," said Mrs. Carroll volubly. "It was a blow he got."

"I struck him wid a chair," said Carroll bitterly.

"Whisht, now, darlin'. You're not to be blamin' yourself at all, at all. Sure, you didn't mane to do it. And what's a bit of discoosion between men? The little Patsy, the brave little heart that he is, run in to help his dad, so he did!" And Mrs. Carroll continued with a description which became more and more incoherent and more and more broken with sobs and tears.

"It's a wonder he didn't kill him," said the doctor.

"Arrah, ye may say it. But they do be tellin' me that his riverence there beyant, he stood in under the blow. God bless his sowl! It's a hairo he is—a hairo!"

She ran toward Shock as if to embrace him, but Shock, who had come to know her ways, avoided her, dodging behind the doctor.

"Not at all," he said. "Any man would have done the same."

"Now, God pardon your riverence for the lie ye've told."

"But how did *you* get into the row?" asked the doctor, turning to Shock.

"And ye may ask," interrupted Mrs. Carroll. "It's all av that squirmin' little worm of a Frenchman. May the divil fly away wid him! I'm not sayin' but Carroll there is quick with his tongue, and betimes with his hands, too—the high spirit that he has! but sure, it's a tinder heart he carries inside av him if they'd lave him be."

Meantime the doctor had been proceeding with his examination.

"He has lain a week like this, eh?"

"Yes, a week, with never a move till him, and niver a look out av his lovely eyes."

"But he takes his nourishment, does he?"

"Yes, once in a while a cup of milk with a wee drap av whisky intill it, doctor."

The doctor nodded.

"Won't hurt him. Not too much, mind. A teaspoonful in a large cup."

The doctor stood for some moments after he had finished his examination, looking down upon the little white face, so wasted, so beautiful. Then he shook his head sorrowfully.

"Ah, doctor, darlin'!" burst out Mrs. Carroll. "Don't say the wurrd! Don't say the wurrd!"

At this Carroll lifted his head and enquired briefly, "Will he get better, doctor?"

"He has a chance. He has a slight chance."

And with a look at Shock he left the room. After speaking a few words of comfort and hope to the mother Shock followed the doctor from the house.

"It is a case for trephining, I fear," said the doctor. "A clear case. It is the only chance he has, and it ought to be done at once."

"You mean to-day?" asked Shock.

"Yes, to-day. But——" The doctor hesitated. "I am not ready."

"I could get your instruments and anything else you might order," said Shock eagerly.

"No, it is not that," said the doctor. "The truth is, I have not the nerve. Nice confession to make, isn't it? Look at that hand."

He held out his hand as he spoke, and Shock saw that not only the hand, but the whole arm, indeed the whole gaunt frame of the doctor, was all in a tremble. Shock's experience in the city wards made him realise something of the shame and humiliation of the moment to the doctor. He hastened to turn his attention in a happier direction.

"You have performed this operation before?"

"Yes, frequently in the old country, once or twice here. I have seen some practice, sir," said the doctor, straightening himself up. "But there it is," holding out again his shaking hand.

"Well," said Shock, "we must wait till—till everything is ready."

"Yes," said the doctor. "Not before three days would I dare to touch a knife. In three days, sir, I shall return, bringing all the appliances necessary, and in the interval the time will not be entirely lost. We shall take every means to tone the boy up. By the way, I suppose there is someone in the village with sufficient nerve to render assistance?"

"I do not know. There is only one man in this country whom I can think of as being reliable for an affair of this kind. Do you happen to know of the cowboy, Ike?"

"The very man," said the doctor. "He lives on the Stanton ranch between this and the fort. We can see him on our way."

Before the doctor left for home he had called to prepare the Carrolls for the operation. At first Tim would not hear of it. He fiercely declared that he would kill any man that dared put a knife on his lad. His wife was equally determined that the operation should not take place.

"Very well," said the doctor, "then your boy will die, and, Carroll, I shall have you arrested for manslaughter forthwith."

This aspect of the case made little impression upon Carroll.

"If the lad dies," he said hoarsely, "divil a care what happens to me."

But Mrs. Carroll became anxiously desirous that the operation should be performed.

"And sure the good God wouldn't be after takin' him from us, for didn't his riverence there put up a prayer that would melt the heart of the angels, and I did promise God meself a rale fast, with niver an egg nor a bit of a fish to my teeth, if he should lave him wid us. And Carroll, darlin', ye'll not be after breakin' ye're wife's heart, nor makin' her a widow? Just ye come on, doctor, and niver a word he'll say till ye."

And so it came, in three days that the doctor returned, clean, steady, and fit for his work, with Ike, Shock, and The Kid on hand as his assistants.

"I asked the doctor if I might come along," said the latter, explaining his presence, "and though he did not encourage me, here I am."

"We will make him nurse or outside guard," said Shock. "We will give him full charge of the family."

"Yes," replied the doctor, in his gentle, professional voice, "the family. Let them be removed to some distance. The house must be kept entirely quiet, entirely quiet. An interruption might be serious. Mr. and Mrs. Carroll and the children had better be taken away to some remote distance, so that we may have in the house perfect peace—perfect peace."

But in Carroll they met an unexpected difficulty.

"Not a fut of me will I lave," he announced, and from this position was immovable.

"Let us say no more at present," said the doctor quietly to his assistants. "There are various methods of removing an obstruction. I have found various methods."

And so The Kid, with Mrs. Carroll, Tim, Nora, Eileen, Jimmie, and little Michael, set off for Jumping Rock at the lake. After the procession had formed, however, another difficulty arose. Michael refused point blank to go, and on being urged threw himself down upon the ground and kicked and yelled vociferously.

"Indade, there's no use of tryin' to make him do what he don't want," said his mother, with a conviction born of long experience of Michael's tempers and ways.

The procession halted, The Kid looking helpless and foolish. In vain he offered his watch, his pistol with the charge drawn. All his possessions availed not at all.

In his desperation he was on the point of proceeding to extreme measures when a voice, singularly sweet and musical, sounded behind him.

"Perhaps I can help," it said.

The Kid swung round, hat in hand. It was Marion, the Old Prospector's daughter.

"I shall be profoundly thankful. And for that matter doubtless he will, too, for I had come to the conclusion that the situation demanded a change of tactics."

The girl sat down beside Michael, and lifting him to her knee began to beguile him from his present misery with promises of songs, and snatches of tales, whose powers of enchantment had evidently been proved in similar circumstances, till finally his interest was diverted, his curiosity excited, and at length Michael was persuaded to join the company with smiling expectation of good things to come.

"I wish you would confide to me the secret of your

power, Miss——" said The Kid, with a most courteous bow.

"I am Marion Mowbray," she said simply.

"Miss Mowbray," continued The Kid, "I know
your father very well, and"—looking into the girl's
eyes, so very piercing and so very black—"I should
like to know his daughter, too."

But Marion devoted herself chiefly to Michael, giving such attention as she could to the older and more
active and more venturous Eileen and Jimmie, and
The Kid found his duties to Mrs. Carroll, Tim, and
Nora so engrossing that he had little time to bestow
any further attention upon the girl.

While Marion with tales and songs held the
younger portion in an enthralled circle about her
upon the Jumping Rock, The Kid upon the lake shore
below was using his most strenuous endeavours to make
the hour pass happily for Mrs. Carroll, Tim, and
Nora.

Meantime, in the back room of the Stopping-Place
Dr. Burton was making his preparations for a very
critical operation. All his movements were marked
by a swift dexterity and an attention to detail that
gave Shock the impression that here was a man not
only a master of his art, but, for the time being at
least, master of himself. He laid out and thoroughly
disinfected his instruments, prepared his lint, band-
ages, sponges, and explained clearly to each of
his two assistants the part he was to take. Shock,
who had had some slight experience in the surgical
operations attendant upon an active football career,

was to be the assistant in chief, being expected to take charge of the instruments, and to take part, if necessary, in the actual operation. Ike was instructed to be in readiness with a basin, sponge, and anything else that might be demanded.

"We shall not give you much to do," said the doctor, "but what you have to do must be done promptly and well. Now, then," he continued, lifting his scissors with a flourish which did not fail to impress Carroll, who was seated near by, "we shall proceed."

"Will it hurt, doctor?" groaned Carroll, gazing upon the row of instruments with fascinated eyes.

"Before we are finished it is quite possible the patient may be conscious of nervous disturbance, accompanied by sensations more or less painful."

"Will it hurt, blank you!" replied Carroll, whose hoarse voice showed the intensity of his repressed emotion.

"As I was saying," said the doctor in his calm, even tone, and examining his instruments one by one with affectionate care, "there is every possibility that the nerve centres may be——"

"Oh," groaned Carroll, still fascinated by the instruments that the doctor was handling with such loving touches, "will someone shut up this blank, blatherin' fool? He'd drive a man crazy, so he wud!"

"Mr. Carroll, we must be calm. We must be entirely calm," observed the doctor. "Now," continuing his monologue, "we shall remove the hair from the field of operation. Cleanliness in an operation of this kind is of prime importance. Recent scientific investigations show that the chief danger in operations is from septic poisoning. Yes, every precaution must be taken. Then we shall bathe with this weak solution of carbolic—three per cent. will be quite sufficient, quite sufficient—the injured parts and the surrounding area, and then we shall examine the extent of the wound. If the dura mater be penetrated, and the arachnoid cavity be opened, then there will be in all probability a very considerable extravasation of blood, and by this time, doubtless, serious inflammation of all the surrounding tissues. The aperture being very small and the depression somewhat extensive, it will be necessary to remove—to saw out, in short—a portion of the skull," lifting up a fierce-looking instrument.

Carroll groaned.

"Let me out!" he whispered hoarsely, rising and feeling his way with outstretched hand to the door. "I can't stand this bloody divil!"

Ike opened the door, while Shock sprang to support the groping man.

"Lave me be!" he said fiercely, with a curse, and pushing Shock back he stumbled out.

"Ah," said the doctor, with evident satisfaction, "there are various methods of removing obstructions, as I have said. We shall now no longer delay." And he proceeded to clip away the golden curls from about the wound. "These," he said, holding them up in his fingers and looking at them admiringly, "we had better preserve. These beautiful locks may be priceless to the mother, priceless indeed. Poor, bonnie laddie! Now we shall prepare, we shall aseptically prepare, the whole field of operation. A sponge—that's it. That will do. Now, let us examine the extent of the injury," feeling with dextrous fingers about the edge of the slight wound, and over all the depressed surface.

"Ah! as I feared. The internal table is widely comminuted, and there is possibly injury to the dura mater. We must excise a small portion of the bone. The scalpel, please." Then, after laying back with a few swift, dexterous movements the scalp from about the wounded parts: "The saw. Yes, the saw. The removal of a section," he continued, in his gentle monotone, beginning to saw, "will allow examination of the internal table. A sponge, please. Thank you. And if the dura mater——" Here the stillness of the room was broken by a sound from Ike. The doctor glanced at him.

"This is a very simple part of the operation," he explained, "a very simple part, indeed, and attended with absolutely no pain. A sponge, please. Thank you. Now the forceps. Yes."

He snipped off a section of the bone. Ike winced.

"Ah, as I feared. There is considerable comminution and extravasation. Yes, and owing to the long delay, and doubtless to the wet applications which the uninitiated invariably apply, pus. Now, the carbolic solution," to Ike, who was standing with white face and set teeth.

"You are doing remarkably well," said the doctor encouragingly to him, "remarkably well. To a novice this at times presents a shocking aspect. Now we shall attack this depression. The elevator, please. No, the elevator, Mr. Macgregor. There it lies. Yes. Now gently, gently. Just hold that in position," offering Shock the end of the instrument which he was using as a lever to raise the depressed portion of the skull. "The other scalpel, please. Now, a slight pressure. Gently, gently. We must be extremely careful of the edges. No, that will not do. Then we must have recourse to the trephine."

He lifted the instrument as he spoke, and gazed at it with every mark of affection.

"This is one of the most beautiful of all the instruments of modern surgery. A lovely instrument, a lovely instrument, indeed. Let us secure our firm surface. That seems satisfactory," beginning to bore.

This was too much for Ike. He hastily set down the basin and sponge on a chair, then straightened up in a vain effort to regain mastery of himself.

"Ah," said the doctor. "Poor Ike! The spirit is willing, but the sympathetic nerve is evidently seriously disturbed, thereby affecting the vasomotor, and will likely produce complete syncope. Lay him down on his back immediately."

"No," said Ike, "I aint no good. I'm going out."

"Now," said the doctor calmly, when Shock and he had been left alone, "I hope there will be no more interruption. We must proceed with the trephining.

Ah, beautiful, beautiful!" his quick moving, deft fingers keeping pace with his monologue.

"There now," after a few minutes' work with the trephine, "the depression is lifted. We shall soon be finished."

With supple, firm fingers he sewed the scalp, dressed the wound, and was done.

"Thank God!" said Shock, with a long breath. "Will he live?"

"It is a question now of strength and vitality. If the inflammation is not too widely extended the child may recover. Young life is very tenacious."

The doctor washed his hands, wiped his instruments, put them carefully away in their case, and sat down.

"Doctor," said Shock, "that is a great work. Even to a layman that operation seems wonderful."

Under the stimulus of his professional work the doctor's face, which but two days before had been soft and flabby, seemed to have taken on a firmer, harder appearance, and his whole manner, which had been shuffling and slovenly, had become alert and self-reliant.

"A man who can do that, doctor, can do great things."

A shadow fell on his face. The look of keen intelligence became clouded. His very frame lost its erect poise, and seemed to fall together. His professional air of jaunty cheerfulness forsook him. He huddled himself down into his chair, put his face in his hands, and shuddered.

"My dear sir," he said, lifting up his face, "it is quite useless, quite hopeless."

"No," said Shock eagerly, "do not say that. Surely the Almighty God——"

The doctor put up his hand.

"I know all you would say. How often have I heard it! The fault is not with the Almighty, but with myself. I am still honest with myself, and yet——" Here he paused for some moments. "I have tried—and I have failed. I am a wreck. I have prayed—prayed with tears and groans. I have done my best. But I am beyond help."

For a full minute Shock stood, gazing sadly at the noble head, the face so marred, the huddling form. He knew something of the agony of remorse, humiliation, fear, and despair that the man was suffering.

"Dr. Burton," said Shock, with the air of a man who has formed a purpose, "you are not telling the truth, sir."

The doctor looked up with a flash of indignation in his eyes.

"You are misrepresenting facts in two important particulars. You have just said that you have done your best, and that you are beyond all help. The simple truth is you have neither done your best, nor are you beyond help."

"Beyond help!" cried the doctor, starting up and beginning to pace the floor, casting aside his usual gentle manner. "You use plain speech, sir, but your evident sincerity forbids resentment. If you knew my history you would agree with me that I state the simple truth when I declare that I am beyond help. You see before you, sir, the sometime President of the Faculty of Guy's, London, a man with a reputation second to none in the Metropolis. But neither reputation, nor fortune, nor friends could avail to save me from this curse. I came to this country in desperation. It was a prohibition country. Cursed be those who perpetrated that fraud upon the British public! If London be bad, this country, with its isolation, its monotony of life, and this damnable permit system, is a thousand times worse. God pity the fool who leaves England in the hope of recovering his manhood and freedom here. I came to this Godforsaken, homeless country with some hope of recovery in my heart. That hope has long since vanished. I am now beyond all help."

" No," said Shock in a quiet, firm voice, " you have told me nothing to prove that you are beyond help. In fact," he continued almost brusquely, " no man of sense and honesty has a right to say that. Yes," he continued, in answer to the doctor's astonished look, " salvation, as it is called, is a matter of common sense and honesty."

" I thought you clergymen preached salvation to be a matter of faith."

" Faith, yes. That is the same thing. Common sense, I call it. A man is a fool to think he is beyond help while he has life. A little common sense and honesty is all you want. Now, let us find Carroll. But, doctor, let my last word to you be this—do not ever say or think what you have said to me to-day.

It simply is not true. And I repeat, the man who can do that sort of thing," pointing to the child lying on the bed, " can do a great deal more. Good things are waiting you."

" Oh, Lord God Almighty!" said the doctor, throwing up his hands in the intensity of his emotion. " You almost make me think there is some hope."

" Don't be a fool, doctor," said Shock in a matter of fact voice. " You are going to recover your manhood and your reputation. I know it. But as I said before, remember I expect common sense and honesty."

" Common sense and honesty," said the doctor as if to himself. " No religion."

" There you are," said Shock. " I did not say that. I did say common sense and honesty. But now, do go and find poor Carroll. He will be in agony."

" Oh, a little of it won't hurt him. He is rather an undeveloped specimen," said the doctor, resuming his professional tone.

In a few minutes he returned with Carroll, whose face was contorted with his efforts to seem calm.

" Tell me," he said to Shock. " Will the lad live? "

" The operation is entirely successful, thanks to the skill of Dr. Burton there."

" Will he live? " said Carroll to the doctor in a husky tone.

" Well, he has a chance—a chance now which before he had not; and if he does, you owe it to Mr. Macgregor there."

" And if he doesn't, I shall owe that to him," hissed Carroll through his clenched teeth.

For this Shock had no reply.

" I shall go for Mrs. Carroll and the children now," he said quietly, and passed out of the room.

" Carroll," said the doctor with stern deliberation, " I have always known you to be a bully, but never before that you were a brute. This man saved your child's life at very considerable danger to his own. And a second time—if the child recovers he has saved his life, for had the operation not been performed to-day your child would have died, and you would have been arrested for manslaughter."

" Doctor," said Carroll, turning upon him, and standing nervous and shaking, " it is that man or me. The country won't hold us both."

" Then, Carroll, let me tell you, you had better move out, for that man won't move till he wants to. Why, bless my soul, man, he could grind you up in his hands. And as for nerve—well, I have seen some in my professional career, but never such as his. My advice to you is, do not trifle with him."

" Blank his sowl! I'll be even wid him," said Carroll, pouring out a stream of oaths.

" Dad." The weak voice seemed to pierce through Carroll's curses like a shaft of light through a dark room.

Carroll dropped on his knees by the bedside in a rush of tears.

" Ah, Patsy, my Patsy! Is it your own voice I'm hearin'? "

" Dad, darlin', ye didn't mane it, did ye, dad? "

" What, Patsy? "

" To hit me."

" Ah, may God forgive me! but it's meself would sooner die than strike ye."

The little lad drew a deep breath of content.

" And the big man," he said. " He put out his hand over me. Ye didn't hurt him, dad, did ye? "

" No, no, Patsy, darlin'," said the big Irishman, burying his face in the pillow. " Speak to your dad again wid your lovely voice."

" Now, Carroll," said the doctor in a stern whisper. " That is enough. Not a word more. Do you want to kill your child? "

Carroll at once with a tremendous effort grew still, stroking the white hand he held in his, and kissing the golden curls that streamed across the pillow, whispering over and over, " Patsy, darlin'! " till the doctor, hardened as he was to scenes like this, was forced to steal out from the room and leave them together.

## XIV.

## THE OLD PROSPECTOR'S AWAKING

FOR six weeks the Old Prospector lay fretting his life away in his shack, not so ill as to be in danger. The pneumonia had almost disappeared and the rheumatism had subsided, but yet such grave symptoms remained as made the doctor forbid his setting forth upon his annual quest of the Lost River. In these days his chief comfort was Shock, whose old habit of sharing his experiences in imagination with those who could not share them in reality, relieved for the Old Prospector many a monotonous hour.

But Shock's days, and most of his nights, even, were spent upon the trail rounding up "strays and mavericks," as Ike said, searching out the lonely bachelor shacks, and lonelier homes where women dwelt whose husbands' days were spent on the range, and whose nearest neighbour might be eight or ten miles away, bringing a touch of the outer world, and leaving a gleam of the light that he carried in his own sunny, honest face.

And so Shock soon came to know more of the far back settlers than did even the oldest timer; and, what was better, he began to establish among them some sort of social life. It was Shock, for instance, that discovered old Mrs. Hamilton and her two sons, and drove her after much persuasion eight miles over " The Rise," past which she had not set her foot for the nine long, sad years that had dragged out their lonely length since her husband left her alone with her two boys of seven and nine, to visit Mrs. Macnamara, the delicate wife of the rollicking Irish rancher, who, seldom out of the saddle himself, had never been able to understand the heart-hunger that only became less as her own life ran low. It was her little family growing up about her, at once draining her vitality but, thank God, nourishing in her heart hope and courage, that preserved for her faith and reason. It was a great day for the Macnamaras when their big friend drove over their next neighbour, Mrs. Hamilton, to make her first call.

Another result of Shock's work became apparent in the gradual development of Loon Lake, or " The Lake," as it was most frequently named, into a centre of social life. In the first place a school had been established, in which Marion had been installed as teacher, and once the children came to the village it was easier for the parents to find their way thither.

Every week, too, The Kid and Ike found occasion to visit The Lake and call for Shock, who made his home, for the most part, with the Old Prospector. Every week, too, the doctor would appear to pay a visit to his patients; but, indeed, in some way or other the doctor was being constantly employed on cases discovered by Shock. The Macnamara's baby with the club-foot, Scrub Kettle's girl with the spinal trouble; Lawrence Delamere, the handsome young English lad up in "The Pass," whose leg, injured in a mine accident, never would heal till the doctor had scraped the bone—these and many others owed their soundness to Shock's prospecting powers and to the doctor's skill. And so many a mile they drove together to their mutual good. For, while the doctor prosecuted with delight and diligence his healing art, all unconsciously he himself was regaining something of his freedom and manhood.

"Digs 'em up, don't he?" said Ike one Sunday, when the second flat of Jim Ross's store was filled with men and women who, though they had lived in the country for from two to twenty years, were still for the most part strangers to each other. "Digs 'em up like the boys dig the badgers. Got to come out of their holes when he gits after 'em."

"Dat's so," said Perault, who had become an ardent follower of Shock's. "Dat's so. All same lak ole boss."

"Prospector, eh?" said Ike.

"Oui. Prospector, sure enough, by gar!" replied Perault, with the emphasis of a man who has stumbled upon a great find; and the name came at once to be recognised as so eminently suitable that from that time forth it stuck, and all the more that before many weeks there was none to dispute the title with him.

All this time the Old Prospector fretted and wasted with an inward fever that baffled the doctor's skill,

and but for the visits of his friends and their constant assurances that next week would see him fit, the
old man would have succumbed.

"It's my opinion," said Ike, who with The Kid had
made a habit of dropping in for a visit to the sick
man, and then would dispose themselves outside for a
smoke, listening the while to the flow of song and
story wherewith his daughter would beguile the old
man from his weariness; "it's my opinion that it
aint either that rheumatism nor that there pewmonia,"—Ike had once glanced at the doctor's label
which distinguished the pneumonia medicine from
that prescribed for rheumatism,—"it aint either the
rheumatism nor that there pewmonia," he repeated,
"that's a-killin' him."

"What then do you think it is, Ike?" said
the doctor, to whom Ike had been confiding this
opinion.

"It's frettin'; frettin' after the trail and the
Lost River. For thirteen years he's chased that river,
and he'll die a-chasin' it."

"Well, he'll certainly die if he starts after it in
his present condition."

"Maybe so, doctor. I wouldn't interdict any opinion of yours. But I reckon he'd die a mighty sight
easier."

"Well, Ike, my boy," said the doctor in his gentle
voice, "perhaps you are right, perhaps you're right.
The suggestion is worth considering."

And the result seemed to justify Ike's opinion, for
from the day that the doctor fixed the time for the

Old Prospector's departure the fever abated, his philosophic calm returned, he became daily stronger and daily more cheerful and courageous, and though he was troubled still with a cough he departed one bright day, with Perault, in high spirits.

"I shall remember you all," he cried, waving his hand gaily in farewell. "Doctor, I shall build you a hospital where your skill will have opportunity and scope. Mr. Macgregor, your heart will be delighted with that church-manse-school building of yours." This was Shock's pet scheme for the present. "To all of you suitable rewards. This time I see success. Farewell."

After he had turned away he reined back his pony and addressed Shock again.

"Mr. Macgregor," he said, with almost solemn earnestness, "I give my daughter into your charge. I am sure you will watch over her. She will be comfortable with Josie, and she will be safe under your care."

His spirit of enthusiastic confidence caught all the crowd standing by, so that they gave him a hearty cheer in farewell.

"Did not say what he would give us, eh, Carroll?" said Crawley, who with Carroll stood at the back of the crowd.

"Blanked old fool!" growled Carroll.

"And yet he has a marvellous instinct for mines," said Crawley, "and this time he has got something more than usual in his head, I believe. He has been particularly secretive. I could not get anything out

of him. Guess he means to euchre us out of our share
of anything big, partner."

"Curse him for an owld thief!" said Carroll. "I'll
have it out av his hide, so I will, if he tries that."

"Then, Carroll, you'll have to do it when his big
friend is not round."

Carroll's answer was a perfect flood of profanity,
copious enough to include not only the Old Prospector, Shock, all the relatives living and dead, but
Crawley, who stood listening with a sarcastic grin on
his evil face.

"Well, well," at last said Crawley soothingly,
"your time will come. And, partner, you may depend on me when it comes. I owe him something, too,
and I would rather pay it than get a mine."

The days that followed the Old Prospector's departure were lonely enough for his daughter. Her
father's illness had brought to them both the ines-
timable boon of mutual acquaintance and affection.
It was the girl's first experience of having near her
one to whom she could freely give the long-hoarded
treasures of her love; and now that he was gone she
could only wonder how she could have lived so long
without him. It was well for her that she had her
school, which she transferred now to her father's
house, for though Shock occupied the inner room he
was very little at home.

In addition to the school there was Patsy, who,
never very strong, had not regained even his puny
strength since the operation. Every fine day Marion
would take the little lad for a glorious canter up the

trail that ran along The Lake, but the day was never complete to Patsy unless it included a visit to the Jumping Rock, and there a tale, and at least one song. In these rides Stanton, as often as he visited the village, would join, and then it was the Swallow that the little cripple would ride, holding his reins in cowboy style high in one hand, and swaying with careless security in the saddle, and all the more because of the strong arm about him.

These were happy days to Patsy, happy to young Stanton, happier than she knew to Marion, and all the happier by contrast to the dark, sad days that followed.

About three weeks after the Old Prospector's departure a half-breed, on a cayuse wet and leg-weary, appeared at the Loon Lake Stopping Place, asking for the preacher.

"Blanked if I know!" growled Carroll. "Off on some fool hunt or other."

"Ask Ike there," said Crawley, who was sitting on the stoop. "You belong to his flock, don't you, Ike? Elder, aint you?"

"His flock?" echoed Ike. "Wouldn't mind if I did. I'd be sure of my company, which I can't always be almost anywhere else. Wantin' the preacher, eh?" turning to the half-breed.

"Letter from de old man."

"What old man? Let me see it," said Crawley quickly. "Ah! 'Rev. Mr. Macgregor, or one of his friends.' Guess this is from the Old Prospector, eh?"

The half-breed nodded.

"Where is he?"

"Way up in mountain," he said, waving his hand toward the hills.

"Well, the preacher isn't here. It must be important," continued Crawley. "I suppose I might as well open it, especially as it is likely it will be something about outfit. Eh, Carroll?"

He was about to tear the letter open when Ike interposed.

"Hold up, there. It strikes me you're a little rapid in your conclusions. Let's have a look at the letter."

Crawley very unwillingly gave it up.

"One of his friends," read Ike, with some difficulty, "You count yourself in there, do you?" to Crawley. "You'd be mighty lucky if he agreed with you on that there point. Now I judge this ought to go to the preacher or, if he aint round, to the young lady."

So saying, Ike, without another glance at the disappointed Crawley, strode away with the letter to find Marion.

He found her busy in the school. She read the letter, looked at Ike with white face and wide-open eyes, read it a second time, and said, "He wants Mr. Macgregor, quick—and me. He is ill. Oh, Ike!" she cried suddenly, "he is ill, and Mr. Macgregor is away."

"Where did he go?" said Ike shortly.

"I heard him say to Willow Creek, to the Martins. The doctor is with him."

"The Martins, eh? Why, that's only eight miles,

I reckon. Well, git yourself ready and your horse. I'll be back in an hour and a half."

He turned away, but after he had gone a few steps he strode back.

"No use lookin' like that," he said almost gruffly. "We'll git a wagon and bring him home easy. A wagon's easier than ridin', though 'taint likely he's very bad."

"Bad!" exclaimed Marion, with a sob. "Oh, Ike, you don't know my father. If he were not bad he would not——" Here her voice failed her.

"Don't you worry, miss. We'll be on the trail in two hours. And look here, we'll want beddin' and lots of things, so hustle." And Ike set off with long strides. "Hustle's the word for her. Got to keep her busy, poor girl!" he said to himself. "Guess he's a goner. You bet that old chap don't weaken for no belly-ache. He's right bad."

The only wagon in the place belonged to Carroll.

"Want your wagon and outfit, Carroll," said Ike briefly. "Old Prospector's pretty bad. Got to get him home."

Carroll growled a refusal. He had never recovered his wonted good nature since his encounter with Shock, and his resentment against the one man seemed to poison his whole nature against all.

"What!" said Ike, amazed at Carroll's refusal. In that country men in need of anything helped themselves without reference to the owner.

"Why, sure, Carroll," interposed Crawley hastily. "You'll let Ike have that wagon. I tell you what,

I'll drive it for him.` (Shut up, Carroll!" he said in an aside. " When do you start, Ike? Two hours? I'll be there."

In an hour and a half, true to his word, Ike was back with Shock and the doctor. Before another half hour had gone past they were all on the trail, Marion riding her pony, Shock and the doctor in the buckboard, and Crawley driving the wagon, in which, besides mattress and bedding, were saddles for use when the trail should forbid wheels.

After long hesitation Ike decided that he ought not to join the party.

" That there Crawley," he argued to himself, " aint to be trusted, especially when he's goin' round lookin' like a blank hyena. But I guess I'll have to let him go and git back to the ranch." And so with an uneasy feeling Ike watched them set off.

Half-way back to the ranch he met his boss.

" Hello, Ike," saluted The Kid gaily. " You're needing a powder. Off your feed, eh? "

" Howdy, boss," replied the cowboy gravely. " I'm feelin' proper enough, but there's others not so frisky."

" What's up, Ike? Your grandmother poorly? "

" Well, do you know," said Ike, watching The Kid keenly with his half shut eyes, " there's been a great mix-up at The Lake there. A breed, half dead with the saddle, came from the Old Prospector askin' for the preacher. Guess the old chap's about quittin' the trail."

The Kid's hand tightened on the reins.

"Hit him there, I reckon," grunted Ike to himself, but the other paid no attention. "So," continued Ike, "they've all gone off."

"Who?"

"Why the hull town, seemingly. There's the preacher, and the doctor, and that there Crawley with Carroll's wagon outfit. They looked a little like a circus, except that there wan't any wild animals. Unless you'd count Crawley for a monkey, which would be rather hard on the monkey, I guess." Ike chuckled, a rare chuckle that seemed to begin a long way below his diaphragm and work slowly up to his lips.

"What the deuce are you talking about?" enquired The Kid. "What has Crawley got to do with this?"

"Why," said Ike in a surprised tone, "dunno, onless he's a friend of the old man's. They do have a lot of business together seemingly. Or perhaps as company for the gel."

"The girl! Steady there, Swallow," to his mare, for Swallow had given a sudden spring. "What girl?" demanded The Kid. "Why don't you talk sense? You didn't say anything about a girl."

"Why, didn't I mention about that gel? Well, I'm gettin' forgetful. Why, what gel do you think? They aint growin' on rose bushes or old willows round here, so far as I've seen. Now, how many gels have you observed in your pilgrimages round that town?"

"Oh, blank you for an idiot!" said The Kid wrathfully. "Do you mean that the—Miss Mowbray has gone off with the rest?" In spite of his splendid self-control, as The Kid spoke the name a red flush on his face could be suddenly seen through the brown tan.

Ike nodded gravely.

"Yes, she's gone. But she'll be all right. The preacher's there. He'll be busy with the old man, of course, but he'll find some time for her. And then there's the other chap, you know. He's been mighty kind to-day, mighty kind, and considerable, too. Can't say as I'd just cotton to him, but when he likes he's ingraciousin' ways, mighty ingraciousin' ways."

"Oh!" roared The Kid. "Crawley——" Then he looked at his cowboy's face. "Confound you, Ike! So you were pulling my leg a little, were you? Never mind, my day will come."

With this he turned the Swallow toward the Lake and set off.

"Good-bye," called out Ike. "Where you going?"

"Oh, I say," cried The Kid, wheeling the Swallow. "What trail did they take?"

"You mean Crawley?" inquired Ike.

With a curse The Kid bore down upon him.

"Which way did they go?" he demanded.

"Okanagan trail," said Ike, with a slow grin. "So long."

"Good-bye, Ike. You'll see me when I come back." And The Kid waved his hand, and gave the Swallow her head.

Ike looked after him, and allowed himself the very unusual indulgence of a hearty laugh.

"Well," he said, "I tried to help Crawley a little, but somehow it didn't seem to go right."

A tail chase is a long chase, and so The Kid found it, for the speed and endurance of the Swallow were both fully tested before the advance party were overtaken.

As he came in sight of them he pulled himself up with the question, "What am I doing here? What is my business with that party?" For a mile or so he rode slowly, keeping out of their sight, trying to find such answer to this question as would satisfy not so much himself but those before him, to whom, somehow, he felt an answer was due. The difficulty of explaining his presence became sensibly greater as he pictured himself attempting to make it clear to Crawley.

"It is none of his business, anyway," at length he said impatiently. "She doesn't want him around. How did he know?"

Crawley was a man of some parts. He had money and ability. He was a scholar, and could talk well about rocks and plants. The Kid had heard him discourse to the Old Prospector and Marion many a day on these subjects, and intelligently, too.

"Well," he said at length, "I may be of some use, anyway. Surely a fellow has a right to offer his services to his friends in trouble."

With this explanation on his lips he sailed down upon the company. Marion and the half-breed were riding far in front, Crawley following as closely as he could with the wagon. Some distance in the rear were Shock and the doctor in the buckboard. The Kid could hear Crawley pointing out to Marion in a loud voice the striking features of the beauty that lay around them in such a wealth and variety of profusion. The words of Ike came to his mind, "mighty ingraciousin'."

"Confound his impudence!" he growled. "I wonder if she knows the kind of snake he is? I believe I'll tell her, for her own sake. No, that won't do, either. Well, I guess I must wait my chance." But the chance seemed slow in coming.

"Thought I would ride after you and offer—see if you—if I could be of service."

"And we are very glad to have you," said Shock heartily.

"Yes, we found you useful on occasion before, and doubtless shall again," said the doctor, in a tone of pleasant sufferance.

The Kid reined up behind the buckboard, waiting for an excuse to ride forward, but for miles finding none.

"I wonder now," said Shock at length, "if we had not better stop and have tea, and then ride till dark before we camp. If Marion is not tired that would be the better way."

"I'll ride up and ask," said The Kid eagerly, and before any other suggestion could be made he was gone.

The proposition found acceptance with Marion,

and, what was of more importance, with the half-breed guide.

If The Kid had any doubt of his reception by the girl the glad, grateful look in her eyes as he drew near was enough to assure him of her welcome; and as he took the guide's place by her side she hastened to say, "I am glad you came, Mr. Stanton. It was very kind of you to come. It was awful riding alone mile after mile."

"Alone!" echoed The Kid.

"Well, I mean—you know he cannot talk much English and——"

"Of course," promptly replied The Kid, "I am awfully glad I came, now. Wasn't sure just how you might take it. I mean, I did not like pushing myself in, you understand."

"Oh, surely one does not need to explain a kindness such as this," said the girl simply. "You see, the doctor and Mr. Macgregor are together, and will be, and the others—well, I hardly know them."

The trail wound in and out, with short curves and sharp ascents, among the hills, whose round tops were roughened with the rocks that jutted through the turf, and were decked with clumps of poplar and spruce and pine. The world seemed full of brightness to the boy. His heart overflowed with kindness to all mankind. He found it possible, indeed, to think of Crawley, even, with a benignant compassion.

Far up in the Pass they camped, in a little sheltered dell all thick with jack pines, through whose wide-spreading roots ran and chattered a little mountain brook. But for the anxiety that lay like lead upon her heart, how delightful to Marion would have been this, her first, experience of a night out of doors. And when after tea Shock, sitting close by the fire, read that evening Psalm breathing a trust and peace that no circumstances of ill could break, the spicy air and the deep blue sky overhead, sown with stars that rained down their gentle beams through the silent night, made for Marion a holy place where God seemed near, and where it was good to lie down and rest. "I will both lay me down in peace and sleep, for thou, Lord, only makest me dwell in safety."

And that sense of security, of being under tender, loving care, did not forsake her all through the long watches of the night, and through the weary miles of the next day's travel that brought them at length to the Old Prospector's camp.

As they neared the camp the trail emerged out of thick bushes into a wide valley, where great pines stood, with wide spaces between, and clear of all underbrush. The whole valley was carpeted thick with pine needles, and gleamed like gold in the yellow light of the evening sun. The lower boughs under which they rode were dead, and hung with long streamers of grey moss that gave the trees the appearance of hoary age.

As they entered the valley instinctively they lowered their voices and spoke in reverent tones, as if they had been ushered into an assemblage of ancient and silent sages. On every side the stately pines led away in long vistas that suggested the aisles of some noble cathedral. There was no sign of life anywhere, no motion of leaf or bough, no sound to break the solemn stillness. The clatter of a hoof over a stone broke on the ear with startling discordance. The wide reaches of yellow carpet of pine needles, golden and with black bars of shadow, the long drawn aisles of tall pines, bearing aloft like stately pillars the high, arched roof of green, the lower limbs sticking out from the trunks bony and bare but for the pendant streamers of grey moss, all bathed in the diffused radiance of the yellow afternoon light, suggested some weird and mighty fane of a people long dead, whose spirits, haunting these solemn spaces, still kept over their temple a silent and awful watch.

Out on the trail they met Perault in a frenzy of anxious excitement.

"Tank de Bon Dieu!" he cried brokenly, with hands uplifted. "Come wit' me, queek! queek!"

"Perault, tell us how your boss is." The doctor's voice was quiet and authoritative. "And tell us how long he has been ill, and how it came on. Be very particular. Take plenty of time."

Perault's Gallic temperament responded to the doctor's quiet tone and manner.

"Oui. Bon," he said, settling down. "Listen to me. We come nice and slow to dis place, an' den we go up dat gulch for little prospect. Good ting, too. Good mine dere, sure. But old boss he can't stay. He must go, go, go. Den we go up 'noder gulch, t'ree, four day more, for 'noder mine. Pretty good,

too. Den one night we comin' back to camp, old
boss feel good. Skeep along lak small sheep. By
gar, he's feel too good! He's fall in crik. Dat's
noting. No! Good fire, plenty blanket make dat
all right. But dat night I hear de ole boss groan,
and cry, and turn overe and overe. Light de fire;
give him one big drink wheesky. No good. He's
go bad all dat night. Nex' day he's het noting.
Nex' day he's worser and worser. Wat I can do I
can't tell. Den de Bon Dieu he send along dat half-
breed. De ole boss he write letter, an' you come here
queek."

"Thank you, Perault. A very lucid explanation,
indeed. Now, we shall see the patient; and you,
Miss Marion, had better remain here by the fire for
a few moments."

The doctor passed with Shock into the Old Prospector's tent.

"Mr. Macgregor," cried the old man, stretching
out both hands eagerly to him, "I'm glad you have
come. I feared you would not be in time. But
now," sinking back upon his balsam bed, "now all
will be—well."

"Mr. Mowbray," said Shock, " I have brought
the doctor with me. Let him examine you now, and
then we shall soon have you on your feet again."

The old gentleman smiled up into Shock's face, a
smile quiet and content.

"No," he said between short breaths, "I have
taken the long trail. My quest is over. It is not
for me."

"Let the doctor have a look at you," entreated Shock.

"Most certainly," said the Old Prospector, in his wonted calm voice. "Let the doctor examine me. I am not a man to throw away any hope, however slight."

As the doctor proceeded with his examination his face grew more and more grave. At length he said, "It is idle for me to try to conceal the truth from you, Mr. Mowbray. You are a very sick man. The inflammation has become general over both lobes of the lung. The walls of the vessels and the surrounding tissues have lost their vitality; the vessels are extremely dilated, while exudation and infiltration have proceeded to an alarming extent. The process of engorgement is complete."

"Do you consider his condition dangerous, doctor?" said Shock, breaking in upon the doctor's technical description.

"In a young person the danger would not be so great, but, Mr. Mowbray, I always tell the truth to my patients. In a man of your age I think the hope of recovery is very slight indeed."

"Thank you, doctor," said the old man cheerfully. "I knew it long ago, but I am content that my quest should cease at this point. And now, if you will give me a few moments of close attention," he said, turning to Shock, "and if you will see that the privacy of this tent is absolutely secure, there is little more that I shall require of you."

The doctor stepped to the door.

"Doctor," said the Old Prospector, "I do not wish you to go. It is more than I hoped, that there should be beside me when I passed out of this life two men that I can trust, such as yourself and Mr. Macgregor. Sit down close beside me and listen."

He pulled out from beneath his pillow an oil-skin parcel, which he opened, discovering a small bag of buckskin tied with a thong.

"Open it," he said to Shock. "Take out the paper." His voice became low and eager, and his manner bespoke intense excitement.

"My dear friend," said the doctor, "this will be too much for you. You must be calm."

"Give me something to drink, doctor, something to steady me a bit, for I must convey to you the secret of my life's quest."

The doctor administered a stimulant, and then, with less excitement, but with no less eagerness, the old man proceeded with his story.

"Here," he said, pointing with a trembling finger to a line upon the paper Shock had spread before him, "here is the trail that leads to the Lost River. At this point we are now camped. Follow the course of this stream to this point, half a day's journey, not more; turn toward the east and cross over this low mountain ridge and you come to a valley that will strike you as one of peculiar formation. It has no apparent outlet. That valley," said the Old Prospector, lowering his voice to a whisper, "is the valley of the Lost River. This end," keeping his trembling finger at a certain point on the paper, "has been blocked up by a mountain slide. The other turns very abruptly, still to the east. Three mountain peaks, kept in perfect line, will lead you across this blockade to the source of the Lost River."

"Mr. Mowbray," said Shock, "Perault tells us you only made short excursions from this point where we are now."

"Listen," said the old man. "I made this discovery last year. I have breathed it to no one. My claim is yet unstaked, but here," said he, taking another small buckskin bag from his breast, "here is what I found."

He tried in vain with his trembling fingers to undo the knot. Shock took the bag from him and opened it up.

"Empty it out," said the old man, his eyes glittering with fever and excitement.

Shock poured forth gold dust and nuggets.

"There," he sighed. "I found these at that spot. Empty the other bag," he said to Shock. "These are the ones given me by the Indian so many years ago. The same gold, the same rock, the same nuggets. There is my Lost River. I thought to stake my claim this summer. I ought to have staked it last year, but a terrible storm drove me out of the mountains and I could not complete my work."

The old man ceased his tale, and lay back upon his couch with closed eyes, and breathing quickly. The doctor and Shock stood looking at each other in amazement and perplexity.

"Is he quite himself?" said Shock, in a low voice.

The old man caught the question and opened his eyes.

"Doctor, I am quite sane. You know I am quite sane. I am excited, I confess, but I am quite sane. For thirteen years and more I have sought for those little pieces of metal and rock, but, thank God! I have found them, not for myself, but for my girl. I ruined her life—I now redeem. And now, Mr. Macgregor, will you undertake a charge for me? Will you swear to be true, to faithfully carry out the request I am to make?"

Shock hesitated.

"Do not disappoint me," said the old man, taking hold of Shock's hand eagerly with his two hands so thin and worn and trembling. "Promise me," he said.

"I promise," said Shock solemnly.

"I want you to follow this trail, to stake out this claim, to register it in your name for my daughter, and to develop or dispose of this mine in the way that may seem best to yourself. I trust you entirely. I have watched you carefully through these months, and have regained my faith in my fellow men and my faith in God through knowing you. I will die in peace because I know you will prove true, and," after a pause, "because I know God will receive a sinful, broken man like me. You promise me this, Mr. Macgregor?" The old man in his eagerness raised himself upon his elbow and stretched out his hand to Shock.

"Once more," said Shock, in a broken voice, "I

promise you, Mr. Mowbray. I will do my best to carry out what you desire, and so may God help me!"

The old man sank quietly back on his couch. A smile spread over his face as he lay with closed eyes, and he breathed, " Thank God! I can trust you as if you were my son."

"Hark!" he said a moment afterwards in an anxious whisper. " There is someone near the tent."

The doctor hurried out, and found Crawley in the neighbourhood of the tent gathering some sticks for the fire. He hastened back.

"It is only Mr. Crawley," he said, " getting some wood for the fire."

A spasm of fear distorted the old man's face.

"Crawley!" he whispered, "I fear him. Don't let him see—or know. Now take these things—away. I have done with them—I have done with them! You will give my love—to my daughter," he said to Shock after some moments of silence.

" She is here," said Shock quietly.

"Here! Now! I feared to ask. God is good. Yes, God is good."

The doctor stepped out of the tent. The old man lay with eager eyes watching the door.

Swiftly, but with a step composed and steady, his daughter came to him.

"Father, I am here," she said, dropping on her knees beside him.

"My daughter!" he cried with a sob, while his arms held her in a close embrace. "My daughter! my daughter! God is good to us."

For a long time they remained silent with their arms about each other. Shock moved to the door. The girl was the first to master her emotions.

"Father," she said quietly, "the doctor tells me you are very ill."

"Yes, my daughter, very ill, but soon I shall be better. Soon quite well."

The girl lifted up her face quickly.

"Oh, father!" she cried joyfully, "do you think——" The look on her father's face checked her joy. She could not mistake its meaning. She threw herself with passionate sobs on the ground beside him.

"Yes, my daughter," went on the old man in a clear, steady voice, "soon I shall be well. My life has been for years a fevered dream, but the dream is past. I am about to awake. Dear child, I have spoiled your life. We have only a few precious hours left. Help me not to spoil these for you."

At once the girl sat up, wiped her eyes, and grew still.

"Yes, father, we will not lose them."

She put her hand in his.

"You make me strong, my daughter. I have much to say to you, much to say to you of my past."

She put her fingers on his lips gently.

"Is that best, father, do you think?" she said. looking lovingly into his face.

He glanced at her in quick surprise. She was a girl no longer, but a woman, wise and strong and brave.

"Perhaps you are right, my daughter. But you will remember that it was for you I lived my lonely life, for you I pursued my fevered quest. You were all I had left in the world after I had laid your mother in her grave. I feared to bring you to me. Now I know I need not have feared. Now I know what I have missed, my daughter."

"We have found each other, dear, dear father," the girl said, and while her voice broke for a moment in a sob her face was bright with smiles.

"Yes, my daughter, we have found each other at length. The doors of my heart, long closed, had grown rusty, but now they are wide open, and gladly I welcome you."

There was silence for some minutes, then the old man went on, painfully, with ever shortening breath. "Now, listen to me carefully." And then he told her the tale of his search for the Lost River, ending with the eager exclamation: "And last year I found it. It is a mine rich beyond my fondest hopes, and it is yours. It is yours, my daughter."

"Oh, father," cried the girl, losing herself for a moment, "I don't want the mine. It is you I want."

"Yes, my daughter, I know that well, but for the present it is not the will of God that I should be with you, and I have learned that it is good to trust to Him, and without fear I give you, my daughter, to His care."

Again the girl grew steady and calm.

"Call Mr. Macgregor and the doctor, my dear," her father said. "These gentlemen alone," he con-

tinued when they had come to him, "hold my secret.
Even Perault does not know all. He knows the valley which we explored last year, but he does not know
it is the Lost River. Mr. Macgregor has promised
to see the claim staked. Perault will guide him to
it. This paper," taking a packet from his breast,
" is my will. In it a full disposal is made of all.
Now I will sign it."

The paper was duly signed and witnessed. With
a sigh of content the old man sank back upon his
bed.

" Now all is done. I am well content."

For some time he lay with closed eyes. Then,
waking suddenly, he looked at Shock and said:
" Carry me out, Mr. Macgregor. Carry me out
where I can see the trees and the stars. Through
long years they have been my best friends. There,
too, I would lie in my long sleep."

They made a bed of boughs and skins for him before the camp-fire, and out into the dry, warm night
Shock carried him. In the wide valley there still
lingered the soft light of the dying day, but the
shadows were everywhere lying deeper. Night was
rapidly drawing up her curtains upon the world.
The great trees stood in the dim light silent, solemn,
and shadowy, keeping kindly watch over the valley
and all things therein. Over the eastern hill the
full moon was just beginning to rise. The mingled
lights of silver and gold falling through the trees
lent a rare, unearthly loveliness to the whole scene.

The Old Prospector, reclining on his couch, let

his eyes wander over the valley and up through the trees to the sky and the stars, while a smile of full content rested on his face.

"It is a lovely night, dear father," said his daughter, quick to interpret his thought.

"Yes, my daughter, a rare night. Often have I seen such nights in this very spot, but never till to-night did their full joy enter my heart. My life was one long, terrible unreality. To-night the world is new, and full of loveliness and all peace."

Then he lay in long silence. The doctor came near, touched his wrist, listened to the beating of his heart, and whispered to his daughter, "It will not be long now."

The old man opened his eyes. "You are near, my daughter," he said.

"Yes, father, dear, I am here," she replied, pressing his hand between hers.

"Could you sing something, do you think?"

The girl drew in her breath sharply as with a sob of pain.

"No," said her father. "Never mind, my daughter. It is too much to ask."

"Yes, yes, father, I will sing. What shall I sing?"

"Sing Bernard's great hymn, 'The world is very evil.'"

It was a hymn she had often sung for him, selecting such of its verses as were more familiar, and as expressed more nearly the thought in their hearts.

As she began to sing the doctor passed out beyond

the firelight to the side of the tent. There he found
Stanton, with his head bowed low between his knees.

"My boy," said the doctor, "that is very beautiful, but it is very hard to bear."

"Yes," said Stanton. "I'm a baby. I would like
to help her, but I cannot."

"Well, my boy, she needs no help that either you
or I can give."

Perault, the half-breed, and Crawley sat in silence
at the other side of the fire. Shock remained near
the girl, wondering at her marvellous self-control.

Verse after verse she sang in a voice low, but clear
and sweet. As the refrain occurred again and
again,

> "O sweet and blessed country, the home of God's elect,
> O sweet and blessed country that eager hearts expect,
> Jesus, in mercy bring us to that dear land of rest,"

the only change was that the song rose a little clearer
and fuller and with deeper tone.

After she had finished the camp lay in perfect
silence.

"Are you asleep, father, dear?" his daughter said
at length, but there was no reply. She touched his
hands and his face.

"Father!" she cried in a voice of awe and fear,
but still there was no reply.

The doctor came hastily into the light, looked into
the old man's face, and said: "He is gone."

With a long, low, wailing cry the girl laid herself
upon the ground by her father's side and put her

arms around him. They all gathered about the couch, with the doctor and Shock standing nearest.

"Poor child!" said the doctor softly. "This is a sad night for her."

"Yes," said Shock, in a voice quiet and steady. "For her the night is sad, but for him the day has dawned and there shall be night no more."

There, in that wide valley where the yellow pine needles lie deep and where morning and evening the mingling lights fall softly through the over-arching boughs, they laid the Old Prospector to rest under the pines and the stars that had been his companions for so long.

# XV

## EJECTED AND REJECTED

IN the main room of the Old Prospector's house some ten or twelve stern-faced men had gathered. The easy, careless manner that was characteristic of the ranchers and cowboys of the district had given place to an air of stern and serious determination. It was evident that they had gathered for some purpose of more than ordinary moment. By common consent Sinclair, a shrewd and fair-minded Scotch rancher who possessed the complete confidence of every man in the company, both for his integrity and his intelligence, was in the chair.

" Where is Mr. Macgregor? " he enquired.

" Gone to the Fort," answered The Kid. " He is on duty there to-morrow. He wished me to say, however, that he has no desire to push this matter, as far as he is personally concerned, but that if the committee thinks the public good demands his presence and his testimony he will appear on Monday."

" He ought to be here," said Sinclair, and his tone almost conveyed a reproof.

" He'll come if he's wanted, I guess," drawled out Ike, quick to take his friend's part.

" Well, then let us proceed. Let us get the facts

first," said Sinclair.   " Stanton, we would like to hear what you have to say."

" Well," said The Kid, " there is not much that I have to tell, but I shall begin at the beginning and give you all I know."   Stanton's air of boyish carelessness had quite disappeared, his voice took a deeper tone than usual, his manner was grave and stern. " It was six days ago that I happened to call at the Old Prospector's house."

" To see the preacher, I guess," interrupted Ike gravely, winking at Macnamara, who responded with a hearty " Ha! ha!  Of course!"

" Quit that, Ike," said Sinclair sternly.   " We have got business on hand."

"As I was saying," continued the Kid, with heightened colour, "I called at the Old Prospector's house and found Miss Mowbray in a state of great anxiety in regard to Mr. Macgregor.   She told me how the doctor had come to see Mr. Macgregor about a week before, in great excitement, and had informed him that Carroll and Crawley had set off for the mountains two days before, and how, upon hearing that, Mr. Macgregor and Perault had hastily followed, having with them about a week's provisions."

" What reason did Miss Mowbray assign for this?" enquired Sinclair.

" Well, I suppose it's no secret, now," said The Kid, with some hesitation. " The Old Prospector, you know, before his death had made a very rich find, but died without staking his claim.   The secret of its location he entrusted to Mr. Macgregor and the doctor.   The doctor, in a fit of drunkenness, gave the secret away to Carroll and Crawley, who, leaving him incapable from drink, set off at once to stake the claim."

"Hold on, Mr. Stanton," said Sinclair. "We must be careful. How do you know their purpose in setting off for the mountains?"

"Well, I think——"

"But," interrupted Sinclair, "we must have statements of fact only."

"Dat's so!" cried Perault excitedly. "Dem feller try to get de Ole Boss show dat mine, for sure. Crawley he's try to mak de Ole Boss tell. I hear heem, me. Dem feller want dat mine bad."

"All right, Perault," said Sinclair quietly. "That doesn't prove they went to stake that claim. Go on, Stanton."

"Well," continued The Kid, "I set off at once, and on my second day out I met these two men, Mr. Macgregor and Perault, exhausted with travelling and faint with hunger."

"Guess you'd better tell how you found them, Kid," said Ike, who had heard the story before.

"Well, gentlemen," continued The Kid, his voice shaking, "it was a pretty tough sight, I can tell you. I first saw them a long way down the trail. Mr. Macgregor was carrying Perault on his back and evidently walking with great difficulty. When I came up to them I found Perault was almost, if not quite, insensible, and Mr. Macgregor in the last stages of exhaustion." The Kid paused a few moments to steady his voice. Low, deep oaths were heard on

every side, while Perault, still weak and nervous from
his recent terrible experience, was sobbing audibly.

"I had plenty of grub," continued The Kid. "I
did my best for them and helped them home. That
is all I have to say."

A deep silence fell upon the group of men.

"Now, Perault," said Sinclair, "tell us your
story."

Perault tried to steady his voice, but, failing
utterly, broke into passionate weeping, Sinclair waiting in grave silence for him to recover. Macnamara,
the soft-hearted big Irish rancher, was quietly wiping
his eyes, while the other men were swearing terrible
oaths.

"Give him a drink," drawled Ike. "Too much
water aint good for no man."

Half a dozen flasks were immediately offered. Perault drank, and, after a few moments, began his tale.

"I can' spik much, me," he said, "when I tink how
dat beeg feller pack me on hees back twenty mile, I
fin' bad pain here," striking his breast, "and den I
can' spik at all." And again the little Frenchman's
voice broke down in sobs.

"Take time, Perault," said Sinclair gravely. "We
want to know all about it. Begin at the beginning and
tell it in your own way." The grave tone, even more
than the whisky he had drunk, steadied Perault, and
he began again.

"Dat's twelve or tirteen day, now. De Preachere,
dat Prospector, I call heem, he's jus' lak de Ole Boss,
for sure—de Prospector he's sen' dat ole fool doctor

for me queek. I come and fin' de Prospector he's ver' mad; mos' awful mad; never see heem lak dat before. 'Perault,' he say, ' get ponee and grub queek. We go for de Los' Reever.'

"By gar! He's mak me scare. I get ponee an' grub and get off queek, *toute suite*, right away. Well, we go two day hard and come to de camp where de Ole Boss he's die, den we climb over de montin. De Prospector he's got map and show me trail. Oui, I know him bon, fus rate. 'Perault,' he say, 'you min' las' year de Ole Boss he's fin' good mine way up in de valley?' 'Oui, for sure.' 'You know de trail?' 'Oui, certainment.' 'Den,' he say, 'we go dere.' Nex' day we strike dat trail and go four or five mile. We come to dat valley—Mon Dieu! dere's no valley dere. We come back and try once more—dat blank valley, she's no dere. De Prospector he look much on dat map. 'Where dose tree peak?' he say. 'Dere sure 'nuff, one, two tree. Dat valley she's right on line of dose peak.' 'Sure,' I say. 'I see heem myself she's gone now for sure! Ah! Voila! I see! Beeg slide feel dat valley up! By gar! Dat's so, dat montin she's half gone, dat valley he's full up. Mon Dieu! De Prospector he's lak wil' man. 'Perault,' he say, 'I promise de ole man I go for fin' dat mine.' 'All right, boss,' I say, 'me too.' We make cache for grub, we hobble de ponee and go for fin' dat mine. Dat's one blank hard day. Over rock and tree and hole and stomp he's go lak one deerhoun.' Next day he's jus' same. For me, I'm tire' out. Well, we come home to camp, slow, slow, hungree, sorefoot—by gar!

Sacre bleu! Dat cache she broke up, de grub he's gone! Mon Dieu! dat's bad—four or five day walk from home and no grub at all."

"What did you think, Perault?" asked Sinclair. "Did you see signs of any beast, bear or mountain lion?"

"Sure, dat's what I tink fus' ting, but de Prospector he's walk aroun' quiet and look everyting. 'Perault, dat's fonee ting,' he say. 'Where dose can' meat, eh?' By gar! dat's so, de bear he can' eat dose can' meat, not moche!"

"Not likely, not bein' a goat," put in Ike drily.

"Well, we look aroun' ver' close, no scratch, no track. By gar! dat's no bear, for sure—dat's one bear on two leg."

"I think," said Sinclair gravely, "that there is no doubt of that. The question is, who did it? Gentlemen, it has been proved that these two men, Carroll and Crawley, were away during the week when this crime took place. We do not know where they were, but we must be fair to them. We may have our opinions about this, but in fixing the responsibility of this crime we must be exceedingly careful to deal justly with every man. I suggest we call Carroll."

Carroll came to the meeting without hesitation, and with him, Crawley.

"We will take you in a few minutes," said Sinclair to Crawley.

"Now," he continued to Carroll, when Crawley had been removed, "we would like to know where you were last week."

" That's nobody's blank business," said Carroll.

An angry murmur arose from the crowd.

" Carroll, this thing is too serious for any bluffing, and we are going to see it through. It is fair that you should know why we ask. Let me give you the facts we have found out." Sinclair gave a brief *résumé* of the story as gathered from Stanton and Perault. As Carroll listened his face grew white with fury.

" Does any blank, blank son of a horse thief," he cried, when Sinclair had done, " say I am the man that broke open that cache? Let him stand up forninst me and say so." He gnashed his teeth in his rage. " Whin Tim Carroll goes to git even wid a man he doesn't go behind his back fur it, and yez all know that! No," he cried, planting his huge fist with a crash upon the table, " I didn't put a finger on the cache nor his ponies ayther, begob!"

" All right, Carroll, we are glad to hear it," said Sinclair, in a cold, stern voice. " You needn't get so wild over it. You cannot frighten us, you know. Every man here can give an account of his doings last week—can you? "

" I can that same," said Carroll, somewhat subdued by Sinclair's tone and manner. " I am not afraid to say that we went up to see a mine we heard of."

" You and Crawley, you mean? " said Sinclair quietly.

" Yes," continued Carroll, " and that's fair enough, too; and we hunted around a week fur it, an' came back."

"Did you find your mine?" asked Sinclair.

"We did not, and it's a blank, blank fool I was to listen to the yarn of the drunken old fool of a doctor."

"Thank you, Carroll. Now, I do not think myself that you touched that cache."

"If he did, he will swing for it," said a voice, cool and relentless, in the crowd.

Carroll started a little as he heard that voice.

"You shut up!" said Ike.

"Now, Carroll, we want you to answer a few questions," continued Sinclair. "Mr. Crawley brought you to the camp where the Old Prospector died—is that right?"

"He did."

"And then you went east from that point over the mountain?"

"We did, and I am telling you we was looking for that mine we heard of."

"All right," said Sinclair. "How long did you stay in that neighbourhood?"

"A week or so."

"Did you see Mr. Macgregor or Perault while you were there?"

"That's none of your business."

"You'd better answer, Carroll."

"It 'll be your business pretty blank soon!" drawled the voice again.

"Shut up!" said Ike. "Give him a chance."

"I think you'd better answer," said Sinclair quietly. "You've nothing to hide, I suppose?"

" I haven't," said Carroll defiantly. "We did see them two walking around, and we soon knew, too, that they didn't know any more than ourselves about that mine. Thin we came away."

" Did you see their camp?"

" We did. We passed it by."

" Did you stop and speak to them?"

" No, we did not; for the good reason they weren't there."

" Did you examine the camp or touch anything?"

" Nivir a touch, so help me God!" said Carroll, with great earnestness.

" Then did you and Crawley come away together?"

" We did."

" Where did you camp that night?"

" Over the mountain beyant, forninst the Old Prospector's grave."

" And you came straight home next day?"

" We did, except for a luk at a couple of prospects we knew of."

" Oh! How long did that take you?"

" It tuk me about a day, and Crawley a little less, I'm thinkin'."

" How was that, Carroll?" enquired Sinclair.

" Well, he tuk one gulch and I tuk the other, and he got through before me, and the next day we came home; and that's the truth of it, so help me."

" Then you were never separated from each other except for that one day?"

" That's true." There was no mistaking the sincerity and honesty of Carroll's manner.

" Any further questions to ask, gentlemen? "

" How long did you stop at Mr. Macgregor's camp when you was passing by? " asked Ike.

" Don't be so blanked smart, Ike! " said Carroll, in savage scorn. " I'm telling you that I didn't stop a fut. We saw their camp and their ponies and we went sthraight past."

" Didn't stop to light your pipe or nothing? " enquired Ike.

" Blank your blank ugly mug! " roared Carroll, " do you mean to say——"

" Oh, nothing," said Ike quietly. " Just wanted to know how long you stopped? "

" And I am tellin' you we didn't sthop atall, atall, not a fut of us! We didn't go near their camp within fifty yards."

" Not fifty yards, eh? Well, that's strange."

Carroll poured out a volley of oaths.

" You're sure about that fifty yards, Carroll? " asked Ike, in insinuating tones.

" I didn't pace it, you blanked fool! but I'll swear it wasn't more than thirty."

" You're dead sure about that thirty yards, Carroll? " persisted Ike.

" I am that, and if you want to say anything more come outside! " said Carroll, glaring wildly at his interlocutor.

" Oh, thanks, I'm comfortable," said Ike mildly, as he sat back in his chair. " Hope you are the same."

" That will do, Carroll," said Sinclair. " I am sure

we all feel much obliged to you for your straightfor-
ward answers. If we want you again we'll send for
you."

"And I'll come," said Carroll, with another oath,
passing out of the room.

"Now," said Sinclair, "we'll have Crawley."

In a few moments Crawley came in, smiling and
self-confident, with plenty of nerve, an abundance of
wit, and a most ingenuous manner. He met the chairman's questions with ready assurance and corrobo-
rated the story told by Carroll. He would frankly
acknowledge that he had heard about the Lost River.
Indeed, he had been more or less interested in it for
some years and, though he did not take much stock in
the doctor's word, still he declared that his own interests and the interests of Miss Mowbray, and indeed
of all concerned, demanded that the thing was worth
looking into. They visited the locality indicated by
the doctor; they spent a week in exploration, but
could find no trace of such a valuable mine as the
doctor had described; and they had come away not
very much disappointed; they had hardly expected
any other result. They had seen Mr. Macgregor's
camp, but they had not approached it; they passed
by at some distance, leaving everything undisturbed.

"You camped that night near the Old Prospector's
grave?" asked Sinclair.

"Yes."

"The next day you set off for home?"

"Exactly."

"You and Carroll were always together?"

"Certainly."

"You came home by the same trail and without any other explorations?"

Here Crawley hesitated a moment. "Well, yes, except that we ran up a gulch to look at some rocks."

"Oh! Did you find anything?"

"Well, we think so," said Crawley pleasantly.

"You went both together up the gulch? You were never separated?"

"We went together, yes."

"Any further questions, gentlemen?"

For a time there was no response, then Ike came slowly forward to the table and stood by Crawley's side.

"You did not go near that cache?"

"No," said Crawley firmly.

"Are you mighty sure about that? Better be sure."

"I am positive we did not go within twenty or thirty yards," said Crawley defiantly.

"All right, Crawley," drawled Ike, "better have a pipe now." And as he spoke he threw down a tobacco pouch on the table.

Crawley turned pale, gripped at the table to steady himself, gazed at the pouch lying before him for a few moments and then enquired in a voice that shook in spite of all that he could do: "Who gave you—where did you get that?"

"It's yours, aint it? Got your name on, any-way," said Ike. "Where did you leave it?"

"Don't know," said Crawley, turning green with terror.

"Gentlemen," said Ike, addressing the crowd, "I aint agoin' to make no speech to this jury, but I want to remark that this here blank reptile is a blank liar, and if he aint a murderer 'taint his fault. That there pouch of his," continued Ike, putting a long forefinger down upon the article lying on the table, "that there pouch of his was found by the 'Prospector,' as Perault calls him, beside that there empty cache. That's all I have to say." And Ike turned and walked slowly back to his seat.

In vain the trembling wretch tried first to bluster and then to explain. Carroll was again summoned and affirmed emphatically that he and Crawley had been separated for the greater part of one day, and that while together they had not approached Mr. Macgregor's camp.

"That will do, Carroll," said Sinclair quietly. "We believe you entirely, and I would like to say that for my part I am mighty glad that you are entirely freed from suspicion."

"That's so, you bet!" came from the men on all sides, as one by one they stepped forward to shake Carroll warmly by the hand.

"Now, gentlemen," said Sinclair, "make your decision. This man," pointing to Crawley, "is charged with a serious crime. What is your verdict?"

One by one the men threw into the hat on the table a bit of paper. In silence Sinclair and The Kid read and recorded the ballots. When they had finished

Sinclair stood up, looking sternly at Crawley, and said:

"Mr. Crawley, this Committee say unanimously that you are guilty. Have you anything to say before sentence is pronounced?"

The wretched creature fell on his knees with tears and cries entreating mercy.

"Take him away," said Sinclair sternly. "Now, gentlemen, what have you to say? What shall be done to this man whom you have decided to be guilty of murder?"

The discussion which followed was long and bitter. Sinclair and those who had come more recently to the country were for handing him over to the police.

"What's the good of that, Sinclair?" demanded Macnamara, one of the old-timers.

"Well, he'll get justice sure; he'll get sent up."

"Don't know about that," said Ike. "You see, you can't prove anything but stealin', and you can't prove that, for sure. They'll take him down to Regina, and they aint going to give him much down there for stealin' a little grub."

"Well, what do you propose?" said Sinclair.

"Well," said Ike, "hangin's too good for him. He ought to be hung, but 'taint the custom in this here country, I understand, and I surmise we'd better scare the daylights out of him and give him twelve hours to get out."

After some further discussion Ike's proposition was accepted. That night four masked men took Crawley out of the room where he had been kept a prisoner and led him out of the village and up the trail to the woods, and there, unheeding his prayers and cries and groans, they made solemn preparations for his execution. In the midst of their preparations Sinclair, with a number of others, came galloping up and demanded the prisoner's release, and after a long and bitter discussion it was finally agreed that Crawley should be given twelve hours to leave the country, which decision was joyfully and tearfully accepted by the terror-stricken wretch.

"Hello, old man, there's a letter for you in my rooms. Thought you'd be in to-day, so took care of it for you." Father Mike drew near Shock's buckboard and greeted him cordially. "By Jove! what's the matter with you? What have you been doing to yourself?" he exclaimed, looking keenly into Shock's face.

"I am rather seedy," said Shock. "Played out, indeed." And he gave Father Mike an account of his last week's experience.

"Great Caesar!" exclaimed Father Mike, "that was a close thing. Come right along and stretch yourself out of my couch. A cup of tea will do you good." Shock, gladly accepting the invitation, went with him.

"There's your letter," said Father Mike, as he set Shock in his deep armchair. "You read it while I make tea."

The letter was, as Father Mike had said, a fat one. It was from his Convener and ran thus:

"MY DEAR MR. MACGREGOR:

"The enclosed letter from the Superintendent will explain itself. You are instructed to withdraw forthwith your services from the Fort. I know you will be disappointed. This is the sort of thing that makes our work in the West depressing: not big blizzards nor small grants, but failure on the part of Eastern men to understand our needs and to appreciate the tremendous importance of these years to the West. Never mind, our day will come. I regret greatly that the Committee should have been influenced by the petition enclosed. Do not let this worry you. The Superintendent's P. S. is due to some misunderstanding. I have written him on this matter. We know some of your difficulties and we have every confidence in you," etc., etc.

From the Superintendent's letter the Convener had enclosed the following extracts:

"It has been decided to withdraw our services from the Fort. I had a stiff fight in the Committee, but failed; they were all against me. Dr. Macfarren especially so—had private information (from his brother, I suppose); presented a petition, which find enclosed; protested against the waste of funds, etc., etc. This precious petition, by the way, seemed to influence the Committee greatly. I need not tell you it failed to influence me, unless indeed as an evidence of the need of our services in that place. You and I have seen this sort of thing before in the West.

Young Lloyd of the Park Church, too, was eloquent in opposing—the old story, funds overlapping, denominational rivalry. These young men, who decline to face the frontier, would show better taste in seeking to learn something of the West than in hampering those who are giving their lives to this work. The upholstered seat of the Park Church pulpit does not induce the liveliest sympathy with the Western conditions. Meantime the Convener sits on the chest, and the rest of the Committee seem to feel that their chief duty lies in cutting down expenses and that the highest possible achievement is their meeting the Assembly without a deficit.

" P. S.—Dr. Macfarren hinted a good deal at want of tact on the part of our Missionary, and young Lloyd, who knows Macgregor, seemed to consider this quite possible. Our Missionary must not antagonise men unnecessarily. Send him this letter if you think well; I always like to deal frankly with our men," etc., etc.

As Shock read the letters and glanced at the petition his look of weariness passed away and the old scrimmage smile came back to his face. " Read that," he said, handing the letters to Father Mike, who read them in silence.

" Withdraw!" he exclaimed in astonishment when he had finished reading. " And why, pray? "

" Oh! don't you see, ' funds overlapping, denominational rivalry '? "

" ' Overlapping, rivalry,' rot! You cannot do my

work here and I cannot do yours. I say, this petition would be rich if it were not so damnable," added Father Mike, glancing at the document. "'Whereas, the town is amply supplied with church services there is no desire for services by the Presbyterians '—or by any others for that matter," interjected Father Mike. "Let us see who signs this blessed paper? Macfarren. He's a beautiful churchman. Inspector Haynes. What's he got to do with it? Frank, Smith, Crozier! Why, the thing is a farce! Not a man of them ever goes to church. 'Whereas, the Presbyterians are quite unable to assume any financial obligation in support of a minister.' Why, the whole outfit doesn't contribute a dollar a month. Isn't it preposterous, a beastly humbug! Who is this young whipper-snapper, Lloyd, pray?" Father Mike's tone was full of contempt.

Shock winced. His friend had touched the only place left raw by the letter. "He is a college friend of mine," he answered quickly. "A fine fellow and a great preacher."

"Oh!" replied Father Mike drily. "I beg pardon. Well, what will you do?"

"Withdraw," said Shock simply. "I haven't made it go, anyway."

"Rot!" said Father Mike, with great emphasis. "Macfarren doesn't want you, and possibly the Inspector shares in that feeling,—I guess you know why,—but you are needed in this town, and needed badly."

But Shock only replied: "I shall withdraw. I

have been rather a failure, I guess. Let's talk no more about it."

"All right, old chap," said Father Mike. "Come along to tea. I wish to Heaven there were more failures like you in the country."

Shock's last service at the Fort marked his emancipation as a preacher of the Gospel. Hitherto the presence of those whom he knew to be indifferent or contemptuously critical had wrought in him a self-consciousness that confused his thought, clogged his emotion, and hampered his speech. This night all was changed. The hall was full; the Inspector and his wife, with the men from the barracks, Macfarren and his followers, General Brady and his gracious, sweet-faced wife, were all there. Ike and The Kid—whose ranch lay halfway between the Lake and the Fort—had ridden in, and far back in the dim darkness of a corner sat the doctor. As Shock stood up and looked into the faces of the men before him and thought of their lives, lonely, tempted, frankly wicked, some of them far down in degradation, he forgot himself, his success, or his failure. What mattered that! How petty seemed now all his considerations for himself! Men were before him who by reason of sin were in sore need of help. He believed he had what they needed. How to give it to them, that was the question. With this feeling of sympathy and compassion, deepened and intensified by a poignant sense of failure, Shock stood up to deliver to them his last message. He would speak the truth to-night, and speak it he did, without a tinge of embarrassment

or fear.  As his words began to flow he became conscious of a new strength, of a new freedom, and the
joy of his new strength and freedom swept him along
on a full tide of burning speech.  He abandoned his
notes, from which he had hitherto feared to be far
separated; he left the desk, which had been to him a
barricade for defence, and stood up before the people.
His theme was the story of the leprous man who dared
to come to the Great Healer in all the hideousness of
his disease and who was straightway cleansed.  After
reading the words he stood facing them a few moments in silence and then, without any manner of introduction, he began:

  " That's what you want, men.  You need to be made
clean, you need to be made strong."  The people
stared at him as if he had gone mad, it was so unlike
his usual formal, awkward self.  Quietly, but with
intense and serious earnestness, he spoke to them of
their sins, their drunken orgies, their awful profanity,
their disregard of everything religious, their open
vices and secret sins.

  " Say," said Ike to The Kid, who sat next to him,
" they'll be gettin' out their guns sure! "  But there
was no anger in the faces lifted up to the speaker;
the matter was too serious for anger and the tone was
too kindly for offence.  Without hesitation Shock
went on with his terribly relentless indictment of the
men who sat before him.  Then, with a swift change
of tone and thought, he cried in a voice vibrating with
compassion:

  " And you cannot help it, men!  The pity of it is,

you cannot help it! You cannot change your hearts; you love these things, you cannot shake them off, they have grown upon you and have become your fixed habits. Some of you have tried: I know you have had your periods of remorse and you have sought to escape, but you have failed."

He paused a moment, and then continued in a voice humble and remorseful:

"I have failed, too. I thought in my pride and my folly that I could help you, but I have failed. We have failed together, men—what then is before us?"

His voice took a deeper tone, his manner was earnestly respectful and tenderly sympathetic, as he set before them the Divine Man, so quick to sympathise, so ready and so powerful to help.

"He is the same to-night, men! Appeal to Him and He will respond as He did to this poor leprous man."

Over and over again he urged this upon them, heaping argument upon argument, seeking to persuade them that it was worth while making the attempt.

"Say, boss, seems reasonable, don't it, and easy, too?" said Ike to The Kid, who was listening with face pale and intent. The Kid nodded without moving his eager eyes from the speaker's face.

"But I can't just git the throw, quite," continued Ike, with a puzzled air.

"Hush, listen!" said The Kid sharply. Shock had paused abruptly. For a few moments he stood looking into the eyes of the men gaping back at him with such intense eagerness; then leaning forward a little he said in a voice low, but thrilling with emotion:

"Does any man here think his father or mother has forgotten him or does not care what happens to him?"

Shock was thinking of his own dear old mother, separated from him by so many leagues of empty prairie, but so near to him in love and sympathy.

"Does any man think so?" he repeated, "and do you think your Father in Heaven does not care? Oh! do not think so!" His voice rose in a cry of entreaty. The effect was tremendous.

"God in Heaven, help me!" cried The Kid to himself with a sob in his voice.

"Me too, boss," said Ike gravely, putting his hand on the other's knee.

Shock's farewell was as abrupt as his beginning. In a single sentence he informed them that the services would be discontinued at this end of the field. He wished he could have served them better; he knew he had failed; he asked their forgiveness as he had already asked it of his God; but, though he had failed, he commended them to Him who had never failed any man appealing to Him for help.

There was no hymn, but in a simple, short prayer the service was closed, and before the congregation had recovered from their amazement Shock had passed out through the back door.

"Well, I'll be blanked!" said Ike, with a gasp.

"Quit that, Ike," said The Kid sharply. "Look here—I am going to quit swearing right now, so help me."

"All right, boss, I'm with you; put it there."

Then above the hum of conversation General Brady's voice was heard:

"Gentlemen, it is my opinion that we have lost a great man to-night, a fearless man and a Christian gentleman."

"That's my entire prognostication, General," said Ike, with great emphasis.

Meantime Shock had gone searching through the hotels for the doctor, whom he had seen slipping out before the closing prayer. But the doctor was nowhere to be seen, and in despair Shock went to Father Mike. He found that gentleman in a state of enthusiastic excitement. "My dear fellow, my dear fellow," he exclaimed, "that was great!"

"What?" said Shock simply.

"That sermon, man. I would give my hand to preach like that."

"Preach?" said Shock. "I didn't preach. Did you see the doctor?"

"Never mind the doctor," said Father Mike. "Come in, I want to talk with you; come in."

"No, I must see the doctor."

"Well, then, wait; I will go with you."

Shock hesitated. "I think I would rather go alone, if you don't mind," he said.

"All right, old chap," said Father Mike, "I understand. The door's always open and the kettle on."

"Thank you," said Shock. "You know how I appreciate that," and he went out.

There was a light in Macfarren's office. Shock

knocked at the door and went in. He found the doctor and Macfarren seated by a table, upon which were glasses and a bottle. The doctor was pale, nervous, shaking.

"Sit down, Mr. Macgregor," said Macfarren, with more cordiality than he had ever shown to Shock before. "I was just saying to the doctor that that was a fine discourse, a very able discourse, Mr. Macgregor."

Shock made no reply, but stood looking at the doctor.

"I would like to say," continued Macfarren, "that I regret your leaving us. I believe, on the whole, it is a mistake; we require preaching like that." There was a touch of real earnestness in Macfarren's tone.

"Mr. Macfarren," said Shock, "I am sorry I have not been able to help you. You need help, you need help badly. Jesus Christ can help you. Goodnight." He took the doctor's arm and, helping him up, walked off with him.

"What do you want?" said the doctor fiercely, when they were outside.

"Doctor, I want your help. I feel weak."

"Weak! Great Heavens above! *You* talk of weakness? Don't mock me!"

"It is true, doctor; come along."

"Where are you going?" said the doctor.

"I don't know," said Shock. "Let us go to your office."

The doctor's office was a cheerless room, dusty, disordered, and comfortless. The doctor sat down in a chair, laid his head on the table, and groaned. " It is no good, it is no good. I tried, I tried honestly. I prayed, I even hoped for a time—this is all gone! I broke my word, I betrayed my trust even to the dead. All is lost!"

"Doctor," said Shock quietly, "I wish that you would look at me and tell me what's the matter with me. I cannot eat, I cannot sleep, and yet I am weary. I feel weak and useless—cannot you help me?"

The doctor looked at him keenly. "You're not playing with me, are you? No, by Jove! you are not. You do look bad—let me look at you." His professional interest was aroused. He turned up the lamp and examined Shock thoroughly.

"What have you been doing? What's the cause of this thing?" he enquired, at length, as if he feared to ask.

Shock gave him an account of his ten days' experience in the mountains, sparing nothing. The doctor listened in an agony of self-reproach.

"It was my fault," he groaned, "it was all my fault."

"Not a word of that, doctor, please. It was not in your hands or in mine. The Lost River is lost, not by any man's fault, but by the will of God. Now, tell me, what do I need?"

"Nothing, nothing at all but rest and sleep. Rest for a week," said the doctor.

"Well, then," said Shock, "I want you to come and look after me for a week. I need you; you need me; we'll help each other."

"Oh, God! Oh, God!" groaned the doctor, "what is the use? You know there is no use."

"Doctor, I told you before that you are saying what is both false and foolish."

"I remember," said the doctor bitterly. "You spoke of common sense and honesty."

"Yes, and I say so again," replied Shock. "Common sense and honesty is what you need. Listen—I am not going to preach, I am done with that for to-night—but you know as well as I do that when a man faces the right way God is ready to back him up. It is common sense to bank on that, isn't it? Common sense, and nothing else. But I want to say this, you've got to be honest with God. You've not been fair. You say you've prayed——"

"God knows I have," said the doctor.

"Yes," said Shock, with a touch of scorn in his voice, "you've prayed, and then you went into the same old places and with the same old companions, and so you find yourself where you are to-night. You cannot cure any man of disease if he breaks every regulation you make when your back is turned. Give God a chance, that's all I ask. Be decently square with Him. There's lots of mystery in religion, but it is not there. Come along now, you are going home with me."

"No, sir," said the doctor decidedly. "I shall fight it out alone.

"Will you walk, or shall I carry you?" said Shock quietly.

The doctor gazed at him. "Oh, confound you!"

he cried, " I'll—— He stopped short and putting his face down upon the table again he burst into a storm of sobs and cried, "Oh, I am weak, I am weak, let me go, let me go, I am not worth it!"

Then Shock got down beside him, put his arm around his shoulder, and said: " I cannot let you go, doctor. I want you. And your Father in Heaven wants you. Come," he continued after a pause, " we'll win yet."

For half an hour they walked the streets and then turned into Father Mike's quarters.

" Father Mike," said Shock, opening the door, " we want coffee, and I'm hungrier than I've been for three days."

" Come in," said Father Mike, with a keen glance at the doctor, " come in, brother mine. You've earned your grub this day."

## XVI

## "STAY AT YOUR POST, LAD"

RELIEVED from his station at the Fort, Shock was able to devote himself entirely to the western part of his field, which embraced the Loon Lake district and extended twenty-five miles up to the Pass, and he threw himself with redoubled energy into his work of exploration and organisation. Long ago his little cayuse had been found quite unequal to the task of keeping pace with the tremendous energy of his driver, and so for the longer journeys Shock had come to depend mainly upon Bob, the great rangey sorrel sent him by the Hamilton boys, the only condition attached to the gift being that he should allow Bob to visit the ranch at least once a month. And so it came that Shock and his sorrel broncho became widely known over the ranges of all that country. Many a little shack in far away valleys, where a woman with her children lived in isolated seclusion from all the world, he discovered and brought into touch with the world about, and by means of books and magazines and illustrated papers brought to hearts sick with longing some of the colour and brightness from the great world beyond, so often fondly longed for. Many a cowboy, wild and reckless, with every link of kinship broken, an unrelated unit of humanity keeping lonely watch over his bunch of cattle, found in Shock a friend, and established through him anew a bond with human society. The hour spent with Shock in riding around the cattle often brought to this bit of human driftwood a new respect for himself, a new sense of responsibility for life, and a new estimate of the worth of his manhood. Away up in the Pass, too, where the miners lived and wrought under conditions wretched, debasing, and fraught with danger, and where in the forest-camps the lumbermen lived lives more wholesome, but more lonely, Shock found scope for the full energy of his passion to help and serve.

" A hospital is what they need up here, doctor! " he exclaimed one day after they had made a tour through the shacks and bunks where men sick and injured lay in their uncared for misery. " A hospital is what they want, and some kind of a homelike place where they can meet together. And by God's help we'll get this, too, when our hands are somewhat free. We have all we can do for the next few weeks." And so they had.

Shock had early recognised that the evils which were so rampant, and that exercised such a baneful influence in the community, were due not so much to any inherent love of vice as to the conditions under which the men were forced to live. Life was a lonely thing on the ranges, without colour, without variety, and men plunged into debauchery from sheer desperate reaction from monotony. Shock believed that, if there could be established a social centre offering intellectual interest and physical recreation, much could be done to banish the vices that were fast becoming imbedded in the very life and character of the people. And so he planned the erection of a building that would serve for church, manse, club-house, school-room, and library, and would thus become a spot around which the life of the community might gather in a clean and wholesome atmosphere. He appealed to the Church Manse Building Fund for a grant, he drew his plans for his building, and throughout the summer quietly set about gathering his materials. One and another of his friends he would persuade to haul a load of logs from the hills, and with good-natured persistence he would get a day's work now and again from the young fellows who frequently had more time on their hands than they knew how to reasonably make use of, with the result that before they were well aware of what was being done a log building stood ready for the roofing and plaster. His success stimulated his friends to more organised and continued effort. They began to vie with each other in making contributions of work and material for the new building. Macnamara furnished lime, Martin drew sand, Sinclair and The Kid, who had the best horses and wagons, drew lumber from the mill at the Fort; and by the time summer was gone the building, roofed, chinked, and plastered, only required a few finishing touches to be ready for the opening. Indeed, it was a most creditable structure. It was a large, roomy, two-story building, the downstairs of which was given up to a room to be devoted to public uses. The upstairs Shock planned to contain four bed-rooms.

" What do you want of four bed-rooms, Mr. Prospector? " said Ike, as they were laying out the space. " You can't sleep in more'n three of 'em at a time."

" No, but you can sleep in one, Ike, and some of the boys in another, and I want one myself."

" Oh!" said Ike, much pleased. " Going to run a kind of stoppin' place, are you? "

" Yes; I hope my friends will stop with me often."

" Guess you won't have much trouble with that side of it," said Ike. " And this here room," he continued, " will do first rate for a kind of lumber-room, provisions, and harness, and such like, I guess? "

" No," said Shock. " This room will be the finest room in the house. See: it will look away out toward the south and west, over the lake, and up to the mountains. The inside of the room won't be hard to beat, but the outside cannot be equalled in all the world, and I tell you what, Ike, it cannot be too good, for this room is for my mother." There was a reverent, tender tone in Shock's voice that touched Ike.

" Is she really goin' to come out here? " he asked.

" I hope so," said Shock. " Next spring."

" I say," said Ike, " won't she find it lonely? "

" I don't think so," said Shock, with a curious smile. " You know, my mother is rather peculiar. For twenty-five years, without missing a single night, she came into my room to kiss me before I went to sleep, and she's just that foolish that if I'm anywhere around I don't think she'll be lonely." And then

Shock proceeded to give Ike a picture of his mother, and all her devotion to him through the long years of his life. The rough but tender-hearted cowboy was more touched than he cared to show.

"Say," he said, when Shock had finished, "how did you ever come to leave her? I couldn't 'a' done it, nohow."

"She sent me," said Shock simply. "There's One she loves better than me." And Ike understood without more explanation.

For the furnishing of the house, and for the equipment of the library and club-rooms, Shock had appealed to his friends in the East through Brown, to whom he gave a full description of the building and the purposes for which it had been erected. The response was so hearty and so generous that, when the loads of house-furnishings, books, magazines, and papers arrived, Shock's heart was full to overflowing with gratitude, and, when a little later he received notice that a cabinet organ had arrived at the railroad depot, he felt that the difficulties and trials of a missionary's life were few and small in comparison with the triumphs and rewards.

At length everything was in place and the building ready for the opening. The preparations for this great event were in the hands of a committee, of which The Kid was chairman; the decorations were left to Ike and Perault; the programme was left to The Kid, assisted by Marion, who had been persuaded not only to sing, herself, but had agreed to train the school children in some action songs. There was to be a

grand supper, of course,—nothing Western would be
complete without that feature,—and in addition to
the ordinary speeches and musical numbers there was
to be a nigger-minstrel show with clog-dancing furnished by the miners and lumbermen from the Pass, at
Shock's urgent invitation. The whole affair was to
be wound up by a grand promenade headed by young
Malcolm Forbes, son of a Highland chief, a shy young
fellow whom Shock had dug up from a remote valley,
and who was to appear in full Highland costume with
his pipes. Small wonder that the whole community,
from the Fort to the Pass, was tingling with delighted
anticipation. Such an event was not only important
of itself, but it was hailed as the inauguration of
a new era in the country, for with church, school,
library, and club they would be abreast of the
most advanced Eastern civilisation.

Not only were the people of the Loon Lake district
stirred with interest in the opening of their new building, but to a far greater extent than they knew their
confidence and even their affection had gathered about
the man to whose energy the whole enterprise was due.
During these months they had come to rely upon his
judgment as a man of affairs, to trust him for his true
human heart, and to regard him with reverence as one
touched with a spirit unlike that of the world with
which they were familiar—a spirit of generous sympathy with them in all their multitudinous trials and
difficulties, a spirit that made him think nothing of
himself and much of them. He represented to them
religion in a manner at once winning and impress-

ive, as few of them had ever seen it represented before.

At length the great day came, and with it the gathering of the people from all parts far and near. A few farmers who lived toward the Fort came with their wives and children in horse-wagons and ox-wagons; the ranchers with their families drove for the most part in *democrats* and buckboards; but many of the ranchers and their wives and all the cowboys came on horseback. There had never been such a gathering at Loon Lake within the memory of the oldest timer. The preparations for supper were elaborate and impressive. It was important that this part of the evening's proceedings should go off well. As Shock, passing up and down, witnessed the abounding hilarity of those who thronged the supper-tables his mind was relieved of all anxiety as to the success of the entertainment to follow. With great difficulty Sinclair, who was a shy man, was persuaded to preside as chairman. It was only the promise of Shock to support him on the one side and of Father Mike, who was almost as much interested in the success of the entertainment as Shock himself, on the other, that induced Sinclair finally to accept this responsible and honourable position. It was indeed an hour of triumph to Shock and his fellow-workers, and as the entertainment progressed they gathered satisfaction to the full from the manifestations of delight on the part of the audience that packed the building to the doors.

After the entertainment had well begun a stranger appeared at the door asking for the minister.

" Well," said Ike, who was performing the responsible duty of door-keeper, " you can't see him, not
now. What's required? "

" I guess it's pretty important," the stranger said.
" It's a telegram. In fact, it's bad news, so Mr. Mc-
Intyre of Big River said."

" Bad news! " exclaimed Ike. " Mighty bad time
to bring bad news. Why couldn't you wait? "

" Some things can't wait," said the man briefly.
" Guess you'd better read it, it's open."

" Not me," said Ike, shrinking from this liberty.
" Send for The Kid."

In a few moments The Kid appeared and, taking
the telegram from Ike, read it.

" The Lord help us! " he exclaimed as he read the
wire. He took Ike to one side away from the crowd
and read him the words: " ' Your mother seriously
ill. Doctors hold out no hope of recovery. Signed,
BROWN.' "

" His mother! Say, boss, what'll we do? He thinks
a mighty lot of his mother. I've heerd him talk. This
will purty nigh kill him, I guess."

They stood for some moments looking blankly at
each other, unwilling to deliver the blow which they
knew would strike deep into the heart of the man they
had come to love.

" He must be told," said The Kid at length. " Let's
see—he'll want to get to the end of the line, anyway,
and that's over a hundred miles from here. I say, Ike,
you'd better tell him, I guess."

" Well," said Ike slowly, " that there's a purty

particular bit of diplomatics, and I aint used to it. I say," with a sudden inspiration, " you tell him."

" Couldn't do it, Ike. How would it do to get Father Mike or Sinclair? "

" Yes," said Ike meditatively, " they'd do all right if we weren't here, but I guess we belong to him 'most more than they do."

" That's so, Ike," said The Kid quickly. " That's so ; it's one of us."

" Yes, it's one of us," said Ike, " and if I could do it well, boss, you wouldn't see no buck."

" All right, Ike," said The Kid, drawing a long breath. " I'll do it."

" I'll remember it, boss," said Ike. " Guess there aint much time to lose. How is he agoin' to git there? "

" Take the Swallow, Ike," said The Kid. " She's good for a hundred miles."

" Mr. McIntyre's team will be ready to go from his place," said the stranger, who had come near.

" Good! " said The Kid. " Where are you going, Ike? "

" To git the horses. He'll want to git right off. I guess I'll put him on Slipper, and I'll take the Swallow. Slipper rides purty easy, and he's a purty big man."

" All right, Ike," said The Kid. " Remember every minute is precious. Here, Mac," he continued, turning to Macnamara, who stood looking in at the door, craning his neck to see and hear what was going on, "slip around to the side door and tell Mr. Macgregor that I want him right away."

In a few minutes Shock came running out in high spirits, elated with the success of the evening. "Hello, old boy!" he cried to The Kid. "It's great, isn't it? You're a great concert conductor! What do you want me for?"

The Kid took him by the arm and led him away in silence toward the Old Prospector's shack, which stood near by.

"What's the matter, Stanton; anything gone wrong?" Still The Kid made no reply; but, walking to the door of the shack, opened it, and went in and lit the lamp. "Sit down," he said, pushing Shock into a chair. "I have something to tell you. There's—there's bad news, I'm afraid. I'll wait outside." He put the telegram down, went hastily out, and closed the door, leaving Shock to face the blow where no eye could see.

It seemed an hour to The Kid before Ike came up with the Swallow and Slipper saddled and ready for the journey.

"Where is he?" said Ike, in a whisper.

"In there," replied The Kid, with a groan. "God help him!"

"I guess He will. He ought to," said Ike gravely.

"Got grub, Ike, and blankets?"

Ike nodded, pointing to the sack strapped to the saddle.

"He ought to start," said The Kid nervously. "That wire's two days old now. It will take till to-morrow night to reach town even if everything goes right, and every moment counts. Better go in," he continued, " and tell him the horses are ready."

Ike nodded and went toward the closed door, opened it softly, and went in. He found Shock sitting at the table gazing vacantly at the telegram in his hand as if trying to take in its meaning. He looked up at Ike as he entered and, handing him the telegram, said:

" It's my mother, Ike. Do you remember my mother? "

" Yes, I know," replied Ike, approaching him timidly and laying a hand awkwardly on his shoulder. " I don't want to presume," he continued, " but I was wonderin' if there was anyone who could help you to stand it? "

" There is, there is One, there is."

" That's all right, then," said Ike, as if an important matter had been settled. " The horses are ready."

" The horses? " said Shock, with a puzzled air.

" Yes; thought you'd want to ride to town to get to send a wire or somethin'."

" Of course I do; thank you. I'll go to her at once. What a fool I am! " He rose hastily as he spoke, changed his coat, and getting his hat and riding gloves came out to where The Kid stood with the horses.

" Why, it's the Swallow, and Slipper! " he said. " Boys, this is good of you."

The Kid stood without a word, looking at Shock's

white, dazed face. He could not trust his voice to speak.

" You'd best get onto Slipper," said Ike. " Rides easy and is mighty sure. The Swallow's all right, of course," he continued apologetically to The Kid, " but a leetle light."

" But I don't want both," said Shock.

" Oh! I guess I'll go along," declared Ike. " I know the trails and short-cuts a little better. Can save time, perhaps. That is," he added, " if you don't mind my goin' along."

" That's awfully good of you, Ike," said Shock. " I shall be glad to have you."

" Good-bye, Kiddie," said Shock affectionately, holding out his hand to The Kid. " I cannot say much just now, but I appreciate this kindness, my boy."

" Don't, don't!" said The Kid, in a husky whisper. " I wish to Heaven I could help you. Good-bye."

" Good-bye," said Shock, taking up the reins. " Oh! I say, Kid, don't tell anyone to-night. Keep the thing going; it would be a pity to spoil their fun, you know. You can do this for me, can't you? "

" I can try," said The Kid, setting his teeth together.

He stood looking after them as they went up the trail in the moonlight. " Oh! this cursed country! " he groaned. " It's so far from any place. He'll never see her again, I'm sure. Well, I must keep this thing going as I promised. But some of the numbers I'll cut out, you can bet."

Straight on through the moonlight rode the two men, the one trying to make real the words that marched with ceaseless tramp across his brain: " Doctors hold out no hope of recovery." They seemed like words of fire written across the prairie. The other, riding a little behind, except where the trail grew difficult or indistinct, silent but alert for opportunity to offer aid or show sympathy, governing carefully the pace so that the best possible speed could be got out of the superb animals that with their swinging lope covered the long slopes up and down. The memory of that ride to Shock in after years was like that of a ghastly nightmare, a strange intermingling of moonlight and shadow; the murmur of the night wind about his ears; the steady beat of the hoofs upon the beaten trail; the pause at midnight by the upper ford of the Black Dog to feed and rest their horses; and then the steady onward push through the night till the grey and gold of the eastern sky told that the morning had come. He could never forget how the first beams of the rising sun smote his eyes like the cut of a whip till he was almost forced to cry out in his pain. He remembered how it seemed to him as if he were in the grip of some mysterious force impelling him onward in that unending, relentless lope. Another pause at sunrise to give the horses breath, and then on again they rode through that terrible red light of the rising sun, till at length in the still early forenoon the manse of Big River was reached. Their horses were jaded and leg-weary, for in the thirteen hours during which they had kept up their long,

swinging gait they had covered more than a hundred
miles.

The McIntyres were expecting them.

"We won't speak about his mother, dear," said the
little woman of the manse, with a warm feeling in her
heart for the missionary who had spent a night with
them some seven months ago, and had told them so
simply and fully of his life, a story of which the
heart and soul had been his mother. "It hurts to
speak of these things for a while," she added.

"Yes, my darling, I know," said her husband,
his eyes lingering tenderly upon the face looking so
sweet, but so wan and pale above the black dress and
*crêpe* collar. "We know, we know, darling," he repeated, taking her in his arms. They were both
thinking of the little mound looking so small upon
the wide prairie, small but big enough to hold all their
heart's treasure. For five months the manse had been
overrunning with heaven's own light; and with joy
that rippled and flowed from baby laughter, that
lurked in dimpled fingers and dimpled toes and dimpled cheeks, every dimple a well of light and joy—
and then the little mound with its white railing, and
only the echoes of the laughter and the memory of
the dimpled fingers, toes, and cheeks,—and the empty
manse! It was this memory that made their welcome
of Shock so full of tender understanding. There is
no speech like heart-speech, and during the hour in
the Big River manse to Shock's heart there came—
how he could not have told—the inarticulate message
of sympathy that healed and comforted, so that he

drove away rested and refreshed as with sleep. As they were hitching up the team Ike found opportunity to whisper to Shock: " I say, p'rhaps you'd rather he'd go with you; he'd help you more, p'rhaps? "

" No, no, Ike; don't leave me; I want you," Shock had replied.

" All right, boss; that suits me," was Ike's answer, glad that his offer had not been accepted.

" Good-bye," said Mr. McIntyre, waving his hand. " Do not spare them, Ike," he continued. " They can make Spruce Creek in two hours and a half easily."

" I'll take care o' them," said Ike, swinging the fiery, half-broken bronchos onto the trail. " They'd ought to do a little better than that, I judge." And they did; for, when the buckboard drew up at the Spruce Creek Stopping Place Ike remarked to Bill Lee, who stood in his usual position leaning against the door: " Two hours from Big River, and not much the worse, I guess."

Bill's welcome of Shock was almost effusive in its heartiness, but Ike cut him short.

" I say, Bill," he called out, walking to the stable; " got any oats in here? "

" Oh, a few. I keep some for thoroughbreds, you know." And he walked after Ike into the stable.

Ike began talking rapidly and in a low tone. As Bill listened he became unusually excited. " Eh! What! No. Say, that's bad, too blank bad! His mother, eh? My team? Certainly. There they are, fit for a good dozen an hour. Put 'em right in."

In ten minutes Bill's team, the pride of his heart, were hitched to the buckboard.

" All right, Bill," said Ike, taking the reins.

" All right, Ike," replied Bill. " Their skin don't say much, but they can talk with their feet a few. Let 'em go. They won't run away."

The performance of Bill's bony, shaggy team more than justified their owner's promise. They did " talk with their feet," and to such good purpose that in less than two hours Shock stood at the door of his Convener's house, his mind bewildered, his senses numbed from the terrible strain through which he had passed.

" Come in, my dear fellow," said the Convener, who had evidently been expecting him, " come right in."

But Shock stood at the door. " Is there any word? " he enquired, with a voice void of all emotion.

" Nothing further."

" When does the train go? "

" The train? Oh, at two in the morning."

" How long does it take? "

" Five days."

" Five days! " echoed Shock, in a voice of despair.

" You might wire a message in the meantime," said the Convener kindly. " We will go down to the telegraph office after you have had a rest and a cup of tea."

" No, no," said Shock, turning eagerly from the door. " I am all right; cannot we go now? "

At the telegraph office a number of men stood laughing and talking. Shock drew a blank sheet toward him and set himself to compose his wire. Again and again he made the attempt, but at length he put down the pen and looked around piteously at his friend. " I cannot say it! " he exclaimed in a hurried whisper.

" Come outside a minute," said the Convener, taking his arm. " Now tell me what you want to say and perhaps I can help you."

" Oh! " cried Shock, wreathing his great fingers in his agony. " I want to say—good-bye—No, no, not that! I want to tell her—give her my love and say I want to see her. She will be wanting me." His breath began to come in great heaving sobs.

" Let me try," said his friend. " You stay out here."

After some moments the Convener returned and handed Shock a paper on which he had written: " God keep you, mother dear. My heart's love to you. Shall I come? "

" Will that do? " he asked.

" Yes, yes; thank you.   That is good."

" Now," said the Convener, when they had reached the house, " you must rest."

" I am not tired," said Shock, as if in surprise.

" My dear fellow, you are half dead."

" No, I am quite right, and besides, there's Ike. I ought to look after Ike."

" Don't you worry about Ike," said the Convener. " He's able to look after himself; besides I'll look him up when I get you to sleep. Come now," and he led him into the tiny bedroom. " You get into bed; I'll bring you a cup of tea and you can sleep. No one will disturb you, and I'll wake you at the right time, never fear."

"I don't think I am sleepy," said Shock; but when in a few minutes his friend came back with his cup of tea he found Shock in a sleep so profound that he had not the heart to wake him. "Poor chap, poor chap!" said the Convener, looking down upon the strong, rugged face, now so haggard. "This is a hard country!"

For hours Shock lay dead in sleep. Before night-fall the Convener went to look up Ike, and on his return found his guest still asleep. "Let him sleep, it will do him good," he said to his kind-hearted wife, who would have wakened Shock to have supper. "We'll let him sleep till an answer comes to his wire."

Late at night he went down to the telegraph office.

"Yes," replied the clerk in answer to his enquiry, "there's a wire for Mr. Macgregor just come in. Bad news, too, I guess."

The Convener took the message and read:

"Your mother passed away in perfect peace this evening. Your message brought her great joy. She wished me to send this reply: 'The Lord is my Shepherd; I shall not want. Stay at your post, lad, till He calls.'                    "HELEN."

"'Stay at your post till He calls,'" read the Convener again. "A great soul that. That word will do him good."

He was right. He found Shock waiting for him, calm, expectant, and ready to bear whatever life might bring, nor did his face change as he read the wire over and over again. He only said: " God is very good to us. She went away in peace, and she got my wire and I hers."

" Yes," said the Convener, " God is always good. We sometimes cannot see it, but," he added, " it was a great matter that your sister could have been there with her."

" My sister? " said Shock. " Oh! " a sudden flush reddening his pale cheek. " She's not my sister —she's my—she's our friend, yes, a dear friend. It would be a great joy to my mother to have her."

There was no sign of grief in his face, but a great peace seemed to have settled upon him. Long into the night he talked over the affairs of his mission field, giving in response to the keen questions of his Convener a full account of the work he had been carrying on, opening up the plans he had made for future work. In particular was he anxious to enlist the Convener's sympathy in his scheme for a reading-room and hospital at the Pass. The Convener shook his head at the plan. " I agree with you entirely," he said, " but the Committee, I fear, will not give you a grant for a hospital. " If it were a church now——"

" Well," argued Shock, " it will serve for a church."

" You may count on me to do my best for you," replied the Convener, " but I am not sanguine. The Committee are extremely cautious and conservative." But when the Convener came to ask about the difficulties and trials of his life his missionary became silent. There were no trials and difficulties to speak of, no more at least than the rest of the people had to bear. They were all good to him.

"That's all right," said the Convener, "but there are difficulties, none the less. It is a hard country, and sometimes it lays burdens upon us almost greater than we can bear. There are the poor McIntyres, now," he continued. "How did you find them?"

"Very well," replied Shock. "But, indeed, I didn't notice much."

And then the Convener told him of the story of their great grief.

"It is a common enough story in this country. The little baby was five months old, singularly bright and attractive. McIntyre himself was quite foolish about it; and, indeed, the whole congregation were quite worked up over it. Took suddenly ill, some mysterious trouble; no doctor within forty miles; before he arrived the baby was gone. They were dreadfully cut up about it."

"I—I never noticed," said Shock, with a sense of shame. "I wasn't thinking."

There was no demonstration of sympathy on the part of his people when Shock returned to his work. One by one they came up after the evening service to shake hands with him and then to leave him alone. But that night, when all had gone except Ike, who was hovering about downstairs within call of Shock,—who was sitting upstairs alone in the room which, in the fulness of his joy, he had set apart for his mother,—a voice was heard asking cautiously:

" Is he in? "

" Yes, but I guess he's pretty tired," replied Ike doubtfully.

" I'd like to see him a minute," replied the voice, with a sudden huskiness.

" Oh! It's you, is it? " said Ike. " Well, come in. Yes, come right upstairs." And Carroll came heavily up the stairs with Patsy in his arms.

" Why, Carroll, this is awfully good of you! " exclaimed Shock, going to meet him.

" It's the little lad," said Carroll. " It's Patsy; he's breakin' the heart av him, an' he wants to see you, and, your riverince, it's meself—I want to——" The voice broke down completely.

" Come in, come in! " cried Shock, his tears flowing fast. " Come, Patsy, do you want to see me? Come on, old chap, I want you, too." He took the little cripple in his arms and held him tight while his tears fell upon Patsy's face and hands.

" Is it for your mother? " whispered Patsy, in an awestruck tone.

" Yes, yes, Patsy dear," said Shock, who was fast losing control of himself, the long pent-up grief breaking through all barriers of self-control. " She's gone from me, Patsy lad."

" But," said the little boy, lifting up his beautiful face in wonder. " Sure, isn't she wid Jesus Himself and the blessed angels? "

" Oh, yes, Patsy, my boy! she is, and it's not right

to grieve too much, but I cannot help it," said Shock, regaining control of himself. "But I am glad you came in to tell me, and we'll all try to be good men so that some day we'll all go there, too."

For a long time they sat looking out on the moon-lit lake and the distant hills, Shock telling the little lad he held in his arms of the beautiful country to which his mother had gone.

That night was the beginning of better things for the big Irishman. The revenge he had cherished for so many months passed out of his heart, and among his closest friends and his warmest companions Shock could count from that time forth Tim Carroll.

## XVII

## BETTY'S LAST WORDS

THERE is a certain stimulus in grief which lends unreal strength to endure, but Nature will be avenged in a physical and emotional reaction, all the more terrible that it is unexpected. Then the full weight of the sorrow presses upon the heart already exhausted, and the sense of loss becomes the more painful because it can be fairly estimated, and the empty place can be more truly measured because it is seen in its relation to the ordinary life.

So it was with Shock. The first sharp stab of grief was over, and now he carried with him the long ache of a wound that would not heal for many a day. His mother had filled a large part of his life. As far back into childhood as his memory could go, there she stood between him and the great world, his sure defence against all evil, his refuge in all sorrow; and as he grew into manhood she made for herself a larger and larger place in his thought and in his life. He well knew how she had toiled and denied herself comforts and endured hardships that he might gain that height of every Scottish mother's ambition for her son, a college education, and he gave her full reward in the love of his heart and the thoughtful devotion of his life. All his interests and occupations, his studies, his

mission work in the Ward, his triumphs on the football
field, all he shared with her, and until the last year no
one had ever challenged her place of supremacy in his
heart.   His future was built about his mother.   She
was to share his work, her home was to be in his manse,
she was to be the centre about which his life would
swing; and since coming to the West he had built up in
imagination a new life structure, in which his mother
had her own ancient place.   In this new and fasci-
nating work of exploring, organising, and upbuilding
he felt sure, too, of his mother's eager sympathy and
her wise understanding.

It had been the happiest of all his fancies that his
mother should preside over the new home, the opening
of which had been attended with such pride and joy.
She would be there to live with him every day, watching him go out and waiting for him to come in.

Now all that was gone.   As his mind ran along its
accustomed grooves every turn of thought smote him
with a pang sharp and sudden.   She was no longer a
part of the plan.   All had to be taken down, the parts
readjusted, the structure rebuilt.   He began to understand the Convener's words, "This is a hard
country."   It demanded a man's life in all the full,
deep meaning of the word; his work, of course of body
and brain, but his heart as well, and his heart's
treasures.

In the midst of his depression and bewilderment Ike
brought him a letter which had lain two weeks at the
Fort, and whose date was now some four weeks old.
It was from Brown and ran thus:

My Dear Old Chap:

I do not know how to begin this letter. The terribly sudden and awful calamity that has overtaken us has paralysed my mind, and I can hardly think straight. One thing that stands out before me, wiping out almost every other thought, is that our dear Betty is no more. You cannot imagine it, I know, for though I saw her in her coffin, so sweet and lovely, but oh! so still, I cannot get myself to believe it. The circumstances concerning her death, too, were awfully sad, so sad that it simply goes beyond any words I have to describe them. I will try to be coherent; but, though I shall give you an account of what happened, I cannot begin to convey the impression upon my mind. Well, let me try.

You know Mrs. Fairbanks has been opposed all along to The Don's attentions to Betty, and has tried her best to block him. After you left, the opposition grew more determined. Why, for the life of me, I cannot say. She had apparently made up her mind that The Don must quit. She worked every kind of scheme, but it was no good. That plucky little girl, in her own bright, jolly way, without coming to an open break, would not give back an inch, and The Don kept coming to the house just because Betty insisted. He would have quit long before, poor chap. You know how proud he is.

Well, Mrs. Fairbanks set to work to gain her purpose. She somehow got wind of the kind of life The Don lived in this city years ago. She set enquiries on foot and got hold of the facts pretty well. You know

all about it, so I need not tell you.  Poor chap, he
had his black spots, sure enough.  She furthermore
got Lloyd somehow to corroborate her facts.  Just
how much he looked up for her I don't know, but I tell
you I have quit Lloyd.  He is a blanked cad.  I
know I should not write this, and you will hate to read
it, but it is the truth.  His conduct during the whole
business has been damnable! damnable! damnable!  I
gnash my teeth as I write.

When she had everything ready she sprung her
mine.  It was in her own house one evening, when
Lloyd, The Don, and I were there, and the Fairbanks'
new minister, Hooper, a young Trinity man, who has
been a close friend of The Don's, I don't know how
long, but some years at least.  A fine fellow.  God
bless him, say I, again and again.

The Don and Betty had been going it pretty strong
that evening, rather unnecessarily so, I think; and
Mrs. Fairbanks got more and more worked up, until
she seemed to lose her head.  As The Don was saying
good night she spoke up and said in that haughty
way of hers, "Mr. Balfour, the time has come when
we must say good-bye, and I must ask you to discon-
tinue your visits to this house, and your intimacy with
my daughter."

Well, we all sat up, I can tell you.  The Don went
white, and red, and white again.  Betty walked over
and stood by his side, her eyes all blazing.
"Mamma," she cried, "what are you saying against
the man I love!  Do you mean to——"

"Betty," said her mother in her haughtiest and

coldest and calmest voice, " before you go any further, listen to me.   I do not choose that my daughter, pure and unsullied, should give herself to a *roué* and a libertine."

The Don took a step toward her and said:  " Mrs. Fairbanks, someone has misled you.   What you say is false, absolutely and utterly false."   Betty glanced proudly up into his face.

" False! " cried Mrs. Fairbanks.   " Then, Mr. Balfour, you force me to ask, did you not live for some months with a woman on Jarvis Street?   Were you not a constant visitor at houses of ill repute for months in this city? "

Poor Don!  I can see him yet.  His face grew livid, his eyes staring, as he stood there without a word.

" Don," cried Betty, " tell her it is false! " and she lifted her little head proudly.  " Tell her it is false, and I don't care who says it is true."   Still The Don stood speechless.

" Alas! my poor child," said Mrs. Fairbanks, " he could not say so.  I have the proof in my hand."   And she pulled a letter out of her pocket.   " It is true, and much more—too true.   Mr. Lloyd here knows this to be true.   Is it not so, Mr. Lloyd?   If this is not true, speak."   The poor old Don turned his eyes imploringly toward Lloyd, like a man hanging on his last hope, but Lloyd, the beast! mumbled and stuttered something or other.   Betty ran to him, caught him by the arm and shook him.   " Speak out! " she said.   " Say it is all a lie! "   The Lloyd said in a thick kind of voice, " I cannot say so."

Betty turned back to The Don, and may God keep me from ever seeing a face like hers again. " Say it isn't true! " she said, putting her hand on his arm; and as he stood still, white and speechless, she gave a kind of cry of fear, and horror, and I don't know what else. " Oh, Don, can this be true—and—you kissed me! "

Then The Don pulled himself together, turned to Mrs. Fairbanks, and began to speak, the words pouring out in a perfect torrent. " Mrs. Fairbanks, you must listen to me. What you say was true of me eight years ago. I came here a mere boy. I fell in with a bad lot—I had plenty of money, and I confess I went bad. That was eight years ago. Then I met your daughters, and came into your home. From that time I have never done a dishonourable thing, my life has been clean. Ever since I touched your daughter's hand my hands have never touched anything unclean. The first day I saw her, eight years ago, I loved her, and since then I have been true in heart and in life to her. For my shameful past God knows I have repented bitterly, bitterly, and have sought forgiveness; and no man lives in this town, or any other, who can point to anything of which I am ashamed to speak here."

Poor Betty! She looked from one to the other in a frightened kind of way, and when The Don had finished his confession she gave a cry the like of which I never heard, " Oh, mother, take me away! " I have heard of hearts being broken. I think hers was broken then.

I tell you we were all in a whirl. The Don fell on

his knees beside her, taking hold of her skirts.  " Oh,
Betty, won't you forgive me? God have mercy on
me! Won't you forgive me? I have done many
things of which I am ashamed, but I have never been
untrue to you in thought or in deed.   Never, never, so
help me God!" He clutched the hem of her dress,
kissing it over and over again.  It was a ghastly
sight, I can tell you.  Betty shrank from him, drawing her skirts away.   " Come away, my daughter,"
said Mrs. Fairbanks.   " There is nothing more to be
said."

As she turned away up spake little Hooper.  God
bless him, the little five-footer, every inch clear grit.
" Mrs. Fairbanks, one minute.   Pardon me if I say a
word.   I am this young man's friend, and I am your
minister.   I have known this man for six years.  I
have known him intimately.   I believe he carries a
clean, pure heart, and he has lived a hard-working,
honourable life.   If he has sinned, he has repented,
and God has forgiven him.   Should not you? "

Mrs. Fairbanks turned impatiently on him.   " Mr.
Hooper, forgiveness is one thing, and friendship
another."

" No, thank God! " cried the little chap.   " No, forgiveness is not one thing and friendship another.
Forgiveness means friendship, and welcome, and love,
with God and with man."   I could have hugged the
little man where he stood.

Then Mrs. Fairbanks seemed to lose her head, and
she blazed out in a perfect fury.   " Do you mean deliberately to say that this man," pointing to The Don,

who was still on his knees, with his face in his hands, "that this man should be received into my house?"

"Mrs. Fairbanks," said Hooper, "is there not a place for the repentant and absolved, even with the saints of God?"

Mrs. Fairbanks lost herself completely. "Mr. Hooper," she cried, "this is outrageous. I tell you, forgiven or not, repentant or not, never will he, or such as he, enter my doors or touch my daughter's hand. Never while I live."

Then Hooper drew himself up. He seemed to me six feet tall. He lifted his hand, and spoke with the kind of solemnity that you expect to come from the altar. "Then listen to me, Mrs. Fairbanks. You say you would not receive him or such as him into your house. You invite me often to your home, and here I constantly meet men who are known in society as rakes and *roués*. You know it, and all society women know it, too. If you cared to take half the trouble you have taken in this case, you could find out all the facts. You are a woman of society, and you know well what I say is true. I have seen you in this room place your daughter in the arms of a man you knew to be a drunkard, and must have suspected was a libertine. These men have the *entrée* to every good family in the city, and though their character is known, they are received everywhere. They have wealth and family connection. Do not attempt to deny it, Mrs. Fairbanks. I know society, and you know it well. If you strike off the names of those men whose lives, not have been in the past, but are to-day unclean and unworthy, you will have to make a very large blank in your dancing list." Then the little fellow's voice broke right down. " Forgive me if I have spoken harshly. I beseech you, hear me. You are doing a great wrong to my friend, a cruel wrong. I pledge you my name and honour he is a good man, and he is worthy of your daughter. God has covered his sin: why have you dared to uncover it? " And then, in the tone that he uses in reading his prayers, he went on, " In the name of the Saviour of the sinful and lost, I ask you, I entreat you, receive him."

You would think that would have melted the heart of a she-devil, let alone a woman, but that woman stood there, cold, white, and unmoved. " Is that all, Mr. Hooper? " she said. " Then my answer is—never! And as for you, his eloquent advocate, I never wish to see you again. Come, Betty."

As they began to move off The Don, who was still on his knees, looked up and reached out his hands toward the poor girl with a cry that stabbed my heart through and through. " I want your forgiveness, Betty, only your forgiveness." She paused, took a step towards him, then putting her hands over her face she stood still, shuddering. Her mother caught her and drew her away.

The Don rose slowly. He seemed stupefied. He turned toward Hooper, and said in a hoarse kind of whisper: " She's gone! Oh, God, I have lost her!" He felt his way out to the hall like a blind man. Helen put out her hand to stop him, but he went on, never

noticing. She followed him to the hall, weeping bitterly, and crying, " Come back, Don, come back ! "

Without waiting to get coat or hat, he rushed out.
" Go and get him," Helen cried to us, and we followed
him as fast as we could. When I got out he had
reached the gate, and was fumbling at the catch.
" Hold on, Don, where are you going? " I cried.
" To hell! to hell! to hell! " My dear chap, that cry
of his made me believe in hell; for, if lost spirits cry
when the devils get hold of them, they will cry like
that. It was the most unearthly, horrible sound I
have ever heard, and may God save me from hearing
the like again.

Next day I tried to see Betty, but it was no use, she
would see no one. And soon after I heard she was ill,
typhoid fever. It had been working on her for some
time. There was almost no hope from the very first.
She became delirious at once, and in her raving kept
calling on The Don for forgiveness. Your mother was
a great help to them, relieving the nurse. They all
seemed to depend upon her. Of course, I was in and
out every day, and brought reports to The Don, who
haunted our house day and night. I never saw a fellow suffer like that. He slept hardly any, ate nothing
at all, but wandered about the town, spending most of
his time at Hooper's when he was not with us.

After the delirium passed Betty asked for me.
When I saw her looking so white and thin—you would
think you could see through her hands—I tell you it
broke me all up. She beckoned me to her, and when
I bent over her she whispered: " Find The Don and

bring him." At first her mother refused, saying he
should never come with her consent. It was mighty
hard, I tell you. But the afternoon of the same day
Helen came flying over to tell us that the doctor had
said there was only a very slight chance for Betty,
and that if her mother persisted in her refusal he
would not be responsible for the consequences, that her
mother had yielded, and I was to bring The Don. I
tell you, I made time down to his rooms, and brought
him to the house.

There was no one in the room but the nurse and the
doctor when he entered. She was expecting us, and
as we entered she opened her eyes and asked, " Is he
here? " The nurse beckoned him to approach, and
The Don came and knelt at her bed. He was very
steady and quiet. She put out her hand and drew him
toward her. She was the calmest of us all. " I want
you to forgive me, Don," she said, and her voice was
wonderfully clear. Poor chap, he went all to pieces
for a minute or two and, holding her fingers, kissed
them over and over again. " I want you to forgive
me, Don," she said again. " I thought I was better
than God." The poor fellow could only keep kissing
her fingers. " My lips, Don, my lips," and The Don
kissed her on the lips twice, murmuring in a broken
voice, " My darling, my love, my love."

Then she looked up and smiled that old smile of
hers—you remember, so bright and so merry? By
Jove, it broke me all up. And she said: " Now we
are all right, aren't we? " The doctor came and
touched The Don. " No, doctor," she said, " I am

quite quiet. See, I am going to sleep. I want you to stay there, Don. Good-night."

Mrs. Fairbanks and Helen came in. Helen gave The Don her hand, but Mrs. Fairbanks paid no attention to him. Betty opened her eyes, saw her mother and smiled. "Dear mother," she said, "see, there's Don." Mrs. Fairbanks hesitated slightly, then reached out her hand across the bed. "Thank you, dear mother," Betty said. "You must be good to him." Then after a little while she said dreamily, like a tired child: "God forgives us all, and we must forgive." She let her eyes rest on The Don's face. "Good-night, Don, dear," she said, "I am going to sleep."

That was her last word, Shock. Just think of it— Betty's last word. I cannot realise it at all.

I wish my story ended there, but it does not. For a time we sat there, the doctor hoping that a turn for the better had come, but in about an hour the nurse noticed a change, and called him. He came quickly, felt her pulse, injected something or other into her arm. She opened her eyes. You remember how she would open those lovely brown eyes of hers when anything surprised her. Well, she opened them just that way, smiled brightly on one and then another, let her eyes rest on The Don, gave a little sigh and closed them, and they never opened again. "She is gone," the doctor said, and we all crowded near. "Yes, she is gone," he said again.

Then The Don stood up, and putting out his hand to Mrs. Fairbanks, said: "Mrs. Fairbanks, I want to thank you for allowing me to come." But she drew herself away from him, refusing to touch his hand, and motioning him off.

Poor chap! He turned back to the bed, kneeled down, touched the soft brown hair with his hands, kissed the fingers again, and then without a word went out. If anyone can tell me what that woman's heart is made of, I would like to know.

The day of the funeral The Don brought me a little bunch of lilies of the valley, saying, " It is for her." I gave them to Helen, and I saw them afterwards in the hands that lay folded across her breast.

I have not seen him since, but Hooper tells me he said he was going out to you. I hope to Heaven he will not go bad. I don't think he will. Of course, he feels very bitterly about Lloyd and Mrs. Fairbanks.

Now, that is all my story. It makes a great difference to all our set here, but I will tell you what I have told no living soul, and that is, that the world will never be the same to me again. I am not much given to sentiment, as you know, and nobody ever suspected it. I do not think she did herself. But I loved that little girl better than my life, and I would have given my soul for her any day.

I know you will feel this terribly. How often I have wished that you could have been with us. The best I could do was to send you this wretched, incoherent scrawl.

Your friend as ever,

Brown.

P. S.—Do you know anything about the British-American Gold and Silver Mining Company, or something like that?   There is a chap here, manager or director, or something.   Ambherg, I think his name is. He speaks as if he knew you, or knew something about you.   He is a great friend of the Fairbanks.   Lots of money, and that sort of thing.   I did not like the way he spoke about you.   I felt like giving him a smack.   Do you know him, or anything about the company?

Your mother has not been very well since Betty's death.   I think she found the strain pretty heavy. She has caught a little cold, I am afraid.        B.

Brown's letter did for Shock what nothing else could have done: it turned his mind away from himself and his sorrow.   Not that he was in any danger of morbid brooding over his loss, or of falling into that last and most deplorable of all human weaknesses, self-pity, but grief turns the heart in upon itself, and tends to mar the fine bloom of an unselfish spirit.

As he finished reading Brown's letter Shock's heart was filled with love and pity for his friend.   " Poor fellow! " he said.   " I wonder where he is now.   His is a hard lot indeed."   And as he read the letter over and over his pity for his friend deepened, for he realised that in his cup of sorrow there had mingled the gall of remorse and the bitterness of hate.

In another week two other letters came, each profoundly affecting Shock and his life.   One was from Helen, giving a full account of his mother's illness and death, telling how beautifully the Superintendent had taken part in the funeral service, and preserving for her son those last precious messages of love and gratitude, of faith and hope, which become the immortal treasures of the bereaved heart. As he read Helen's letter Shock caught a glimpse of the glory of that departing. Heaven came about him, and the eternal things, that by reason of the nearness of the material world too often become shadowy, took on a reality that never quite left him. Where his mother was henceforth real things must be.

The letter closed with a few precious sentences of love and sympathy from Helen, but in these Shock, reading with his heart in his eyes, and longing for more than he could rightly find in them, thought he could detect a kind of reserve, a reserve which he could not interpret, and he laid down the letter with painful uncertainty. Was her love more than she cared to tell, or was it less than she knew he would desire?

From Helen's letter Shock turned to Mrs. Fairbanks' and read:

My Dear Mr. Macgregor:

We all deeply sympathise with you in your great loss, as I know you will with us in our grief. We can hardly speak of it yet. It is so new and so terribly sudden that we have not been able fully to realise it.

My great comfort in this terrible sorrow is my daughter Helen. Mr. Lloyd, too, has proved himself a true friend. Indeed, I do not know what we should have done without him. We are more and more com-

ing to lean upon him.    You will not have heard yet
that we have been so greatly attracted by Mr. Lloyd's
preaching, and influenced by our regard for him personally, that we have taken sittings in the Park
Church.

Helen, I am glad to say, is beginning to take an
interest in the church and its work, and as time goes
on I think her interest will grow.    I should be glad
indeed that it should be so, for our relations with Mr.
Lloyd are very close; and, in fact, I may tell you what
is yet a secret, that he has intimated to me his desire
to make Helen his wife.    Helen is very favourably disposed to him, and all our circle of friends would re-
joice in this as an ideal marriage.    Mr. Lloyd belongs
to her own set in society, is a gentleman of culture and
high character, and in every way suitable.    As for
myself, in my loneliness I could not endure the thought
of losing my only daughter, at all, and her marriage
would be a great blow to me were it not that her home
is to be so close at hand.

There is one thing, however, about which Helen is
sensitive.    She cannot rid herself of a feeling that she
is in a manner bound to you on account of her foolish
and impetuous words, uttered under the excitement of
your departure; but I am sure you would never think
of holding her because of those words, uttered in a
moment of great feeling, and I also feel sure that you
would not in any way interfere with her happiness, or
do anything that would hinder the consummation of a
marriage so eminently suitable in every way.

We hear of you and of your work occasionally.    It

must be a terrible country, and a very depressing life. The loneliness and isolation must be well-nigh overwhelming. I am sure you have all our sympathy. I suppose work of this kind must be done, and it is a good thing that there are men of such rugged strength and such courage as you have, who seem to be fitted for this kind of work.

Now, my dear Mr. Macgregor, in your answer I think that a few words of assurance to Helen on the points I have suggested would be greatly appreciated, and would do much to remove difficulties that now stand in the way of her happiness and mine.

Yours very sincerely,

E. FAIRBANKS.

It was then that Shock drank to the dregs his full cup of bitter sorrow. The contrasts suggested by Mrs. Fairbanks' letter stood out vividly before him. He thought of Helen's beautiful home, where she was surrounded with all the luxuries of a cultured life; he thought of her circle of friends, of the life work to which, as Lloyd's wife, she would be permitted to take up; he thought, too, of her mother's claim upon her. And then he looked about upon his bare room, with its log walls, its utter absence of everything that suggested refinement; he thought of the terrible isolation that in these days had become so depressing even to himself; he thought of all the long hours of weary yearning for the sight and touch of all that he held dear, and for the sake of the girl to whom he had given his heart's love in all its unsullied purity and in

all its virgin freshness he made his decision.  He took
up his cross, and though his heart bled he pressed his
lips upon it.

His letter to Mrs. Fairbanks was brief and clear.

" I thank you for your sympathy," he wrote, " and
I grieve with you in your great sorrow.

" In regard to what you write concerning Miss
Helen, you have made yourself perfectly clear, and I
wish to repeat now what I said on the morning of my
leaving home: that Miss Helen is to consider herself
in no sense bound to me.  She is perfectly free, as
free as if she had not spoken.  I fully realise the
possibility of mistaking one's feelings under the stress
of such emotional excitement.  The sphere of work
opening out before her is one in every way suited to
her, and one in which she will find full scope for her
splendid powers of heart and mind, and I shall be
glad to know that her happiness is assured.  At the
same time, truth demands that I should say that my
feelings toward her have not changed, nor will they
ever change ; and, while I cannot ask her to share a life
such as mine, I shall never cease to love her."

In Shock's preaching, and in his visitation of his
people, a new spirit made itself felt.  There was no
less energy, but there was an added sweetness, and a
deeper sympathy.  He had entered upon the way of
the Cross, and the bruising of his heart distilled all its
tenderness in word and deed.  His preaching was
marked by a new power, a new intensity ; and when,

after the evening service, they gathered about the organ to spend an hour in singing their favourite hymns, then most of all they were conscious of the change in him. The closer they drew toward him the more tender did they find his heart to be.

The loneliness of the days that followed was to Shock unspeakable. There was no one to whom he could unburden himself. His face began to show the marks of the suffering within. Instead of the ruddy, full, round, almost boyish appearance, it became thin and hard, and cut with deep lines.

The doctor, who now made his home in Loon Lake, became anxious about his friend, but he was too experienced and too skilled a physician to be deceived as to the cause of Shock's changed appearance.

" It is not sickness of the body," he remarked to Ike, who was talking it over with him, " but of the mind, and that, my friend, is the most difficult to treat."

" Well," said Ike, " when I hear him speak in meetin', and see him git on one of them smiles of his, I come purty nigh makin' a fool of myself. I guess I'll have to quit goin' to church."

" No, I do not think you will quit, Ike, my boy," said the doctor. " You have become thoroughly well inoculated. You could not, if you tried."

" Well, I surmise it would be difficult, but I wish somethin' would happen."

# XVIII

## THE DON'S RECOVERY

IKE had his wish; for, when one day his business took him to the Fort, the stage brought a stranger asking the way to Mr. Macgregor's house, and immediately Ike undertook to convoy him thither. It was The Don.

Shock's shout of welcome did Ike good, but the meeting between the two men no one saw. After the first warm greeting Shock began to be aware of a great change in his friend. He was as a man whose heart has been chilled to the core, cold, hard, irresponsive. Toward Shock himself The Don was unchanged in affection and admiration, but toward all the world he was a different man from the one Shock had known in college days.

In Shock's work he was mildly interested, but toward all that stood for religion he cherished a feeling of bitterness amounting to hatred. True, out of respect he attended Shock's services, but he remained unmoved through all; so that, after the first joy in his friend's companionship, the change in him brought Shock a feeling of pain, and he longed to help him.

" We will have to get him to work," he said to the doctor, to whom he had confided The Don's history in part, not omitting the great grief that had fallen upon him.

"A wise suggestion," replied the doctor, who had been attracted by his young brother in the profession, " a wise suggestion. This country, however, is painfully free from all endemic or epidemic diseases."

" Well, doctor, you know we ought to get that hospital going in the Pass. Let us talk it over with him."

At the first opportunity Shock set forth his plans for the physical and moral redemption of the lumbermen and miners of the Pass.

"I have seen the most ghastly cuts and bruises on the chaps in the lumber camps," he said, " and the miners are always blowing themselves up, and getting all sorts of chest troubles, not to speak of mountain fever, rheumatism, and the like. There is absolutely no place for them to go. Hickey's saloon is vile, noisy, and full of bugs. Ugh! I'll never forget the night I put in there. I can feel them yet. And besides, Hickey has a gang about him that make it unsafe for any man to go there in health, much less in sickness. Why, the stories they tell are perfectly awful. A fellow goes in with his month's pay. In one night his fifty or sixty dollars are gone, no one knows how. The poor chap is drunk, and he cannot tell. When a prospector comes down from the hills and sells a prospect for a good figure, from a hundred to five hundred dollars, and sometimes more, these fellows get about him and roll him. In two weeks he is kicked out, half dead. Oh, Hickey is a villain, and

he is in league with the *red-light* houses, too.  They
work together, to the physical and moral damnation
of the place.  We want a clean stopping-place, a
club-room, and above everything else a hospital.  Why,
when the miners and lumbermen happen to get off the
same night the blood flows, and there is abundant
practice for any surgeon for a week or so."

"Sounds exciting," said The Don, mildly interested.
"Why don't you go up, doctor?"

"It is not the kind of practice I desire.  My tastes
are for a gentler mode of life.  The dangers of the
Pass are too exciting for me.  They are a quaint people," the doctor continued, "primitive in their ideas
and customs, pre-historic, indeed, in their practice of
our noble art.  I remember an experience of mine,
some years ago now, which made a vivid impression
upon me at the time, and indeed, I could not rid myself of the effects for many days, for many days."

"What was that, doctor?" enquired Shock, scenting a story.

"Well, it is a very interesting tale, a very interesting tale.  Chiefly so as an illustration of how, in
circumstances devoid of the amenities of civilised life,
the human species tends toward barbarism.  A clear
case of reversion to type.  There was a half-breed
family living in the Pass, by the name of Goulais, and
with the family lived Goulais' brother, by name Antoine, or, if you spelled it as they pronounced it, it
would be 'Ontwine.'  The married one's name was
Pierre.  Antoine was a lumberman, and in the pursuit of his avocation he caught a severe cold, which

induced a violent inflammation of the bowels, causing very considerable distension and a great deal of pain. Being in the neighbourhood attending some cases of fever, I was induced by some friends of the Goulais to call and see the sick man.

"The moment I opened the door I was met by a most pungent odour, a most pungent odour. Indeed, though I have experienced most of the smells that come to one in the practice of our profession, this odour had a pungency and a nauseating character all its own. Looking into the room I was startled to observe the place swimming with blood, literally swimming with blood. Blood on the floor, blood upon the bed, and dripping from it.

"'What does this mean? Is someone being murdered? Whence this blood?'

"'Non! non!' exclaimed Mrs. Goulais. "There is no one keel. It is one cat blood.'

"Approaching the bed to obtain a nearer view of the patient, I discovered the cause. Turning down the bed quilt to make an examination, you may imagine my surprise and horror to observe a ghastly and bloody object lying across the abdomen of the sick man. A nearer examination revealed this to be an immense cat which had been ripped up from chin to tail, and laid warm and bleeding, with all its appurtenances, upon the unhappy patient. All through the day the brother, Pierre, had been kept busily engaged in hunting up animals of various kinds, which were to be excised in this manner and applied as a poultice.

" In uncivilised communities the animal whose healing virtues are supposed to be most potent is the cat,
and the cure is most certainly assured if the cat be
absolutely black, without a single white hair.   In this
community, however, deprived of many of the domestic
felicities, the absence of cats made it necessary for
poor Pierre to employ any animal on which he could
lay his hands; so, throughout the day, birds and beasts,
varied in size and character, were offered upon this
altar.   The cat which I discovered, however, was evidently that upon which their hopes most firmly rested;
for, upon the failure of other animals, recourse would
be had to the cat, which had been kept in reserve.
The state of preservation suggested this.

" A very slight examination of the patient showed
me that there was practically no hope of his recovery,
and that it would be almost useless in me to attempt
to change the treatment, and all the more that I should
have to overcome not only the prejudices of the patient and of his sister-in-law, but also of his very able-
bodied brother, whose devotion to his own peculiar
method of treatment amounted to fanaticism.   However, I determined to make an attempt.   I prepared
hot fomentations, removed the cat, and made my first
application.   But no sooner had I begun my treatment than I heard Pierre returning with a freshly
slaughtered animal in his hand.   The most lively
hope, indeed, triumph, was manifest in his excited
bearing.   He bore by the tail an animal the character
of which none of us were in doubt from the moment
Pierre appeared in sight.   It was the mephitis me-

phitica, that mephitine musteloid carnivore with which none of us desire a close acquaintance, which announces its presence without difficulty at a very considerable distance; in short, the animal vulgarly known as the skunk.

"'Voila!' exclaimed Pierre, holding the animal up for our admiration. 'Dis feex him queek.'

"'Ah! Mon Dieu!' exclaimed his wife, covering her face with her apron. But, whether from devotion to his art or from affection for his brother, Pierre persisted in carrying out his treatment. He laid the animal, cleft and pungently odorous, upon the patient. Needless to say, I surrendered the case at once."

The doctor's manner of telling the story was so extremely droll that both The Don and Shock were convulsed with laughter.

"Yes, they need a hospital, I should say," said The Don, when they had recovered.

"Well," said Shock, "we shall go up and have a look at it."

The result of their visit to the Pass was that within a few weeks a rough log building was erected, floored, roofed in, chinked with moss, and lined with cotton, lumbermen and miners willingly assisting in the work of building.

The Don became much interested in the whole enterprise. He visited the various lumber camps, laid the scheme before the bosses and the men, and in a short time gathered about two hundred dollars for furnishing and equipment.

Shock left him to carry out the work alone, but after two weeks had passed he was surprised to receive a message one day that the young doctor was cutting things loose up in the Pass. With a great fear at his heart Shock rode up the next day.

The first man whom he met in the little, straggling village was Sergeant Crisp of the North-West Mounted Police, a man of high character, and famed in the Territories alike for his cool courage and unimpeachable integrity.

" Up to see the young doctor? " was the Sergeant's salutation. " You will find him at Nancy's, I guess," pointing to where a red light shone through the black night. " Do you want me along? "

" No, thank you," said Shock. " I think I had better go alone."

For a moment he hesitated.

" How does one go in? " he enquired.

" Why, turn the handle and walk right in," said the Sergeant, with a laugh. " You don't want to be bashful there."

With a sickening feeling of horror at his heart Shock strode to the red-light door, turned the handle, and walked in.

In the room were a number of men, and two or three women in all the shameless dishabille of their profession. As Shock opened the door a young girl, with much of her youthful freshness and beauty still about her, greeted him with a foul salutation.

Shock shrank back from her as if she had struck him in the face. The girl noticed the action, came

nearer to him, and offered him her hand.   Shock, over-
coming his feeling of shame, took the hand offered
him, and holding it for a moment, said:   " My dear
girl, this is no place for you.   Your home waits for
you.   Your Saviour loves you."

In the noise that filled the room no one save the girl
herself heard his words; but two or three men who
knew Shock well, amazed at his appearance in that
place, exclaimed:   " It's the preacher! "

Nancy, the keeper of the house, who was sitting at
one of the tables gambling with some men, sprang to
her feet and, seeing Shock, poured out a torrent of foul
blasphemy.

" Get out of this house!   Get out, I say!   You've
no business here.   Go, blank your blank soul!   Take
yourself out of this! "

She worked herself into a raging fury.   Shock
stood quietly looking at her.

" Here, Tom! Pat!   Put this blank, blank out, or
you'll go yourselves.   What do I keep you for? "

Three or four men, responding to her call, approached Shock.

Meantime The Don, who had been sitting at one of
the tables with three others, a pile of money before
him, stood gazing in amazement at Shock, unable to
believe his eyes.

As the men approached Shock The Don came
forward.

" Stop! " he said.   " This man is my friend."

" Friend or no friend," shrieked Nancy, beside herself with rage, " out he goes.   He called me names in

this town. He threatened to drive me out of the town."

"Come, Don," said Shock, ignoring Nancy. "I want you."

"Wait one moment and I am with you," replied The Don, going back to the table where he had been sitting. "We will finish this game again, gentlemen," he said. "Hickey, that's my money. Hand it over."

"You lie!" said Hickey. "Curse you for a blank, blank swell! You can't come that game over us. It aint your money, anyway, and you know it. That's money you raised for the hospital. Come on, boys, let's clean them out. They don't belong to us."

With these words he sprang at The Don, but The Don's training in the 'Varsity gymnasium had not been in vain, and he met Hickey with a straight left-hander that sent him into the corner upon his shoulders, with his feet in the air.

Simultaneously with Hickey's atttack, Nancy, shrieking "Kill him! kill him!" flew at Shock, and fastening her fingers in his hair dragged his head downward. Taking advantage of this attack a man from the crowd rushed in and struck him a heavy blow on the neck, and as he was falling kicked him full in his face. Immediately another, jumping on Shock's prostrate form, began kicking him savagely with his heavy calked boots.

"Give it to him!" yelled Nancy, dancing about like a fiend.

"Stop! Stop! You have killed him!" shrieked

the young girl, Nellie by name, throwing herself upon Shock and covering him with her body.

"Get up, you blank fool!" yelled Nancy, seizing her by the hair.

At this moment, however, The Don, freed from Hickey, sprang to Shock's side, seized Nancy by the back of the neck and hurled her across the room, caught the man who was still trying to kick Shock to death, by the throat, and holding him at half arm struck him a terrific blow and threw him like a log against his companion, who came rushing to his assistance.

Meantime Nancy, still shrieking her refrain, "Kill him! kill him!" was dragging forward Hickey, who had partially recovered from The Don's blow, to renew the attack.

"Come on, you cowards!" she cried to the other men. "What are you afraid of? Come on."

Stung by her taunts the men, led by Hickey, prepared to rush, when the door opened and Sergeant Crisp appeared. Immediately the men who had attacked Shock vanished through the back door.

"Hickey, I want you. Stand where you are. You too, Nancy, and every man of you. What's this? Someone hurt? Why, it's the preacher. This may be serious," he continued, drawing his revolver. "Don't move. Not a man of you. What does this mean?" he asked, addressing The Don.

"My friend there," said The Don, "came for me. We were going out when they attacked us."

"Go and get help," replied the Sergeant. "We

will carry him to the hospital. You would, eh?" to one of the men who started for the door. "Here, put up your hands. Quick!" There was a flash and a click, and the man stood handcuffed.

In a few moments The Don came back with help, and they carried Shock, groaning and bleeding, to the hospital, while the Sergeant, putting a man in charge of Nancy and her gang, accompanied The Don.

In an agony of remorseful solicitude for his friend, and cursing himself for his folly, The Don directed the movements of the bearers.

In the darkness behind them came the girl Nellie, following to the door of the hospital.

"What are *you* after?" said Sergeant Crisp sharply. "We don't want you here."

"I want to see the doctor," she said earnestly.

"Well?" said The Don, facing round to her.

"Let me nurse him," she said in a hurried, timid voice. "I have had training. You can depend upon me."

The Don hesitated, glancing at her dishevelled, gaudy attire, painted cheeks, and frowsy hair.

"Well," he said, "you may come."

The girl disappeared, and in a very few minutes returned dressed modestly and quietly, the paint and pencilling washed from her face, her hair smoothed behind her ears. The Don looked her over, and nodding approval said: "That is better. Now, hold the light for me."

His examination revealed serious injuries about the head and face, three ribs broken, one piercing the lungs. With Nellie's assistance he managed to dress the wounds and set the broken bones before Shock regained full consciousness.

As they were finishing Shock opened his eyes and fixed them enquiringly upon The Don's face.

"Well, how do you feel, old chap? Pretty sore, I guess," enquired The Don.

Shock tried to speak, but his attempt ended in a groan. Still his eyes remained fastened enquiringly upon The Don's face. The Don bent over him.

"The money, Don," he said with great difficulty. "Hospital?"

The Don groaned. He understood only too well; and unable to escape the insisting eyes, replied: "Yes, Shock. But I will make it all right. Hickey has it now."

Shock closed his eyes for a few minutes, and then, opening them again, compelled The Don's attention.

"Send for Ike," he whispered. "Right away."

Next day Ike appeared in a cold, white rage at The Don. He had got the whole story from the messenger, and blamed no one but The Don.

As Shock's eyes rested upon Ike's lean, hard face, bent over him so anxiously, he smiled a glad welcome.

"Don't look like that, Ike," he said. "I'll soon be fit."

"Why, you just bet!" said Ike, with a loud laugh, deriding all anxiety.

"Ike," whispered Shock. Ike bent over him. "I want two hundred dollars at once. Don't tell."

Without a word of questioning Ike nodded, saying:

" In half an hour, I guess." But in less time he appeared and, slipping the roll of bills under Shock's
pillow, said: " It's all there."

" Good old boy," said Shock, trying to offer his
hand.

Ike took his hand carefully. " Is there anything
else? " he said, his voice grave and hoarse.

" No, old boy," said Shock. " Thank you."

" Then," said Ike, " you'll keep quieter without me,
I guess. I'll be on hand outside." And with a nod he
strode out of the room, his face working with grief and
rage.

For a week Ike remained at the Pass in hourly at-
tendance at the hospital, looking in at every chance
upon the sick man. In Shock's presence he carried an
exaggerated air of cheerful carelessness, but outside
he went about with a face of sullen gloom. Toward
The Don, with whom he had previously been on most
friendly terms, he was wrathfully contemptuous, disdaining even a word of enquiry for his patient, pre-
ferring to receive his information from the nurse. In
Ike's contempt, more than in anything else, The Don
read the judgment of honourable men upon his conduct, and this deepened to a degree almost unendurable
his remorse and self-loathing.

One morning, when the report was not so favourable,
Ike stopped him with the question: " Will he git
better? "

" Well," said The Don gloomily, " I have not given
up hope."

" Look here," replied Ike, " I want you to listen to

me." His tone was quiet, but relentlessly hard. "If he don't, you'll talk to me about it."

The Don looked at him steadily.

"Would you kill me?" he asked, with a quiet smile.

"Well," drawled Ike slowly, "I'd try to."

"Thank you," said The Don. "That would save me the trouble." And, turning on his heel, he left the cowboy in a very puzzled state of mind.

But Shock did not die. His splendid constitution, clean blood, and wholesome life stood off the grim enemy, and after two weeks of terrible anxiety The Don began to hope, and insisted on the nurse allowing herself some relaxation from her long watch.

But as Shock grew stronger The Don's gloom deepened. He had determined that once his friend was fit for work again he would relieve him of the burden of his presence. He had only brought trouble and shame to the man who was his most trusted, almost his only friend.

Life looked black to The Don in those days. Lloyd's treachery had smitten him hard. Not only had it shaken his faith in man, but in God as well, for with him Lloyd had represented all that was most sacred in religion. Death, too, had robbed him of his heart's sole treasure, and in robbing him of this it had taken from him what had given worth to his life and inspiration to his work. Of what use now was anything he had left?

He was confronted, too, with the immediate results of his recent folly. The hospital funds, of which he was the custodian, had disappeared. He knew that

Hickey had robbed him of most of them, but in order to recover them he would have to acknowledge his crime of using them for his own ends. As he moved in and out among the men, too, he had caught murmurs of a charge of embezzlement that in his present condition filled him with shame and fear. If the thing could be staved off for a month he could make it right, but he knew well that the gang would give him as little respite as they could. Indeed, it was only Sergeant Crisp's refusal to entertain any formal charge while Shock's life was in danger, that had saved The Don so far. But while Sergeant Crisp had stood between him and his enemies thus far, he knew that a day of reckoning must come, for the Seregant was not a man to allow considerations of friendship to interfere with duty. With Sergeant Crisp duty was supreme.

But more than The Don was Shock anxious to have this matter of the hospital funds cleared up, and he only waited an opportunity to speak to The Don about it. The opportunity was forced on him unexpectedly.

One day, as he lay apparently asleep, the Sergeant called The Don into the next room. Through the paper and cotton partition their voices came quite clearly.

" I have been wanting to speak to you about a matter," the Sergeant said, with some degree of hesitation. " Hickey's friends are saying nasty things about you."

" What do you mean? " said The Don, knowing only too well.

" About the hospital funds, you know. In fact, they are saying——"

At this point the nurse came running in.

"Mr. Macgregor wants you, doctor, at once," she cried, and The Don hurried in to him.

"Go and tell the Sergeant to wait," Shock said to the nurse, and she went out leaving The Don alone with him.

"Don," said Shock, "I know all about it. Don't speak. Here," taking the roll of bills from under his pillow, "here is the hospital money. Quick! Don't ask questions now. Go to the Sergeant. Go! go!"

"Nothing wrong?" asked the Sergeant anxiously, when The Don had returned.

"Oh, no," said The Don. "Nothing serious. You were speaking about some hospital funds?"

"Why, yes, the fact is, they are—it's an ugly thing to say—they are charging you with misappropriation of those funds."

"Oh, they are?" said The Don, who had by this time got back his nerve. "Well, Sergeant, let them come on. The accounts will be ready. And, indeed, I shall be glad to turn over the funds to yourself now. Excuse me a moment." He went to his desk and brought out a pass book. "This shows all the subscriptions, about two hundred dollars, I think. And here," he said, drawing the bills out of his pocket, "you will find the whole amount."

"Not at all," said the Sergeant, "not at all, my dear fellow. I thought it right you should know—be prepared, you understand."

"Thank you, Sergeant," said The Don. "Any time my books can be seen. Good-bye."

The Don went in to Shock, sent the nurse out for a walk, shut the door, and then, returning to the bed, threw himself on his knees.

"Oh, Shock," he said, "this is too much. What can I say?"

"Nothing at all, old chap. Don't say anything. What is that between us? We have been through too many things together to have this bother us."

"Shock! Shock!" continued The Don, "I have been an awful fool, a blank, cursed fool!"

"Don't swear, old chap," said Shock.

"No, no, I won't, but I curse myself. I have been waiting for this chance to tell you. I don't want you to think too badly of me. This thing began in Hickey's saloon some days before that night. He was playing some fellows from the camp a skin game. I called him down and he challenged me. I took him up, and cleaned him out easily enough. You know my old weakness. The fever came back upon me, and I got going for some days. That night I was called to visit a sick girl at Nancy's. The gang came in, found me there, and throwing down their money dared me to play. Well, I knew it was play or fight. I took off my coat and went for them. They cleaned me out, I can't tell how. I could not get on to their trick. Then, determined to find out, I put up that—that other money, you know—and I was losing it fast, too, when you came in."

As Shock listened to The Don's story his face grew brighter and brighter.

"My dear fellow," he said in a tone of relief, "is

that all? Is that the whole thing? Tell me, as God hears you!"

"That's the whole story, as God hears me!" said The Don solemnly.

"Oh, thank God!" said Shock. "I thought—I was afraid——" He paused, unable to go on.

"What! You thought I had forgotten," cried The Don. "Well, I confess things did look bad. But I want to tell you I am clean, and may God kill me before I can forget! No, no woman shall ever touch my lips while I live. Do you believe me, Shock?"

Shock put out his hand. He was still too much moved to speak.

At length he said: "Nothing else matters, Don. I could not bear the other thing."

For some minutes the friends sat in silence.

"But, Don," said Shock at length, "you cannot go on this way. Your whole life is being ruined. You cannot draw off from God. You have been keeping Him at arm's length. This will not do."

"It is no use, Shock," said The Don bitterly. "My head is all right. I believe with you. But I cannot get over the feeling I have for that——" He broke off suddenly.

"I know, I know. I feel it, too, old chap, but after all, it is not worth while. And besides, Don,—forgive me saying this—if it had not been true about you he could not have hurt you, could he?"

The Don winced.

"I am not excusing him, nor blaming you," continued Shock eagerly, "but a man has got to be honest. Isn't that right?"

"Oh, yes, it is true enough, Shock. I was a beast, as you know, at that time in my life, but I had put it all past me, and I believed that God had forgiven me. And then those two raked it all up again, and broke my darling's heart, and drove me away, an outcast. He is a minister of the gospel, and she is a member of the Christian Church."

"Don," said Shock gravely, "that won't do. You are not fair."

The door opened quietly, and the nurse came in and sat down out of Shock's sight behind the bed.

"Now, Don, I want you to read for me that tale of the Pharisee and the woman who was a sinner. For my sake, mind you, as well as for yours, for I was wrong, too, on this matter. I confess I hated him, for I cannot help thinking that he has done me a great wrong, and I have found it hard enough to say the Lord's Prayer. Perhaps you had better read this letter so that you may understand."

He took from under his pillow Mrs. Fairbanks' letter and gave it to The Don, who read it in silence. Poor Shock! He was opening up wounds that none had ever seen, or even suspected, and the mere uncovering of them brought him keen anguish and humiliation.

As The Don read the letter he began to swear deep oaths.

"Stop, Don. You mustn't swear. Now listen to me. I think she has a perfect right to do as she has been doing. But—Lloyd "—Shock seemed to get the name out with difficulty,—" was my friend, and I think he has not been fair."

" Fair! " burst out The Don. " The low down villain! "

" But listen. The question with me has been how to forgive him, for I must forgive him or keep far from Him who has forgiven me, and that I cannot afford to do. Now read." And The Don took up the Bible from the little table beside Shock's bed, and read that most touching of all tales told of the Saviour of the sinful.

" ' Wherefore I say unto thee, her sins, which are many, are forgiven, for she loved much: but to whom little is forgiven, the same loveth little. And he said unto her, Thy sins are forgiven. Thy faith hath saved thee; go in peace.' "

As The Don finished reading, a sound of sobbing broke the silence in the room.

" Who is that? Is that you, Nell? " said Shock. " What is the matter, Nell? That is for you, too. Now we will have Don read it again." And once more, with great difficulty, The Don read the words, so exquisitely delicate, so divinely tender.

" That is for you, too, Nell," said Shock.

" For me? " she cried. " Oh, no, not for me! "

" Yes, Nell, my sister, it is for you."

" Oh," she cried, with a tempest of sobs, " don't call me that. It cannot be. I can never be clean again."

" Yes, Nell, He says it Himself. ' Her sins, which are many, are forgiven,' and He can make you clean as the angels. We all need to be made clean, and He has undertaken to cleanse us."

It was a very humble and chastened man that went out from Shock's presence that evening. Through the days of the week that followed The Don went about his work speaking little, but giving himself with earnestness and in a new spirit, more gentle, more sympathetic, to his ministry to the sick in the camps and shacks round about. But still the gloom was unlifted from his heart. Day by day, however, in response to Shock's request he would read something of the story of that great loving ministration to the poor, and sick, and needy, and of infinite compassion for the sinful and outcast, till one day, when Shock had been allowed for the first time to sit in his chair, and The Don was about to read, Shock asked for the story of the debtors, and after The Don had finished he took from his pocket Brown's letter and said: "Now, Don, forgive me. I am going to read something that will make you understand that story," and he read from Brown's letter the words that described Betty's last hour.

The Don sat white and rigid until Shock came to the words, "God forgives us all, and we must forgive," when his self-control gave way and he abandoned himself to the full indulgence of his great sorrow.

"It was not to grieve you, Don," said Shock, after his friend's passion of grief had subsided. "It was not to grieve you, you know, but to show you what is worth while seeing—the manner of God's forgiveness;

for as she forgave and took you to her pure heart again without fear or shrinking, so God forgives us. And, Don, it is not worth while, in the face of so great a forgiveness, to do anything else but forgive, and it is a cruel thing, and a wicked thing, to keep at a distance such love as that."

"No, no," said The Don, "it is not worth while. It is wicked, and it is folly. I will go back. I will forgive."

# XIX

## THE REGIONS BEYOND

THE visit of the Superintendent to a mission field varied according to the nature of the field and the character of the work done, between an inquisitorial process and a triumphal march. Nothing escaped his keen eye. It needed no questioning on his part to become possessed of almost all the facts necessary to his full information about the field, the work, the financial condition, and the general efficiency of the missionary. One or two points he was sure to make inquiry about. One of these was the care the missionary had taken of the outlying points. He had the eye of an explorer, which always rests on the horizon. The results of his investigations could easily be read in his joy or his grief, his hope or his disappointment, his genuine pride in his missionary or his blazing, scorching rebuke. The one consideration with the Superintendent was the progress of the work. The work first, the work last, the work always.

The announcement to Shock through his Convener, that the Superintendent purposed making a visit in the spring, filled him with more or less anxiety. He remembered only too well his failure at the Fort; he thought of that postscript in the Superintendent's

letter to his Convener; he knew that even in Loon
Lake and in the Pass his church organization was not
anything to boast of; and altogether he considered
that the results he had to show for his year's labour
were few and meagre.

The winter had been long and severe. In the Pass
there had been a great deal of sickness, both among
the miners and among the lumbermen. The terrible
sufferings these men had to endure from the cold and
exposure, for which they were all too inadequately
prepared, brought not only physical evils upon them,
but reacted in orgies unspeakably degrading.

The hospital was full. Nell had been retained by
The Don as nurse, and although for a time this meant
constant humiliation and trial to her, she bore herself
with such gentle humility, and did her work with such
sweet and untiring patience, that the men began to
regard her with that entire respect and courteous consideration that men of their class never fail to give to
pure and high-minded women.

The Don was full of work. He visited the camps,
treated the sick and wounded there, and brought down
to the hospital such as needed to be moved thither,
and gradually won his way into the confidence of all
who came into touch with him. Even Ike, after long
hesitation and somewhat careful observation, gave him
once more his respect and his friendship.

The doctor was kept busy by an epidemic of diph-
theric croup that had broken out among the children
of the Loon Lake district, and began to take once
more pride in his work, and to regain his self-respect

and self-control. He took especial pride and joy in the work of The Don at the Pass, and did all he could to make the hospital and the club room accomplish all the good that Shock had hoped for them.

But though the hospital and club room had done much for the men of the Pass, there was still the ancient warfare between the forces that make for manhood and those that make for its destruction. Hickey still ran his saloon, and his gang still aided him in all his nefarious work. Men were still " run " into the saloon or the red-light houses, there to be " rolled," and thence to be kicked out, fit candidates for the hospital. The hospital door was ever open for them, and whatever the history, the physical or moral condition of the patient, he was received, and with gentle, loving ministration tended back to health, and sent out again to camp or mine, often only to return for another plunge into the abyss of lust and consequent misery; sometimes, however, to set his feet upon the upward trail that led to pure and noble manhood. For The Don, while he never preached, took pains to make clear to all who came under his charge the results of their folly and their sin to body and to mind, as well as to soul, and he had the trick of forcing them to take upon themselves the full responsibility for their destiny, whether it was to be strength, soundness of mind, happiness, heaven, or disease, insanity, misery, hell. It was heart-breaking work, for the disappointments were many and bitter, but with now and then an achievement of such splendid victory as gave hope and courage to keep up the fight.

At Loon Lake during the winter Shock had devoted himself to the perfecting of his church organization. A *Communion Roll* had been formed and on it names entered of men and women whose last church connection reached back for ten or fifteen or twenty years, and along with those the names of some who had never before had a place in that mystic order of the saints of God. And, indeed, with some of these Shock had had his own difficulty, not in persuading them to offer themselves as candidates, but in persuading himself to assume the responsibility of accepting them. To Shock with his Highland training it was a terribly solemn step to " come forward." The responsibility assumed, bulked so largely in the opinion of those whom Shock had always regarded as peculiarly men of God, that it almost, if not altogether, obliterated the privilege gained.

When a man like Sinclair, whose reputable character and steady life seemed to harmonize with such a step, he had little difficulty; and had the Kid, with his quick intelligence, his fineness of spirit and his winning disposition, applied for admission, Shock would have had no hesitation in receiving him. But the Kid, although a regular attendant on the services, and though he took especial delight in the Sabbath evening gatherings after service, had not applied, and Shock would not think of bringing him under pressure; and all the more because he had not failed to observe that the Kid's interest seemed to be more pronounced and more steadfast in those meetings in which Marion's singing was the feature. True, this peculiarity the Kid shared with many others of the young men in the district, to Shock's very considerable embarrassment, though to the girl's innocent and frank delight; and it is fair to say that the young men, whom Shock had put upon their honor in regard to one who was but a child, never by word or look failed in that manly and considerate courtesy that marks the noble nature in dealing with the weak and unprotected.

The truth about the Kid was that that gay young prince of broncho busters, with his devil-may-care manner and his debonair appearance, was so greatly sought after, so flattered and so fêted by the riotous and reckless company at the Fort, of which the Inspector and his wife were the moving spirits, that he was torn between the two sets of influences that played upon him, and he had not yet come to the point of final decision as to which kingdom he should seek.

It was with Ike and men like Ike, however, that Shock had his greatest difficulty, for when the earnest appeal was made for men to identify themselves with the cause that stood for all that was noblest in the history of the race, and to swear allegiance to Him who was at once the ideal and the Saviour of men, Ike without any sort of hesitation came forward and to Shock's amazement, and, indeed, to his dismay, offered himself. For Ike was regarded through all that south country as the most daringly reckless of all the cattlemen, and never had he been known to weaken either in " takin' his pizen," in " playin' the limit " in poker, or in " standin' up agin any man that thought he could dust his pants." Of course he was " white." Everyone acknowledged that. But just how far this quality of whiteness fitted him as a candidate for the communion table Shock was at a loss to say.

He resolved to deal with Ike seriously, but the initial difficulty in this was that Ike seemed to be quite unperplexed about the whole matter, and entirely unafraid. Shock's difficulty and distress were sensibly increased when on taking Ike over the " marks " of the regenerate man, as he had heard them so fully and searchingly set forth in the " Question Meetings " in the congregation of his childhood, he discovered that Ike was apparently ignorant of all the deeper marks, and what was worse, seemed to be quite undisturbed by their absence.

While Shock was proceeding with his examination he was exceedingly anxious lest he should reveal to Ike any suspicion as to his unfitness for the step he proposed to take. At the same time, he was filled with anxiety lest through any unfaithfulness of his on account of friendship a mistake in so solemn a matter should be made. It was only when he observed that Ike was beginning to grow uneasy under his somewhat searching examination, and even offered to withdraw his name, that Shock decided to cast to the winds all his preconceived notions of what constituted fitness for enrollment in the Church of the living God, and proceeded to ask Ike some plain, common sense questions.

" You are sure you want to join this church, Ike? "
" That's what," said Ike.

"Why do you want to join?"

"Well, you gave us a clear invite, didn't you?"

"But I mean, is it for my sake? Because I asked you?"

"Why, sure. I want to stand at your back."

Shock was puzzled. He tried another line of approach.

"Do you know, Ike, what you are joining?"

"Well, it's your church, you said."

"Supposing I was not here at all, would you join?"

"Can't say. Guess not."

Shock felt himself blocked again.

"Ike, do you think you are really fit to do this?"

"Fit? Well, you didn't say anything about bein' fit. You said if anyone was willin' to take it up, to stay with the game, to come on."

"Yes, yes, I know, Ike. I did say that, and I meant that," said Shock. "But, Ike, you know that the Apostle calls those who belong to the church 'saints of God.'"

"Saints, eh? Well, I ain't no saint, I can tell you that. Guess I'm out of this combination. No, sir, I ain't no paradox—paragon, I mean." Ike remembered the Kid's correction.

His disappointment and perplexity were quite evident. After hearing Shock's invitation from the pulpit it had seemed so plain, so simple.

His answer rendered Shock desperate.

"Look here, Ike, I am going to be plain with you. You won't mind that?"

"Wade right in."

" Well, you sometimes swear, don't you? "

" Yes, that's so. But I've pretty much quit, unless there's some extraordinary occasion."

" Well, you drink, don't you? "

" Why, sure. When I can git it, and git it good, which ain't easy in this country now."

" And you sometimes fight? "

" Well," in a tone almost of disappointment, "there ain't nobody wantin' to experiment with me in these parts any longer."

" And you gamble? Play poker for money, I mean? "

" Oh, well, I don't profess to be the real thing," replied Ike modestly, as if disclaiming an excellence he could hardly hope to attain, " but I ginerally kin stay some with the game."

" Now, Ike, listen to me. I'm going to give it to you straight."

Ike faced his minister squarely, looking him fair in the eyes.

" You have been doing pretty much as you like all along. Now, if you join the church you are swearing solemnly to do only what Jesus Christ likes. You give your word you will do only what you think He wants. You see? He is to be your Master."

" Yes," said Ike. " Yes, that's so. That's right."

" In everything, remember."

" Why, sure." That seemed quite simple to Ike.

" Swearing, drinking, fighting, gambling," Shock continued.

Ike hesitated.

"Why, you don't suppose He would mind a little thing like a smile with the boys now and then, or a quiet game of poker, do you?"

"What I say, Ike, is this—if you thought He did mind, would you quit?"

"Why, sure. You just bet! I said so."

"Well, Ike, supposing some one of those chaps from the Pass, say Hickey, should walk up and hit you in the face, what would you do?"

"What? Proceed to eddicate him. Preject him into next week. That is, if there was anything left."

Shock opened his Bible and read, " 'But I say unto you, That ye resist not evil; but whosoever shall smite thee on thy right cheek turn to him the other also.' That is what Jesus Christ says, Ike."

"He does, eh? Does it mean just that?" Ike felt that this was a serious difficulty.

"Yes, it means just that."

"Are all you fellers like that?"

This wrought in Shock sudden confusion.

"Well, Ike, I am afraid not, but we ought to be, and we aim to be."

"Well," said Ike slowly, "I guess I ain't made that way."

Then Shock turned the leaves of his Bible, and read the story of the cruel bruising of the Son of Man, and on to the words, "Father, forgive them." Ike had heard this story before, but he had never seen its bearing upon practical life.

"I say," he said, with reverent admiration in his voice, "He did it, didn't He? That's what I call pretty high jumpin', ain't it? Well," he continued, " I can't make no promises, but I tell you what, I'll aim at it. I will, honest. And when you see me weaken, you'll jack me up, won't you? You'll have to stay with me, for it's a mighty hard proposition."

Then Shock took his hands. " Ike, you are a better man than I am, but I promise you I will stay all I can with you. But there will be days when you will be all alone except that He will be with you. Now listen," and Shock, turning over the leaves of his Bible, read, " Lo, I am with you always," and a little further over and read again, " I can do all things through Christ that strengtheneth me."

" That is His solemn promise, Ike. He has promised to save us from our sins. Do you think you can trust Him to do that? "

" Why, sure," said Ike, as if nothing else was possible. " That's His game, ain't it? I guess He'll stay with it. He said so, didn't He? "

" Yes," said Shock, with a sudden exaltation of faith, " He said so, and He will stay with it. Don't you be afraid, Ike. He will see you through."

The Communion Roll when it was completed numbered some eighteen names, and of these eighteen none were more sorely pressed to the wall in God's battle than Ike, and none more loyally than he stayed with the game.

Owing to miscarriage in arrangements, when the Superintendent arrived at the Fort he was surprised to find no one to meet him. This had an appearance of carelessness or mismanagement that unfavorably

impressed the Superintendent as to the business capac-
ity of his missionary. He was too experienced a trav-
eller, however, in the remote and unformed districts
of the West, to be at all disconcerted at almost any
misadventure.

He inquired for Mr. Macfarren, and found him in
Simmons' store, redolent of bad tobacco and worse
whiskey, but quite master of his mental and physical
powers. The Superintendent had business with Mr.
Macfarren, and proceeded forthwith to transact it.

After his first salutation he began, "When I saw
you last, Mr. Macfarren, you professed yourself
keenly desirous of having services established by our
church here."

" Yes."

" Why this sudden change, represented by your
letter to the Committee, and the petition, which I
judge was promoted by yourself? I placed a man
here, with every expectation of success. How can
you explain this change in you and in the people you
represent? "

The Superintendent's bodily presence was anything
but weak, and men who could oppose him when at a
distance, when confronted with him found it difficult
to support their opposition. Macfarren found it so.
He began in an apologetic manner, "Well, Doctor,
circumstances have changed. Times have been none
too good. In fact, we are suffering from financial
stringency at present."

" Mr. Macfarren, be specific as to your reasons.
Your letter and your petition were instrumental in

persuading the Committee to a complete change of policy. This should not be without the very best of reasons."

"Well, as I was saying," answered Macfarren, "finances were——"

"Tut! tut! Mr. Macfarren. You do not all become poor in six months. Your cattle are still here. Your horses have suffered from no plague."

"Well," said Mr. Macfarren, "the people have become alienated."

"Alienated? From the church?"

"Well, yes. They seem to be satisfied with—to prefer, indeed, the Anglican services."

"Mr. Macfarren, do you mean to tell me that the Presbyterians of this country prefer any church to their own? I fear they are a different breed from those I have known, and unworthy to represent the church of their fathers."

"Well, the truth is, Doctor," said Macfarren, considerably nettled at the Superintendent's manner, "the people consider that they were not well treated in the supply you sent them."

"Ah! Now we have it. Well, let us be specific again. Is Mr. Macgregor not a good preacher?"

"No, he is not. He is not such a preacher as many of us have been accustomed to."

"By the way, Mr. Macfarren, what do your people pay toward this man's salary? Five hundred? Three hundred? We only asked you two hundred, and this you found difficult. And yet you expect a two-thousand-dollar preacher."

" Well, his preaching was not his only fault," said
Macfarren.  " He was totally unsuited to our people.
He was a man of no breeding, no manners, and in this
town we need a man——"

" Wait a moment, Mr. Macfarren.  You can put
up with his preaching? "

" Yes."

" Did he visit his people? "

" Yes, goodness knows, he did that enough."

" Was his character good?"

" Oh, certainly."

" Then I understand you to say that as a preacher
he was passable, as a pastor and as a man all that
could be desired? "

" Oh, yes, certainly.  But he was—well, if you have
met him you must know what I mean.  In short, he
was uncouth and boorish in his manners."

The Superintendent drew himself up, and his voice
began to burr in a way that his friends would have
recognized as dangerous.

" Boorish, Mr. Macfarren?  Let me tell you, sir,
that he is a Highland gentleman, the son of a Highland gentlewoman, and boorishness is impossible to
him."

" Well, that may be too strong, Doctor, but you do
not understand our society here.  We have a large
number of people of good family from the old country
and from the East, and in order to reach them we require a man who has moved in good society."

"Well, sir," said the Superintendent, "Jesus Christ
would not have suited your society here, for He was

a man of very humble birth, and moved in very low circles." And without further word he turned from Macfarren to greet Father Mike, who had entered the store.

"Delighted to see you again, Bishop," said Father Mike. "We are always glad to see you even though you are outside the pale."

"Depends upon which pale you mean, Father Mike," said the Superintendent, shaking him warmly by the hand.

"True, sir. And I, for one, refuse to narrow its limits to those of any existing organization."

"Your principles do you credit, sir," said the Superintendent, giving his hand an extra shake. "They are truly Scriptural, truly modern, and truly Western."

"But, Doctor, I want to ask you, if I may without impertinence, why did you do so great an injury to our community as to remove your missionary from us?"

"Ah, you consider that a loss, Father Mike?"

"Undoubtedly, sir. A great and serious loss. He was a high type of a man. I will quote as expressing my opinions, the words of a gentleman whose judgment would, I suppose, be considered in this community as final on all such matters—General Brady, sir. I think you know him. This is what I heard him say. 'He is an able preacher and a Christian gentleman.'"

"Thank you, sir. Thank you, sir," said the Superintendent. "I thank you for your warm apprecia-

tion of one whom, after short acquaintance, I regarded as you do."

It was Father Mike who drove the Superintendent
to Loon Lake next day, only to find Shock away from
home.

"We will inquire at the stopping-place," said
Father Mike.

"Let us see," said the Superintendent, who never
forgot a name or a face, "does Carroll keep that still?
He did five years ago."

"Yes, and here he is," said Father Mike. "Hello,
Carroll. Can you tell me where your minister is?"

"Be jabers, it's a search warrant you'll need for
him, I'm thinkin'. Ask Perault there. Perault, do
you know where the preacher is?"

"Oui. He's go 'way for prospect, sure."

"Prospecting?" inquired Father Mike.

"Oui," grinned Perault, "dat's heem, one prospector. Every day, every day he's pass on de trail,
over de hill, down de coulee, all overe."

"He does, eh?" said Father Mike, delighted at the
description of his friend. "What is he after?
Coal?"

"Coal!" echoed Perault with contempt. "Not
moche. He's go for find de peep'. He's dig 'em up
on de church, by gar."

"You see, Doctor," said Father Mike, "no one has
any chance here with your fellow. There's Carroll,
now, and Perault, they are properly Roman Catholic,
but now they are good Presbyterians."

"Bon, for sure. Eh, Carroll, mon garçon?"

" Bedad, an' it's thrue for ye," said Carroll.

It was no small tribute to Shock's influence that
the ancient feud between these two had been laid to
rest.

" Well, do you know when he will be home? " asked
Father Mike.

" I go for fin' out," said Perault, running into his
house, and returning almost immediately. " To-morrow for sure. Mebbe to-night."

" Well, Carroll, this is your minister's bishop. I
suppose you can look after him till Mr. Macgregor
comes home."

" An' that we can, sir. Come right in," said Carroll readily. " Anny friend of the Prospector, as we
call him, is welcome to all in me house, an' that he is."

That afternoon and evening the Superintendent
spent listening in the pauses of his letter writing to
the praises of the missionary, and to a description,
with all possible elaboration and ornament, of the
saving of little Patsey's life, in which even the doctor's
skill played a very subordinate part.

" An' there's Patsey himself, the craythur," said
Mrs. Carroll, " an' will he luk at his father or meself
when his riverince is by? An' he'll follie him out an'
beyant on that little pony of his."

The Superintendent made no remark, but he kept
quietly gathering information. In Perault's house
it was the same. Perault, Josie, and Marion sang in
harmony the praises of Shock.

Late at night Shock returned bringing the doctor
with him, both weary and spent with the long, hard

day's work. From Perault, who was watching for his return, he heard of the arrival of the Superintendent. He was much surprised and mortified that his Superintendent should have arrived in his absence, and should have found no one to welcome him.

"Tell Josie and Marion," he said to Perault, "to get my room ready," and, weary as he was, he went to greet his chief.

He found him, as men were accustomed to find him, busy with his correspondence. The Superintendent rose up eagerly to meet his missionary.

"How do you do, sir, how do you do? I am very glad to see you," and he gripped Shock's hand with a downward pull that almost threw him off his balance.

"I wish to assure you," said the Superintendent, when the greetings were over, "I wish to assure you," and his voice took its deepest tone, "of my sincere sympathy with you in your great loss. It was my privilege to be present at your mother's funeral, and to say a few words. You have a great and noble heritage in your mother's memory. She was beautiful in her life, and she was beautiful in death."

Poor Shock! The unexpected tender reference to his mother, the brotherly touch, and the vision that he had from the Superintendent's words of his mother, beautiful in death, were more than he could bear. His emotions overwhelmed him. He held the Superintendent's hand tight in his, struggling to subdue the sobs that heaved up from his labouring breast.

"I suppose," continued the Superintendent, giving him time to recover himself, "my last letter failed to reach you. I had expected to be here two weeks later, but I wrote changing my arrangements so as to arrive here to-day."

" No, sir," said Shock, " no letter making any change reached me. I am very sorry indeed, not to have met you, and I hope you were not much inconvenienced."

" Not at all, sir, not at all. Indeed, I was very glad to have the opportunity of spending a little time at the Fort, and meeting some of your friends. By the way, I met a friend of yours on my journey down, who wished to be remembered to you, Bill Lee of Spruce Creek. You remember him? "

" Oh, perfectly. Bill is a fine fellow," said Shock, enthusiastically.

" Yes, Bill has his points. He has quit whiskey selling, he said, and he wished that you should know that. He said you would know the reason why."

But Shock knew of no reason, and he only replied, " Bill was very kind to me, and I am glad to know of the change in him."

" Yes," continued the Superintendent, " and I spent some time at the Fort meeting with some of the people, but upon inquiries I am more puzzled than ever to find a reason for the withdrawal of our services, and I am still in the dark about it."

Shock's face flushed a deep red.

" I am afraid," he said, in a shamed and hesitating manner, " that I was not the right man for the place. I think I rather failed at the Fort."

" I saw Macfarren," continued the Superintendent,

ignoring Shock's remark. "He tried to explain, but seemed to find it difficult." The Superintendent omitted to say that he had heard from Father Mike what might have explained in a measure Macfarren's opposition. But Shock remained silent.

"Well," continued the Superintendent, "now that I am here, what do you wish me to do?"

"First," said Shock, "come over to my house. Come to the manse. Carroll will not mind."

The Superintendent put his papers together, and Shock, shouldering his valise and coat, led the way to the manse.

As they entered the big room the Superintendent paused to observe its proportions, noted the library shelves full of books, the organ in the corner, the pictures adorning the walls, and without much comment passed on upstairs to Shock's own room. But he did not fail to detect a note of pride in Shock's voice as he gave him welcome.

"Come in, come in and sit down. I hope you will be comfortable. It is rather rough."

"Rough, sir," exclaimed the Superintendent. "It is palatial. It is truly magnificent. I was quite unprepared for anything like this. Now tell me how was this accomplished?"

"Oh," said Shock, diffidently, "they all helped, and here it is."

"That is all, eh?"

And that was all Shock would tell. The rest of the story, however, the Superintendent heard from others. And so, throughout his whole visit the Superintendent found it impossible to get his missionary to tell of his own labours, and were it not that he carried an observant and experienced eye, and had a skilful and subtle inquisitorial method, he might have come and gone knowing little of the long, weary days and weeks of toil that lay behind the things that stood accomplished in that field.

It was the same at the Pass. There stood the hospital equipped, almost free from debt, and working in harmony with the camps and the miners. There, too, was the club room and the library.

" And how was all this brought about? " inquired the Superintendent.

" Oh, The Don and the doctor took hold, and the men all helped."

The Superintendent said nothing, but his eyes were alight with a kindly smile as they rested on his big missionary, and he took his arm in a very close grip as they walked from shack to shack.

All this time Shock was pouring into his Superintendent's ear tales of the men who lived in the mountains beyond the Pass. He spoke of their hardships, their sufferings, their temptations, their terrible vices and their steady degradation.

" And have you visited them? " inquired the Superintendent.

He had not been able to visit them as much as he would have liked, but he had obtained information from many of the miners and lumbermen as to their whereabouts, and as to the conditions under which they lived and wrought. Shock was talking to a man of like mind. The Superintendent's eye, like that of his missionary, was ever upon the horizon, and his desires ran far ahead of his vision.

It was from The Don that the Superintendent learned of all Shock's work in the past, and of all that had been done to counteract the terrible evils that were the ruin of the lumbermen and miners. Won by the Superintendent's sympathy, The Don unburdened his heart and told him his own story of how, in his hour of misery and despair, Shock had stood his friend and saved him from shame and ruin.

" Yes, sir," The Don concluded, " more than I shall ever be able to repay he has done for me, and," he added humbly, " if I have any hope for the future, that too I owe to him."

" You have cause to thank God for your friend, sir," said the Superintendent, " and he has no reason to be ashamed of his friend. You are doing noble work, sir, in this place, noble work."

A visit to the nearest lumber camp and mines, a public meeting in the hospital, and the Superintendent's work at the Pass for the time was done.

As he was leaving the building The Don called him into his private room.

" I wish to introduce you to our nurse," he said. " We think a great deal of her, and we owe much to her," and he left them together.

" I asked to see you," said Nellie, " because I want your advice and help. They need to have more nurses here than one, and no one will come while I am here."

The Superintendent gazed at her, trying to make

her out. She tried to proceed with her tale but failed, and, abandoning all reserve, told him with many tears the story of her sin and shame.

" And now," she said, " for the sake of the hospital and the doctor I must go away, and I want to find a place where I can begin again."

As the Superintendent heard her story his eyes began to glisten under his shaggy brows.

" My dear child," he said at length, " you have had a hard life, but the Saviour has been good to you. Come with me, and I will see what can be done. When can you come? "

" When the doctor says," she replied.

" Very well," said the Superintendent, " I shall arrange it with him," and that was the beginning of a new life for poor Nellie.

The last meeting of the Superintendent's visit was at Loon Lake, after the Sunday evening service. The big room was crowded with people gathered from the country far and near, from the Fort to the Pass, to hear the great man. And he was worth while hearing that day. His imagination kindled by his recent sight of the terrible struggle that men were making toward cleanness, and toward heaven and God, and the vision he had had through the eyes of his missionary of the regions beyond, caused his speech to glow and burn.

For an hour and more they listened with hearts attent, while he spoke to them of their West, its resources, its possibilities, and laid upon them their responsibility as those who were determining its future for the multitudes that were to follow. His appeal for men and women to give themselves to the service of God and of their country, left them thrilling with visions, hopes and longings.

In the meeting that always followed the evening service, the people kept crowding about him, refusing to disperse. Then the Superintendent began again.

"Your minister has been telling me much about the men in the mountains. He seems to have these men upon his heart."

"Sure," said Ike. "He's a regular prospector, he is."

"So I have heard, so I have heard," said the Superintendent, smiling, "and so I should judge from what I have seen. Now, what are you going to do about it?"

They all grew quiet.

"You know about these men, no one else does. Are you going to let them go to destruction without an attempt to prevent it?"

The silence deepened.

"Now, listen to me. This will cost money. How much can you give to send a man to look them up? Two hundred and fifty dollars?"

"Count me," said Ike.

"Me, too," echoed Perault. "And me, and me," on all sides. In ten minutes the thing was arranged.

"Now, there is something else," said the Superintendent, and his voice grew deep and solemn. "Can you spare me your man?"

"No, sir!" said the Kid, promptly.

" Not much!" echoed Perault, and in this feeling all emphatically agreed.

" Do you know where we can get such a man? " said the Superintendent, " such a prospector? " There was no answer. " I do not either. Now, what are you going to do? "

Then Sinclair spoke up.

" Do you mean, Doctor, to remove Mr. Macgregor from us? That would seem to be very hard upon this field."

" Well, perhaps not; but can you spare him for six months, at least? "

For some minutes no one made reply. Then Ike spoke.

" Well, I surmise we got a good deal from our Prospector. In fact, what we ain't got from him don't count much. And I rather opine that we can't be mean about this. It's a little like pullin' hair, but I reckon we'd better give him up."

" Thank you, sir," said the Superintendent, who had learned much from Ike throughout the day. " Your words are the best commentary I have ever heard upon a saying of our Lord's, that has inspired men to all unselfish living, ' Freely ye have received, freely give.' "

## XX

## THE NEW POLICY

IT was still early spring when Shock received a letter from Brown, a letter full of perplexity and love and wrath.

"Something has gone wrong," he wrote. "You have got to come down here and straighten it out. I can plainly see that Mrs. Fairbanks is at the bottom of it, but just what she is at I cannot discover. Helen I do not now see much. The changes in our life, you see, have been very great. I cannot bear to go to the house now. The associations are too much for me. Besides, Lloyd seems to have taken possession of the whole family. The old lady flatters and fondles him in a manner that makes my gorge rise. It is quite evident she wants him for her son-in-law, and more than evident that he entirely concurs.

"Just what Helen thinks of it I am at a loss to know, but I cannot believe she can stand Lloyd any more than I can. Up till recently she was very open with me and very loyal to you, but of late a change has taken place, and what in thunder is the matter, I cannot make out. Have you done or said anything? Have you been guilty of any high-falutin' nonsense of giving her up, and that sort of thing? I fear she is avoiding me just now, and I feel certain she has been misled in some way, so you must come down.

377

You really must. Of course you will say you cannot afford it, but this is too serious a thing for any
excuse like that. Will not your confounded Highland pride let me loan you enough to bring you down.
Anyway, come, if you have to walk."

It must be confessed that Brown's letter produced
little effect upon Shock's mind. The bitterness of
his surrender was past, so, at least, he thought. The
happy dream he had cherished for a year was gone
forever. He was quite certain that it was not Brown's
but the Superintendent's letter that determined him
to accept appointment as a delegate to the General
Assembly.

"I have no right to command you in this," the
Superintendent wrote. "I wish I had. But I need
you, and for the sake of the men you and I know,
I wish you to come down to the Assembly and meet
the Committee."

It was undoubtedly the Superintendent's letter,
and yet that sudden leap of his heart as he read his
chief's entreaty startled him.

"Nonsense!" he said, shutting his jaws hard together. "That is all done with." And yet he knew
that it would be a joy almost too great to endure to
catch a glimpse of the face that still came to him
night by night in his dreams, to hear her voice, and
to be near her.

So Shock came down, and his coming brought very
different feelings to different hearts, to Brown the
very news of it brought mad, wild delight. He rushed
to find Helen.

"He is coming down," he cried.

"Is he?" replied Helen, eagerly. "Who?"

"I have seen his chief," continued Brown, ignoring the question. "He has had a wire. He'll be here day after to-morrow. Oh, let me yell! The dear old beast! If we could only get him into a jersey, and see him bleed."

"Don't, Brownie," said Helen, using her pet name for her friend. They had grown to be much to each other during the experiences of the past year. "It suggests too much."

"I forgot," said Brown, penitently. "Forgive me. It will be hard for you."

"And for him. Poor Shock," said Helen. "Don't let him go to his home."

"Not if I can help it," replied Brown.

"And don't—don't—talk about me—much."

"Not if I can help it," replied Brown again, this time with a suspicion of a smile.

"Now, Brownie, I want you to help me," said Helen. "It is hard enough. There is nothing between us now. He wishes it to be so, and after all, I do too."

"You do? Look me in the face and say you do."

Helen looked him steadily in the face, and said, quietly, "Yes, I do. In all sincerity I believe it is far better so. Mother is quite determined, and she has only me. It is the only thing possible, so I want you to help me."

"And all that—that—that thing last spring was a farce—a mistake, I mean?"

"Yes, a mistake. An awful mistake. You see," explained Helen, hurriedly, "I was dreadfully excited, and—well, you know, I made a fool of myself. And so, Brownie, you must help me."

"Help you—how? To keep him off? That won't be hard. Tell him it was all a mistake last spring and that you regret it, and you won't need to do anything else, if I know him."

"I have—at least mother has told him."

"Your mother?" gasped Brown. "Then that settles it. Good-by. I did not expect this of you."

"Come back, Brownie. You know you are unkind, and you must not desert me."

"Well, what in heaven's name do you want me to do? Keep him off?"

"Oh, I do not know," said Helen, breaking through her calm. "I don't know. What can I do?"

"Do?" said Brown. "Let him tell you." He had great faith in Shock's powers.

But the next two days were days of miserable anxiety to Brown. If Shock would only do as he was told and act like an ordinary man, Brown had no doubt of the issue.

"Oh, if he'll only play up," he groaned to himself, in a moment of desperation. "If he'll only play up he'll take all that out of her in about three minutes."

The only question was, would he play. Brown could only trust that in some way kind Providence would come to his aid. On the afternoon of the second day, the day of Shock's arrival, his hope was realized, and he could not but feel that Fortune had condescended to smile a little upon him.

Shock's train was late. The Superintendent had sought Brown out, and adjured him by all things sacred to produce his man at the committee meeting at the earliest possible moment, and this commission Brown had conscientiously fulfilled.

Toward evening he met Helen downtown, and was escorting her homeward when they fell in with Tommy Phillips, a reporter for the *Times*. He was evidently in a state of considerable excitement.

" I have just had a great experience," he exclaimed. " I was down this afternoon at your church committee, and I tell you I had a circus. There was a big chap there from the wild and woolly, and he made 'em sit up. Why, you know him, I guess. He's that 'Varsity football chap the fellows used to rave about."

" Oh, yes, I know," said Brown. " Macgregor. Shock, we used to call him."

" Yes, of course. I remember I saw him last year at the McGill match."

" Well, what was up? " said Brown, scenting something good. " Let us have it. Do the reporter act."

" Well, it's good copy, let me tell you, but I don't want to allow my professional zeal to obliterate my sense of the decencies of polite society."

" Go on," said Brown, " I want to hear. You know, I played quarter behind him for three years, and Miss Fairbanks is interested, I know."

" You did? Well, if he bucked up as he did this

afternoon, you must have had good hunting. Well, then, when that committee met you never saw a more solemn-looking bunch in your life. You would think they had all lost their mothers-in-law. And when they broke up they didn't know but they were standing on their heads."

" What was the matter? "

" Oh, there was a big deficit on, and they had to go up to your big council—conference—what do you call it in your pagan outfit? Assembly? Yes, that's it—and take their medicine. Twenty thousand dollars of a debt. Well, sir, on the back of all that didn't their Grand Mogul—archbishop—you know, from the West—no, not Macgregor—their chief pusher. Superintendent? Yes—come in and put an ice pack on them in the shape of a new scheme for exploration and extension in the Kootenay country, the Lord knows where, some place out of sight. Well, you ought to have heard him. He burned red fire, you bet. Pardon my broken English, Miss Fairbanks."

" Go on," said Helen, " I like it," and Brown gave himself a little hug.

" I am glad you do," continued Tommy, " for it is bad enough to write copy without having to speak it. Well, the war began, some in favour of the scheme, some against, but all hopeless in view of the present state of finances. Better wait a little, and that sort of talk. Then, let's see what happened. Oh, yes. The question of the man came up. Who was the man? The Superintendent was ready for 'em. It was Macgregor of some place. Frog Lake? No, Loon Lake. Then the opposition thought they had him with a half-nelson. Old Dr. Macfarren jumped on to the chief with both feet. His man was no good, a flat failure in his field, no tact. Beg your pardon, Miss Fairbanks. What did you say?"

"Oh, never mind," said Helen. "Go on."

"He appealed for corroboration to his friend, the chap up at Park Church, you know, that sleek, kid-gloved fellow."

"Burns?" asked Brown, innocently, delighted in the reporter's description of Lloyd and desiring more of it.

"No. You know that orator chap, liquid eyes, mellifluous voice, and all the rest of it."

"Oh, Lloyd."

"Yes. Well, he took a whirl and backed up Macfarren. Evidently didn't think much of the Superintendent's choice. Remarked about his being a Highlander, a man of visions and that sort of thing."

"What else did he say?" inquired Brown, who was in a particularly happy mood.

"Oh, a lot of stuff, in his most lordly, patronizing tone. Macgregor was a very good, earnest fellow, but he should judge him to be lacking in tact or adaptability, fine sensibilities, and that sort of rot. But never mind. Didn't he catch it! Oh, no. My Sally Ann! Boiling lard and blue vitriol, and all in the chief's most sweet-scented lavender style, though all the time I could see the danger lights burning through his port-holes. I tell you I've had my diminished moments, but I don't think I was ever reduced to such a shade as the Park Church chap when the Superintendent was through with him. Serve him right, too."

"What did the Superintendent say?" continued Brown, delighted to find somebody who would express his own sentiments with more force and fulness than he could command.

"Say! Well, I wish I could tell you. 'Mr. Lloyd says he is a Highlander. Yes, he is, thank God. So am I. He is a man of visions. Yes, he has vision beyond the limits of his own congregation and of his own native cross-roads, vision for what lies beyond the horizon, vision for those men in the mountains who are going to the devil.' A quotation, Miss Fairbanks, I assure you. 'These miners and lumbermen, forgotten by all but their mothers, and God.' Say, it was great. If I could reproduce it there would be a European trip in it. Then he turned on Dr. Macfarren. It seems that Macgregor somehow had to quit some place in the West on the plea that he was not adaptable, and that sort of thing. 'Dr. Macfarren says he was a failure,' went on the old chief, using at least five r's, 'Mr. Lloyd says he is not adaptable, he is lacking in fine sensibilities. It is true God did not make him with sleek hair'—which, by Jove, was true enough—'and dainty fingers. And a good thing it was, else our church at Loon Lake, built by his own hands, the logs cut, shaped and set in place, sir, by his own hands, would never have

existed. He was a failure at the Fort, we are told.
Why? I made inquiries concerning that. I was
told by a gentleman who calls himself a Presbyterian
—I need not mention his name—that he was not suitable to the peculiarly select and high-toned society of
that place. No, sir, our missionary could not bow
and scrape, he was a failure at tennis, he did not shine
at card parties,' and here you could smell things
sizzling. ' He could not smile upon lust. No, thank
God!' and the old chap's voice began to quiver and
shake. ' In all this he was a failure, and would to
God we had more of the same kind!' 'Amen,'
' Thank God,' ' That's true,' the men around the
table cried. I thought I had struck a Methodist re-
vival meeting."

"What else did he say?" said Brown, who could
hardly contain himself for sheer delight.

"Well, he went on then to yarn about Macgregor's
work—how a church and club house had been built
in one place, and a hospital and all that sort of thing,
in another, and then he told us stories of the different chaps who had been apparently snatched from
the mouth of hell by Macgregor, and were ready to
lie down and let him walk over them. It was great.
There was an Irishman and a Frenchman, I remember, both Roman Catholics, but both ready to swallow
the Confession of Faith if the Prospector ordered
them. Yes, that was another point. Macgregor, it
seems, was a regular fiend for hunting up fellows and
rooting them out to church, and so they dubbed him
' the Prospector.' The old chief stuck that in, I tell

you. Then there was a doctor and, oh, a lot of chaps,
—a cowboy fellow named Ike, who was particularly
good copy if one could reproduce him. And then—"
here Tommy hesitated—" well, it's worth while telling. There was a girl who had gone wrong, and had
been brought back. To hear the chief tell that yarn
was pretty fine. I don't turn the waterworks on without considerable pressure, but I tell you my tanks
came pretty near overflowing when he talked about
that poor girl. And then, at the most dramatic moment—that old chap knows his business—he brought
on Macgregor, announcing him as ' the Prospector
of Frog Lake, no, Loon Lake.' Well, he was not
much to look at. His hair was not slick, and his
beard looked a little like a paint brush, his pants ran
up on his boots, and bagged at the knees."

" He had just come off the train," hastily interposed Brown, " He hadn't a moment to dress himself."

" Well, as I say, he wasn't pretty to look at, and
they gave him a kind of frosty reception, too."

" Well, what happened? " inquired Brown, anxious
to get over this part of the description.

" Well, they began firing questions at him hot and
fast. He was a little rattled for a while, but after
a bit he got into his stride, put down his map, laid
out his country and began pouring in his facts, till
when they let him out they looked for all the world
like a lot of men who had been struck by a whirlwind
and were trying to get back their breath and other
belongings."

" Well, what did they do then? "

" Oh, the thing passed, I guess. I left 'em and went after the man from the West. I thought I had struck oil. I had visions too."

" Well, did you get him? "

" I did, but there was not any oil. It was rock, hard, cold Scotch granite. I'm something of a borer, but I tell you what, he turned my edge. It was no use. He wouldn't talk."

" Good by. Come around and see your man at my rooms," said Brown heartily. " I'll pump him for you, and you can catch the oil."

" You will, eh? All right, set a mug for me."

" Great boy, that Tommy," said Brown, who was smitten with a sudden enthusiastic admiration for the reporter. " Clever chap. He'll make his mark yet."

Helen walked for some distance in silence.

" Is—is he—is Mr. Macgregor with you? " she inquired at length.

" Yes, Mr. Macgregor is with me," mimicked Brown. " Will you send him a card? "

" Now, Brownie, stop," said Helen in distress. " He has not been home yet, has he? "

" No. Why? "

" Could you keep him away till about eleven to-morrow? "

" Yes, I suppose I might. He has got to get some clothes and get some of the wool off him. But why do you ask? "

" Well, I thought I would just run in and dust, and

put some flowers up, and, you know, make it a little more homelike."

" Helen, you're a brick. I had decided to drop you because I didn't love you, but I am changing my mind."

" Well, do not let him go before eleven. Everything will be right by that time."

" Good!" said Brown, with an ebullition of rapture, which he immediately suppressed as Helen's eyes were turned inquiringly upon him. " You see," he explained hurriedly, " he has been in the West and will need to get a lot of things, and that will give you plenty of time. There's my car. Good-by. We have had a happy afternoon, eh? "

" Oh, yes, very happy, thank you," said Helen, but she could not quite suppress a little sigh.

" Well, good-by," said Brown, and he went off jubilant to his car.

He sat down in a corner, and thought hard till he came to his street. " If he'll only play up we'll win, sure thing. But will he, confound him, will he? Well, the kick-off will be to-morrow."

He found Shock waiting in his rooms, with a face so grave and so sad that Brown's heart grew sore for him.

" Come on, old chap, we'll go to grub. But first I am going to groom you a bit. We'll take a foot or two off your hair since the football season is over; and I think," examining him critically, " we can spare that beard, unless you are very fond of it."

Shock protested that he had no particular love for

his beard; it was better for the cold weather, and it was not always convenient for him to shave.

When the barber had finished with Shock, Brown regarded him with admiration.

" You are all right, old chap. I say, you've got thin, haven't you? "

" No, I am pretty much in my playing form."

" Well, there is something different." And there was. The boyish lines of his face had given place to those that come to men with the cares and griefs and responsibilities of life. And as Brown looked over Shock's hard, lean face, he said again, with emphasis, " You'll do."

After dinner Shock wandered about the rooms uneasily for a time, and finally said, " I say, Brown, I would like to go up home, if you don't mind." They had not yet spoken of what each knew was uppermost in the other's mind.

"All right, Shock. But wouldn't it be better in the morning? "

" I want to go to-night," said Shock.

" Well, if you are bound to, we will go up in an hour or two. There's a lot of things I want to talk about, and some things to arrange," replied Brown, hoping that in the meantime something might turn up to postpone the visit till the morning.

For a second time that day Fortune smiled upon Brown, for hardly had they settled down for a talk when the Superintendent appeared.

" I am glad to find you in," he said, giving Shock's hand a vigorous shake. " I came to offer you my congratulations upon your appearance this afternoon, and also to tell you that the Committee have appointed you to address the Assembly on Home Mission night."

" Hooray! " cried Brown. " Your Committee, Doctor, is composed of men who evidently know a good thing when they see it."

" Sometimes, Mr. Brown, sometimes," said the Superintendent, shrewdly.

But Shock refused utterly and absolutely.

"I am no speaker," he said. "I am a failure as a speaker."

" Well, Mr. Macgregor, I will not take your refusal to-night. It is the Committee's request, and you ought to hesitate before refusing it."

"A man can do no more than his best," said Shock, " and I know I cannot speak."

" Well, think it over," said the Superintendent, preparing to go.

" Oh, sit down, sit down," cried Brown. " You must want to have a talk with Shock here, and I want to hear all about this afternoon."

" Well," said the Superintendent, seating himself, " it is not often I have a chance to talk with a Prospector, so I will accept your invitation." And by the time the talk was done it was too late for Shock to think of visiting his home, and Brown went asleep with the happy expectation of what he called the " kick-off " next day.

# XXI

## THE WAITING GAME

**B**ROWN was early astir. He knew that he could not keep Shock so fully employed as to prevent his going home long before ten o'clock, and it was part of his plan that Shock's first meeting with Helen should take place in his own mother's house.

" The first thing we must do," he announced, " is to see a tailor. If you are going to address the General Assembly you have got to get proper togs. And anyway, you may as well get a suit before you go West again. I know a splendid tailor—cheap, too."

" Well, he will need to be cheap," said Shock, " for I cannot afford much for clothes."

" Well, I will see about that," said Brown. So he did, for after some private conversation with the tailor, the prices quoted to Shock were quite within even his small means.

It was half-past nine before they reached Shock's home. Brown took the key out of his pocket, opened the door, and allowed Shock to enter, waiting outside for a few moments.

When he followed Shock in he found him still standing in the centre of the little room, looking about

upon the familiar surroundings, the articles of furniture, the pictures on the wall, his mother's chair
beside the table, with her Bible and glasses at
hand.

As Brown came in Shock turned to him and said,
" Is this some more of your kindness, Brown? Have
you taken this care of everything? "

" No," said Brown, " that is not my work. Every
week since the house was closed Helen has come over
and kept things right."

Without any reply Shock passed into his mother's
room, leaving Brown alone.

When half an hour had passed, Brown, glancing
out of the window, saw Helen approaching.

" Thank goodness! " he exclaimed, " here she is at
last."

He opened the door for her.

" Oh, good morning," she exclaimed in surprise.
" I am sure this is very kind of you."

" Yes, I thought I would help," said Brown in a
loud voice. " You see, Shock was anxious to come,
and I thought I would come up with him. He is in
the next room. He will be out in a minute. We were
coming up last night, but could not get away. The
Superintendent dropped in, and we talked till it was
too late." Brown kept the stream of his remarks
flowing as if he feared a pause.

Helen laid the bunch of flowers she was carrying in
her hand upon the table.

" Oh, Brown," she exclaimed, " how could you!
This is very unkind." She turned to go.

" Hold on," said Brown in a loud voice. " Shock will be here in a minute. He'll be sorry to miss you, I am sure."

For a moment Helen stood irresolute, when the door opened and Shock, pale, but quiet and self-controlled, appeared. He had just been face to face for the first time with his great grief. The thought that filled his mind, overwhelming all others, was that his mother had passed forever beyond the touch of his hand and the sound of his voice. Never till that moment had he taken in the full meaning of the change that had come to his life.

During the minutes he had spent in his mother's room he had allowed his mind to go back over the long years so full of fond memory, and then he had faced the future. Alone henceforth he must go down the long trail. By his mother's bed he had knelt, and had consecrated himself again to the life she had taught him to regard as worthy, and with the resolve in his heart to seek to be the man she would desire him to be and had expected him to be, he rose from his knees.

When he opened the door the dignity of his great grief and of a lofty purpose was upon him, and he greeted Helen unembarrassed and with a serene consciousness of self-mastery.

" I am glad to see you, Miss Fairbanks," he said, taking her hand. " I am glad that we meet here, for it was here, in this house, that you gave such loving and tender care to my dear mother. However long I may live, whatever may come to me, I shall never forget what you did for her through all the year, and at the last."

His quiet dignity restored to Helen her self-possession.

"I did all I could for her. I was glad to do it, because I loved her. But she did more for me than ever I could have done for her. Her last illness was very brief, and her death was full of peace."

"Tell me," said Shock, placing a chair for her. "I want to know all."

With gentle, sweet sympathy the story was told in all its beautiful details, till the very end. Instinctively Helen seemed to know the points that Shock would desire to hear, and he listened to her with his heart shining through his eyes.

"Thank you, thank you," he said. "Never can I thank you enough for all that you have done. And you, too, have had your great sorrow. Brown told me about it all."

At this Brown rose hastily, and looking out of the window, exclaimed, "I say, there's Boyle. Wait for me."

"Yes," said Helen, when Brown had gone, "it was a terrible grief, and mother has never recovered from it, nor will she. Betty was the life of our house. She was so bright."

"Oh, bright, indeed. How well I remember her brightness that night in your home."

"I remember," said Helen. "And Mr. Balfour," she continued, "The Don. He has been with you?"

" Yes, indeed, poor chap.   And nobly he has done,"
and Shock told of The Don and of his work in the
Pass.

" How good you have been," exclaimed Helen, " and
how much you have done.   I am so thankful, and so
proud.   We are all so proud of you."

" No," said Shock gravely, " that is not the word,
Miss Fairbanks.   There is no room for pride."

" Well, we think so," replied Helen.   " You will
come to see us?   Mother will be so glad."

Helen was wondering at her own calmness.   She
could hardly make herself believe that she was talking to Shock, and so quietly, in this room where so
short a time ago he had held her in his arms.

" I do not know," replied Shock.   " It may be as
well not to—not to see much—to see you."

Shock became unexpectedly conscious of their
previous relations.   The memory of that scene in
which they had been the chief actors came vividly
before him.   For weeks he had dreaded this interview,
and now it was almost over.   He felt like a man who,
in the hour of victory, is unexpectedly threatened with
defeat.   Well, sooner or later he must speak his mind
plainly; there would never be a better chance than
now, and though he wished he could get back that
perfect self-mastery of the past few minutes, he resolved to go through with it now.   He took hold of
himself with a stern grip.

Helen saw it in his face.   A great fear seized her.
She started up.

" Oh, I must run! " she exclaimed.   " You will be

sure to come and see us, Mr. Macgregor. Indeed, you must come."

Her manner was light, almost frivolous. Shock felt the change instinctively, read her fear, and decided that the moment for speech had passed.

"Good-by," he said, looking steadily into her eyes. "Good-by. God bless you for your kindness to—to us both."

The little catch in his voice reached the girl's heart, and the tears sprang to her eyes.

"Good-by," she said hurriedly. "Good-by," and was gone.

A little way down the street she met Brown.

"Well?"

"Well, it is all over. I am thankful, too. Yes, so thankful."

"Well, I'll be—" Brown left his sentence unfinished and turned away from her impatiently.

He found Shock still sitting at the table, unspeakable misery showing in his eyes.

"Well, old chap," Brown said kindly, putting his hand upon his friend's shoulder.

"That is over, thank God!" said Shock. "I was afraid of it, but it is over now."

"It is, eh?" said Brown crossly. "Well, let's go. You're two of a kind. Come on. You'll have to get at your speech now."

"My speech?" said Shock, rising wearily. "No speech for me."

"I tell you what, Shock," said Brown, with a touch of impatience, "you think too much of yourself."

" Do I, Brown? Well, perhaps so," said Shock, humbly.

" Oh, confound your old carcass!" cried Brown, throwing his arm round Shock's neck. " You'll be my death yet. At the same time, you ought to speak, and I believe you will. If I know your conscience it won't let you rest."

It turned out that Brown was right, for when the Superintendent wrote a note to Shock asking him formally on behalf of the Committee to address the Assembly on Home Mission night, the last sentence in his letter determined Shock to accept.

" I know what this will cost you," the Superintendent wrote, " but the cause is not yours nor mine. It is His. And for His sake I believe you will do this."

" I knew you would, old chap," said Brown exultantly. " If a fellow could get the combination of your conscience he could do what he liked with you."

" Well, I suppose if they wish me to make an exhibition of myself I should not refuse, and after all, what matter how I speak? I will fail, I know, but I will do my best."

" Never a fail," cried Brown. " Don't preach at them. Tell them yarns. That's what your chief does. Now you hear me."

This proved to be good advice, for when the chairman introduced Shock as the Prospector from Loon Lake, Shock simply began, as Brown said, to " yarn."

" That is what Perault and Ike called me," were his first words, and from that moment till the close of his speech he had his audience leaning forward and listening with ears and eyes and heart. He made no attempt at fine speaking, but simply told them of his friends in the West, of the men he had come to love as brothers, and who had come to love him.

As they came down the steps of the Park Church, where the meeting was held, Brown could hardly keep pace with Helen as she danced along beside him.

"Oh, wasn't he splendid!" she cried, "wasn't he splendid!"

"Splendid?" said Brown. "There's not a word big enough left."

"Oh, I am so happy," sang Helen.

"Why, what's the matter with you?" cried Brown.

"Oh, nothing, nothing," and she bubbled over with happy laughter until Brown grew gloomy and cross. But Helen deigned him no further explanation of her overflowing joy, and left him, still sullen and somewhat indignant, at her door.

Her radiant face caught her mother's eye as she entered the room.

"Well, my child, you are looking very happy. I have not seen you look so bright for months. You are very beautiful, my daughter," said her mother, putting her arm around her daughter as Helen stooped to kiss her.

"Oh, mother," cried Helen, "I am very happy."

"Well, darling, it makes me happy to hear you say so. Has—has Mr. Lloyd spoken to you?"

"Mr. Lloyd?" Helen laughed gleefully. "No, mother, he knows better than that. Oh, mother, Shock loves me."

"What! Has he dared to speak—after promising——?"

"No, mother, he has not spoken, not with his lips. But I know it, I know it, and oh, I am so glad."

"What of his plain declaration to me that he had given you up?"

"Oh, I don't care, mother. He has not changed," cried the happy girl. "He loves me just the same as ever."

"And what of the girl Mr. Ambherg told us of?"

"No, mother, there is no other girl," cried Helen. "I don't care who told you."

"Helen, I am ashamed of you," exclaimed her mother, angrily.

"Dear mother," said Helen, falling on her knees and putting her arms about her mother, "I cannot help loving him, and I cannot help being happy. Oh, mother, he is splendid. You ought to have heard him to-night, and you ought to have seen the people. Why, the ministers almost hugged him. And oh, mother, mother, as he came down and passed my seat, he turned and looked at me. He did not expect to see me, and he was off his guard, and then I knew, oh, I knew. He is just the same. Oh, mother, be happy with me."

Her mother burst into tears.

"Oh," she sobbed, "I thought I was to have one child left. I am indeed bereaved."

"Hush, mother," cried Helen. "I will not leave you."

"But you love him?"

" Yes, yes. With all my heart."

" He will not give up his work in that awful country? "

" No," said the girl proudly, " he will not, not even for me. But he will love me always and I will love him, and that is enough just now."

" Helen, listen to me. You will never marry him with my consent," said Mrs. Fairbanks, determinedly.

" And he would never marry me without," replied Helen.

" What, then, is your future to be? "

" Oh, I will stay with you, mother darling."

" And he? " inquired Mrs. Fairbanks.

" He? Oh, I don't know, but he will always love me, mother."

In desperation Mrs. Fairbanks sent next day for Shock. Her one hope lay in his fine sense of honour, and in his generosity.

" Mr. Macgregor," she said, when Shock stood before her, " I want to appeal to your generosity. You will not stand in the way of my daughter's happiness? "

" Mrs. Fairbanks, I thought I had made myself clear. What more can I say or do? "

" She fancies you still love her. Could not you disabuse her of her foolish fancy? "

" Tell her I do not love her? " asked Shock. " That I cannot do. It would be false."

" Oh, Mr. Macgregor," cried Mrs. Fairbanks, weeping, " if you force my child from me I will die."

Shock was greatly disturbed at her tears.

"Mrs. Fairbanks, I could never force your daughter away from you, but I shall always love her. Can I say more?"

"I have told her," said Mrs. Fairbanks between her sobs, "I will never consent to her marriage with you."

Shock's heart gave a leap.

"And what did she say?" he inquired in an unsteady voice.

"She said you would not marry her without my consent."

"And that is true," said Shock.

"And what, then, will you do?" inquired Mrs. Fairbanks.

Shock threw up his head, with joy illumining his face.

"I—we—" changing the pronoun with a sudden ecstasy of rapture, "we can wait."

"And how long, pray?" inquired Mrs. Fairbanks, scornfully.

"How long?" He paused as if pondering the question. "Forever!"

"Shock!"

He turned quickly. There at the door, in all her glorious beauty, her eyes luminous with the light of love, stood Helen.

"Helen!" he cried aloud, in his surprise. "You heard! Can you? Can we?"

With a movement of ineffable grace she was at his side. He put his strong arms about her. She looked into his eyes.

"Yes, Shock, we can wait—now."